When the Owl Sings

WHEN THE OWL SINGS

David C. Maloney

Two Harbors Press | Minneapolis

Two Harbors Press
322 First Avenue N, 5th floor
Minneapolis, MN 55401
612.455.2293
www.TwoHarborsPress.com

ISBN-13: 978-1-63505-052-3
LCCN: 2016902225

Distributed by Itasca Books

Cover Design by Penterra Design
Typeset by Mary Kristin Ross

Printed in the United States of America

To Tatum

Thank you for being an inspiration to me. Your love of life, endearing spirit, and radiant smile are forever etched on my heart. You're a blessing I could never have imagined.

Cheers!

Chapter One

Temple Ball
Altun Ha
899 AD

Sweat mixed with blood ran down Ma'xu's forehead and dripped into his eyes. The salty, burning sensation made the long rectangular playing field difficult to see. A hot midafternoon sun scorched the players and added to their battle fatigue. The mental and physical rigor of Temple Ball would challenge every ounce of willpower the players could muster. The annual match would, in any ordinary year, dictate who went on the village hunts. This, however, was no ordinary year. This year, the village would welcome its newest warrior. The two captains, Ma'xu and Kanul, were vying for the right to take the village offering to Tikal. The winner of this year's match would meet the gods in Tikal and the loser would meet the gods in paradise. One way or the other, each of their destinies would be fulfilled this day.

Jul'bul gasped for air as he tried to counsel his leader, "Ma'xu, I don't know how much longer we can go. Kanul's team has the will of a panther. Some of our teammates can hardly walk."

"I know; we need to make one final push," Ma'xu said, patting Jul'bul on the shoulder and taking a deep breath himself. "Get B'aku and tell him to be ready for our play. The next run we make may be our last," Ma'xu warned.

Surveying the large playing field, Ma'xu locked his sights onto the stone ring suspended ten feet in the air. The ring at the end of the field represented both victory and death. His legs, tight from an entire day of fighting, were starting to cramp. He sensed an end to the game was drawing near. At some point, one of the teams would be forced to concede.

Bloodied and bruised, Ma'xu and Kanul fought each other as if their lives depended on it, because it did. Their forearms and elbows swung fiercely as they fought for the ball. What Ma'xu gave up in size to Kanul, he more than made up for in speed and agility. With one swift move, he stole the ball from Kanul and made his way up the field. Ma'xu's speed created distance from Kanul. Ma'xu watched as B'aku raced ahead of him on his right toward the ring.

"Ma'xu, pass it!" B'aku shouted.

Instead of passing the rubber ball to his teammate, Ma'xu shuffled the ball across the field with his feet. He weaved in and out of Kanul's players as if they were standing still. One after another, players from Kanul's team tried in vain to knock Ma'xu out of the match. One by one, they failed.

Ma'xu slowed down and angled for a shot at the ring. His mind raced as he anticipated his shot. I'm still too far away, but I must try. I must not fail. I cannot shame my father. Ma'xu could feel his heart pump like a hunted jaguar running for its life.

He focused on the ring and pulled his right foot back. His eyes grew wide. His face tensed. With his mouth open, his foot came forward to kick the ball. Before his foot could make contact, Kanul caught up and planted a forearm into Ma'xu's back, knocking him to the ground.

When Ma'xu stopped rolling, he noticed blood pouring out of his nose. He looked up and met his father's eyes watching from the throne on the side of the field. He could see the disappointment in the king's face and fear in the queen's. Ma'xu looked down in shame. He knew he had missed his chance. He quickly realized the wise choice would have been to pass to

B'aku. Before he could get up, defenders from Kanul's team descended on top of Ma'xu, pummeling him further into the ground. One by one, they made sure Ma'xu would not get another shot at the ring.

Unable to expand his lungs, Ma'xu gasped for air at the bottom of the pile. With each warrior piling on top of him, a commensurate amount of air was forced out of his lungs until every bit was gone. A rush of panic overcame him. He opened his mouth, but couldn't make any sounds. He couldn't call for help. He couldn't move. His chest began to convulse trying to get air. The weight was too much.

He teetered between this world and the next. His eyes fluttered. His stomach tightened. A sharp pain suddenly penetrated his chest. His eyes slowly closed. Calm, peaceful sleep approached. His body ceased all instinctual efforts to sustain life. What will the other side be like? would be his final thought.

As his life force evacuated his body, the weight on top of him became lighter. His lungs, not yet asleep, expanded with air. With every mouthful of air, he could feel life return to his body. As the last player from Kanul's team was thrown off Ma'xu, he could see his friend towering over him.

"Ma'xu, I don't know about you, but I don't feel like having you sacrificed today; get up," Jul'bul said, pulling Ma'xu up by his arm.

"Thank you, Jul'bul, I thought I was on my way to the underworld." His gasping breaths rhythmically matched his rebounding heartbeat. He shook life back into his legs and arms. Ma'xu's senses returned. The smell of hot, humid, salty air never smelled so good. His lungs were alive again, his erratic respirations recovered.

"I don't know if we can beat them, they're too big," Jul'bul said with desperation.

Escaping death rejuvenated Ma'xu. His eyes glistened with fury. Ma'xu found the resolve he needed.

"Indeed, Kanul's team may be bigger, but we're faster. Remember, Jul'bul, the larger and stronger tapir doesn't hunt the jaguar, the jaguar hunts the tapir."

Ma'xu looked down the field. Some of his teammates were on the ground and some were being beaten by Kanul's team. Ma'xu felt born again. A rush of energy flowed through Ma'xu's body. Like his teammates', Ma'xu's leather-hide chest protector and arm pads were torn and covered in blood and sweat.

"We need to finish this game, Jul'bul," Ma'xu said as a crooked grin crept across his face. His eyes grew wide as if possessed by the god of pain himself. With a crazed look, Ma'xu took off in pursuit of Kanul. Ma'xu tackled Kanul and threw him to the ground, but not before Kanul kicked the ball at the suspended ring. The ball sailed through the air. For the first time that day, the players stopped in their tracks. Silence enveloped the three thousand-plus villagers watching the match.

The queen dug her fingernails into the king's arm as they watched the ball heading straight for the ring. A score would end the game, and her son's life. The ball hit the inner edge of the ring and circled the rim. Time stopped while everyone waited and watched. Would it fall through or not?

"Stay out, stay out . . ." Ma'xu whispered from his knees, clenching his fists.

"Come on, come on," Kanul said, fanning the air as if trying to help blow the ball through the ring. Everybody waited. The ball finally slowed down. Half of the spectators let out a moan, while the other half cheered as the ball fell back into the playing field.

"You can let go of my arm, my queen," the king said, pulling the queen's fingernails out of his forearm.

"Sorry, that was close," she replied, wiping the king's blood from her hand onto her tan hide dress.

"Yes, too close."

Kanul's team was dumbfounded. They stared at the ring in disbelief. It was as if they had fished all day and lost their catch.

Ma'xu's heart pounded again. It's not over, he thought. He couldn't let Kanul's team take another shot. He jumped up, ran to the ball, and kicked it out toward the opposite side of the field. Ma'xu's enthusiasm was contagious. His team found their second wind and pursued the ball. The game continued.

"Get them and kill them!" Kanul ordered his team, now in pursuit of Ma'xu's team. The game turned into war.

"Jul'bul! Keep them back," Ma'xu called out.

Jul'bul used his massive arms to knock the players from Kanul's team down, while Ma'xu moved the ball up the field with his feet. He fought off attacks from Kanul's team. Ma'xu delivered a crushing elbow to a player trying to steal the ball; trying to steal his honor; trying to steal his destiny. Not this year, he thought. This year was special. There was far too much at stake.

"Ma'xu, pass!" B'aku said as he ran up the side of the field. This time, Ma'xu passed the ball without hesitation. Kanul's team swarmed B'aku like a swarm of killer wasps. Ma'xu broke to the center of the field and called out to Jul'bul.

"Now!" Ma'xu yelled.

Jul'bul nodded and ran to the center of the field. He positioned himself in front of the ring. Hunched over, he placed his hands on his knees and braced himself.

Kanul's team descended on B'aku and crushed him, but not before he was able to center the ball back to where Jul'bul was hunched over waiting for Ma'xu. Kanul's team stopped, turned, and followed the ball's trajectory high above the playing field. They realized that in their angst at Ma'xu's team, no one was guarding their ring. A strategic mistake; a potentially deadly mistake.

Kanul and his team watched in disbelief as Ma'xu ran up the back of Jul'bul and leapt from his shoulders. The crowd went silent for the second time of the day. Ma'xu was fifteen feet in the air laid out horizontally. Sailing fast and straight, the ball showed no sign of coming down to earth. Ma'xu flew through the air to intercept the ball. He let out an ear-piercing battle cry and with one swift motion he punted the ball, redirecting its path toward the ring. The ball never touched the edges as it soared through. A perfect shot. The game was over.

The crowd let out a thunderous applause as Ma'xu's team mauled him in celebration. Kanul's team dropped their heads. They knew what defeat meant.

Moments later, standing at an altar positioned in front of the king's throne on the north side of the field, a straight-faced high priest shook a collection of bones that let out a haunting dull pitch. Silence quelled the celebration. Kanul and Ma'xu knew the tradition and walked up to the altar.

"Ma'xu, you will deliver the village gift to the gods in Tikal!" The high priest yelled out. "Kanul, you will dine with the gods this day in paradise."

Turning to Ma'xu, Kanul offered reconciliatory words: "My young friend, be brave on your journey. I will be one of many protecting you from the darkness. Bring honor to our village."

"As you do for us in paradise, my friend."

After a brief embrace with Ma'xu, Kanul climbed onto the altar. With no fear or hesitation, he laid on his back. Slow rhythmic drumbeats echoed through the jungle silencing the villagers and players again as the high priest began the ritual. The villagers and players watched with anticipation.

After reciting a prayer, the high priest raised his dagger high in the air over Kanul with both hands. Kanul's eyes focused on the point of the dagger. He was too much of a warrior to close his eyes. The high priest looked to the heavens and, in one swift motion, plunged the dagger deep into Kanul's chest, penetrating his heart.

Kanul's chest rose off the altar slightly to meet the instrument of his fate. His lips tensed. He struggled to keep them closed. He didn't dare make a sound. He didn't dare disrespect the gods by crying out, not before entering paradise. His eyes winced, then grew large as his heart shuddered. After a final breath, Kanul closed his eyes and his body went limp.

Warm blood flowed freely over the high priest's hands as he held the dagger in Kanul's chest and moved it back and forth.

With the precision of a seasoned hunter, the high priest cut away Kanul's flesh from his chest and exposed his now still, filleted heart.

"Kanul, enter paradise!" the high priest called out, raising his arms and looking skyward. Kanul's blood ran down the high priest's forearms and dripped off his elbows. Ma'xu thought he saw Kanul's spirit ascend upward out of his opened chest cavity. Ma'xu looked up and realized the importance of Kanul's sacrifice. Kanul had transcended the small village.

For a moment, Ma'xu's stomach clenched and his chest tightened. Ma'xu bowed his head. Thank you for your sacrifice, Kanul. Honor is yours, my friend.

Ma'xu thought he heard Kanul's voice say, "Peace be with you, Ma'xu."

The slow and steady beat of tribal drums began. On cue, some of the women of the village rushed and encircled the altar. Standing with their arms outstretched, they closed their eyes and tilted their heads back. The slow sway of their bodies allowed them to absorb every beat from the drums. As if in a trance, they began to slowly and rhythmically move around the altar. Their gyrations matched every strike of the drums. The pulsating beat increased until the women were no longer in control of their bodies. Like gods, the drummers possessed the women with every beat. In perfect synch, the dancers were slaves to the rhythm. The watching villagers could no longer hold back. They joined in and a celebration ensued. They too began to chant and sway to the beat of the drums as the high priest led the crowd away from the field. They followed him to the village where a bonfire had been started. The celebration had begun and would continue for three days.

Chapter Two

The Pulitzer
Low Library, Columbia University, New York
May 19, 2017

The annual Pulitzer awards luncheon at Columbia University was blessed with warm temperatures, clear skies, and plenty of alcohol. The annual recognition of top journalists would again stroke the egos of the chosen. A veneer of politeness enveloped the ballroom and concealed the secret individual validation many writers searched for. Champagne and wine flowed as freely as the compliments. Mason Rhimes wanted no validation. As an investigative journalist for the *Chicago Sun*, he exposed a corrupt city alderman that led to a corrupt police chief, which led to a corrupt judge and trickled down from there. It involved corrupt police officers and assistant district attorneys. Some writers in the business accused him of having a death wish, or that he was reckless and was going to get a lot of people hurt. Still others believed he was selfish and it was his ego that was driving him.

None of those reasons were what drove Mason. Only a select few friends he worked with knew the truth. It was his way of dealing with grief.

Most people knew him and his tragic story, but not well enough to discuss it with him. People didn't know how to handle him. They eventually learned to leave him alone.

The *Chicago Sun* has three nominations this year, an average year for Chicago's largest newspaper. Mason had no intention of attending the ceremony, but his newspaper wasn't going to let him miss this one. He knew he wasn't going to weasel out of it and willingly succumbed to peer pressure. They watched the ceremony and waited patiently until the moderator at the podium began to announce Mason's category.

"The next Pulitzer Prize is awarded for the category of: 'A distinguished example of investigative reporting, using any available journalistic tool.' The prize for this outstanding journalism category is awarded to an individual who overcame great personal sacrifice to expose corruption at nearly every level of city government and has made the city of Chicago much safer. Ladies and gentlemen, the Pulitzer Prize award for Excellence in Investigative Reporting is awarded to Mason Rhimes from the *Chicago Sun* for his series entitled Internal Affairs: The Depth of Corruption."

The crowd let out a roaring applause as they rose out of their chairs and stood for Mason. Although his peers were somewhat envious, they knew this award was one that was truly earned. It was the final chapter to a rough year.

With both inner pride and resolved purpose, Mason quickly walked from his round table of ten and made his way around three more tables, toward the stage. Before climbing the three steps up to the stage, Mason stopped to shake the hand of Jim Stevens, the president of the White House Press Corps. Given the forty-plus-year career of Stevens, Mason felt obligated to acknowledge one of the few remaining relics who knew what it meant to be a good journalist. Mason was not eager to be in the spotlight, but deep down he appreciated the recognition.

"Congratulations, Mason. Would you like to say a few words?" the moderator asked.

"No, thank you. I'll write one," Mason said, taking his prize and trying to avoid a speech. Mason was a good writer, but a bad politician.

"They're on their feet, Mason, you really should say something," the moderator reiterated into Mason's ear. As he placed his hand on Mason's shoulder, they both experienced a shock that penetrated their bodies. Their eyes grew large as the intensity of the shock grew. Their eyes were drawn to each other's. Time stopped. Neither of them could breathe. The moderator was powerless to stop the spiritual assault on his now exposed soul. Mason knew what the pulsating energy meant. Something he hadn't experienced in over a year. The fate of the moderator was clear. Information was now burned into Mason's mind. The shock stopped abruptly as the moderator removed his hand from Mason's shoulder. They both took deep breaths. The moderator's confusion quickly began to subside with each breath.

"What was that?" he asked Mason.

"Static electricity I guess," Mason replied, knowing well it was not. "You'll be okay, just be sure to call your children when you get home."

"All right," he said calmly, "I will." Not sure what had happened, the moderator stepped back and tried in vain to figure out what Mason meant.

Mason caught his breath and sheepishly stepped up to the microphone. His broad shoulders and thin six-foot-tall frame dwarfed the podium. A navy blue blazer that covered his wrinkled white dress shirt hung on him as if he were merely a coat rack. His black eyebrows accentuated his deep-set, piercing brown eyes. Smooth facial skin wouldn't allow him to grow anything but patchy facial hair. Silky jet-black hair covered his ears and hung to the nape of his neck. He surveyed the ballroom and realized everyone was watching and waiting on him. With a deep breath he collected his thoughts, cleared his throat, and began to speak.

"I want to just say thanks to everyone who helped me on this project. Although I ended up with the award, there are so many people from the Sun that helped in various capacities; I couldn't possibly mention all of them. Thanks to Dom, for letting me run with the story, and thanks to the team at the Sun for their support."

Mason retreated down the steps to a second standing ovation. As Mason traversed the crowd, he stopped and shook hands with dozens of people, some of whom he had never met in his life. Funny, they were never that interested in what I had to say before, he thought.

"Nice job, Mason," Dom and his wife Elena said as Mason returned to the table.

Michelle, one of the proof editors, gave Mason a hug. "Congratulations Mason, we're all proud of you."

Michelle was a good person on whom he had relied on countless occasions to conduct discreet inquiries in various city offices. Her athletic figure, fiery red hair, and sea-blue eyes augmented her twenty-something mannerisms. Taken as a whole, her physical appearance camouflaged her aggressive and competent instincts. Few could resist her wiles.

"Yeah, congrats Mase. Now aren't you glad we talked you into coming?" Al said, raising his glass of champagne to Mason.

"Yes, I guess so." Mason looked down and placed on the table, the crystal plaque that from this day forward would collect dust. He didn't like to be the center of attention.

Dom turned to Mason and with a wink and a Cheshire-cat smile announced, "I have a surprise for you, Mason; we'll talk later."

"Oh, I can hardly wait," Mason replied, knowing that Dom's surprises usually ended up with more work and shorter deadlines.

"You'll see," Dom said as his voiced faded. "Just wait . . ."

When the ceremony ended, the mob of people began their trod out of the dining room and into the lobby. Joining the lobotomy parade, Mason made his way into the lobby with the rest of the Sun staff. Mason took comfort in his conclusion that unlike some of his peers, he presented the truth. Nothing more. Nothing less.

"Well, Mason," Michelle said, "that was way cool. Kelly would've been proud of you." Mason looked down, Al made a beeline for the bar, and everyone gave her "the look." Picking up on their "don't bring up Kelly's name" hint, she tried to backpedal. "Mason, I'm sorry. I—"

"No Michelle," Mason cut her off and continued, "it's all right. Kelly? Yes, she would've enjoyed this." A group of people from the local Fox affiliate stopped and interrupted their conversation to congratulate Mason, and in doing so bailed out Michelle.

Al walked up and handed Mason a drink and pulled Michelle out onto the patio, away from the group. The fresh air brought color back into her otherwise pale complexion.

"Thanks for saving me," Michelle said.

"Don't ever say there's never a cop around when you need one," Al replied, handing Michelle a Jameson and Coke.

"You know Mason pretty well, don't you?" Michelle asked.

"Mason and I have been friends since we were kids. We grew up on the west side together. I probably know him better than anyone."

"Do you think I offended him when I asked about Kelly?" she asked.

"No way. Kelly was a big deal to him, but I wouldn't worry about it."

"I remember when she died. He took it pretty hard," Michelle said.

"I think he still takes it pretty personal, but he's getting better. Sometimes he's hard to read. When the Sun didn't really support him, it reminded him of issues he had when he was a kid."

"Like what?" Michelle asked.

"That's a lot more complicated than we have time for. Let's just say that he's no stranger to abandonment and ridicule."

"That's horrible; he's so nice."

"There are some things that are complicated about him, and he doesn't like to discuss it." Al sensed he was probably saying too much and clammed up. He knew better than most the remorse that Mason felt about Kelly's death. He also knew he was going down a road he didn't want to go with Michelle. He did a classic redirect.

"So what's your story, Michelle?"

Mason walked up before Michelle could answer. "Michelle, is he bothering you? I can call the police."

"No Mason, I think I can handle this one," she said with a flirtatious grin. "However, I'll leave you boys to talk about guy stuff." She could feel their eyes burning her back as she walked away smiling.

"Way to go Mase, I was just about to move in for the 'Al your pal' move."

"Sorry; and for the record, that never works."

"Yeah, you're right," Al conceded.

Noticing the gaggle of women smiling at Mason from the bar, Mason asked Al, "Any idea why those women over there keep looking at me weird?"

"Nope. I have no idea. Maybe they like you," Al replied, knowing that Mason knew better.

"Right, what am I now, a massage therapist?" Mason asked.

"Mase, I don't know what you're talking about. They probably think you're a stallion or something like that," Al said with a chuckle.

"Great! Thanks. That would explain the winks."

"See, it works, as long as we work together," Al said, lowering the pitch in his voice. His words oozed sarcasm.

The two of them retreated with their drinks into the courtyard overlooking the mature red sunset maple trees. Violet Weigela bushes were in full blossom. The grounds were accented with perfectly trimmed variegated dogwood hedges and perennials that acknowledged summer was close at hand. The old brick buildings scattered across the campus reeked of academics and tradition. Leaning over the railing, they took in the beauty of the university campus.

"The drawback to burning the candle at both ends is at some point it stops burning," Al said. "Then you have to regroup. You know, slow things down and start living again."

"I guess so. You really don't realize how busy you get until you stop and look around," Mason replied.

"I don't know how you did it and managed to stay alive, but it was a hell of a year for you," Al said, raising his glass to Mason's. Mason drank the cool, smooth Irish whiskey. It felt like soft hand-brushed silk as it warmed his throat. Coke was the perfect complement to the Jameson. Just then a large white owl flew by and caught their attention. They watched as it flew up and perched up on a corner of a building.

"Mason, that's not for you, is it?" Al asked cautiously.

"I don't know; I don't think so. I haven't seen him in a long time." Mason gazed at the bird. His thoughts raced. What now? Why now?

The owl looked down at them with its blood-red eyes. It opened its massive wingspan and let out an ear-piercing screech that quieted the entire patio instantly. Then it leapt from its perch and flew off with its black talons dangling in the air. Dom spotted Mason and Al watching the owl as it disappeared into the horizon and walked over to them.

"You guys see that owl? I've never seen anything like that," Dom said in amazement.

Mason and Al looked at each other and Al excused himself. Mason spoke up.

"Yes, kind of weird," he replied.

Dom quickly dismissed the odd bird. "Mason, what you said in there was very nice, and not entirely true. You know as well as I do that most of the people who worked with you did very little to help out. In fact, most people tried to sabotage your work. No, you did this one on your own."

"Look, whether anyone realizes it or not, it helped having somewhere to go and keep busy. I know a lot of people don't understand me, and that's fine, I'm not even sure I do sometimes."

"Reporters deliberately tried to mislead and derail you and you're all right with that?"

"What am I supposed to do, Dom, hate everyone?" Mason said, throwing his arms up.

"No, but get a little pissed, you know, vent a little. It'll liberate you."

Mason knew Dom was right; however, Mason had enough personal issues to dwell on and chose not to worry about work things. "No, I'm done with it. Water under the bridge."

"Look Mason, you exhibited real class. You and I know you did this one on your own. It wasn't until you had enough proof that I bought off on the project; and I knew it would sell papers. I don't tell many people this, but thank you for taking the high road. I was wrong."

"Dom—" Mason started, but was immediately cut off.

"No, I'm sorry for making your life harder than it needed to be. You're an outstanding journalist and we're lucky to have you on our staff."

"Thanks Dom. That means a lot to me."

"You've had a heck of a year, and the city is indebted to you. So here's the surprise. You're going to take a month off with pay; you deserve it."

"Thanks Dom, but I don't—" Mason tried again.

"No Mason; this one's not negotiable," Dom interrupted. "I was a jerk when you lost Kelly. I was a jerk when you came to me with the story. In fact, I was jerk to you most of the last year. It's the least the Sun can do. Take it as a 'thank you' from me," Dom insisted.

Mason looked around and was curiously at a loss for words. "I don't know what to say."

"Say you'll do something fun."

"All right, I'll try."

"Remember, success can be fleeting," Dom reassured. "Make sure you enjoy it a little."

"Thanks, I will. It's been a long time since I've done anything, fun or otherwise. So, yes, I will," Mason said, trying to reassure himself.

"That's the spirit, Mason," Dom said, raising his glass to Mason's.

Chapter 3

The Almazorians
Rabwah, Pakistan
May 20, 2017

The brilliancy of the stars pierced the cool nighttime shroud that encompassed the town square. The surrounding mountains provided a backdrop of majesty, a constant reminder of the arduous culture they lived in. With restless anticipation, the people waited to be enlightened as to the nature of the last-minute assembly. The low rumble from the gathered villagers erupted into cheers as Ahmed Mirza Almazor walked up to the elevated stage and stood at the podium. He looked up at the cloudless night and out over the thousands of villagers gathered in the square to hear their leader speak. When Ahmed raised his arms, a hush came over the crowd. No one dared make a sound when Ahmed spoke. He began to deliver his scathing proclamation.

"Tonight Allah bestows great favor on us, my fellow Almazorians. I come to you as the last of many great prophets. Allah has revealed to me that some of you question his will for us. I assure you that Allah will give a great sign that you will believe we are his favored people." He waited for the crowd's cheers to subside before continuing.

"He will deliver to us our enemies, and we will be victorious!" he shouted to the masses. "No longer will evil nations disrespect our culture. Infidels will bow down to us or they will perish!" he continued.

The loud cheering crowd fed off every word Ahmed delivered. Their shouts became louder. His words were like verbal cocaine. The villagers held their rifles and guns in the air in elation as they listened to their leader.

"Our time draws near, my brethren, when Allah will call on us to act. Prepare yourselves physically and mentally. For the spawn of Satan prepares his armies for battle. We will attack any infidel nation that will not bow down to Allah, especially the Americans. The eagle will bow down or become extinct. Feast now, for soon we go to battle and claim what is ours. All hail Allah! All hail Allah!" Ahmed concluded and exited the stage with his advisors. His vocal orgy transformed the crowd into a spectacle second only to Sodom and Gomorrah.

Ahmed hurriedly climbed into his chauffeured limousine with his brother Macmul.

They drove thirty minutes through the Suleiman Mountains to his lavish palace secluded in the Suleiman mountain range. The guards stood at full attention and saluted the limousine as it passed through the entrance gates. The limousine pulled up to the front of the house; Ahmed and his brother climbed out and entered the palace through the large front doors. They sat down in oversized plush chairs and watched the party on their television set while his servant girls brought them *Khamr*.

"You! Come here," Ahmed said, pointing to a young Muslim serving girl. She walked over and bowed down, "Yes, King?"

"My beautiful flower, let me show you how much Allah loves you," Ahmed said, pulling the young girl onto his lap and kissing her roughly. Macmul smiled and called one of the other girls and began to grope her as well.

"Bring more drink," Ahmed ordered.

"And send for more girls," Macmul added as they looked at each other and laughed.

The villagers partied and drank all night, celebrating. Most did not know what exactly they were celebrating, but they enjoyed the revelry nonetheless.

The nighttime debauchery was extinguished by the advent of dawn, at which time General Aleem, who had been keeping watch all night, rushed to the front door of Ahmed's palace and knocked.

A servant answered the front door. "Sir, they are sleeping and not to be disturbed," the servant told a nervous General Aleem.

"I know, but this is of utmost importance."

"Wait here, I will check if he will see you." Aleem walked in and waited inside the front door while the servant went to disturb Ahmed, a duty he knew was a risky proposition. As the servant opened the large double doors to Ahmed's bedroom, allowing light to illuminate the huge room, the occupants all shielded their eyes as if the light burned.

"What, what do you want!" Ahmed yelled.

"Your highness, I beg your forgiveness, but General Aleem requires your immediate attention."

"What does the general want?" Ahmed asked, trying to gather his senses.

The servant looked around the room. The long red drapes covering the windows barely let in enough light to observe numerous nude women strewn around like laundry. "I don't know sir, but he said it was of the utmost importance."

"Bring him to me," Ahmed ordered while he sat up in bed.

"Excuse me sir, here?" the servant asked.

"Perhaps I cut off your ears since they do not work; yes here!" Ahmed scolded.

"Of course my lord, my apologies," he said, bowing and backing out of the room. He returned to the general.

"The king will see you; follow me. He's in there," the servant said, pointing down a long corridor lined with portraits of past leaders that led to Ahmed's bedroom.

"He wants me in there?" the general asked curiously.

"Yes, and I pity you if it's not important," the servant said as he walked away, leaving the general to enter alone. With a deep breath, Aleem walked nervously down the hall and entered Ahmed's bedroom.

"Your highness, I apologize for the intrusion."

"Get on with it, what do you want?" Ahmed bellowed.

"My lord, perhaps we can talk in private," he said, looking at the nude and partially nude women scattered throughout the room sleeping.

"Ah, you like, no?" Ahmed said, changing his tone, looking at the women as if they were candy.

"Yes, lord, they are quite beautiful, but this matter is of utmost importance."

"I'll tell you what, my friend," Ahmed said from his bed. "If what you tell me is worthy, you can have any one of them; but if you waste my time I cut your throat right here."

"As you wish, my lord," the general said with a deep swallow and a long nervous breath.

"All of you, go to the pools. Leave, get out, all of you!" Ahmed ordered the women.

"All right my friend, what is so important as to wake a prophet and make him remove his conquests?"

"Sir, intelligence from the field indicates that the Americans might be planning an attack."

Ahmed's ears perked up. "Where?"

"We believe right here in Rabwah, sir."

"How did you obtain this information?"

"One of our confidential sources in the US Army told us."

"And this source is credible?"

"Yes sir, he is an officer."

"Did he say what they are going to do?"

"Yes sir, they are going to send a recon team in to scout the area. The next course of action depends on what they report back."

"What do you recommend, general?" Ahmed asked.

"We either attack them or we cease all training, pull back all military, and hide what we can until they leave."

"How did they find us?"

"We're not sure sir. We know there's a lot of activity in the region searching for al-Qaida or ISIS. More than likely, it's not us they're looking for."

"Al-Qaida; those greedy bastards. I should show the Americans their base myself, just to show the world they are but a pimple on the ass of a donkey compared to me!" Ahmed exclaimed.

"My king, what will you have us do? Should we attack them? Certainly Allah will protect us?"

"Patience, general, today we hide and plan. Don't let on that we know anything. Let them see that we are a peaceful village, for soon we will be silent no more," Ahmed ordered.

"As you wish," Aleem said as he bowed and backpedaled to the door.

"Wait!" Ahmed ordered.

Aleem stopped in his tracks and froze. A nervous tightening overcame his stomach. "Yes, Ahmed?"

"General, what about the other matter, in London?" Ahmed asked.

"Sir, the final plans are in order; tomorrow we attack Victoria Square," Aleem replied with a sense of relief.

"Very good Aleem. Allah has assured me that the attack on England will get the Americans' attention. Then we hit the Unites States and cripple them. Only then will we take our rightful place as a world power."

"Yes, my lord. We are in exciting times thanks to your greatness," Aleem said while trying to conceal his great concern.

"General, go to the pool. Eat, drink, and have as many women as you want, for you are a good and trustworthy man."

"Thank you, your highness," the general said with a sigh of relief and bowing to Ahmed.

"And general, be sure to tell people how good and generous your king is. Allah will take care of anyone who bows to me. Those that do not will perish."

"Hail Allah," General Aleem said, leaving the king's quarters. As he walked quickly down the hallway out of Ahmed's room, he passed Macmul heading toward Ahmed's room.

"Greetings Ahmed," Macmul said, bursting into Ahmed's bedroom.

"Ah Macmul, how are you this fine morning?" Ahmed asked, sitting up in his bed.

"My head pounds like a jackhammer," Macmul answered as he poured himself into an oversized chair and threw his right leg up over the armrest. "Ahmed, I must apologize for the servant girl—"

"No Macmul, not again," Ahmed said, cutting off his brother.

"I'm sorry, it got crazy. I won't do it again, I promise," Macmul said.

"You better not, Macmul," Ahmed scolded. "You have to stop killing my servant girls. People will start asking questions." Ahmed's reprimand was abruptly interrupted by a servant who brought the two of them breakfast. Ravenously attacking their food, Ahmed ordered Macmul, "Save your aggression for the battlefield, my brother."

"I know, I'm sorry. I'll try to stop before cutting them too deep," Macmul said regretfully. "At least until tonight," he laughed.

"Macmul, you are an animal," Ahmed said, throwing a piece of toast at him and shaking his head. Macmul changed their conversation to General Aleem.

"Hey, I saw General Aleem going to the pool; what did he want?" Macmul asked.

"He warned us of the Americans possibly attacking."

"Attacking us?" Macmul said, laughing with Ahmed.

"Yes, I thought that was good intelligence to leak to the general," Ahmed said. "We just needed to buy some time; this will give us all of the time we need," he continued.

"But what happens when our soldiers don't see any American soldiers?" Macmul asked.

"Then we start killing them one by one until someone sees something. After two or three, they will all have seen the Americans, trust me," Ahmed said with a smile on his face. "Then because they are gone, we'll take credit for chasing them out of our city."

"Nice plan, Ahmed, but brother, I have a serious question."

"What is it, Macmul?"

"We've made a name for ourselves and our people over the last several years attacking small targets; do you really think we should hit London?"

"I can assure you, Macmul," he said, looking intently into Macmul's eyes, "we will never get the respect from our Muslim brethren if we don't go bigger."

"Yes, but England are allies with America."

"That is precisely why we hit America after London," an impassioned Ahmed said, standing up and throwing his arms up in the air. "Nobody could deny us after that—nobody," he said.

"I hope you are correct, Ahmed."

"I am; now let's finish breakfast and go to the pool for dessert."

Chapter 4

Spirit of the Jaguar
Altun Ha
899 AD

Shortly after midnight on the third day after Ma'xu's victory, the familiar sounds of the high priest's rattling string of bones made their way to Ma'xu resting in his hut. He was still recovering from the injuries handed out during the life-altering game of Temple Ball.

He got up and walked outside to see the gauntlet of villagers waiting for him. He was unsure if it was the dark eyes of the high priest or the head of the jaguar on top of the high priest's head that peeled back the protective layers of flesh and penetrated the depths of Ma'xu's soul. Without hesitation, Ma'xu followed the high priest to the village center. Ma'xu anticipated the bestowed glory that would forever be associated with his family lineage.

With every step, Ma'xu's heart beat faster. I must not disrespect my father, he reminded himself. He had seen the village blessings before, but had never participated in them. I must be strong, like Kanul. I must be a warrior.

The cool night air was singed with the scent of wood from the bonfire. Glowing embers ascended into the air as if showing the way to paradise. The high priest led Ma'xu to a large stone altar in the center of the village. The altar was stained with blood from previous sacrifices. Unlike the altar on which Kanul was ushered into paradise, this altar was for more significant village sacrifices. Stopping at the altar and raising his arms, the high priest looked to the night sky. Everyone and everything stopped instantly as his arms dropped.

"Ma'xu, you have been chosen by the gods to go to Tikal!" he yelled out. "You will need protection from the gods on your journey." The high priest raised his right arm. Receiving the cue, four tribal warriors carried a live jaguar up to the altar behind the high priest. The jaguar growled in protest. His trembling jowls muzzled, the jaguar gnawed on the leather straps that silenced his plea for freedom. The jaguar now knew what it meant to be hunted. His days of hunting prey were over. The jaguar sensed his impending doom as he thrashed about in full survival mode.

A hush came over the villagers as they watched the warriors slam the jaguar onto the top of the altar. Blood leaked out of the arms of the transporters as the jaguar used its sharp claws to slice the arms of the men as they struggled to hold it down. In an act of defiance, the jaguar's pink tongue licked their blood through its muzzle as if making its last stand.

The high priest looked up to the night sky with the familiar dagger in both hands, closed his eyes, and said a prayer. He then leaned in and looked into the jaguar's black eyes. The jaguar went still as the mesmerizing glare of the high priest controlled the beast. Their eyes stared intensely into each other's. In another time or dimension, these two would have been siblings. Tonight the high priest would seize the jaguar's spirit and channel it into Ma'xu.

With one smooth motion, the high priest plunged the stone dagger deep into the belly of the jaguar. The jaguar writhed in pain and let out an ear-piercing cry that echoed through the jungle. The jaguar's confusion was short-lived. With a final whine, its life bled away. The high priest reached into the open belly of the now motionless jaguar and ripped out the animal's lifeless heart with his bare hands.

"Receive the spirit of the jaguar!" he said, handing it to Ma'xu. Ma'xu held the jaguar's stagnant heart, still warm and dripping with blood, in his hands. He looked at his father for approval. The king nodded and extended his arms toward Ma'xu. The king could not have been more proud.

Raising the heart to his mouth, Ma'xu bit into it and ripped a piece off. He chewed the warm tough flesh and resisted the impulse to gag. His stomach turned to knots. Fighting back the urge to throw up, Ma'xu tightened his stomach and prevented it from convulsing. As the soft flesh made its way down Ma'xu's narrowing throat, he felt empowered. He did not disgrace his father, his people, or the gods by throwing up the raw meat. The high priest then dipped a cup into the animal's open cavity and filled it with the jaguar's blood for Ma'xu to drink.

The warm metallic taste of the jaguar's blood made Ma'xu's own heart beat faster. It was like nothing he had ever tasted before. It was the taste of being a warrior, of being a leader. With most of the blood running down Ma'xu's face and chest, the villagers cheered louder with every succession of Ma'xu's throat. All eyes were locked onto Ma'xu. When he finished drinking the blood, the villagers let out a frenzied applause. Ma'xu had passed his test. The village had a new warrior amongst them.

Ma'xu's father approached Ma'xu and applied village war paint to Ma'xu's blood-drenched face while the high priest continued to pray over him. Retrieving a handful of powder from a leather pouch, the high priest blew the powder into Ma'xu's face and said, "The powder will protect you from the evil spirits, Ma'xu."

"Why does it burn?" Ma'xu asked while wincing and tossing his head back and forth.

The high priest's eyes grew wide. "Because it cleanses your soul," he said, followed by an uproarious, eerie laugh.

Ma'xu's vision began to fade in and out. His head began to spin. "What's happening?" he called out. The villagers laughed as Ma'xu began to hallucinate. The drums started beating again and the women began to dance. In the clear night sky, he could make out a large white bird circling.

"Ma'xu," the bird called to him. Dropping to his knees and looking up, he heard the bird call him again, "Ma'xu!"

"Ma'xu! Wake up," his mother said, shaking him from his sleep.

"What!" Ma'xu said, jumping up off the ground in his stone hut. "What? What's going on?"

"Ma'xu, relax, you were having a dream."

"No, it was an owl," Ma'xu said, looking around frantically, trying to gather his senses.

"No Ma'xu, it was the gods," his father said, entering the hut. "It is the spirit that will guide you today."

"Today? What happened last night?"

"After you received your blessing, you went to sleep. Now you are ready for your journey."

"Tikal; yes, I'm ready," he said, as if trying to convince himself. He caught his breath and reassured himself, "Yes, I'm ready."

Chapter 5

New Beginnings
Chicago, Illinois
May 20, 2017

With every step Mason took, running through the tropical forest, the screech of the large white bird was getting closer. The faster he ran, the closer it got. He couldn't see the bird. He could only hear its terrifying screech echoing through the woods. He knew it was coming for him.

I've got to hide, he thought. Seeing a small cave, he sprinted for it. Turning slightly over his left shoulder, he saw the large white owl emerge from the trees. Locked onto Mason like a laser-guided missile, the owl let out an ear-piercing screech and flapped its wings faster, heading for Mason. Mason ran into the cave and stopped. Standing in the dark, he could now see the owl stopped at the entrance. Perched on a rock, the owl was going to wait for Mason to come out.

I have to keep going, he thought. Deeper and deeper into the dark cave he went. The blackness of the cave rendered his vision useless. He stumbled into the wall of the cave, disturbing sleeping bats. Thousands of them at once made a mass exodus out of the cave. Every bat that bumped into him was like someone sticking him with a hot poker. Mason's heart pounded as he ducked for cover.

I must continue on, he reassured himself. As he straightened up, he felt spiders begin dropping onto his head and shoulders. They crawled on his neck and arms. They were everywhere. Panic set in. He began smacking himself, yelling, and shaking like a possessed person. He started running blindly, banging into the walls of the cave. Finally, a light. Hope overcame him as he ran to it.

He emerged from the cave and was stunned. He walked out onto a beach. It was serene, tranquil, and soothing. It was like walking into another world. Dropping to his knees exhausted, he shook one last spider out of his hair. As he tried to regain his breathing, he noticed a large shadow move over the sand. Looking up to confirm what he dreaded, he saw the large white owl circling. His heart pounding again, but too tired to run any further, he accepted defeat.

"What do you want?" he yelled, throwing his arms up in the air.

While looking up at the bird, he hadn't noticed that he was being dwarfed by a large shadow. He could feel someone standing behind him. He turned slowly and saw a large Indian standing behind him holding a staff. Falling backwards onto his back, Mason froze. He stared up at the Indian. If he wanted me dead, he'd already have done it, he thought. What does he want?

The owl opened its massive wingspan and landed on the Indian's staff. Its black talons dug into the wood while it tucked away its bright-white perfect feathers. Its ruby red eyes stared at Mason. He was paralyzed.

"Fear not," the Indian said. "Soon he comes for you."

"Who?" Mason asked as he trembled.

With that, the Indian let out a deafening laugh and the owl leapt from its perch straight at Mason's face.

"Whoa!" Mason leaped out of bed panting like one of Pavlov's dogs. "What the hell?" he said, patting himself down, looking for injuries or spiders.

With each ring of the phone, Mason heard five more in his head. Between the pounding hangover and the bizarre dream, he finally managed to find the phone. Still deeply confused, "Yeah?" was all he could muster into the phone.

"Hey, wake up," the voice on the other end of the phone said.

"What? Are you crazy, do you know what time it is?" Mason shot back, looking at his alarm clock.

"Yes, I know what time it is; the question is, do you?" the vaguely familiar voice responded.

Looking at the clock, Mason said in a rude voice, "It's one o'clock in the freaking morning!"

"No, it's one o'clock in the afternoon," the now familiar voice said.

Mason moved his window shade aside and looked outside. The blinding light confirmed his father was right. "Sorry Dad, late night," he replied. Patrick Rhimes was no stranger to late night parties. After Mason's mother died, he spent many nights drinking away the pain. Drinking away parental responsibility. Drinking away his relationship with Mason.

"No problem Mase. Then I guess you probably don't remember calling me at 3:30 in the morning?"

Rubbing his throbbing head in confusion, he remorsefully replied, "No I don't, sorry."

"Don't worry about it, you sounded like you were having fun, a sound I haven't heard from you in a long time."

"I think it was fun, from what I remember of it," Mason said as his eyes began to focus clearly now. "We got in last night and went to a party for the paper and everyone had to buy me a shot."

"Sounds painful; congratulations again then, I'm really proud of you."

"Thanks, it was pretty incredible. I feel like the last year was a blur, like I just woke up from a weird dream." Wait a minute, he thought, I did just wake from a weird dream, huh?

"Last year *was* a blur; you buried yourself in your work so much that you really didn't live much. Sounds like this year's going better for you."

"Yes, maybe," Mason replied. "I must've caught Dom in a good mood; he gave me a month off with pay."

"Wow! I'd take him up on it before he changes his mind, or conveniently forgets that he gave it to you."

"Yes, I'll confirm it with him later. Although, I'm not sure what I'll do with that much time off."

"Great! Why don't you come down to Arizona for a couple of weeks and we'll play some tennis; that is, if you still remember how."

"I'll see. I'm not sure what I've got going, but maybe," Mason said while actually thinking about it.

"I've been retired six years now and you've come down what, twice?"

The words his father said struck Mason deep. There are a few reasons I don't go down, Mason thought. There's the little thing about my childhood. There's the thing with Mom's death. There's the thing with Kelly's death.

"So what do you say?" his father said, interrupting his temporary internal regression.

"Look, Dad, let me call you later, I have to get up and get some aspirin." After Mason hung up, he pondered the possibility of going to see his dad in Arizona. He had always hoped that one day he would see his father and he'd understand Mason's issues. Instead, his father always feared what he didn't understand. We get along great as long as it doesn't involve someone dying, he thought. A byproduct of him being an engineer, Mason concluded.

While retrieving a Red Bull from the refrigerator, the phone rang again. Being more awake and expecting this one, he answered the phone, "Hello Al—yes, I'm up."

"Wow, miracles never cease to amaze me," Al said on the other end of the line. "How are you feeling?" he continued.

"Like my brain simply stopped working. It's been a long time since I've been to a party like that. I feel as if I've been on a bender," Mason said.

"Yeah, it kind of was a bender," Al said. "Are we on for Gino's?"

"Yes, I'm starving; I'll meet you there in an hour," Mason said.

"Great, that'll give me time to complete the trifecta with Michelle."

"A trifecta! What, are you training for porn star auditions?" Mason joked.

"It's an alter ego thing, you wouldn't understand—or actually, I guess you would," Al said, laughing.

"Funny; even if it's true. I'll see you at Gino's," Mason said.

After he hung up the phone, Mason sat down on a padded Adirondack chair on his balcony and inhaled the fresh springtime air. Mason sipped a well-known cure for the common hangover, a Red Bull. It tasted like strawberry Mountain Dew. He loved Mountain Dew as a child. Memories of his childhood crept into his consciousness. A sobering chill went through his body as he closed his eyes and reminisced about the sixth grade.

While walking his bike home from school because some older kids released all the air out of his tires, some other kids started picking on a twelve-year-old Mason.

"Hey, Mason, you kill anyone today?" one boy shouted at him.

Another said, "Yeah, you really see ghosts? You freak." Mason tried to ignore them and go around, but they wouldn't let him pass. They circled him and started pushing him. One after another, they pushed and taunted him until he fell to the ground.

"Leave me alone!" he yelled, but that just egged them on more. Large pimple-faced Ricky Heinz walked up to hit him.

"Here loser, let me know if you see a ghost now." As he raised his clenched fist and prepared to punch Mason, a boy from the seventh grade walked up behind Ricky and knocked him to the ground next to Mason. The older boy, who was much larger then Ricky, threatened them all.

"If you ever touch this kid again, I'll pound you into the dirt! Got it?" With that, they all agreed and took off running.

"Hey kid, are you all right?" he asked Mason as he held out his hand to help him up.

"Yeah, thanks," Mason said, shamefully taking his hand.

"Don't worry about those jerks," the stranger said. "They won't be bothering you any time soon."

"It's all right; I'm used to it. It seems like trouble just follows me."

"Well, I should hang out with you more often because I love trouble," the large, intimidating boy said with a smile. "Come on. I'm Al, what's your name?" the boy asked as they started to walk. Mason found a smirk creep across his face. For the first time in his new town, his new school, and his new life, he felt a little at ease.

As Mason sat on his balcony and reflected on one of the most defining moments in his life, he smiled. What he remembered next about meeting Al for the first time removed the smile.

While walking down the road, Al stopped and pointed to a bird perched on top of a utility pole across the street. "Hey Mason, check out that huge bird. What is it?" he asked.

"I don't know, but it's huge," Mason said as they stood looking at it. "Maybe it's an eagle."

"It's just staring at us; maybe it's a vampire bat and it wants to suck our blood," Al said naively.

"No, those are black and they can't come out during the day," the twelve-year-old Mason said nonchalantly. Just then the large white bird opened its enormous wingspan and flew off, followed by a loud screech.

"That was cool, huh Mason?" Al said with excitement as he tried to follow it down the street.

"Yeah, that was awesome; I can't wait to tell my mom," Mason said as they continued their walk up the street.

"Hey, what did those guys mean when they asked if you saw ghosts?"

"I don't want to talk about it."

"Cool. Do you like sports?" Al asked, changing the subject. He was just content talking to a new friend. That was the first time someone actually didn't care about Mason's uniqueness.

Back on his balcony, Mason remembered the bird. A white owl. That was the first time he remembered seeing it, but not the last. What was it doing at Columbia? he wondered. Ah, the moderator he remembered; he's already dead. He tried to recall his dream; however, the jackhammer in his head would not allow it. "Weird" was the only descriptor his pounding head could garner. Then he looked at the copper oil lamp hanging on the balcony patio wall and remembered when Kelly brought it home two years ago.

"Hey Mase, check out this oil lamp, I found it down on Maxwell Street," Kelly said to Mason, who was sitting on the balcony, reading.

"Wow! Oh my God," Mason said. "It looks like, like, like an oil lamp," he stuttered sarcastically, followed by an outburst of laughter.

"Funny," Kelly said, laughing as well. "They don't make this kind of quality anymore, and besides, it could be magic."

"I'm kidding; it's nice," Mason said, examining the lamp.

"Well, I like it, and it stays here," she said, hanging it on an old nail in the center of the outside wall on their balcony. That night, they had the first of many romantic candlelight dinners on their balcony with their magical oil lamp. Mason prepared a pepper cream sauce with shallots and drizzled it over roasted beef medallions and crumbled blue cheese. Kelly made the brown rice and warm spinach salad with bacon and almonds topped with raspberry vinaigrette dressing. Of course, Kelly's favorite red zinfandel, Tobin James French Camp Vineyard, perfected the evening.

It was definitely a magical lamp, he thought, staring at it hanging slightly crooked on the wall. As soon as the thought entered his mind, however, it was erased with the memory of Kelly's death one year earlier. It wasn't supposed to happen. I made sure of it. He continued to struggle with the fact that it didn't make any sense.

When Kelly was around, the world made sense for him, and when she died, all sense of the world died. The confusion and restlessness that he suffered throughout his entire life resurfaced. He was alone again. Between the deaths of Kelly and his mother, Mason learned not to dwell on things he couldn't change. Some might call it denial. Others might call it apathy. To Mason, it was coping.

As the Red Bull coursed through his veins, a tranquil calm came over him like a hippie in an opium den. The light springtime breeze blowing across his eighteenth story balcony felt cool on his face, and the sound of downtown life going on around him calmed his nerves. He could feel his hangover disappear with every sip. For a small moment in time, he was at peace with the world instead of fighting it.

The weight of grief, guilt, anger, and pressure was hoisted off his back. For the first time in a year, he didn't have a deadline to meet, he wasn't scared of people getting killed, he wasn't chasing leads, he wasn't being harassed or threatened, and, most importantly, he was relaxed. As he closed his eyes, his mind began to fade away into his safe place. Random thoughts came and went like channel surfing on late night television. On one channel, the Stone Sheet from Pampered Chef promised perfect pizza every time. A pizza would be great right now.

"Pizza! I'm late!" Mason crash-landed on his return back to earth. Just as quickly as serenity settled upon him, it had eluded him. He again was forced to substitute peace and quiet for hustle and bustle. His heart rate jumped into overdrive. He banged his shin into the corner of the coffee table on the patio trying to hurry back into the apartment. He stopped. Wait a minute. This was different, he thought. This wasn't distress, this was eustress. A good stress. Strange?

He took a deep breath and grinned. A renewed sense of optimism and confidence overcame Mason. The day was looking up.

Chapter 6

Journey to Tikal
Altun Ha
899 AD

The early morning sun creeping over the horizon illuminated the village and alerted Ma'xu that the wait was over. Standing in front of the villagers, the king gave his son a final blessing before sending him on his journey to Tikal. Ma'xu focused on every word his father said.

"Remember, you must not disrespect the gods by being careless; it is a great honor to deliver the tribal offering to the gods," the king said.

"I know, I know," Ma'xu said, thrusting his pack onto his shoulder.

"To anger Ah Puch will bring great misfortune to our people and shame to our tribe," the king continued.

"I will deliver the offering, father," Ma'xu reassured.

"Very good, Ma'xu. Like your ancestors before me, I too made the journey to the city of the gods. It is nothing like this small fishing village. The structures are large; there are multitudes of people, great fortune, and food fit for kings. Beware, though; there is also wrongdoing, treachery, and deceitfulness. Heed this warning: be strong and do not fall under its spell. It is said that if you get lost there, you can never be found."

"But father, if I get lost surely someone will help me?"

With his right index finger, the king pointed to Ma'xu's heart. "When you get lost here, nobody can help you."

"I understand, father, I will not fail you," Ma'xu said.

"Good. Keep pure your heart and the gods will favor you."

"When I get there, how will I know where to go?"

"Go to the largest building; it is the temple. That is where Ah Puch will be; deliver the onyx owl to him there. If he is pleased, he will bless our village with abundant rains, prosperous fishing, and riches from the earth. You will bring greatness to your tribe, Ma'xu."

"Thank you, father," Ma'xu said as they walked down the path that led out of the village.

"Fear not, Ma'xu, the god Itzamn will protect you," his worried mother said, checking his warrior face paint and wiping dried blood off his chin from the night before.

"Be on your way, and may the gods protect you," Ma'xu's father said.

Ma'xu walked until he was out of sight of the village; then he began to run. The lush, dense rain forest was no match for the new warrior. He dodged vines and trees, and weaved in and out of the brush without missing a step. He was the fastest boy in the village, and his pace proved it. He was determined to get to Tikal as fast as he could. He ran until nightfall, until he could no longer run. Exhausted, he made a small fire, ate some bread, and soaked in the mystery of the jungle.

He had never been so far from the village by himself. No one was there to protect him. He was on his own for the first time in his young life. As night settled in, the jungle came alive.

Ma'xu heard sounds he never heard before. The wind blowing through the trees whispered his name, making it impossible to sleep.

Through the rustling of bushes, he saw two eyes reflect off the small crackling fire. The eyes stared at him. Maybe they're not eyes, he hoped— until they blinked, reassuring him that they were definitely eyes. Something was watching him. His heart raced. He sat still, not moving a muscle. The more he tried not to breathe, the more he needed to. I'm being hunted, he thought.

A somber chill moved down his spine. The hair on the back of his neck rose. He knew he was a visitor in an unfamiliar world. A hostile world. A world that put him at a severe disadvantage—a potentially deadly disadvantage.

He knew from his village hunts that if he didn't do something, it would attack. He slowly removed a stick out of the fire and waved it in the direction of the menacing eyes. In the other hand, he held his dagger tightly. He could see the eyes move down to the ground, not wanting to be seen. It was waiting; waiting for the right time to attack.

A loud shrill pierced the silence, nearly knocking Ma'xu out of his leather-hide booties. Looking in all directions, Ma'xu couldn't find where the terrifying scream came from. He was sure that something had been killed; he was grateful it wasn't him. He redirected his attention back to the present danger in the bush.

He took a deep breath and walked closer to the bush. His sweaty hand held the dagger tight. He knew he couldn't wait any longer; his father always told him to strike first and catch his enemy off guard.

With one motion, he lunged at the bushes with the fire and yelled. A large black panther leaped from its hiding place and retreated. Ma'xu stumbled back and continued to yell. The panther was gone. Ma'xu sat down and started to breathe again. His heart still beat like the rhythmic drums from his village. He passed yet another test. In an attempt to calm his nerves, he laid down and turned his thoughts to Tikal.

He closed his eyes and pictured pyramids of gold, clear rivers, multitudes of people, enormous gods, and vast prosperity. The women were beautiful, to please the gods. The people lived in large stone huts, ten times larger than what Ma'xu saw in his village. What was it going to be like to meet a god? Ma'xu thought about this as he fell into a deep sleep.

Ma'xu found himself on a hunt with some warriors from his village. They stalked a grazing tapir and planned their attack. They made their way through the waist-high prairie grass strategically encircling the animal, not making a sound. With the tapir in their sights, they were positioned for the kill.

The sky turned dark and the wind began to howl. Ma'xu looked up at the swirling dark clouds multiplying above them. Immediately, torrential rains pelted the warriors as they scattered to take cover. The crash of lightning and thunder drove Ma'xu to the ground, covering his head. A series of ear-piercing screeches permeated his ears.

Out of the corner of his eye, he saw a flock of large owls circling overhead. He tried to make himself flat and small on the ground. Then, with one loud screech, the birds ravenously descended in unison onto the warriors. The sound hurt Ma'xu's ears. He could hear the muffled cries of his fellow warriors being slaughtered by the birds. One after another, their screams tormented his mind.

I'm going to die, he thought. Tensed and frozen on the ground, he waited for his death.

Then it stopped. As quickly as the storm came in, it was gone. An eerie dead calm came over the prairie. Now in a curled up position on the ground, Ma'xu hesitantly looked up and saw a quiet, clear sky. He stood up and looked around. Did anyone else survive? Where were they? He couldn't see anybody. The tapir was in the same spot still grazing as if nothing had happened. The other warriors were all dead.

Ma'xu's heartbeat pounded like he had just played another game of Temple Ball. He looked in all directions, not wanting to accept what just happened, but he saw no one. The realization set in; he was alone.

I must return to the village, he told himself. He turned around to leave and was knocked to the ground by a tall figure towering directly over him.

Lying on his back, he stared up at the emotionless, perfectly still figure wearing full headdress and warrior face paint and holding a staff. It must be a tribal leader, he thought. The two stared at each other until the Indian spoke.

"It's coming," the Indian calmly said to Ma'xu, breaking the silence.

"What's coming?" Ma'xu replied, his voice quivering.

With that, the Indian started to laugh uproariously and pointed out over the horizon. From the ground, Má'xu turned and looked behind him. The dark clouds on the horizon were slowly approaching. He turned back around to face the Indian and started to ask, "What is com—?" He stopped midsentence. The large tribal leader was gone.

Má'xu stood up. As he turned back once more to see how far off the dark clouds were, it was as if a steed had just trampled his chest. A large white owl was heading straight for his face. Paralyzed by the mesmerizing blood-red eyes of the rapidly approaching owl, his feet felt as if they were stuck in the tar pits. The owl's black talons dangled in the air beneath it. It screeched and opened its snarling beak, revealing jagged sharp teeth.

Má'xu threw his arms up at the last second and blocked the beast just before it hit his face.

He awoke with a scream and as he sat up. He froze almost instantly. A hissing yellow and black snake hung from a tree branch six inches in front of his face.

Still shaken up by his dream, Ma'xu sat still, not moving a muscle. He and the snake stared at each other. A steady bead of sweat ran from his forehead down his face. Daring not to move, he let the sweat sting his eyes. With every hiss from the poisonous snake, the serpent's pink split tongue came closer to Ma'xu's face. Ma'xu stared into its sloped black glossy eyes and started to come to his senses. The snake opened its mouth and raised its upper lip, exposing two fangs, each dripping clear, deadly venom. The snake slowly pulled its head back away from Ma'xu, preparing for a strong lunge forward.

Without moving any part of his body but his hand, Ma'xu felt the ground around him, trying to find his dagger. Come on, where is it? he said to himself.

Before he could find his dagger, the snake hissed and shot itself forward at Ma'xu with its mouth open and fangs extended. With his hands, Ma'xu grabbed the snake by its thick throat and fell backwards.

His hands barely made it around the snake's muscular neck. Struggling to keep its head inches from his face, Ma'xu fought with the snake. The remaining coiled six feet of the snake's body fell out of the tree and landed on Ma'xu.

The snake began to unravel and work its way around Ma'xu. Feeling the snake's body begin to squeeze around him, he knew he had to find his dagger. He freed his right arm and felt his chest compress.

The snake squeezed every drop of air out of Ma'xu's lungs. He could no longer breathe at all. The snake squeezed tighter and tighter. White spots flashed. Ma'xu blinked faster and faster. He was completely immobilized. His consciousness began to fade away until the snapping of his ribs painfully brought him back.

The snake rolled him over, almost offering him his dagger lying on the ground, daring him to try to get it, mocking him.

With one final effort, Ma'xu rolled just close enough to grab the dagger. He grabbed it and, with no time to think, he sliced off the snake's head. Green ooze shot out of the serpent's neck and covered Ma'xu's face. The vise grip the snake had around Ma'xu instantly ceased, allowing his lungs to expand. He could breathe again.

He breathed the cool morning air faster and faster. His heart pounded, trying to keep up with his respirations. Inhaling the thick jungle air, he tasted the element of life again, in a way so few people ever do. He would never again take something as simple as breathing for granted. His organs immediately came out of their suspended state and functioned once again. The life force that was slowly being squeezed out of him quickly returned.

Ma'xu pushed the snake's undulating carcass off him. He looked at the headless snake's body. His brief insight into the world around him in the last two days made him see a seriousness he had not previously seen. His survival was dependent on his ability to adapt, something no one could have prepared him for.

He wiped the snake's essence off his face. At the same time, he wiped away the memory of the village celebration. He wiped away the dream. He wiped away his boyhood. He acknowledged his duty and the importance of his responsibilities. His new reality terrified him. As he wiped the snake off himself, he wiped away his confidence.

Still anxious to get to Tikal, he stood up. His legs trembled. He couldn't run, not yet, but every breath re-energized his body. Much wiser than he was eight hours earlier, he continued his journey to Tikal.

After running for hours in the light tropical afternoon rain, a drenched Ma'xu stopped at the edge of a cliff. It gave him a chance to catch his breath, nurse his sore ribs, and formulate his plan for the dangerous descent ahead of him. Jagged rocks covered the face of the cliff and would be unforgiving if he made a mistake. The treacherous cliff would slow his pace. Now was not the time to be reckless. From his perch high above the valley, he looked in awe at the lush green foliage of the land. A low layer of fog was beginning to break. The peaceful sound of running waterfalls and the brilliantly colored tropical flowers eased his mind. The emerging sun warmed his bronzed skin.

He pulled out the polished chunk of black onyx and admired it. Soon it would belong to a god. The black onyx resembled an owl. Found by a villager in a remote area of the surrounding mountains, it was polished by the village women. When the king saw it, he knew it was meant for Ah Puch, the god of death.

In the distance across the valley, Ma'xu saw something sparkle. He strained to see it more clearly through the clearing fog. His heart began to beat faster in anticipation. It must be Tikal, the city of the gods, he thought. He was an entire day early. Revitalized, Ma'xu began his descent down the perilous cliff wall.

Chapter 7

Gino's Pizza
Chicago, Illinois
May 20, 2017

Mason offered Al an apology for his lateness as he rushed into Gino's. Al knew better. An hour always meant an hour and a half. The welcoming embrace of basil, oregano, garlic, and fresh-baked pizza quickly aroused their senses and made them brush off Mason being late. Helen, their usual waitress, greeted them at the door.

"Ah, they finally come back. Where have you two been? I was getting worried about you," she said in a loud, thick, hospitable Italian voice while hugging them.

"Too much work and not enough play," Al said.

"Congratulations on your award, Mason," she said. Then, turning to the kitchen, she yelled, "Hey Tony, we have a famous person out here, come here!"

"Ah Mason, you're not too big for us after all, eh!" Big Tony said with a large smile, bursting through the stainless steel double doors from the kitchen.

"Hi Tony," Mason said. "It's good to see you."

"You too," Tony said, embracing each of them. "We're so proud of you, Mason; you're a good soul. God smiles on you, you know that?"

"Sometimes it's hard to see," Mason replied as if he didn't believe it.

"God has plans for all of us, Mason, you remember that."

"I will, Tony," Mason said, discounting it. "But right now I think he wants us to eat."

"Fair enough," Tony replied. "Today, it's on me, boys," he continued with authority.

"No, Tony—" Mason tried to say.

"Naaaa!" Tony cut him off. "Today is on me, tomorrow you pay again."

Mason and Al both knew there was no arguing with Tony. "Thanks, Tony, that's really cool of you," Al said.

"You're welcome, boys." Turning to Helen and raising his right hand with his index finger extended, he proclaimed, "Today the Chicago police think I'm cool!" He made his way back to the kitchen through the kitchen doors, shaking his head in agreement, and shouted, "Amen to that, boys, amen to that."

Mason and Al climbed into a booth and asked Helen for "the usual."

"You got it," she said. "One sausage deep dish and two Jameson and Cokes?"

"No, just Coke for me," Mason said, correcting the order. "Rough night."

"I'll do the same," Al added.

"What? You boys aren't so young anymore, huh?" Helen razzed.

"Hangovers aren't the same when you're thirty-one as they were when you're twenty-one," Al said painfully. Mason nodded in agreement.

Helen walked away and shook her head. "Thirty-one? You're still pups."

Gino's was regarded as the best pizza in Chicago. It was as therapeutic as it was appetizing. Going there to vent, relax, and eat became a weekend ritual for Al and Mason during high school and continued throughout college. There wasn't anything that couldn't be solved over a pizza. It was their place and their thing to do. It was only natural to celebrate Mason's award there.

"So what's the deal," Al said. "Did you get laid last night and not tell me?"

"What? Not that I know of, why?" Mason replied.

"You look like your old self, not so uptight."

Although he did feel different, Mason played it off. "No, I'm fine."

"Come on, you look like the weight of the world has been lifted off of your back."

"Well, to a degree, it has. I mean I was so burnt out on work, it just brought me down. I guess I kind of feel like I got a new lease on life."

"That's the spirit."

"Al, do you think things happen for a reason? I mean, there are so many events in my life that are caused by other events that were caused by other events, and it goes on and on."

"That's pretty deep for a Sunday afternoon," Al said.

"I know; I was thinking earlier about how we met. Remember that little jerk Ricky Heintz?"

"Yeah, I loved beating his ass."

"Yeah, me too. But that's not what I mean. Had he not picked on me and you not being in the exact place you were, we may never have met. We would've gone to the same school, been in different grades, and probably never have hung out. I would've continued to get bullied, probably avoided school, eventually dropped out, not have gone to college, and ultimately, never have researched that project."

"Look," Al said. "As much as I would love to take credit for your success, you would've figured it out eventually. Me, on the other hand, I probably wouldn't have graduated from high school and then not gone to college."

"You're one of those guys that are good at everything they do," Mason said.

"When my old man was around, the only thing he could've helped me with was drinking. He couldn't help me with school. Hell, he dropped out in the seventh grade," Al replied.

"Yes, but you always land on your feet no matter what you're doing. Academically, your dad may not have helped you, but he taught you how to survive. My dad taught me how to hide."

"I guess we learn from them whether we want to or not," Al said. "All I know is if you wouldn't have helped me through school, I wouldn't be here today. I may not even be alive."

"I can assure you, you would've still been alive," Mason said.

"Don't even go there," Al said, raising his eyebrows. They both knew there were some things that were off limits, and that was one of them.

"Sorry, I know," Mason replied, nodding his head in agreement. "Anyway, I guess we helped each other."

"Okay, I know you, Mase, so what's going on upstairs? What are you thinking?" Al questioned.

Looking out the window, Mason watched a street performer banging on white buckets as if they were drums. He could hear the muffled beat through the window. "I'm always amazed at how good those guys are," he said, as if buying time.

"Mase?"

"I had another weird dream last night," Mason said, bringing his attention back into the restaurant.

"Whoa, maybe we do need some Jameson in these Cokes," Al said.

"No, it's not a big deal," Mason said, not wanting to discuss it. "Changing the topic. Dom gave me a month off. I talked to my dad earlier; he wants me to visit him in Arizona."

"That's a great idea; you should do it."

"Maybe. I think I'm ready to get over things. I mean, part of me never forgave my dad for not helping me when I was a kid."

"Mase, that was some weird shit, nobody knew how to support you."

"My mom did," Mason said, reflecting on his emotional protector. She defended him when others ridiculed him, encouraged him when others discouraged him, and always believed Mason was special. He knew he was different, but not more special than anyone else; he was special to her, and that's all that mattered to him. When his mother died, his support system died with her.

"I guess I always wished he understood me like my mom did. It seemed that as long as we didn't talk about it we were fine. I just learned not to expect anything from him."

"Maybe it's time to give him another chance," Al said.

"Yes, probably. I'm not even sure it's that big of a deal any longer. I haven't talked to him in months and haven't seen him in over a year, since Kelly's funeral; he probably doesn't care either."

"You know that's not true. There are two sides to that coin. You didn't give him much to work with. You get so deep in your world that nobody else gets in."

"You're right; Kelly got in, though," Mason admitted. Kelly and Mason had a connection that only they understood and a bond that Mason always cherished, which made Kelly that much more special and the loss of her that much more painful.

"She was awesome, but maybe it's time to start living again. You know, meet some ladies and start dating again," Al offered.

"I don't know if I'm ready to move on that way yet," Mason said. "But what do you think about this?" Mason regressed slightly. "Had she not died, there may not have been last night."

"I don't know which is worse, my pounding headache or your mental aerobics," Al said. "I know you feel like your award has her blood on it, but it doesn't. Just because we deal with something doesn't mean we like it. That story came after she was gone, not *because* she was gone."

"You're right," Mason agreed. "I just have to remember that."

"I bet it would mean a ton to your dad," Al said. "Put it this way: my dad was a drunk who really didn't care about anything; your dad cares, and it's not too late to square things up with him. You ought to go see him."

"All right, Dr. Al," Mason said. "I probably will. It'll be good to get away," Mason said, as if convincing himself.

Chapter 8

The Briefing: A New Threat
The Pentagon, Washington, DC
May 22, 2017

"Good morning, ladies and gentlemen; at ease," Colonel Mike Austin said, crashing into the briefing hall at 0900 sharp. The sixty-plus civilian and military officers on hand immediately quieted down and gave their undivided attention to the NSA senior intelligence director.

"People, I've called this briefing to introduce you to a potential new threat. Our intelligence officers have received credible information from the field about a relatively new Islamic extremist organization poised to make their mark on the world. I've asked Special Agent Brian Dougherty to bring us up to speed on this outfit. Brian, please," Austin said, moving away from the podium and gesturing for Dougherty to approach.

"Thank you, colonel. The organization I'm going to talk to you about is called the Almazorians. They are a small Islamic organization that resides in a village in the Suleiman mountain range of Pakistan called Rabwah. Much like some other Islamic extremists, they want to be respected by the world. However, rather than create a productive state, they prefer to bomb civilian targets. Thus far, their targets have been small open-air markets or vehicles, with not too many casualties. However, recently acquired intel indicates that they are stepping up their game. We believe they may be plotting an attack somewhere in London. We're working with MI6 to figure this out. We need to obtain assets that can deliver intel so we can begin building a file on this group. Are there any questions?"

"Sir, do we know what sect of Islam they are?" asked a standing gentleman wearing a highly decorated army uniform.

"Excellent question, thank you. They are actually not recognized by the mainstream Islamic religion, but they do adhere to similar ideologies like world conversion to Islam, theocratic government, and the removal of Christianity. Generally, mainstream Islam does not acknowledge them."

"Brian, why don't the mainstream Islamic organizations simply kill them like they do anyone else who disrespects their religion?" a younger gentleman wearing a black suit asked.

"In short, for two reasons: Number one, they pose no credible threat to the mainstream Islamic religion. They are so different that they are not even viewed as Muslims, by real Muslims. Secondly and more importantly, they are out there bombing and killing 'infidels.' They're essentially carrying out the other extremists' missions. In fact, a bombing in Israel in 2002 had four different extremist organizations trying to take credit for what was eventually learned to be an Almazorian bombing."

Another question from the back of the hall was asked. "Brian, do they pose any immediate threat to the US?"

"We don't believe they pose an imminent threat, at the present time. However, remember the reason we're interested in them is because the tapes they've been releasing to the media have been increasingly outspoken and impudent in their criticism of the US. They are trying to compete with large extremist organizations. Since they don't have the organizational structure nor advanced technology, they must respond in numbers killed. In the end, they're really a nuisance that we can't underestimate."

"Anything else?" Dougherty hesitated but could see the gears grinding in their heads as many were frantically writing notes. The silence in the hall made it clear this threat had the potential to be on our front door relatively quickly. His concluding statement drove home his point. "It's paramount that we gather intel on this group ASAP. We have to develop an action plan and institute preemptive action before they decide to act. Without it, this could get real ugly real quickly. Thank you for your time."

"Thank you, Brian," Colonel Austin said while walking back to the podium. "If anyone gathers any information on this group, please forward it to Brian's team, where the central file is being maintained. His group will act as the central repository of intelligence on this organization and subsequently disseminate the information through the different intelligence agencies via intelligence bulletins. Thank you all for your time." As the meeting ended, the low rumble of people standing up and talking began as they cleared the hall.

Chapter 9

The City of the Gods
Tikal
899 AD

Ma'xu walked out of the forest with a full view of the brilliance of the city. The irregular expansion of structures surrounding and radiating from the main temple reinforced that Ma'xu had indeed arrived in Tikal. The sprawling city of pyramid-shaped limestone structures, waterways, and other large huts was now directly in front of him.

He felt small and humble as he entered the city through the massive entryway. He had never seen structures that climbed so high. The straight limestone structures, elaborate and complicated, lined the main dirt roadway. There's no way people built these, he thought. This was the work of the gods. But where were all the people? The other warriors and his father all said there would be many people. Instead, it was quiet. The only sound he could hear was his heartbeat.

There was nobody in sight. He began to doubt himself. This has to be the right city, he thought. Am I in the wrong place? Is that why I'm early? He searched for answers to questions that made no sense.

The main roadway of crushed rock led directly to the temple. It was exactly as his father had described it: large, impressive, and in the center of the city. Steep stairs led to the flat top section where the gods lived. No, this was Tikal. It had to be, he reassured himself, but why are there no people?

He continued slowly walking toward the temple. Concern overcame him. Questions continued to race through his mind. Am I not supposed to be here? Were the people somewhere else? Why was this huge city deserted? This was not like his father had explained.

Ma'xu walked up to the base of the towering temple and gazed up at the monstrosity in awe. The pit in his stomach reminded him how small he was. His heart raced. Not wanting to disturb the gods in case they were sleeping, Ma'xu cautiously walked around the temple to the other side. As he emerged around the backside of the temple, he could feel his body begin to buckle. He was overcome with fear. His breath escaped him. He had undeniably found the people.

As far as he could see, mangled dead bodies lined the blood-red dirt roadway.

Embers from a dying bonfire burned in the middle of the complex. Large black crows picked at the rotting, decaying corpses. He turned in all directions but couldn't escape the rancid, gut-wrenching smell. The stale, bitter stench of thousands of dead bodies knocked him to his knees. The pungent odor was permanently burned into his senses. It was the smell of death, a foulness he would never forget.

His mouth began to salivate. Without warning, his stomach started to convulse. Within seconds, he vomited like never before. At that moment, his innocence was ripped from his soul. If being a warrior meant having to do this, he wanted no part of it.

On his knees, trembling, something caught his eye. He looked past the limestone structures and into the adjacent forest. Squinting, he saw something move. Scared that he, too, would be killed, he ran and took cover in a nearby stone hut. While looking out across the carnage trying to catch his breath, sweat poured out of his body. He noticed a young boy in the street move. Is he still alive? Ma'xu wondered as he ran to him.

"Boy, are you alive?" Ma'xu asked, trying to awaken the blood-covered child.

"Huh? Who are you?" the child stuttered, coming in and out of consciousness.

"I am Ma'xu," he said, cradling the boy in his arms. "What is your name?"

"I am Catika."

"Catika, what happened?" Ma'xu asked, trying to remain strong.

"I am cold; can you stay with me?"

"Of course I will," Ma'xu said, fighting back tears, knowing that the boy's time was close. "Catika, can you tell me who did this? Catika? Catika, stay with me!" Ma'xu said, brushing the long black hair out of Catika's face.

"Tunkuruchu . . . Kinsik . . . Masewal . . ." the boy whispered, regaining consciousness.

"Owl kill people?" Ma'xu asked, his eyes growing large while thinking about the birds in his dream.

"Tunkuruchu Kinsik Masewal!" Catika said as he grabbed Ma'xu's arm tightly. With his last breath, Catika's eyes closed and his body went limp.

"Catika? Catika!" Ma'xu said as his eyes welled up. Holding the boy's head and covered in his young blood, Ma'xu looked up to the sky and called out, "Why?"

Chapter 10

The Trip
Chicago, Illinois
May 22, 2017

Mason pulled an old green beat-up suitcase out of his bedroom closet and began to fill it with clothing. He had never taken a month-long vacation in his life. How many clothes do you bring for a month? he pondered. No dress clothes, no long pants, and no work. This was a vacation, a retreat, a chance to reconnect with his father, or go insane because of his father.

As he retrieved his tennis racket out of the back corner of the bedroom closet, he saw something behind the racket that stopped him dead in his tracks.

He felt his heart pound like a pile driver. He started breathing harder, but couldn't get enough air to his lungs. His head hummed in a fever pitch as time slowed. His focus became razor sharp. He felt as if he was in the sixth grade again and Ricky Heinz had just punched him in the chest. Fear disabled him. He could now hear the deafening silence inside his bedroom.

His vision was locked onto it like a deer in headlights—something that he hadn't seen in over a year; something he never wanted to see again. With the closet door open, he slowly backed up until he hit his bed. He carefully sat on the edge, not taking his eyes off it. It was a crushing blow to his otherwise renewed self. Confusion set in as his mind raced with questions.

How did it get there? Who put it there? When was it put there? Where was it for the last year? More concerning, whoever had it, did they see what was inside? A black attaché case was resting against the back wall of the closet. The case contained his personal diaries, newspaper clippings about him, and doctor evaluations. Essentially, everything that cursed his life was inside that case. He stared at the black attaché case from the edge of the bed. The case stared back at him, cursing him, mocking him, offering him pain, daring him to open it. It wasn't supposed to be there. It was supposed to be gone forever. He made sure of it.

The vexing problem was he would have to look inside to see if everything was there. There was no way that was going to happen. Not now, not ever. Just as he was about to get up off the bed and close the closet door, the phone rang and startled him to the point he fell off the bed onto the floor. "Good God!" he yelled, breathing even harder than before. He made his way to the nightstand and answered the phone.

"Hello!"

"Man, you sound like you just ran a marathon," Al said on the other end of the phone. "Are you okay?"

"Yes, you just startled me. I'm fine. What's up?"

"I'll be there in ten minutes."

Mason hung up the phone and tried to gather his thoughts. Puzzled on how the case resurfaced, he resigned himself to throwing it away again. I'll do it later, he thought and closed the door. He finished getting ready and was about to sit down when the apartment buzzer sounded and Al's muffled voice came over the speaker: "You coming, sunshine?"

"I'm coming!" Mason sent back over the speaker. He stuck his head into the bedroom one last time. He looked at the closed closet door. Although he had no desire to see anything inside that case again, he knew he'd have a month to himself in Arizona and probably time to sort things out. Besides, he rationalized, he could always throw it away down there. Against better judgment, Mason opened the closet door, grabbed the case by its handles, threw it inside his luggage, and ran for the elevator.

"Hey, sorry I'm late," Mason said, jumping into Al's car in anticipation of his lecture.

On cue, Al started in, "You know why you have a hard time with the ladies? Because you're supposed to be waiting on them; instead, they're always waiting on you."

"I didn't realize you were a lady," Mason replied.

"Oh you're funny. You'll see," Al said, acknowledging Mason's touché.

"Yeah, yeah, I'll just have to find one who's later than me," Mason said back, adding, "no big deal." Knowing that Al would continue his lecture most of the way, Mason had to redirect Al to food. "Hey, you want to hit Pete's Kitchen on the way?"

"Sure, you buying?" Al asked, knowing exactly what Mason was doing.

"Of course," Mason said with a smirk.

As they drove off, Mason noticed the dumpster in the alley next to his apartment complex. He thought about the attaché case. He closed his eyes and pictured himself lifting the dumpster lid, looking around, and with no one watching, throwing it in the dumpster. The lid closed and he went to catch the bus to go to work. As the bus drove by the alley a few minutes later, looking out the bus window, he saw the dumpster being emptied. He remembered it so vividly because that was the day Kelly died.

"Earth to Mason, are you out there?" Al said to a catatonic Mason.

"Yeah, I'm here, just thinking about things," Mason replied.

"You have to relax; you're on vacation now. Pretty soon you'll be hanging out in the sun, maybe catch some Diamondback games, play a little tennis, or, should I say, get beat really bad in tennis," Al said, kidding with Mason.

"Yes, you're right."

"Something else going on, Mase?" Al asked.

Explaining the case would take a lot longer than they had time for. Mason didn't want to start something he couldn't finish; and telling Al the entire story about the case would lead to questions that Mason didn't want to get into.

"No, just nervous about the trip," Mason said. Al assumed Mason was hiding something, but he'd grown accustomed to him doing that. He also knew when to leave things alone.

As part of Chicago's west side backdrop for over fifty years, Pete's Kitchen was a twenty-four-hour greasy dive that was usually packed any time of the day, and any day of the week. Popular with inebriated college kids, it was the place to go after the clubs closed.

"Ah, Pete's Kitchen, are you having flashbacks yet?" Al said to Mason. They were like two people possessed. Pete's Kitchen was the White Castle of eggs.

"You bet; this place is awesome," Mason answered back. "Fortunately, they're not too busy. We kind of need to eat and run," he continued. They inhaled their breakfast like two drunken college students at 3 a.m. and hit the road to Midway Airport.

Al prided himself on being able to read people. He could see sincerity in Mason and could tell Mason was in a different place than a year ago. One thing Al was taught in his police training was to recognize when someone was ready to talk. He sensed it in Mason, something he had waited a long time to see. Unfortunately, the other side of the "ready to talk" coin was setting the proper environment to talk. Pulling into the airport was neither the right time nor place, and they both knew it.

Mason had bought himself a thirty-day reprieve. Disappointed and feeling like he had just lost a confession from a suspect, Al said, "Why do I feel like you just lawyered up?"

"I wouldn't sweat it, officer; I think my days are numbered," Mason joked as he pulled his luggage out of the backseat.

Chapter 11

Dealing with the Past
Flight to Phoenix, Arizona
May 22, 2017

When Mason reclined his seat next to the window on the airplane, he finally found the peace and quiet he sought. With the flight not being very crowded, he was able to have a three-seat row to himself. The stress of seeing his father was not as stressful as checking bags, getting through airport security, and boarding the airplane.

That was all behind him now. When the pilot came over the intercom and welcomed everyone aboard, Mason felt as if the pilot was talking directly to him. Furthermore, when he said to "recline your seat and enjoy the flight," that was exactly what Mason had in mind. He was as content as he had been in a year. As the white noise of the airplane's pressure system rhythmically soothed Mason, he closed his eyes and let his thoughts slowly drift to his mother.

Elaine Rhimes died the summer after Mason completed the seventh grade. She was a fighter. She had beat cancer for several years before it finally got the better of her. Mason remembered the last time he saw her.

Mason was thirteen years old and Chicago was experiencing a severe heat wave. His mother lied in a sterile, cold hospital bed in the intensive care unit of the Mercy Medical Center in downtown Chicago. Wires and tubes went from her body to different machines, all making beeps and other sounds. Her complexion was pasty white and she had a Memorial Crusader bandana covering her hairless head. It had been given to her by Mason's older brother Sean, from his high school.

She was not in good shape, although no one could tell by speaking to her. The family members and relatives were waiting for visitation hours to begin. Mason couldn't wait any longer, however, and had to see her now. While the nurses and doctors were talking, a thirteen-year-old Mason snuck into her room.

"Mom, are you awake?" Mason quietly asked her from her hospital bed.

"Yes dear, I'm here." She opened eyes and tried to sit up, but didn't have the strength. "How's my special boy?" she asked him, mustering all the energy she could.

"I'm fine, Mom. I wish you were better," he said sadly, looking at the floor.

She reached over and held his hand. Her touch was soft. Her grip was frail. "Don't be sad, Mason, be happy for the time we had together." Her smile instantly warmed the room.

"I am, Mom; I just wish you didn't have to go yet."

"I guess it's that time, isn't it?" she said rhetorically. "You're the one person I can't fool. You know what's going on, don't you?"

"Yes, I do, but I wish I didn't," he said.

"It takes a special person to carry that, Mason. Be strong and know that there's a purpose for you," she told him softly.

"I'm scared, Mom, nobody understands except you. Dad says to forget about it and Sean thinks I make it up. I don't know what to do anymore," Mason said.

"Don't worry about your father or your brother. They don't understand that we all have a purpose. Yours is just more special. It's something that is very private, Mason. Most people will be scared by it, so keep it to yourself and some day, when the time is right, you'll know what to do with it."

"I'll try."

"Remember, embrace your gift. Until then, be happy and come give your mother one last hug." As Mason held his mother for the last time, tears began to pour down his face. She kissed him on his cheek and told him she loved him.

"I love you too, Mom. Have a safe journey and tell Grandma hi for me?" he said, holding his mother.

"I will, honey. I will always be with you, Mason. Tell Dad and Sean I love them." With her last breath, she said, "Good-bye, honey." With that, she passed away. Mason continued to hold his mother until his father and the rest of the family came into the room. They could tell by Mason's sorrow that the woman they all loved had passed on. They surrounded the bed and began to mourn quietly, holding each other.

It wasn't long after that Mason's father began to emotionally withdraw from Mason. When Mason's mother died, his father stopped communicating on an intimate level. Mason felt as if his dad thought he had something to do with her death because of Mason's past, a feeling that his dad never really dismissed or denied, although it couldn't be further from the truth.

His father was an introvert and kept his feelings inside. To a thirteen-year-old, it felt as if their relationship was contingent on not discussing Mason's mother, so they never did. Elaine Rhimes was the glue that kept the family together. After she left, that role remained vacant.

Although there was always the underlying passive threat of conflict between Mason and his father, Mason found himself mildly excited and was looking forward to seeing him. On a subconscious level, perhaps it was because for the first time in Mason's life, he felt as if *maybe* his father would be proud of him.

The last thing Mason wanted to do was let his dad down; he felt like he'd done that enough. Mason wasn't sure if either one of them could handle that again. In the end, he realized his dad tried, but their relationship wasn't like it was with his mother.

Although eighteen years had passed since his mother's death, she was in his thoughts daily. The positive side of seeing his father was no deadlines, no work, and most importantly, no pressure. Their relationship had been strained for a long time. Despite that, there seemed to be a glimmer of hope as age and distance seemed to have quelled some of their discontent. For the first time in many years, they were genuinely excited about visiting each other.

Chapter 12

The Cleansing
Victoria Square, London, England
May 23, 2017

Rain from the previous two days made London, England, cool and humid. This day, however, was a rare cloudless day. The welcomed warm temperatures were gradually drying out the city. Early summertime weather had people flocking to Victoria Square in central downtown London. Sitting on a park bench across from Victoria Square, Hamed and Ishmail watched the crowded marketplace with disdain. Infidels, carrying on as if they had not a care in the world. Talking; laughing; working. The audacity of people going about their business. They pay no attention to their sins. They care not about repenting. They disrespect Allah constantly. The humid air calmed Hamed's nerves. The warm sun high in the cloudless sky was a sign from Allah that the infidels' impending fate was indeed a blessing.

Hamed sat erect on the bench with both hands on his knees, staring straight-faced at the marketplace. His glazed-over, defiant stare removed any semblance of emotion. He fought all psychological attacks on his mindset. He was a disciplined disciple of Allah. His mental preparation was interrupted temporarily by Ishmail.

"Hamed, are you ready?"

"They keep themselves so busy," Hamed said, watching the people with disgust. The sight of fellow Muslims wearing suits and mingling with Christians while rushing to work reinforced his conviction. I must set my imprisoned brethren free from their bondage, he told himself. He could feel his heartbeat immediately increase. The rage growing in his stomach made it tighten instantly. Breathing harder and faster, he knew the battle was at hand. His eyes blinked away all hesitation as he intensified his focus.

"Yes they do, so not to be reminded of their pathetic existence," Ishmail said, feeding the growing contempt inside Hamed. "They have made their choice to disrespect Allah. That is why our mission is so important."

"Yes, Ishmail, we will save them from themselves. It will be a cleansing. They will soon know the power of Allah," Hamed concluded. His surreal tone spoke volumes to Ishmail.

"Now is the time, Hamed."

"Yes it is, Ishmail," he replied as they stood up from the bench. Hamed thrust the black backpack over his right shoulder and gave one last look around. Nerves were replaced with anticipation.

"Remember, once you activate the device, you have sixty seconds to get away, so take your time. You do not want to draw attention to yourself by looking nervous or running. You'll be two hundred meters away before it goes off. Now, you know what to do, right?" Ishmail asked.

"Yes, I got it. I reach into the backpack, flip the switch, zipper the backpack closed, and set it down. Then I slowly start counting. After I reach ten, I start to walk away slowly, not drawing attention to myself. After sixty seconds it will explode."

Ishmail shook his head in agreement and said, "Good, Hamed; very good. Remember, this will bring great honor to your family and to all Almazorians. Ahmed will personally bestow upon you the blessing from Allah. You and your family will have great riches, and your descendents will be many!" Ishmail continued. "Once you put the backpack down and are in the clear, I will cause a distraction so people will not notice you. Then you must disappear. I will see you back in Rabwah for our celebration."

"But Ishmail, what if they catch you?"

"My friend, do not worry about me. Save only yourself. If they catch me, it will be an honor to die for Allah. You have a wife and children to take care of, I have no one," Ishmail proudly said to Hamed.

"I pray that we both do right in Allah's eyes," Hamed said.

"All for Allah, my brother. Now, let us cleanse the market from its infidels. Let the mission begin."

With a deep breath, they embraced each other. They stared deeply into each other's eyes. Ishmail placed his hands on Hamed's shoulders and continued the mental preparation.

"Do not think of those swines as people; they are demons, Hamed. We are the sword of Allah. The more demons we send to hell, the more our reward in heaven will be. Be strong, Hamed, let nothing stand in your way. This is what we've trained for. Victory will be ours," Ishmail continued. "Now, in the name of Allah, let us carry out his will."

"In the name of Allah," Hamed replied, scowling as he watched the people in the square. His anger had become visible. He was ready to complete his mission. Looking back at Ishmail as if possessed himself, he declared, "I will destroy the infidels; nothing can stop me."

"Go, and Allah be with you, Hamed."

Ishmail watched as Hamed made his way directly to the market square, intent on carrying out Allah's will. Hamed made no eye contact with anyone, so as not to be distracted and fall under their evil spell, just like he was trained to do. In his mind, he kept repeating to himself, "Allahu Akbar; Allahu Akbar," over and over, so that the demons could not possess his mind. He must remain focused.

When Hamed arrived in the middle of the square, without thinking for a second, he unzipped the black backpack, reached in, and flipped the switch to activate the bomb. He zipped the backpack back up and set it on the ground. He had executed the plan flawlessly. He closed his eyes and began counting, "One, two, three, four—" but before he could get to five, the ground shook with a thunderous *boom*! The backpack exploded, sending shrapnel and fire in all directions. Hamed was incinerated instantaneously. The hot, positive pressure wave sped though the people in the square, sending debris like daggers through the crowd. Anyone within three hundred feet was involuntarily knocked to the ground.

The market square erupted into chaos as people lay dead and injured on the ground. With the sound of sirens nearing, Ishmail calmly walked to the opposite side of the park as far away from the market square as he could and drove away in a stolen vehicle he acquired the previous day. With his cell phone in hand and straight-faced, he made a call.

"I think you may want to turn on the news," he said into the mouthpiece. "Yes, I'll see you in a few days," he continued and hung up.

Chapter 13

The Valley of the Sun
Phoenix, Arizona
May 22, 2017

As the aircraft began its initial descent into the Phoenix area, the flight attendants began their prelanding cabin checklist. Mason's restful sleep would all too soon come to an end as well, as a flight attendant attempted to wake him up.

"Excuse me, sir? Would you please move your seat to its upright position for landing?" the flight attendant said, shaking Mason's shoulder to wake him up.

"Ouch! I'm sorry," the flight attendant said, shaking off the shock she got when she touched Mason's shoulder. "Are you all right?"

"Ouch! Yes, sorry," a startled Mason said, taking a deep breath and sitting up. He looked around as if he had done something embarrassing. He knew what the strong shock he received from the flight attendant was. "Are you okay?" he asked.

"Yes, it's all right; must be the dry air," she offered. It wasn't the dry air. The flight attendant smiled and continued up the aisle, rubbing her hand. He stared at her as she walked away. He knew she would be dead soon.

After the plane landed, Mason made his way to the baggage claim. He could hear someone calling his name.

"Mason! Mason! Over here," his father shouted as he recognized Mason's tall, slender frame. Wandering among throngs of people through the endless field of luggage carousels, Mason's eyes found his father.

"Hey, Dad!" Mason said as he waved to his dad. They shook hands and gave each other a brief one-armed half embrace.

"It's good to see you," his father said, looking over Mason.

"Yeah, it's good to see you too," Mason said back. "You look good; do you just work out all day?" Mason said, observing that his father had aged quite a bit since the last time they saw each other at Kelly's funeral.

"Just living right, I guess," his dad said.

"It feels like more than fourteen months, doesn't it," Mason said.

"Yes it does, and that's way too long," his dad replied. The pitch in his voice trailed off.

Recognizing the slight undertone of regret from his dad, Mason said to him, "That just means we have some catching up to do."

"I'd like that," his dad replied.

When they had spoken on the phone over the last year, his father sounded fine and never let on that there were any problems with him. After seeing him, however, Mason could tell something was different about his dad; he was getting older.

For the first time in Mason's life, he felt empathy for his dad. He was now faced with the harsh reality of his father's own mortality, something he assumed he would never have to do. He also realized that all the tough talk on the phone over the last year was his dad trying to maintain an air of vigor that had, in reality, slipped away like the sun setting over the Rocky Mountains.

"How's everything going?" Mason asked.

"Things are good. I have a few aches and pains that I never had before, but I still get around the court better than these old guys down here," he said.

"I'm sure you do," Mason said, believing every word. Mason was surprised that his father would even admit he had aches and pains. Additionally, Mason was pleasantly surprised at his dad's humility and openness. That could only mean one thing. "So I'm guessing you've met a lady?" Mason asked.

"Yes, I have; how'd you know?" he asked Mason.

"I can just tell," he said with a smirk.

"I'm not getting soft, am I?"

"No, no, you're definitely not soft," Mason reassured. "You actually just look happy."

"I am, Mase. Irene's a widow also; you'll meet her later. We've been living together for a few months now. I hope that's all right with you."

"Yes, that's great; I look forward to meeting her. Anyone that could slow you down must be pretty amazing."

"Trust me, it's not her slowing me down, it's more the other way around," his father joked.

Mason's father wasted no time on the drive to Chandler to start in on Mason's shoulder-length black hair. "I know a good barbershop if you want to get a haircut," he said to Mason.

"Dad, I'm going to grow it while I still can, and besides, I just got one," Mason replied, cutting that one off at the knees.

"No problem, just offering," he replied.

The entry gates of the Pelican Reef Adult Community were a welcoming sight. They were home. They waved to the elderly security guard in the guard shack talking to a bicyclist. The main entrance was highlighted with palm trees lining both sides of the road and the center median. Water fountains and vividly colored flowers accented the drive through the community.

Although they called the Pelican Reef an "adult" community, they really meant "retirement" community, Mason thought. The people that lived there, however, were anything but old and frail. The road paralleled a perfectly manicured golf course. The scent of fresh paint hit Mason as they drove by the navy blue and green tennis courts. Driving past a retired couple riding their bikes, Mason was reminded of the relaxation he so desired.

As his father was pulling into the driveway, Mason commented on his landscaping: "The lemon trees look good."

"It's all in the fertilizer. If you don't fertilize, you don't get any fruit," he replied. "Come on in and get settled. I'm going to change, then Irene is meeting me at the courts. You are more than welcome to come with us if you'd like," Mason's dad offered.

"No, you go ahead. I'm going to chill out for a while," Mason said back.

"It's your vacation; you do whatever you want. If you want to take off, take the other car. Otherwise, I'll see you later." his father said.

"What do you mean, 'the other car'?" Mason asked with a befuddled look on his face.

"Yes, take the Mustang; it's running great," his dad laughed.

"I think the sun is playing tricks on you," Mason said, surprised. "Because I thought you said to take the convertible 1965 blue Ford Mustang, and I know nobody drives Blue Lightning."

As his father chuckled, he told Mason, "If you do go out, make sure you come back with her."

"That could be tough, but I'll try. Anyway, thanks, I'm not sure I'm ready for the Lightning just yet; I might walk over to the pool and crash. However, I'll hold you to that offer later."

"I'm counting on that," Mason's dad said, smiling as he left.

Mason walked out onto the concrete patio and looked out at the trees and bushes sparsely populating the small rock yard. A look in either direction revealed tropical flowers, cactuses, water fountains, beautifully landscaped yards, and stucco-clad houses. A flagstone walkway divided his dad's backyard and led to a cement walkway that snaked its way along the backyard property lines of the houses and ultimately led to the main pool and clubhouse area.

Mason thought to himself, Eighty-five degrees, sun, and nowhere to be; I need to visit more often. It had been almost three years since Mason had been down to Arizona, and that was for a short visit. He found himself appreciating the beauty of it more and more—something he never really paid much attention to before. This was a good idea, he reassured himself. Now I need the pool.

While he unpacked his suitcase, he grabbed the attaché case. As much as he vowed to forget that part of himself, he would have to examine the contents at some point, but not today. It was much too nice of a day to ruin it with that stuff. He put it in the closet and took off for the pool.

The tennis courts were adjacent to the pool and clubhouse. When his father and Irene finished their tennis match, they went to the pool bar to get a drink. They saw Mason sleeping in a lounger and made their way over to him.

"Don't wake him, he's sleeping," Irene said.

"How can you tell?" Patrick asked.

"What do you mean, how can I tell? Look at him, he's sleeping," she snapped back.

While they were bickering over whether to wake him up or not, their voices woke him up.

"Hey, what's going on?" Mason interrupted.

"See, he's not asleep," Mason's dad said to Irene.

"Not anymore," she politely said in a stern voice.

Again, Mason interrupted. "I take it you're Irene? I'm Mason; nice to meet you," he said while sitting up and shaking her hand.

"Hi. Yes, I'm Irene. Nice to meet you, too. I've heard so much about you. Congratulations on the award."

"Thanks."

"I'm sorry we woke you; your dad—"

Mason cut Irene off. "No worries, it's no big deal. I have a month to sleep. What time is it, anyway?" he asked.

"It's 5:30," his dad replied.

"Wow, I've actually been sleeping for two hours. I needed to get up anyway," Mason said.

"We're going to head home and get the grill fired up. Ray and Gina and a few other friends are coming over," his dad said.

"God, I haven't seen them in ages. How are they?" Mason asked.

"They're doing great," his dad replied. "Ray's had some problems with his heart, but he's hanging in there."

"Great; it'll be good to see them," Mason said.

"It was nice to finally meet you, Mason," Irene added.

"Yes, you too. I'm going to walk back, so I'll see you at the house," Mason said, shaking her hand again. As his father and Irene walked away, Mason could hear Irene say, "You didn't tell me he was so handsome."

"Well, he takes after me, what did you expect?" his dad replied.

Mason watched as they walked to the car. They seemed happy. His father could dish it out, but Irene dished it right back.

As Mason walked into his father's house from the patio, he looked around at the three-bedroom, two-bathroom, ranch-style house decorated with Southwest art and Southwest colors. Mason's dad always loved the southwestern part of the United States and decided long ago he'd end up living there—a dream that he shared with Mason's mother. A dream that he partly fulfilled for her after she was gone. Mason's father made friends wherever he went, and Arizona was no different. Although he never remarried, he'd always had people in his life, just nothing too serious; at least that's what Mason thought.

Chapter 14

A Few Friends
Chandler, Arizona
May 22, 2017

A knock on Mason's bedroom door broke his thoughts. He closed up his laptop and put away the *USA Today* newspaper he was reading. Another government shutdown on the horizon, he thought. When are these politicians going to start actually running the country instead of destroying it? he wondered.

"Hey Goldilocks, you about ready?" his dad said through the door.

"Yes, I'll be out in a minute!"

As Mason made his way out into the main room of the house, he was surprised to see about fifty people drinking and talking.

"Hey, there he is!" Mason's dad said while pointing out Mason to his friends. His father came across the room and handed Mason a Jameson and Coke. Putting his arm around Mason, he introduced Mason with one announcement.

"Everyone, this is Mason; yes, the Pulitzer award-winning Mason. I would like you to join me in proposing a toast. To Mason: congratulations on your award and welcome back to Arizona!"

"Hear, hear!" the crowd said in unison and took a drink.

After the drink, Mason's dad added, "I'm not going to introduce all of you, just take a minute and introduce yourselves, and drink up!" As his father ended his emcee duties, Mason, completely taken aback, leaned in and whispered to his dad, "This is a few friends?"

"Yeah, some people couldn't make it," his dad replied. "Have fun; I have to get the grill going." As his dad walked away, Mason stared in disbelief.

Where the hell is my dad and when did he become a socialite? Mason thought. He's having a blast down here. How come I didn't know about this? Where have I been? Mason wasn't sure what happened to his dad or when it happened, but he welcomed the change. Feeling somewhat overwhelmed, he drank his liquid courage and began to enter his father's world, head first.

Mason met his father's friends, one after another. In a way, he was getting to know his father all over again. People were telling him stories about his dad, especially ones that probably should have remained untold. John Mueller told him how his father would fly to Milwaukee on weekends during college, party all weekend, and steal street signs. Dan Raraten bragged about how he and his dad flew on Continental Airlines without tickets. It seemed his dad had a much more colored past than he had previously thought. His father's friends congratulated him and drank. They were partiers, Mason thought—not exactly the stereotypical old retirement community he thought it was. Mason found himself having a lot more fun than he thought he would.

The sounds of Glenn Miller, Tommy Dorsey, and Ralph Flanagan resonated through the house. Big band? I've never really liked it before, he thought, but then again I've never listened to them turned up loud on a Definitive Technology sound system. Maybe all music is better loud, he thought. Either way, he experienced firsthand what a party was like back in the '40s. Psychedelics were not necessary.

When the night drew to an end, people began to leave. As the party thinned, Ray Reed finally got a chance to talk to Mason before he left.

"Congrats, Mason, we're really proud of you," Ray said.

"Thanks Mr. Reed, it's nice to see you guys."

"How many times do I have to tell you, call me Ray."

"Sorry, Mr. Ree— eh, Ray, old habits," Mason stumbled, "Hey, how's Lori?"

"She's doing great; she's a physical therapist living in Colorado with Colton and the kids."

"That's terrific; tell her hello for me when you talk to her," Mason said.

"I will; she always asks about you. It'll be nice to actually tell her something for once other than, 'I don't know, I think he's fine.' So, your dad wants to play doubles this weekend and Gina can't play. What do you say we partner up and teach him a lesson?"

"That would be fun. Playing on your team might be my only chance to beat him. Just not too early. I am on vacation, you know," Mason pleaded.

"I'm not a morning person either, Mason, so we'll tell them to wait until 7:30," Ray offered.

"7:30? Thanks a lot; I knew you'd understand," Mason said with a sigh.

"Well, we have to get going, Gina's getting loose lipped; too much wine, if you know what I mean," Ray said, rolling his eyes. "I'll see you in a couple of days, Mason."

"Sounds good; it was nice seeing you guys," Mason said with a wave.

Mason looked out from the kitchen into the family room; a strange familiar feeling came over him. He looked around at the empty beer and liquor bottles on the counters, the trash can overflowing, the Billy May Orchestra still playing, and half-eaten plates of food left throughout the house. It looked as if he was at a fraternity party. The only thing missing were people passed out on the floor, vomit in the plants, and the lingering odiferous remnants of marijuana in the air. He saw Irene and his father cleaning up and started to help.

"No you don't," Irene insisted, ushering Mason and his dad to the living room. "You guys go in and sit down; I'll clean up," she continued.

"I don't mind helping. I've been to college parties that weren't this trashed," Mason said.

"But were they as fun?" his father asked.

"From what I can remember, no they weren't," Mason said. "In fact, I can't remember when I had this much fun. I think I've been missing out on something," Mason continued.

"That's what counts," Patrick said, nudging Irene. "Right?"

"Yes, Pat," Irene said, rolling her eyes. Turning to Mason, she continued, "You see, Mason, when these guys get together, it is kind of a fraternity and they regress accordingly."

"All I know is you guys have put retirement in a whole new light for me. I hope my retirement is half as fun as yours. Hell, I wish my life *now* was half as fun as yours," Mason said, surprised.

"All it takes is a decision," his father said, walking him to the sofa in the living room with Irene. "Make the decision that you're going to live happy and then do it."

"I wish it were that easy; maybe someday," Mason said. "Hey, let me help clean up," Mason offered again to Irene.

"Nope, thanks, I got it," she insisted again.

"Mason, trust me, you're not going to win this one," his father said.

"Well thanks," Mason said. He was touched by the effort that his father put into his party. He continued, "This was a great party; I certainly was not expecting it. So thank you both."

"You're welcome. We had as much fun as you did," Irene said.

"If it's all right with you, then I'm going to crash. I'm beat," Mason said.

"By all means, we'll see you in the morning," Irene said.

"You bet, Mase. Good night," his father said.

As Mason lay down to sleep, he reminisced about the party. Seeing a sixty-five-year-old man shot-gunning a beer brought a smile to his face. *I could've done without seeing the Stotts making out, though,* he thought.

On the other hand, good for them. He had never thought that being retired would be that fun, and yet seeing retired people act as if they were twenty-five was a refreshing thought. His eyes were opened to a whole new dimension of life that he had never given much thought to. He was as content as he'd been in a long time. He was pleasantly surprised how his reunion with his father had turned out. His father had obviously changed. Maybe it was time for Mason to change as well. He faded into a deep sleep.

Chapter 15

Welcome Back, Old Friend
Chandler, Arizona
May 23, 2017

Mason found himself on the 384th floor of a skyscraper, running frantically from office to office telling people to leave the building. The building was swaying in the wind and nobody recognized it except Mason. People were laughing at him and mocking him. He looked out the window. He was so high up he could barely see the street below. His heart pounded harder and harder. He could see the storm growing in intensity and heading straight for the building.

He could hear the wind howling and felt the building start to sway even more. It was getting harder for him to get oxygen into his lungs. Gasping for air, he was torn between continuing to try in vain to help the people in the office building and saving himself.

A blanket of night descended over the building. He could see stars falling from the sky. The earth began to tremble. Finally, the people in the office began to notice what was going on. It was too late. The building began to crumble and people started to scream as they fell from the building. Their hopeless screams shattered the night. During the chaos, a white owl with dark-red, piercing eyes flew into the office through a broken window. Mason stopped and noticed that the storm had no effect on the owl. He then saw his father calling his name with his arms outstretched, "Mason! Mason!"

He yelled back to his father, "Dad!" As he started to run toward his father, the wind slammed Mason into the wall before throwing him to the floor. As a piece of the crumbling building was about to crush Mason, he woke up to his father shaking him and calling his name.

"Mason! Mason, wake up!" his father shouted as he ran into Mason's room and turned on the light.

Sweating profusely and heart pounding, Mason jumped nearly off the bed and sat up. The light added to his confusion. "What! What! What's going on?"

"Slow down, you were having a dream. Relax, Mason; you must've been having some dream." While Mason recovered and got his bearings back, his fathered assured him again, "It's just a dream, Mason. You're okay."

His eyes now adjusted to the light. "Yeah, yeah, I'm okay," Mason said, sitting on the edge of the bed. "A little confused, but I'm okay."

"What's going on?" Irene said as she rushed into the room.

"Mason just had a dream," Patrick replied.

"A dream? It sounded like someone was being tortured," Irene said.

"Mason has the most intense dreams I've ever heard of. He always has. I guess they haven't gone away?" he asked Mason.

"No, but it's been a long time since I've had anything this intense."

"You know, Mason," Irene said, "dreams are just a form of communication from the subconscious to the conscious. The more intense they are, the more important they are. You can't ignore them."

"It was pretty intense, but pretty ridiculous too. I'm not sure how important it is."

"Usually, if the subconscious sends a message to your conscious over and over, and you don't listen to it, it will send the message to you in a violent way so that you'll remember it," she continued.

"Well it made damn sure I'd remember this one," Mason said, finally starting to catch his breath. "And please don't tell me you're a shrink?" he asked Irene with caution.

"No, I've always been intrigued by dreams and studied them in college; and oh yeah, I *used* to be a shrink, but I'm not any longer," she said with a glimpse at Patrick. "I'm retired."

"Great," Mason sighed. His experiences with psychologists were not always pleasant experiences.

"I'd like to talk to you about them some time; maybe I can help," Irene said.

"Believe me, these will blow your mind," Mason replied.

"I'd love to hear about them. Think about it and you let me know," Irene offered.

After they left Mason's room, Mason thought about what Irene had said. The last one I had like this, Kelly died, he remembered. But this one had Dad in it. That doesn't make any sense; it's not his time.

As Irene and Patrick slipped back into bed, Irene probed Patrick further: "What's going on with Mason's dreams?"

"I remember the nightmares he had when he was a kid," he replied. "They would scare Mason to death. I would have to sit with him sometimes all night, so he could sleep. I figured, or hoped, Mason would grow out of them."

"It sounds like he didn't."

Mason's father searched for answers. He hoped the dreams were over and neither of them would have to deal with it again. That, however, was apparently not the case. It would appear they would both get the opportunity to relive the tumultuous experience that drove them apart so many years ago. Was this a chance to have a do-over? A second chance to be there for his son? A chance to right a wrong?

"He said he hadn't had one like this for a while," Patrick thought out loud. "Maybe they stopped for a while and now they're starting again."

"Maybe there's some similarity between now and when he had them before," Irene replied, nodding in agreement.

Chapter 16

Beautiful Anomaly
Chandler, Arizona
May 23, 2017

Feeling a little awkward from all of the attention the preceding night, Mason hesitantly entered the pool area. The hot sun was high in the sky. Immediately, he recognized several people from the party lounging. With his sunglasses on, a beach towel draped over his shoulder, and a Chicago White Sox hat just above his eyes, he tried to slip into a lounge chair unnoticed, but they were too quick.

"Hey! There's the man of the hour," a familiar voice shouted from across the pool, walking over to Mason.

"Hi Ray, hi Gina," Mason replied with a slow wave.

"That was a fun party, huh Mason?" Ray asked.

"Yeah, what I can remember of it. I'm a little hungover, I think."

"Well, get that out of your system today, because tomorrow's the big day," Ray said with a quirky looking grin.

What does he mean by that? Mason thought. "Oh I will, don't worry about that. Wait, tomorrow? What about the weekend?"

"Oh, we'll play on the weekend also. Tomorrow is just a warm up," Ray said. The bartender from the party walked up and interrupted them.

"Hey, there's a couple of partiers!" he said, greeting the Reeds and Mason.

"Mason, you remember Ed Berms; he was mixing your drinks last night," Ray said, reminding Mason.

"Of course, and as I recall, mixing quite a few of my drinks," Mason replied.

"They were good, right?" Ed asked, taking pride in his mixological prowess.

"Yes, they were great, thanks."

"Hey Mason, did you really take down the entire Chicago Police Department by yourself?" Ed asked. Before Mason could answer, however, Ray jumped in.

"Of course he did! They don't just hand out Pulitzers. That's serious business."

"I know that," Ed replied. "I just wanted to know how dangerous it was."

"He put his life on the line," Ray replied. Mason and Gina watched as Ray and Ed continued their discussion about Mason as if he wasn't there. The embellishing began a little quicker than I thought it would, Mason said to himself. Heck, I didn't think I'd be in front of them while they did it.

Finally, Gina rudely interrupted them. "Look, the guy just got here; he's hungover and just wants to relax. Give it a rest, will ya."

Ed and Ray looked at Gina, then at Mason, then at each other, and they all started to laugh.

"Sorry Mason, Gina's right. We love to discuss things down here," Ed offered, with Ray shaking his head in agreement.

"Yeah, get some rest Mason, you'll need it tomorrow," Ray added again.

"Thanks guys," Mason replied. As Gina led Ray and Ed away from Mason, still talking, she turned back toward Mason and winked at him to acknowledge his plight.

He reclined his lounger and finally found the peace and quiet that he sought. Until he was abruptly summoned by his father. "Mase, come here; quickly."

"Good God, do these people ever relax?" he mumbled. He could see people gathering at one end of the pool staring upward toward some trees and pointing.

"Mason, come here before you miss it," his father called out again. Mason sat up and walked over to where everyone had gathered. "Hey guys, what's up?"

"Check that out; there's a huge white owl over there in the trees," his father said, pointing to a tree outside of the pool area.

Mason removed his sunglasses and asked, "What? Where?" His ears perked up. The massive bird that had drawn so much attention jumped from its perch and flew out of the trees, across the pool, and over the heads of the people.

"No way," Mason said under his breath.

"Oh my! Look at how big that thing is," Irene said, watching the owl glide gracefully overhead.

"I've never seen anything like that," Patrick said. "Have you, Mason?"

"Not exactly," he replied, although he did in fact recognize the owl. It was the same owl he saw when he met Al. It was the same owl that was in his dreams, and more importantly, it was the same owl that he saw before Kelly died. Mason's face went pale. What was it doing here? Why was it following him?

"I wonder what he's doing out in the middle of the day and around people," Irene said.

"Not very common, that's for sure," Patrick said.

Mason watched as the bird flew away. His gaze was interrupted by his father,

"Pretty wild, huh Mason?"

"Yes, pretty wild," he replied as he intently watched it disappear into the horizon. Was this another dream? Is it the same one from my dreams? Mason wondered.

As quickly as the owl showed up, it was gone. Everyone went back about their day. People went back to playing tennis, swimming, and eating lunch, with not so much as a second thought about the unique owl. I can't ignore it, Mason thought as he climbed back into his lounge chair. I have a pretty good idea of why it was there; the plaguing question is, who was it there for? And, what am I supposed to do about it? What *can* I do about it?

When Patrick and Irene finished their tennis match, Patrick noticed Mason getting ready to leave the pool. He handed Irene the car keys and instructed her, "You take the car; I'm going to catch up and walk with Mason." He cut across the pool area and caught up with Mason finishing the last of a Coors beer. Pure Rocky Mountain spring water, he thought. The banquet beer indeed.

The walk along the path back to the house was filled with the sweet scent of pink bougainvillea. The flowers and the hot, dry air couldn't overshadow whatever troubled Mason's mind.

"So what's going on with the nightmares, Mason?"

"I don't know; I haven't had one since before Kelly. Now all of a sudden, they start up again, and maybe even a little more intense," Mason answered.

"Was it like the other ones where people were dying all over the place?" his father asked.

"Kind of, but it's more this time. This one was different. It wasn't like when I was a kid. This one dealt more with choices; maybe that's what it's about, choices," Mason said.

"Well, you are older now and the issues may be more adult-oriented. Then again, I don't know what the hell I'm talking about. You really should talk to Irene. I'm telling you, she's really approachable and has a great way about her in dealing with people. In fact, all the old people down here think she's their personal shrink," his father said.

"She seems really nice. I guess it wouldn't hurt to get her take. I mean hell, if she can deal with you, she must be good," Mason said, pushing his dad and lightening the air.

"Hey, what do you mean by that?" his dad said back, laughing.

They found themselves talking for what seemed like hours. It was the first time in Mason's life that he felt as if his father was really trying to understand. As they entered the house, Irene heard Patrick tell Mason, "We'll see what Irene says."

"See what Irene says about what exactly?" she said to them, catching the last part of their conversation.

"Mason wants to get your take on his nightmares," Patrick said.

"Mason, I'd be happy to talk to you about it. But don't let your father talk you into it. You have to want to do it, and it has to be in private. In other words: no Pat," she said, looking at Patrick.

"I won't say anything," Patrick said, but was immediately cut off by Irene.

"No! End of discussion. That's how this stuff works, Pat, and you know it," she kindly scolded him.

"All right, fine," Patrick said. "I've got things to do anyway," he continued.

"Look, it's not a big deal, I don't want to make a mountain out of a mole hill," Mason said. "I don't need major therapy—yet, anyways. I just want to get your take on the dreams."

"We'll talk after dinner, Mason, and we'll only do what you're comfortable with, no pressure. Deal?" she asked.

"Sounds great," Mason replied.

"That works fine with me also; it'll give me time to work on my scrapbook," his father interjected, acting as if he wasn't being left out.

"Did I hear a 'scrapbook' in there somewhere?" Mason razzed.

"No, it's more of a photo album," his father said, realizing what he said and trying to save face.

"I'm pretty sure I heard 'scrapbook,'" Mason said, not letting it go.

"Well, you should listen closer," his dad said firmly, not giving an inch.

With Mason grinning, Irene saved Patrick by telling him, "It's okay honey, it's for me."

"It's not a scrapbook, it's a photo album!" Patrick said adamantly.

"I think scrapbooks are cool," Mason said, laughing.

"Me too," Irene said, also smiling, trying to hold in her laughter. She'd never seen Patrick turn red with embarrassment. It was cute, she thought.

"It's not a scrapbook!" Patrick said again. "Ah, forget it. Let's eat," he continued, dismissing them both and getting the dishes out of a kitchen cabinet.

After dinner, Patrick excused himself to work on his "photo album" and Mason and Irene sat down in the living room to discuss Mason's dreams.

"Mason, I'll let you start where you want to and we'll go from there. Usually we have to delve into childhood, family, rearing, among other things. However, under the circumstances and because we're not doing a formal therapy session, I don't think that's necessary. So why don't you tell me about the dream."

"I was in a building on the 384th floor running from cubicle to cubicle trying to get people to leave the building because it was going to be destroyed by a storm. Nobody would listen to me; instead they were laughing at me. I looked out the windows and saw a dark storm approaching and the building was swaying more and more. As the storm got closer, the building started to fall apart. The stars started falling from the night sky, and I couldn't decide whether to try to help the people or get out and save myself. In my indecision, I was thrown against a wall and fell to the ground, and that's when my dad woke me up."

"Have you ever seen the building before? Maybe in an ad or somewhere in town?" she asked.

"No, I've never seen it before."

"The reason I asked is because if it's a familiar building it changes the meaning. If you've never seen it before, it symbolizes you or a part or your life. If it was something you've seen before, then it's the feeling or thought being conveyed that it gave you when you first experienced it.

"Since you've never seen it before, it symbolizes you or a belief that you have. The bigger the building, the more deep-rooted the emotion or feeling, or the bigger the aspect of you."

"It must be a pretty big aspect then, because it was a huge building. When I looked out the window I could barely see the street, we were so high up," Mason said.

"Dreams are also very current. Typically, they convey current information or issues your subconscious wants you to recognize. There was major destruction caused by an event in your dream. The Pulitzer could be the event, and perhaps it's 'breaking down some walls' or destroying some of the patterns or beliefs that have become so ingrained and have grown into very large 'buildings,' something almost impossible to break down."

"That makes sense," Mason agreed.

"You see, Mason, sometimes dreams that seem terrible may actually be good news. Death in a dream doesn't always mean bad things; it just means that something is ending. It could be a relationship, job, car payment, or anything that is ending or has ended. It sounds to me like there are some changes taking place inside of you, and some of those changes may have been things that were there for a very long time."

Mason considered what Irene had said. Everything she was saying made sense, even if she didn't have all the information. Maybe that is what was happening, he wondered. I needed to accept the changes that were happening around me. Maybe now was the time to accept some change.

"Wow Irene, I think you might be right on. Everything you've said really makes sense. When I finished my article for work, it was like an enormous weight was lifted. I was so burnt out, and then seeing my dad, maybe I am looking at things a little differently right now."

"In the end, Mason, only you can know for sure if the dream interpretation is accurate. Typically, dreams are like wheels. There is a central theme like the center of the wheel. The spokes lead to and from the central theme and surround it. But to know if the interpretation is correct, you have to ask yourself, 'Does it click?' Usually, the right interpretation will click to the dreamer."

"It totally clicks," Mason said.

"Well good, I hoped I've helped a little," Irene said.

"You have helped a ton. I really just need to think about that for a while."

"All right, if you have anything else, please feel free to ask me anytime," Irene said.

"Thanks, I appreciate that. I'm sure I will."

When Mason got to his room, he opened the closet door and again saw the dreaded attaché case. He laid down and again contemplated its existence. His thoughts soon turned to what Irene said.

It made a lot of sense, with the information she had. He wished it was that simple; however, in his experience it was more complicated than that. I wonder if I gave her more information if she would change her assessment, he thought. No, instead I'll keep it to myself, like I've always done, he decided.

If he explained other things, it would lead to other questions, and that would require more explaining and he didn't want to go down that road. This was vacation; he didn't want to stir up old problems. The attaché case, however, was eventually not going to let him *not* deal with it.

Tennis, he thought; it's what was keeping his father ticking. He thought about people who couldn't do things with their parents when they got old. I should be grateful that we're able to hang out and do something fun instead of just playing cards, he told himself. A final peaceful thought came over him as he faded to sleep. Dad is still going to kill me tomorrow, and I'm okay with that.

Chapter 17

The Quickening
Chandler, Arizona
May 24, 2017

A clear, warm Wednesday morning with no wind—a perfect day for tennis. Patrick and Irene were the epitome of the stereotypical senior tennis players. They wore matching tennis outfits, headbands, and wristbands. Mason and Ray warmed up on the court next to Patrick and Irene. Both teams slammed balls back and forth. What speed Mason's father lost due to his age, he more than made up for in his accuracy. Mason noticed how formal the pregame warm-up was. He was used to hitting a little and then starting the game. Usually, it wasn't until the third game before he felt warmed up. Not down here. There was a routine. Protocols to follow.

They warmed up practicing all facets of the game, until they broke a sweat. Although new to Mason, he liked the extra practice. After they were done warming up, each team went over their strategy.

"All right Mason, here's the deal; your dad is going to try and cover for Irene as much as he can. We need to make him run as much as possible to wear him down; otherwise, we're toast."

"Do you think they're saying the same thing about me? Keep me running to try and wear me down?" Mason asked.

To which Ray sternly replied, "Hell no, you're what they're going to try and exploit. You just keep the ball in play and hit it to Irene."

"Man, I feel like Mrs. McEnroe," Mason said.

"You shouldn't; she's much prettier than you and much better in tennis than you are," a quick-witted Ray said back, equally as sarcastic.

"Touché! Thanks for the pep talk; you really know how to motivate people. I can see the Tony Robbins tapes have really been paying off for you," Mason said.

"Tony who? Ah, doesn't matter. Get your head in the game; they're ready to start," Ray replied.

"Hey, if you two are done making love to each other over there, maybe we can get started!" Patrick yelled from the opposite end of the court.

"There's my dad! He's finally arrived; I wondered when he'd show up!" Mason yelled back while Ray laughed.

"All right, love-love, here we go," Patrick said as the match got under way.

Although Patrick and Ray were more serious about the match than Mason and Irene, they were still pretty lighthearted with each other.

Mason noticed that his father was more concerned about having fun than winning. He noticed his father hitting shots to keep the ball in play instead of hitting kill shots. Mason found himself having fun playing tennis instead of the usual stressful experience that accompanied their tennis games. Usually, Mason likened their matches to that of a prostate exam instead of a game, but not this time.

To Patrick and Ray, bragging rights were worth their weight in gold. At parties, barbeques, card games, or any other gathering, tennis always came up. They'd also been friends for more than forty years. Most of their lives they worked hard and played hard. Now they partied hard and played harder. With the second set winding down and the heat getting more intense, everyone was getting more fatigued.

Mason noticed Ray squinting and rubbing his eyes. With Ray's head hanging and Ray having difficulty breathing, Mason was sure that Ray was exhausted. "Dad, let's take a break; this heat is killing me," he said, trying to help Ray.

"Yeah, it's hot. Let's finish this set and call it a day," his father replied.

"Look Dad, you won the first set and are up 4–1 in this one. Let's call it," Mason said again.

Observing that Ray didn't look so good, Patrick asked, "Ray, what do you think? You want to finish or call it?"

"I'm good; let's finish," Ray struggled to say.

Irene also noticed Ray was breathing harder, looked flushed, and seemed to be having a difficult time focusing when he spoke. She could tell he was done. She turned to Patrick and shook her head back and forth, indicating no more. Patrick acknowledged Irene and the two of them walked toward the net. As they approached the net, Patrick asked Ray again, "Are you okay, Ray? Why don't we take a breather?"

It was obvious to everyone that Ray was done playing. He now started to slouch over with his hands on his knees and he hung his head down. He was indeed worn out.

"Yeah, maybe we'll finish tomorrow," Ray said, straightening up and trying to not look like he was in too much pain.

"That sounds good. Let's gather up the balls and get a drink," Patrick said. His friend wasn't feeling right and he wanted to get him out of the sun. "Ray, sit down. We'll get the balls and get going," Patrick ordered.

Mason picked up the balls on his side of the court while Ray slowly began making his way to the bench on the side at midcourt. As Mason got closer to Ray, he saw Ray stumble. Dropping his racket and balls, Mason raced to Ray's side to assist him to the bench. As Mason grabbed Ray's arm, he experienced a strange but familiar sensation.

Time came to a complete standstill. An eerie chill moved through Mason's body as he made contact with Ray. As he held Ray's arm, he looked at his father and Irene walking toward them and noticed they were moving in slow motion. He noticed that he, too, was walking in slow motion. There was no sound, no senses. Everything was dead calm. He could see his father's mouth moving, but couldn't hear anything. Perplexed by the complete and utterly peaceful sensation, Mason questioned what was going on.

He looked back at Ray. Ray simultaneously turned and looked at Mason. Their eyes intensely locked onto one another's as if they were seeing into each other's souls. Still holding Ray's arm, Mason began to recognize the sensation. He had experienced this before.

As it became more familiar to Mason, he began to realize his plight. His eyes grew larger and his muscles tensed in preparation for what he knew was coming. Before he could break contact with Ray's arm, the sense of time that had slowed almost to a standstill quickly accelerated. Sound came crashing back, as did all of his senses, simultaneously. With a deafening boom, a sharp jolt of electricity pierced both Mason and Ray. The jolt ran the length of Mason's body, knocking them both to the ground.

Mason was three feet behind Ray on the ground. With a surprised look and a vain effort, Ray turned around to see what happened to Mason. Mason was lying on his side. He sat up and shook his head to clear out the residual electricity. He looked up at Ray and saw blood dripping from Ray's nose.

"Are you all right, Mason?" Ray asked.

"Yeah Ray, I'm fine. Are you okay?"

"I'm not sure. I feel kind of weird," Ray said.

Patrick and Irene arrived within seconds. "Are you guys all right?" Irene asked.

"Yeah, we're fine," Ray said as Patrick helped him up.

"What just happened?" Irene asked, looking at Mason sitting on the court.

"I tripped," Mason said, "but I'm fine."

"That didn't look like a trip," Irene said.

As the four of them speechlessly walked over to the bench, Ray began to black out. His eyes blinked rapidly in an attempt to regain his sight. A sharp pain penetrated his chest as if someone had driven a knife through it.

He dropped his racket and, in a split second, his body collapsed out from underneath him and slammed onto the hot tennis court.

"Ray!" Irene yelled as they tried to grab hold of him.

"Ray! Wake up! Are you okay? Ray! Ray!" Patrick shouted at him.

Mason backed up and watched his father trying to revive Ray.

"We need to call 911," Mason said, still groggy from his own experience. Before his father could answer, Ray started to regain consciousness. He opened his eyes and became more alert.

"Hey, I'm fine, just a little heat stroke. Give me a minute, I'll be fine."

They helped Ray up and got him the last few feet to the bench and handed him some water.

"You gave us a little scare, Ray," Irene said.

"Oh, I'll be fine. It's going to take a lot more than that to get rid of me," Ray said.

In an attempt to talk to his father in private, Mason pulled his father off to the side, away from Ray. "Dad, we need to get him to a hospital."

"He's fine, Mason, just give him a minute to catch his breath. He does this all the time. It's heat stroke; that's why we don't play in the middle of the day," his father told him.

"Dad, you don't get it. We need to get him to a hospital and we need to call his family and get them down here," Mason demanded.

Trying to reassure Mason, his father replied, "Look Mason, I know Ray; he'll be all right. He just needs some rest and fluids."

Irene walked up and interrupted them. "Guys, we need to get going."

They both stopped talking and looked at her. Being very perceptive, Irene picked up on their private conversation.

"I get it. What's going on?" she asked.

"Irene, we need to get Ray to a hospital and we need to contact his family," Mason said, unyielding.

"What? He's done this before, granted this was a bit scarier. But he seems all right," she said.

"He's not all right! He needs to get to a hospital," Mason demanded.

"What makes you so sure, Mason?" Irene asked.

Somewhat at a loss for words, Mason offered more calmly, "Look, I can't explain it. If I'm wrong, he gets a night in a hospital and his family gets a small vacation, nothing hurt. If I'm right, his family will want to be here, trust me."

"Well, we can't argue with that logic, Pat. Let's get him to Saint Joseph's," Irene said. "We'll just get him looked at."

"But he's fine, he—" Patrick tried to explain, but Irene cut Patrick off midsentence. "It's not up for discussion; let's go."

Chapter 18

Dodging Bullets
Chandler, Arizona
May 24, 2017

A cautiously optimistic aura filled the waiting room outside the emergency room on the first floor of Saint Joseph's Hospital. Gina, Patrick, Irene, Mason, and some of Ray's other friends were gathered there awaiting word from the doctors about Ray's status. The more time that transpired, the more concerned they became. After four hours of waiting with trepidation, the doors finally opened. An exhausted older gentleman in a white lab coat and green scrubs entered the waiting area and walked over to Ray's group.

"Good evening everyone. Here's where we're at. Ray had a moderate heart attack that was exacerbated by heat stroke. There is some blockage to some of the arteries around the heart and once he's a little more stable, I'd like to go in and clear them out. Then, we'll have to run some tests to determine the extent of damage to the heart. That may take a few days to show up. For the next few days, we'll keep him in the ICU to make sure he's monitored. Right now he needs rest. You should be able to visit him tomorrow."

"Is he going to be all right?" Gina asked.

"Right now, he's stable. However, we won't know the full extent of the damage until we run more tests. It'll be touch and go for the next few days until we can get more information. Keep praying for him; he needs that as well."

"Thank you doctor," Gina said, shaking his hand.

As the doctor left the room, the heavy air was replaced by lighter, more optimistic air. Gina was thankful for all of the support everyone offered as people began to head home after the long night. The drive home from the hospital was a quiet one. They were thankful that it appeared like Ray was going to be all right and that he had dodged the proverbial bullet. Patrick broke the silence in the car.

"Well, Mason; good call," his father said.

"Yeah Mason, thanks to you it looks like he's going to make it," Irene added.

Mason always hated this part. People tended to grasp onto any thread of hope, and in doing so, they dismissed the possibility of the inevitable. They fight tooth and nail to deny it. Death however, invited or not, inserts itself in our lives like the tax man on steroids. There is no convenient time for his visit, but rest assured, he will visit. It was easier to not go there. Mason downplayed his part. "I thought he needed medical attention, that's all."

"Mason, you may have saved his life," Irene said.

Mason adamantly rebutted Irene and said, "No I didn't. Suggesting someone go to the hospital is not saving a life. In fact, Dad, are Lori and the other kids coming down?"

"I don't know, I think they're waiting to get more information."

"Dad, you have to do everything in your power to convey to them that they need to be here. Will you promise me you'll do that?" Mason begged.

"I'll try, Mason. I can't make them come if they don't want to," his father replied.

Irene interjected, "Mason, the doctor said he'll probably be all right."

Finally conceding with "I know," Mason asked his father one more time. "Just try, Dad, will you?"

"Yes Mason, I will try. You have my word on that."

After they arrived home, they were all exhausted. The emotional toll of the hospital visit was more taxing than any workout. They all retired for the night. Mason, still terribly concerned about what happened earlier, was reminded of Kelly, and he knew how that turned out. Lying in bed, he couldn't get his mind off of Ray. It's happening again, he thought. He slowly began to wane out of consciousness and fell asleep.

It was a hot sunny day and he was walking on a beach holding hands with Kelly. The waves were rolling up onto the sand, barely getting their feet wet. Laughing and talking, they were having fun. There was no doubt in either of them that they would spend the rest of their lives together.

The waves started to roll in a little harder. Looking out over the water, Mason saw the waves increasing in size. Churning clouds formed and blocked out the sun. It became dark. The temperature dropped and the wind started blowing. Their hands released their grip on each other to block the sand from blowing into their faces. As the wind and the waves intensified, Mason lowered his head. The clouds swirled faster, multiplying on top of themselves. It got dark quickly. The storm that had blown in without warning was getting worse.

Mason tried to look up to get Kelly to safety, but she was nowhere to be found. He started calling her name, but his voice was being drowned out by the howling wind. His heart started pounding. I can't lose her again, he thought. He then started getting pelted with hail and rain. He dropped to his knees and covered his head with his arms to protect himself.

As quickly as the storm blew in, suddenly everything stopped. Mason stayed kneeling on the sand, afraid to look up for fear of something else happening. While on his knees trying to get the strength to rise, a strange pungent odor overcame him. The odor got worse to the point he thought he was going to vomit. He looked up. The storm was gone. He stood up and looked around. He saw dead fish covering the beach. Surrounding him. He counted 384.

Then he looked out over the now calm waters and saw a large white bird circling above two dead floating bodies in the water. He ran out into the shallow waters, and as he reached them, they turned over one at a time. One was Kelly and the other was Ray Reed. He started to sob when all of a sudden Kelly sat up in the water. Mason's heart nearly jumped out of his body. She looked at Mason and said, "Help them." Then she and Ray sank underwater and disappeared.

"No!" Mason cried out. "Come back!"

With that, he awoke again, sweating and breathing hard. He looked at the clock that read 3:18. Holy crap! he thought. What the hell is going on? He got up and went into the kitchen to get a drink and noticed his father sitting on the sofa in the family room.

"Hey, what are you doing up?" he asked his father.

"Couldn't sleep; you?"

"Another dream," he replied, sitting on the adjacent loveseat. "I wish they'd go away. This one had Kelly in it."

"I thought I heard you call her name. I figured you were dreaming."

"Yeah, it was another doozy. They always start good and end up bad."

"I wish I could help explain it, but I just don't have a clue about it."

"That's all right, neither do I. I know that Irene had a pretty good explanation, and there is probably some truth to what she said. But you and I know there's more to it; I know that for sure," Mason said.

"You know, all those years when I denied what was happening to you, I think I knew deep down that you were right. I just didn't want to admit it," his father confessed.

Mason reassured his father that it was all right. "I figured you did, but at the end of the day, I had to figure out what to do myself. So I was all right with us not talking about it."

"Your mother always believed you had a gift, but I saw the pain it caused you and maybe helped you believe it was a curse. Maybe it *is* a good thing?" his father suggested.

"If it is, I haven't seen any good come of it yet," Mason said.

"That's not entirely true. If it wasn't for you, Ray may not have made it."

"Dad, I'm not completely sure how to tell you this."

"Tell me what?"

Mason hesitated, took a deep breath, and regrettably told his dad, "Look, you know I wish it weren't so. I'm not trying to get attention. I'm not trying to scare anyone. If it was anyone except Ray, I wouldn't say anything; I'd just ignore it, like I always do. But here it goes; Ray's not going to make it."

Mason's father looked down and consciously stopped himself from saying anything. He had to gather his thoughts. If there was anything he'd learned in his years, it was to not fly off the handle and say things that typically he'd regret one minute after he said them. With an open mind and in the spirit of trying to connect with Mason, he calmly asked, "That's what your dream told you?"

"Kind of. I can't really explain it, but yes, that's part of it," Mason said in sobering tone. He continued, "Look, I know how hard it is for you to not go off on me, but remember, I'm not causing it, I'm just reporting it. You know, 'Don't shoot the messenger.' I know how you feel about Ray; do you think I'd mess with you about this? I would rather be wrong and have you see him through it and be there for him, rather than keep it to myself and see you wish you had known."

Mason's father recognized that Mason was right. Mason did put himself out there and opened himself up to be ridiculed yet again. But he did it out of love for his father and nothing else. With a renewed attitude, Mason's father was going to work with Mason, whether he was right or wrong. He was once again happy that he held his tongue and actually listened and thought, before he spoke.

"Do you really believe that, Mason?" he asked.

"I wish I didn't, but yes, I do," Mason replied.

Mason's father sat up and in a grateful but serious manner proclaimed, "Well then, we'd better get some sleep; we've got a busy day ahead of us tomorrow. I mean today. We have to make some calls and get some people moving for Ray's sake."

"All right," Mason said. As they were walking out of the family room Mason's dad reassured him, "And Mason, no matter which way this thing goes, whether you're right or wrong, we'll ride it together."

"Thanks Dad; see you later."

Chapter 19

The Aftermath
The Pentagon, Washington, DC
May 23, 2017

"Sir, I think you need to see this," an intern said, bursting into Colonel Austin's office and turning on his television. The no-knock entry got the attention it needed from Austin.

"What the hell," Austin started to say, jumping up from his desk, until he realized the importance of the intrusion.

"This is coming out of London minutes ago, sir," the intern said as he turned on the television to the news.

"The only thing we know for sure was that it was a suicide bomber in the middle of the Victoria Square marketplace in downtown London. Preliminary results have at least twelve dead and over forty injured by what witnesses say was evil incarnate. Sarah, we'll have more for you when the chief inspector releases their statement shortly. Back to you in the studio . . ."

Austin sat back down behind his desk and ordered, "Get Dougherty here, ASAP."

"Yes sir."

The intern left the office as quickly as he entered. The colonel stared out his fifth floor window weighing the implications of the new direction the "war on terror" just took.

"Colonel, I guess you've seen the news?" Brian Dougherty asked, walking into Colonel Austin's office.

"Yes, come in and close the door please. Here, sit down," the colonel said, gesturing to a burgundy colored leather chair.

"Not twenty-four hours ago you briefed us as to a possible attack in London."

"Yes sir."

"Did we send that intel to MI6?"

"Yes sir, we sent them what intel we had. We didn't know the location or the time; we were still working on that. This attack happened very quickly, sir. I'm not sure we could've stopped it."

"What concerns me, Brian, is what that means."

"I know, sir. If they would hit our allies, would they hit us?" The realization hit them simultaneously. Their silence was like a wrecking ball in their minds. The answer was undeniably clear.

"Exactly; so would they?" the colonel asked, hoping for anything but the obvious.

"We just don't know yet, colonel. We know they couldn't pose a very large threat to our country as a whole, but explain that to the 3,000 families from 9/11."

"We can't allow one American to die because of these jackasses, Brian." The colonel's resolve was that of a fighter. This was a personal shot to him. It was his watch and he'd be damned if his country wasn't going to prevail.

Brian tried to help with strategy. "The problem is that they are unorganized and, therefore, they don't have prescribed patterns that can be predicted. In fact, that's what makes them unpredictable. Couple that with the fact that they're so small, and it makes them tough to fight."

"I want everyone we got working on this group," Austin ordered.

"We have operatives working on it as we speak, sir."

"We need that intel, Brian; we can't let this happen here. We are one of the few countries left where suicide bombers and terrorist bombings really haven't hit. If we show them that we're vulnerable, God knows where that ends."

"All of our intel indicates that it's not a matter of 'if,' sir, it's a matter of when."

"We need to put it off as long as possible. And if we can't put it off, we need to know where and when."

Brian stood up and took a deep concerned breath. "We're on it, sir. As soon as I get any info, you'll be the first to know."

Chapter 20

Small Victories First
Rabwah, Pakistan
May 24, 2017

"Ah, right there, my flower, that's the spot," Ahmed said to the scantily clad servant girl giving him a massage by the pool. "Your hands are soft, fit for a god, my dear," he continued as he groped her at will. The warm oil she poured on his back made him tense up. A warm breeze cooled the oil almost immediately. Relaxing traditional Islamic hymns by Mishary Rashid Al-Afasy playing over the speakers complemented the serene sounds of the waterfall next to the pool. A small glimpse into paradise, Ahmed thought, until his quietude would be ripped from his being.

"Your highness, my apologies for the intrusion," General Aleem said, barging into the pool area where Ahmed was receiving his daily massage. A risky proposition to do on any day.

"What is the meaning of this?" Ahmed yelled.

"Sir, we have word from London."

Ahmed looked around and struggled with whether or not to continue his massage. He finally decided to excuse the servants.

"All of you, leave us. Wait, my flower," he said to the girl massaging him. "I want you to wait for me in the messiah's quarters. Allah wants me to give you a special blessing," he said with a perverted smile.

"As you wish, lord," she said, bowing out of the spa.

"Now, what is it, general?" Ahmed said, as if he had no patience for being disturbed.

"Hamed, the young man has completed his mission in London."

"How many dead?"

"Twelve now and forty injured."

"Could we not have killed more, general?"

"Perhaps if we used a vehicle or multiple bombers?" General Aleem said.

"It doesn't matter anyway. It's a small victory today, but after next week's meeting, we will have the entire Muslim world on our side."

"Sir?" Aleem questioned. "What meeting?"

"Aleem, we can only do so much by ourselves. We will join forces with the Muslim world and destroy Satan's playground once and for all."

"But I thought—" Aleem was cut off by Ahmed.

"Next week you'll see. Now you must excuse me, I have an indoctrination to attend to."

Chapter 21

Denial
Chandler, Arizona
May 25, 2017

Mason looked at the clock again and it read 11:05. He could hear voices out in the kitchen. I'd better see what they're up to now, he thought. He wondered if the conversation he had earlier in the morning with his father really happened. He hoped it did. He knew his father was going out on a limb trusting him. Usually, Mason would hope that he didn't make an ass out of himself, but this time, for Ray's sake, he would gladly be wrong. Stumbling into the kitchen, he saw several people that he recognized from the party. "Hey, good morning, Mason," Irene said.

"Yeah, hi Mason!" the Waltons from next door said.

"Hi everyone, what's going on?" Mason asked.

"We're organizing," his father replied.

"Organizing what?" Mason asked.

"A party for Ray," his father said with a grin.

"Do you think that's a good idea?" Mason asked his father as if he had forgotten what they had discussed earlier in the morning.

"Apparently Ray had a great night and they're letting him come home later today," Irene said.

"What about all the testing?" Mason asked.

His father interjected, "They said they can do that as outpatient care. We just need to get him to his appointments."

"That's good," Mason said slowly, as if he was not really sure it was good.

His father walked over to him and said, "I've made some calls and convinced the kids to come down and visit him. We decided to maybe have it as a surprise party."

"A surprise party?" Mason questioned. "Is that a good idea with his heart?"

"Doc says he'll be fine; he's a real fighter," Gina said.

"Dad?" Mason asked, giving him "the look."

"Mason, come help me move some boxes in the garage," his father said to get him alone.

As the door to the garage started to close behind Mason, the voices in the kitchen faded until the door was completely closed. Mason and his father were alone in the garage.

"Look Mason, I am sticking to what I said this morning. I meant what I said. But you've got to admit, this is great news."

"It is, Dad, but he's not out of the woods yet."

"I know, but this is the only way to get his family down here; then we play it by ear. If he's doing good, maybe we don't make it a surprise, we just make it a regular party. At least it gets his family interacting with him."

"All right, I'll buy some of that," Mason said.

"Oh, by the way, Mason, how much time do we think we have before we know he's out of the woods?"

Mason was wondering when that question would come up and dreaded it. Not sure how to respond, he tried to dance around it.

"If we're having this talk next weekend, I think we're good. So get people down here, but don't plan a party until the end of next week," Mason replied.

His father then asked Mason, more rhetorically than not, "We'll plan it for next Friday then, is that good?"

Mason could tell it wasn't that his father was skeptical; he just didn't believe Mason. It dawned on Mason that his father was appeasing him and that they were going to do the party regardless of what Mason thought. Although it was somewhat disheartening, Mason put himself in their shoes and understood their reaction. He also thought that scheduling a party would get Ray's family down there, and that was the goal. Not letting his father know the jig was up, he played along.

"Next Friday would be perfect; that'll give Ray a little time to rest," Mason said, not believing it for a second.

Ray was released from the hospital and was home resting while the circus came to town around him. Over the next three days, between running back and forth to the airport, seeing Ray, and making party arrangements, Mason hardly saw his father. His dad took the reins for essentially planning a family reunion for Ray. It gave him a purpose, and because it was for his friend, he was that much more passionate about it. The constant barrage of friends and family kept Ray's spirits high. It was indeed turning into quite the production.

Mason recognized his father was coping with it the best way he could. Instead of moping around and being sad and depressed, his father turned the situation around and energized people. An interesting approach, Mason thought. The proverbial "glass half full" axiom.

Chapter 22

Logical Conclusions
Chandler, Arizona
May 28, 2017

After walking into the backyard after a late afternoon run, Mason saw his father and Irene sitting on the back patio sipping lemonade. He stopped. Not having been seen yet, he watched them. Talking; happy; alive. The run couldn't shake the torture from Mason's mind of what was to come. Mason's father was proud of himself for arranging the party for Ray on Friday. However, it was Sunday, May 28, 2017. There would be no party for Ray on Friday. No laughing. No drinking. No life.

Mason slowly walked up to the patio. He hid the remorse he felt inside. He had a lifetime of hiding his feelings. He learned to be a verbal chameleon.

"Hi guys, are you finally taking a break?" Mason asked.

"Nope, we're waiting on you. We're going to Ray's house tonight for pizza."

"All right. I'll get cleaned up and we can go."

Mason's gift would again be a testament to the logical conclusion to life. A witness to the foregone conclusion we all have. The harsh reality that all people will cease to live some day. For Ray, this would be his special night.

Another spectacular Arizona sunset highlighted the drive to the Reeds' house. Pizza was the last thing on anyone's mind. Both Mason and his father were content, yet for two completely different reasons. Both of them had the goal to reunite Ray with his family, but their objectives couldn't have been more polarized. Patrick made the drive to Ray's house a thousand times. This drive seemed different, though the quietness in the car was peaceful. Patrick and Irene couldn't put their finger on it. Mason could. Maybe on some level they all knew how special this night was.

"Now Pat, take it easy on Ray. Remember, he's recuperating," Irene said, sitting in the car parked in front of Ray's house checking her makeup.

"I know, I know; you've reminded me ten times today."

"I know how you guys are. If he starts it, let it go," she commanded.

"I know. Now come on; let's go."

While they walked up the walkway to the house, the front door opened and a smiling Lori ran out to greet them.

"Hi guys!" Lori said, hugging them each in turn and getting to Mason last.

"Hi Lori, it's good to see you," Mason said.

"You too, and congratulations on the award. That's great! Now come in," she said, ushering them into the house. Inside the house were Ray's closest friends, his children and grandchildren, his brother and sister and their families, and one of his cousins, who made it from New Haven, Connecticut. It really did turn out to be a family reunion. Ray greeted everyone as they entered the house. He looked good and sounded even better. It was hard to believe that a week earlier, he had a heart attack and heat stroke. He was indeed a fighter. He was happy to have his friends and family there with him. They found themselves having a wonderful reunion rivaling that of any Thanksgiving. The pizza gave the turkey a run for its money.

After a couple of hours, Patrick and Irene stood in the kitchen marveling at the interaction of Ray's family. "I think it turned out bigger than we had anticipated," Irene said.

The air of Ray's family connecting permeated the house. After catching up with many of Ray's relatives that Patrick hadn't seen in years, Patrick noticed several of Ray's friends began departing the party, leaving Ray's family to catch up with each other.

Patrick leaned in and whispered in Irene's ear, "You know, most of Ray's friends have left. Why don't we let him spend some time with his family?"

"Great idea," Irene replied.

They walked into the family room and announced to the Reeds they were leaving. They said good-byes to everyone and followed Ray and Gina to the front door, where they all stopped.

"Ray, this has been a great night, but we have to get the youngster to bed," Patrick said, pointing to Mason with his thumb. They all laughed, including Mason.

"Thanks for everything, guys," Ray said to the three of them. His eyes watered up; he was deeply moved by all of the effort people put in on his behalf. Looking at Patrick, he added, "You've been a good friend, Pat, and I'm blessed to be able to say that. You know I love you guys."

Rather than give the usual sarcastic comment, Patrick could tell that Ray was more serious.

"Ray, we love you too and would do anything for you," Patrick said back to him.

"I know; we've been pretty fortunate to have been friends for as long as we have," Ray said.

"We've been more than friends—we've been brothers."

"Yes we have, brother!" Ray said back in an attempt to lighten the mood.

This was no ordinary night. Ray gave them heartfelt hugs and told them good-bye. Turning to Mason, Ray joked with him. "You're not going to trip, are you?" he asked as he went to hug him.

"No Ray, I'm okay now," Mason said as he embraced him. They both felt the shock go through their bodies.

Ray whispered something in Mason's ear.

Mason looked down and humbly whispered back, "Thank you."

Ray continued to whisper in Mason's ear while Mason just nodded his head in acknowledgment. Mason then looked up and whispered back sadly with a smile, "Yes, I know, Ray."

As they separated, their eyes were deeply intent and locked on each other's like at the tennis court. They both nodded their heads in acknowledgement and smiled as if they had a secret; perhaps they did. With that, Patrick, Irene, and Mason left the house and drove home, not saying anything to each other. They all felt something strange was going on, but no one could put their finger on it. Although Mason could, he tried to avoid it. Once they arrived home, Irene wasn't one to employ avoidance.

"All right Mason, what was all that about?"

"What was what all about?"

"You know exactly what I'm talking about; with Ray."

"Oh that. Nothing. He just thanked me for helping."

"Mason, I analyzed people for a living for thirty years. That was no 'thank you.' There's more to it; what's up?" she continued.

Mason contemplated how to answer Irene. If he avoided her question all together, it could be construed as extremely rude. If he minimized it or was too misleading, it would insult her. However, giving them the truth could crush them, and after the night they just had, he couldn't do that to them. Although, he suspected they already knew.

"Look, why don't we talk about it tomorrow," Mason said calmly.

Irene, getting more concerned, asked again. "Mason, if there is something we need to know, please, let us help."

"Trust me, there's nothing you or anyone can do," Mason said. "Ray is still pretty sick; you really just need to understand that."

"We do understand that, Mason," his father interjected. "Do we need to get him to a hospital or get him anything?"

Mason realized that his father and Irene were holding on pretty tightly. He also knew they weren't going to let him off the hook that easily. When people get that age, they don't want the games, they want the truth. Mason negotiated a compromise.

"You've got him everything he needs: his family and friends. I know this stinks, but I don't know how else to dance around it. He's not going to be here much longer. There is nothing else anyone can do for him, it's simply his time. I'm sorry. I wish it wasn't so, but it is," Mason said remorsefully.

The silence reinforced the finality of what Mason said. Breaking the long, painful quiet, Irene, not wanting to believe Mason, asked despairingly, "Are you sure? How do you know? Is he all right?"

"He's fine; let him be with his family. He knows his time is coming, and that's what he wants," Mason said.

Patrick observed the exchange between Mason and Irene and intervened, "Hey, let's drop it. We'll play it by ear, check in with him tomorrow, and go from there. How does that sound?" he asked.

"That's fine," Mason said.

"Yes, that's fine," Irene said, and then turned to Mason to apologize. "I'm sorry Mason, I didn't mean to drill you like that. I'm just really concerned about Ray. I didn't mean to offend you."

"No, you didn't; don't worry about it," Mason offered. "You didn't offend me and I completely understand; you care about Ray. Usually, I just keep my mouth shut, but this time I wanted to help. Actually, it's probably me who should apologize."

"Nonsense," his father said, reassuring Mason. "We know you were trying to help and we appreciate that, Mason. It's just that Ray is a very good friend and you're never prepared to get that kind of news. It kind of took us by surprise."

"Let's talk about it tomorrow," Mason said.

No one was going to sleep well tonight.

Chapter 23

The Owl Cometh
Chandler, Arizona
May 29, 2017

Tossing and turning in bed, Irene couldn't find the right position to get comfortable. Every time she thought she had found it, her racing thoughts and the rustling of sheets from Patrick's restlessness made it clear she had not. Her body temperature soared. Burning up, she'd throw the covers off of her, only to pull them back minutes later when she was cold. She couldn't calm her breathing. Every time she nodded off, she was quickly prodded back to consciousness by her anxiety. She knew this was simply one of those nights. Fed up with her intermittent five-minute power naps, she sat up in bed and let out a long frustrated sigh. Patrick recognized her abrupt movement and rolled over toward her.

"Hey, you all right?"

"Yes, I can't sleep," Irene answered.

Sitting up, Patrick agreed, "Me too. I don't know what's going on. I hope Mason's wrong about this."

"What's going on with Mason? I mean, Ray's doctor's report was pretty good. I'm concerned that Mason has an attention-seeking thing going on."

"Is this your idea of pillow talk?" Patrick joked. "Just kidding, he's fine. He's just always had a quirky thing about him and his dreams. I don't understand it and I'm not sure he does. At first we thought it was just an overactive imagination, until some pretty weird things started to happen."

"Like what?" Irene said.

Patrick hesitated and thought about what to say. He knew how it was going to sound. "I'm not sure exactly how to explain it, but he had some dreams that came true and it scared a lot of people."

"Scared people?" Irene perked up.

"People were scared because people died. In fact, some people even blamed him for the death of a boy at his school. Mason said he was playing football at school and a boy tackled him and started picking on him. He told the boy he was going to die the next day. The next day the boy was climbing a street sign and fell into the street and was killed. Ever since then, people blamed him as if he caused it. Eventually, he believed he *did* cause it, and it scared the tar out of him. So he withdrew and never really spoke of it again."

"My God, that must have crushed him. Did you ever get him therapy?" Irene asked.

"We tried; he didn't respond to it and wouldn't open up. We moved to a new town, got a fresh start, and he started to improve. He made friends, did good in school, so we thought things were better."

"Didn't you wonder what it was?"

"Sure, but when it went away and he started to improve, we thought it was better to let a sleeping dog keep sleeping."

"That may have been best for him then, but that sleeping dog may have been awakened, and it might behoove him to confront that beast now. Maybe I'll try and talk to him tomorrow."

"I'm sure it would help him. I know this much, he's definitely not looking for attention. I can assure you of that. I guess if anyone can get him to talk, it's you," Patrick said.

A loud screech pierced the quiet night air and interrupted their talk. It echoed through the house. Irene winced as her muscles tensed up. "What the hell was that?" Irene asked.

"I don't know, sounded like a cat being mutilated. Maybe a coyote got a hold of one."

"That was kind of creepy." A chill shot up her spine. "I've never heard anything like that," Irene said.

"Neither have I. You get some sleep. I'm going to go get a drink and look around," Patrick continued.

Patrick walked out into the kitchen and noticed Mason standing in the family room staring out the window up at the cloudless night sky. The light from the full moon reflected off the trees in the backyard.

"Peaceful down here, isn't it, Mason?" his father said, walking up behind Mason.

"Yes, as long as you rule out the weird sounds of the night."

"That was strange, wasn't it? Must've been an animal killing a cat or something?" his father offered.

"The last time I heard that sound, Kelly died."

Taken aback, his father asked, "You've heard that before?"

"Unfortunately yes. I think it's an owl."

"Like the white one we saw at the pool?"

"Yes," Mason replied in a monotone voice, while staring out the window. He thought to himself, in fact, I've heard that screech many times, and it never ends good for someone.

"He must have been hungry, by the sound of that scream."

"I'm not sure he was here for an animal."

"What do you mean?" his father asked. Although he knew exactly what Mason meant. They both knew. Neither would openly admit it, but they knew. Neither of them felt the need to discuss what was apparent. Instead they both politely changed the emerging surreal tone to one more positive. There would be time to discuss the gravity of the situation later.

"Nothing," Mason finally said, turning his gaze from the moon and directing it inside onto his father. "Other than that, it's quite beautiful down here. You picked a great place to retire," he continued.

"I love it here, Masc."

"I wish Mom could've seen it." Mason looked back out at the night. In the distance, he saw the silhouette of an owl fly across the moon.

His father reflected for a moment and nodded his head in agreement. "She would've loved it." He continued, "You know what's going to happen to him, don't you?"

"I guess I thought that deep down we all knew."

"Knew, as in past tense?"

Mason turned his gaze from the bright shining moon and fixed it on his father, and with a sympathetic smile, he told his father, "Ray's already told Mom 'hello' for us."

Patrick shook his head slowly in acknowledgement as he turned and stared up at the moon through the window. A tear crept out of his right eye. A peaceful, sad calm came over him as he said good-bye to Ray. He turned back to Mason, who was somewhat humbled at how his father had taken the news.

"Mason, I have no idea what gift, or ability, or whatever it is you have; but I can assure you, it is a gift, not a curse. You will never know how much you coming here and helping us deal with this has helped me. If you hadn't come down here, this would've taken all of us by surprise. You gave us all a chance to say good-bye the right way. Embrace your gift, Mase, and then figure out how to use it to help people. Don't be afraid of it anymore."

Mason waited twenty years to hear his father say those words. They were comforting to him. So different than before. Genuinely touched, Mason felt more at peace with his father than he had in years. "Thanks, Dad. That means a lot to me."

"No, thank you," his father consoled. "Now let's get some sleep; it sounds like we have a wake to plan."

Chapter 24

Kelly's Plight
Chandler, Arizona
May 31, 2017

Another cloudless Arizona afternoon. Irene, Mason, and Patrick retreated to the covered patio after returning home from the funeral of Ray Reed. A slight breeze offered a reprieve from the heat. The thick orange-striped outdoor sofa cushions were a soft and comfortable alternative to the hard wood pews from the church. As they sank into the cushions, they could feel the closure of Ray's death begin to settle in. The tartness of the fresh squeezed, ice-cold lemonade was perfect. Picking homegrown lemons off their trees was a welcome reminder that summer had arrived.

"That was a nice mass," Irene said.

"Yes, he will be missed, that's for sure," Patrick added.

"Gina's got a ton of friends and family, a good support system," Mason said.

"I'm happy that his family got to see him before he left us," Irene said. "Thanks to you, Mason," she continued.

"No, I didn't—"

"Yes Mason," his dad said, cutting him off midsentence. "You did have something to do with it. You demanded that we get him to a hospital, that we get his family, and that we spend time with him."

"That's true, Mason," Irene said, siding with Patrick.

"In fact," Patrick continued, "you said the opposite of what the doctors were telling us."

"The bottom line, Mason, is that you *do* have a gift and can probably do a lot of good with it," Irene said.

"I don't know; it can do a lot of damage as well," Mason responded cautiously.

"How's that, Mason?" Irene asked.

"Well, it didn't help Kelly. In fact, it quite possibly caused her to die."

"Mason, you didn't cause Kelly to die, just like you didn't cause Ray to die," Patrick said.

"I know, but had I not said anything to her, she may still be alive," Mason said.

"You know, I keep hearing bits and pieces of what happened to Kelly. Could you fill me in?" Irene asked. Then she realized she might have put Mason on the spot she quickly recanted, "Unless you don't want to, that's okay too."

"No, it's all right. I knew she was going to die but I wanted so badly to change it. I thought if I kept her home, maybe she wouldn't . . . die. In a nutshell, here's what happened. We had just finished dinner and were arguing over her going to work the next day . . ."

"Mason, I'm not going to call in sick tomorrow because you had a dream," Kelly said.

"Look, do it for me this one time," Mason emphatically asked.

"You still haven't even told me what the dream was," Kelly said.

"It's not important; you have to trust me on this one. Believe me, after this I won't hassle you ever again about it."

"I don't know. I'll sleep on it and let you know."

"Kel, I'm not crazy, but if you trust me, if you love me, take tomorrow off and play hooky: please!" Mason pleaded.

"You must be pretty serious to pull out the trump card. Fine, I'll stay home and take a mental health day. Just promise me that some day, you'll tell me why?" Kelly asked.

"After tomorrow, I'll tell you everything, I promise," Mason reassured.

Just then, a loud ear-piercing screech resonated off the apartment buildings.

"Good God, what was that?" Kelly said.

"I don't know," Mason said, going to their patio door and opening the curtains.

"Whoa! What's that?" Kelly said, hiding behind Mason.

"It's a white owl perched on our railing."

"It's beautiful. Look at him just checking out the city," Kelly said. "That must've been what we heard." The bird then turned its head and looked at Mason and Kelly standing on the other side of the glass. The owl was confident and aware. Its red eyes burned right through them. Then it opened its beak, screeched again, and flew off.

"Damn, you don't see that every day," Mason said, watching it fly off through the city.

"That was awesome," Kelly said. "He was there to see my magical lamp."

"You're probably right," Mason said, still staring out at the night, wondering what that owl was doing on his balcony.

"Now that I'm off tomorrow, I think I can stay up late," Kelly said, breaking Mason's thought. She gave him a sleek look and a sultry grin as she walked toward the bedroom.

He walked up slowly behind her and moved her black hair off her shoulders. He kissed her on the back of her neck. A strong shock hit Mason as he kissed her.

"Ouch! You shocked me," Kelly said with a laugh, moving away from Mason, completely shattering their moment.

"I think you shocked me," he replied, trying to turn it around on her. Although he knew what it meant. It was a painful reminder of what was to come, and soon. Mason wasn't going to let this happen. He took measures to stop it. It has to work, he thought. If it didn't, he'd lose the one person in the world he loved the most.

"God, I love you," Kelly said, trying to reel Mason back in. She always could take his mind off anything by her mere presence. The door to the bedroom closed behind them.

The next morning

"Well, what are you going to do on your mental health day?" Mason asked while getting ready for work.

"I'm not sure. What *can* I do, warden?"

"Not funny. It's for your own safety," he said.

"Yes sir," she said with a military salute. She wasn't completely buying into the whole thing, but she knew it was important to Mason, and for better or for worse, she went along with it to appease him.

"I'm serious," Mason said.

"Mason, I'll be fine; stop worrying."

"I know, but I'll feel better tomorrow," Mason said.

"I'm going to get a latte, read the paper, and chill out, okay?"

"Yes, thanks. I know it's a pain, but it's important to me. Remember, don't go anywhere. Get your latte and come right back up," Mason said.

"The coffee cart is right outside our building door. I'll come right back up, I swear," Kelly said, comforting Mason. She could tell whatever it was, he was terribly troubled by it.

Irene took a sip of her lemonade, not taking her eyes off Mason as he relayed the events of what happened to Kelly.

"So you see, Irene, I was adamant about her staying home, because I thought . . . I knew something was going to happen to her at school. I was so sure of it."

"Well what happened?" Irene asked.

Mason continued, "Later in the morning, she went down to the coffee cart outside our building to get a latte. While she was waiting in line, a car pulled up. Some guys in the car started arguing with the guy working the cart. A guy in line was getting irritated and started to mouth off to the guys in the car. Someone in the car pulled out a gun and started shooting at the guy in line. He hit Kelly instead. She died that day."

"Oh Mason, that's horrible," Irene said. "But there was no way you could've controlled what those idiots did. You can't blame yourself," she continued.

"The only reason she was there was because I made her stay home. Any other day at ten, she would have been rounding up the children from recess."

"Yes, but—" Irene tried to console but was cut off by Mason.

"I know, but you have to admit, if you asked someone to do something purely for you and then that happened, how could you not accept some responsibility? I mean, was my dream or vision a self-fulfilling prophecy? Had I not believed or paid attention to it and not tried to change it, where would she be today?"

"Mason, you're not responsible for the actions of those guys. I understand how bad you must feel, but remember, the shooters are the ones that did it, not you. You don't know what might have happened all day long. There are simply too many variables to try and control," Irene tried to explain.

"I know; but essentially there is nothing anyone can tell me to take away the guilt. I put her there and will never forget that. That's why I'm convinced that this 'gift' is not good. Had I just blown it off and not given it a second thought, she'd be fine. But I got caught up in it, didn't understand it, and tried to change things that have nothing to do with me," Mason continued.

Irene realized she was dealing with something outside her comfort zone. Meanwhile, Mason's father sat contently watching the dialogue between Mason and Irene and learning more about each one of them with every exchange.

"You know, Mason, I have a friend who specializes in premonitions and people with special abilities that might help you understand yours better if you're interested," Irene offered.

"Maybe someday. For now I'm not going to give it any attention. The things I do know about it don't seem to help too many people," Mason said.

"Well, whatever you knew about Ray was a big help to us, and we appreciate it," his father chimed in.

"Mason, he's a doctor of psychiatry at the University of Oklahoma and specializes in special abilities and he owes me big time; I helped him with his daughter once. Put it this way. If there is anyone who can help you with this, it's Max, and I guarantee he'd talk to you." Retrieving his business card from her purse, she handed it to Mason. "Here's his card. Give him a call; he's great to work with," Irene said.

"Thanks, I'll think about it. Right now, though, I'm going to go to the pool. See you guys later," Mason said and excused himself.

After Mason left, his father approached Irene. "You know, I never knew that about Kelly. I knew he felt responsible, but I had no idea why. It makes a lot of sense on why he withdrew from everyone after she died."

"There's no way you could've known, and even if you did, he probably wouldn't have leveled with you. He wasn't ready to discuss it, but I think he might be now," Irene said.

"What should I do?"

"Just let him know you're available, but don't push it; let him open up on his terms."

"All right, I will. Besides, I've got the surprise for him," Patrick said.

"I love it when you get something up your sleeve," Irene said playfully.

"Lately, it seems that I've always got something up there," he replied.

"Yes, you do," Irene said, accompanied by a mischievous grin.

"We'll do it tomorrow at breakfast," Patrick said. "Now what do you say we go and knock some balls around before we go to the movie?" he continued.

"That's not exactly what I had in mind," she replied, looking back over her shoulder while walking toward the bedroom.

"Can we still make the movie?" a smiling Patrick asked as if he had no say in the matter.

Chapter 25

All Good Things Must End
Chandler, Arizona
June 1, 2017

The day after the funeral proved therapeutic for Mason. He got up early and went for a run. When he was done, he walked in from the back patio. He wiped sweat from his forehead before it ran into his eyes and greeted his father and Irene.

"You must've caught up on your sleep finally. This is the earliest you've been up since you got here," his father said, turning his attention from the newspaper to Mason.

"Yes, maybe. I just needed to get a run in. You know, clear out the cobwebs."

"Oh, we know what you mean. There's nothing like a workout to start your day," Irene said.

"I've been here for two weeks and I feel like I've been gone for two months."

"That just shows how bad you needed a vacation," his father added. "We're fixing breakfast; sit down and have some juice. After breakfast we need to run an errand," he continued.

"An errand?" Mason asked. "You're not going to berate me on the tennis court again, are you?"

Laughing, his father replied, "No no, quit being paranoid. Sit down, before I burn your omelet."

"All right, something's always up with you. I give up trying to figure you out," Mason said, observing the unusually excited nature of his father.

"You're better off, trust me," Irene said back to Mason.

"All right, here's your omelet," his father told him, pouring it onto his plate. "First of all, I've offered it before and I'll do it again. If you want to talk about things, I'm all ears. Secondly, we have a small business matter that needs our attention."

"Do you need money?" Mason asked jokingly.

"Yeah, I can always use more of that," his father shot back. "But no, that's not it. It has to do with the future," he continued.

"Good God, Patrick, enough with the suspense, just get to it already," Irene said.

"All right, fine. Here it goes. Mason, I want you to have Blue Lightning."

"What? No, I can't, that's your baby," Mason said.

"No, there's no discussing this, Mason. We've decided and that's the end of it. You've always loved that car and I always knew I was always preserving it for you. You are the only other person besides me who would appreciate it. After breakfast, we need to go by a bank and notarize the title."

"Dad, seriously I can't, it wouldn't be right," Mason explained. His heart began beating as if he had just run another five miles.

"Mason, there will never be a better time. We don't drive it, and I really want you to have it."

"I don't know what to say. I mean, it's a collector's dream."

"Then say you'll take it," his father pleaded.

"Are you really sure?"

"I've never been more sure of anything. I want you to have it," his father reassured Mason.

"Wow. Well then, thank you. This is really unexpected. If you change your mind, just let me know and you can keep it."

"I'm not going to change my mind, Mason, it's yours. Finish up and let's go do it."

As Mason finished his breakfast, his mind raced with questions. How do I get it back to Chicago? Do I just have it shipped with a freight company? Where am I going to park it?

"Any idea how I get it back to Chicago?" Mason asked.

"Hell, I'd drive it back. You have another two weeks of vacation left, just leave a few days early," his father offered.

"Boy, that's a long drive. I don't know if I can handle that," Mason replied.

"It's a three or four day trip. I'd take my time and turn it into five or six."

"If you do drive, we belong to AAA and can get you maps and anything else you need," Irene offered.

"Thanks. If I drive, I'll probably take you up on that. Right now, I gotta call Al; he isn't going to believe this. In fact, I'm not sure I do yet. Thanks again, Dad. I'll see you later."

A road trip, Mason thought to himself. That's exactly what I need. Pulling up a lounger in a shady, secluded corner of the pool and soaking up the warm, dry air, Mason pondered the logistics of the trip. He slowly faded away into a tranquil sleep.

Mason walked aimlessly through a densely populated forest with lush vegetation surrounding him. The longer he walked the more concerned he became, because he had no idea where he was going. As he approached the edge of the forest, he could see an urban development in a clearing on the other side. A small feeling of relief came over him as he felt a glimmer of hope that maybe he wasn't lost.

When he emerged from the protection of the tropical forest, he was hit with a dry, hot blast of air. He saw people fanning themselves from an apparent heat wave. In the distance, he could see smoke moving toward him. As it got closer, he could tell that it was fire and it was engulfing everything in its path. The heat from the fire was so intense it was drying out the vegetation and burning it almost instantly. He ran toward the houses to try and get people to evacuate, but no one would listen to him. He was forced to retreat away from the fire as houses were spontaneously exploding in the heat.

People began to panic. They recklessly ran into each other and screamed. The entire development burned. Flames reached high and scorched the sky. Then as quickly as the fire moved in, clouds formed overhead and a steady rain began to fall, extinguishing the fires. After the fires were out, Mason overheard a fire marshal say that 384 homes were burned to the ground.

When Mason heard that, he looked out over the smoldering homes and noticed the familiar large white owl flying over the remains, as if it were surveying the damage. As Mason was looking at the smoldering homes, he felt a tap on his shoulder. When he turned around it was Kelly. Startled, he stumbled back. He woke up to a little girl tapping him on his shoulder.

"Hi mister," the little girl said as he woke up.

"Hi," Mason replied, still a bit confused.

"It's time to go," she said with an expressionless face. Her pasty white complexion was accented by her light blonde hair bleached almost white by the sun. Her green and blue sundress was accentuated by her white patent leather shoes.

"Excuse me? What did you say?"

"I said, it's time to go."

"Go where?" he asked.

"Home."

"Why is that?" Mason asked.

"Because the bird told me to tell you."

"What? What bird?"

"The pretty white one."

"Really?" Mason said sarcastically. "What kind of bird was it?"

"I think it was an owl, with red eyes."

Mason sat up, a little more concerned now. "And when did the bird tell you that?"

"In my dream. He said when I see you here, wake you up and tell you that."

"Did the bird tell you why I have to leave?"

"So you don't miss it."

"Miss what?"

"Sorry, I have to go too," the little girl said, running away.

"Wait!" Mason called out. "What about—" Before he could finish, he watched her jump into the pool and go under water. He waited for her to come up. When she didn't emerge, he jumped out of his lounger and ran to the edge of the pool. He couldn't see anyone under the water. He dove in and searched for her on the bottom. There was no one there. He dove under several times, but could not see anyone. He climbed out of the pool and hurried to an elderly couple sitting by the pool.

"Did you see the little girl who jumped into the pool climb out?"

"No. But we didn't see a little girl jump in, either."

"The little girl that I was just talking to. You didn't see her?"

"I saw you sleeping. Then you jumped up and ran into the pool. Didn't see a little girl though, and we've been here for an hour," the man said.

"Okay," Mason said, trying to gather his composure. "Sorry, I must've been having a crazy dream."

"It's all right, sometimes the sun plays tricks on us," the elderly lady said, trying to save Mason from any further embarrassment.

Puzzled, Mason left the pool and walked back to the house. With every step, Mason found himself looking for the little girl as if she were hiding from him behind every tree he passed. He thought he heard every bird that flew by him whisper his name. Not a stranger to odd events, Mason decided maybe it was time to head back to Chicago.

When he arrived back to the house, he could hear his father talking to the television as if it were a two-way discussion. It broke his thoughts about his dream; he welcomed the redirect.

"What did you expect, you moron? You left the scene of an accident and almost killed someone. We should lock you up and throw away the key," he heard his father say to the television.

"You do realize they can't hear you, right?" Irene said, sitting down in a recliner to watch the news with Patrick.

"If they would just listen to me, we would have less problems in the world."

"In world news today, Ahmed Mirza Almazor, leader of the extremist Almazorian Islamic sect and self-proclaimed messiah, released another tape claiming the United States will soon pay for their sins that they've perpetrated on the world. This is the third such statement that Almazor has released in the past year.

"In the tape, he claims that Allah's patience with the United States is growing thin.

Additionally, he claims that Allah has revealed to him directly that unless the United States changes their ways he will destroy them. Defense Secretary Giuliani has cautioned Almazor in the past from using language that may be construed as hostile or inflammatory, however, his threats have obviously fallen on deaf ears. The White House reports that they're monitoring the situation. Elsewhere, Canada's crumbling healthcare system is looking at a major overhaul this year. We send it up to Kathy Burke, on our Fox affiliate in Toronto . . ."

"We should go and kick their butts just like we did with Saddam! I get so sick of Islamic extremists, forcing their B.S. on the world. I don't even know why we're giving them air time. We should just ignore them completely," Patrick said, with the vein in his forehead becoming more pronounced.

"I can see you're still a news junkie," Mason said calmly. He continued, "The problem with the smaller Islamic sects is that they all want to make a name for themselves. So they have to do something big and stupid to get noticed, like that will automatically give them credibility."

"There's nothing good about Islam, Mase. They reduce Jesus to a prophet, but then say, 'If you follow that prophet we'll cut your head off.'

It's ridiculous. You have to know what's going on in the world; this is no age to be ignorant."

"Oh believe me, I agree. Heck, I make a living at reporting what's going on in the world."

"Yes, I guess you're right. Now if we can just get Irene more involved," Patrick said, calming down slightly.

"Oh Patrick, you know they only report things to get your blood pressure up," she teased.

"Yes, I suppose," Mason's father said, actually contemplating his own sincerity.

Changing the topic before his father could go off on another verbal bender, Mason announced his bombshell.

"I need to get back to Chicago, so I have to leave tomorrow. That'll give me time to drive back."

"I wish you could stay longer, but we understand," his father said.

"I'd like to stay, but I want to get a head start."

"It'll be a nice drive; we've done it several times," Irene said.

"It still gives us time to get some tennis in this afternoon," Patrick said, looking for the silver lining. Mason knew there was no fighting it. He simply accepted his fate. "I can hardly wait."

Chapter 26

Seven Deadly Sins
Rabwah, Pakistan
June 1, 2017

General Aleem arrived at Ahmed's palace precisely at 8 a.m. for the emergency meeting. He could hear the guards slam the two iron security gates behind him as they drove through. Although all meetings with Ahmed had a degree of stress associated with them, this particular one had heightened concern because of its last minute request. Ahmed prided himself on being unpredictable, so although the meeting was not necessarily a surprise, the urgency was. Aleem had no idea what this meeting was about. He knocked at the front palace doors and nervously waited. He tried to focus his attention on the perfectly trimmed hedges that lined the security fence and gave seclusion to the estate. When the doors rushed open, Ahmed was there to greet him.

"Good morning Aleem, come in. We're waiting for one more person and we'll get started," Ahmed said while ushering Aleem into the large marble-cased entryway.

"Who are we waiting for, Ahmed?"

"You'll see," he said with an excited, devious smile. "Ah, here he comes now. Let's meet him outside," he said, rushing back to the front doors. Ahmed was more anxious than usual, almost nervous. Unusual for Ahmed, Aleem noticed. Whatever this was, it was big. A black limousine pulled into the roundabout driveway and stopped at the front door. The driver hurried around the vehicle to open the back door. A short stocky man with a long black and gray beard, dark sunglasses, and a white turban emerged from the passenger compartment behind two personal guards. He surveyed the grounds for security threats, as he always did.

He spotted two men with rifles draped over their shoulders on the top balcony, two more walking with German shepherds around the side of the palace, and a handful more securing the perimeter from various points. His guards stayed at the vehicle with their AK-47s in hand. Slightly more at ease, Rahim walked toward the front door. In Rahim's world, trust was not a luxury many people had, and it most certainly was not taken for granted. He knew that doing so could get him killed.

"Welcome Rahim!" Ahmed said, bursting though the front door, rushing to meet him. "It's nice to see you," he said, struggling to get his arms around his rotund cousin.

"Ahmed, it's good to see you too," Rahim replied in a soft voice.

"Rahim, this is General Aleem; he controls the warriors."

"You made no mention of anyone else being here," Rahim questioned in a concerned voice.

"I assure you, Aleem will be instrumental in the execution of the plan. He must be informed if we are to be successful. I trust him with my life."

"Very well. Peace be with you, Aleem," Rahim said with a slight bow, but didn't take his eyes off of Aleem.

"And with you, Rahim." The two sized each other up. Aleem knew from the chauffeured vehicle and the bodyguards Rahim was someone important. Someone dangerous. Someone that could make people disappear with the wave of a hand. He could barely make out Rahim's dark eyes through the sunglasses, but he saw enough to know Rahim didn't trust him.

"Let's sit out back by the pool," Ahmed said, interrupting the two nonverbal interrogations taking place. He shifted their focus to the topic at hand and said, "Rahim brings good news I hope?"

Rahim shifted his focus back to his cousin. His demeanor relaxed a bit and he assured Ahmed, "Yes cousin, good news indeed."

Ahmed led them through the palace corridors to the back pool area where numerous young women were lounging. They sat at a table next to a slow moving waterfall that gave off a tranquil sound of running water. Two servants quickly approached and put plates of fruit and breads down and served them juice and tea.

Finding it difficult to break his gaze off the young women, Rahim finally turned his attention to Ahmed. "Our leader Asaad was pleased with your work in London. He has agreed to your request."

"*The* Asaad?" Aleem interjected, now getting a better grasp of the situation.

"Yes Aleem, we will be working with Asaad," Ahmed replied.

Asaad trained with al-Qaida for years and was one of Osama Bin Laden's top generals, until they had a falling out after the attacks on the United States on 9/11. Asaad wanted to apply more pressure on the United States by continuing with more attacks. He wanted to essentially kick them while they were down. Osama, on the other hand, retreated and gave the US breathing room. An unforgivable action, in the mind of Asaad. Now that Bin Laden was gone, Assad planned on finishing the job. He was positioning himself to take the place once held by al-Qaida as the number one freedom fighting group by making al-Qaida insignificant.

Rahim continued, "We have a shipment of supplies being smuggled into the United States this week. We can get the packages on that shipment and to your coordinates in two weeks. Then what you do with it is up to you," he said, knowing full well what Ahmed intended to do with it.

"Very nice, Rahim. Asaad has made a wise choice. America will fall after this attack."

"If they don't, you know they will step up their efforts to find you," Rahim warned.

"Yes. However, the worst case scenario is that we kill as many of them as possible and we are heroes to our Islamic brethren."

"Ahmed, if you fail and get caught, you know you're on your own. No one will come to your side," he cautioned.

"But if I succeed, I will have the respect of many, no?"

"Ah, *if* you succeed, cousin, Asaad will welcome you and all Almazorians. For even al-Qaida will finally be insignificant compared to you. You will have proven your worth as a legitimate leader."

"*When* I succeed! Yes!" Ahmed said confidently with a crazed laugh as red juice ran down his chin after he bit into a guava.

"Ahmed, what are you talking about?" General Aleem asked rhetorically as he started to put the pieces together. "You aren't thinking of attacking the United States, are you?"

"Aleem, we are going to hit a target inside the United States. We have purchased a Serbian ALAS short-range missile from Rahim's organization that we will fire from within their own country. Our men will work with theirs to smuggle it into America. Is that not exciting?"

"Yes, but how are you smuggling a missile into the United States?" Aleem asked. "Are you using the submarine?"

"No submarine," Rahim replied. "We have a proven route that we use along their northern border. Don't worry about that, my friend; we've been using it for years. We'll get it in."

Turning to Ahmed, a nervous Aleem asked, "Ahmed, why not use a young martyr to hand carry a bomb, like in London? Perhaps we should work up to an attack of this magnitude?"

Ahmed looked him in the eyes and explained, "Because, Aleem, we need this to be big. If we keep doing small things then we will always be small. The only way we get the respect of the world is to go after the Americans. Like a prizefighter, you won't get respect until you fight the champion. Well, my friend, the champion has become drunk in his success. He has rested on his past accomplishments and it is time for a new champion."

Aleem stood up and began to pace, staring at the floor. His mind raced. He could feel his heart rate speed up. His breathing became more erratic as he began to comprehend what Ahmed had proposed. Rahim and Ahmed glanced at each other and watched Aleem process the enormity of what Ahmed was planning. Aleem's lips began to move, but no sounds came out of his mouth. It was as if he was having a conversation with himself. Not wanting to disrespect Rahim or Ahmed, Aleem took a deep breath, turned to Ahmed, and asked, "Should we not take more time to consider the plan further?"

Ahmed stood up and walked to Aleem. He appreciated the due respect Aleem gave his plan. He placed his hands on Aleem's shoulders, looked him in the eyes, and said, "No, my friend, this is the perfect time to enter the world arena. The Americans are a confused nation. They live and breathe the seven deadly sins. Their greed is bankrupting their economy, their thirst for lust has removed all sense of morality, their gluttonous and slothful ways have made them soft and ill-prepared, their pride and envy has removed all sense of humility and principles, and the wrath of their behavior has consequences all over the world."

"This will cause an international incident," Aleem replied.

Ahmed agreed, "Exactly, it will expose America as the playground of Satan for all to see. While they try to figure out whether a man should marry a man, or whether they should kill their innocent unborn young, we will—no, we *must*—strike at this most opportune time. While they are sympathetic to sin, Allah shall not be sympathetic to them."

Turning his concern to Rahim, General Aleem asked, "Rahim, what does Asaad say to this?"

"Asaad is watching carefully. We recognize that this is a bold step, one that our Islamic brethren have not yet taken. This will pave the way for the conversion of America to Islam. Once we show the world that America is not impenetrable, the Islamic community will join forces and subsequently destroy Satan and cleanse the United States of their sins."

Ahmed then interjected, "Aleem, the dumb Americans will spend years suing each other over whose fault it was. They'll make new laws that are impossible to enforce, and in the mean time, not secure their borders any better. They are so concerned with issues in the Middle East that they are not watching their own backyard."

Aleem listened to Ahmed's rationalization. Although he knew what Ahmed said was true, he knew there could be grave consequences for their village. He walked back to the table and sat down. Gathering his senses, he sipped his tea.

"The Americans will turn this into a religious attack. Do you think they'll implore the Vatican to get involved?" Aleem asked.

"The Vatican? Catholics are leaving the church in droves. The Vatican can't get their people to give one hour a week to their God, let alone die for him. No, the Vatican will be no threat. They seem to be playing checkers in a chess game."

Aleem thought a possible outcome of this type of attack could result in a holy war. He also knew that a holy war would be the war to end all wars. He was not convinced that the time was right to initiate this kind of action. After all, the final war could be the end of mankind. He didn't want to be disrespectful, but this was a serious move and he was compelled to make Ahmed aware.

"What if they unite all Christians? Surely it will result in a holy war?" Aleem said.

"Aleem, Christianity is a splintered religion. They have diluted the original text of the bible so much that they can't even agree on what it says. Instead of focusing on the commonalities of their churches, they focus on their differences. The different Christian denominations interpret the bible in different ways to accommodate their beliefs."

Ahmed could see that he was finally breaking through to Aleem. He could see Aleem begin to believe and fed off of his emotion. He continued his sales pitch.

"Their egos will never allow them to agree and unite. As long as they don't agree, there will always be conflict within Christianity. Besides, their church has become politically charged, and we all know politics and war go hand in hand. Christianity could not possibly organize a counteroffensive.

Their own president denounced that they are even a Christian nation. No Aleem, now is the perfect time to strike the Americans."

The gears in Aleem's head were grinding. He contemplated what was said and knew Ahmed was right. The Americans were at their weakest point in their history. If not us, someone else will hit them and they will get the credit, he thought. Although hesitant, Ahmed was about to raise the ante, and if he wasn't with Ahmed, he would be considered against him. The consequences were big, but so was the payoff if they were successful. Knowing he was not going to talk Ahmed out of the attack, the wise move was to join him. He had but one choice and conceded. He needed to know more.

"All right, what are we hitting, Ahmed?"

"That's the spirit, Aleem. I'll tell you that when I hear from my contact. This is a very exciting time for us, my friend. We will do what no other country has ever done to them. This will cripple the Americans and put us in our rightful spot in the world."

"This attack will be construed as an act of war on the United States," Aleem said.

"I know! Isn't it exciting!" Ahmed said, discounting Aleem's statement.

"But Ahmed, we don't have the defenses built up and we can't sustain a counterattack."

"Our Islamic brothers will join us, Aleem. There is no need to worry," Ahmed said, looking at Rahim for tacit approval.

"As long as you are successful, Ahmed," Rahim added cautiously.

"Oh, we will be. So many are afraid to give the order, Rahim, but I am not. I do not fear the American pigs. They are as incompetent as they are arrogant. Everybody knew where Osama was, and yet it took them years to find him. No, my friends, we will not fail. This time we hit them in their genitals. They will be forced to succumb, for they will have no choice; it will be checkmate! Now, who's up for a little indoctrination training?" Ahmed said, devilishly looking at the girls from across the pool.

With that, Ahmed and Rahim began to laugh as they selected their girls and retreated to their quarters. Aleem gave an insincere laugh, being very concerned with what Ahmed was planning. People in their village could be killed. Indoctrination training was the last thing on his mind, but he could not question Ahmed too much. If he did, Ahmed and Rahim would consider it disrespectful. Remorsefully, he grabbed a girl and retreated as well.

Chapter 27

The New Millennium
Chandler, Arizona
June 2, 2017

As Mason packed up his freshly laundered clothes, he saw the black attaché case resting safely against the wall in his bedroom. Stopping what he was doing, he slowly began to digress on the history of the case. Maybe I should just toss it, he thought, knowing well that he couldn't. On the other hand, the road trip might be a good time to look at it, he continued. As he played "point-counterpoint" with himself, his father interrupted his thoughts.

"Hey, getting ready to roll?"

"Yes, just finishing up packing."

"Can I give you a hand carrying this stuff out?" his father offered.

"No thanks, Dad, I got it."

"Okay, I'll see you outside."

Grabbing his suitcase and the attaché case, Mason went to load the car and walked up on his father looking perplexed at the interior of the car.

"What did you do to the dash?" his father asked Mason.

"Oh that. Well, after I had a tune-up done yesterday I stopped by Car Toys and had them change out the stereo."

"There was nothing wrong with the one that was in there," his father said.

"I know, I kept it. I just thought she needed to be welcomed to the new millennium."

"Part of the appeal is being from the old one."

"Here, check this out," Mason said to his father, directing him to the 2-DIN size monitor sunk into the dash of the Mustang. "It has Sirius satellite radio so no commercials, and it has a GPS navigational system with updated maps of the entire country. Plus a 200-watt amplifier and six new speakers with a subwoofer," he continued. "It's a great system."

"Sounds like it. The nav system will be nice, but we got you some maps just in case."

"Thanks. I'll take them."

"Well, I can't tell you how nice it was to see you, Mase."

"Yes, it was a really great little vacation for me too," Mason said to his father.

"Well, don't take so long next time, you know you're always welcome."

"Thanks. I'll try not to."

"By the way, when you get up to Oklahoma, call Max; he'd love to talk to you," Irene said.

"I probably will. I mean, what have I got to lose? My mind's already going. Thanks again for everything," Mason said while backing out of the driveway.

"Have a safe trip; if you need anything, give us a call," his father continued, trying not to let go.

"I will," Mason said while slowly pulling away from the house, waving through the open top of the car.

As they watched Mason drive away, Patrick asked Irene, with his eyes welling up, "Do you think he knows how much I love him?"

"You bet he does. You know how much he loves you too, right?"

"I do now."

Chapter 28

Opening Old Wounds
Tatum, New Mexico
June 2, 2017

Instead of driving north along the main highways, Mason departed the Phoenix area to the east through the White Mountains into New Mexico. He felt as if his personal walls were destroyed, his defenses were down, and yet another tremendous burden was lifted off his shoulders. He also knew that there was one thing left that he needed to do to make his makeover complete. He had to come to terms with what was inside the attaché case.

Like the cold jagged edge of a steel knife penetrating his nirvana, his undirected thoughts turned somberly painful. In the rearview mirror, he could see the attaché case sitting quietly on the rear seat begging to be opened, laughing at Mason, mocking him, taunting him with painful memories. He knew the contents of the case would control him as long as he avoided it. "No more," he said aloud, looking at the case. The case would no longer control or torment him, he decided. The new Mason would confront that demon head on. As quickly as the troubled thoughts of his childhood impregnated his blissful drive, Mason redirected his thoughts to his route through the mountainous scenery.

Welcome to Tatum, New Mexico, Elev. 3986', the welcoming sign along the highway read.

This is as good a stop as anywhere, Mason thought to himself while pulling into the Scorpion Motel.

"Good evening, sir. What can we do for you?" the strange old man said, coming out from behind a wall where he was watching the television.

"Do you have any rooms available for the night?" Mason asked.

"Sure do; just one person?"

"Yes, just me."

"Fill out this form and we'll get you squared away. There's a diner down the street with good food if you're interested," the old man offered.

"Thanks. Yes, I'm starving."

"Go to Mabel's; she'll fill you up, and try her homemade cherry pie, best in the state. It's a ten minute walk down Main Street."

"Sounds good. I will, thanks."

"All right, here you go. Room number 384 is around the back side of the building. If you need anything, give me a call," the attendant said, looking at Mason with an eerie glare.

"Thanks," Mason said, staring at the old man and then at the key with number 384 stamped on it. Again with the 384, Mason thought to himself. "What the . . ."

"You all right, mister?" the old man said, seeing something was bothering Mason.

"Yeah, no, I'm fine. Thanks." Mason said, reassuring himself that it was no big deal.

Sitting in his car pondering the room number again and the strange old man giving him weird looks, he wondered if he was just getting paranoid. After storing his luggage in his room, he walked through town to Mabel's.

Walking down Main Street was like stepping out of a history book. Old buildings with signs that had names like "Saloon," "Blacksmith," and "Ranchers Bank" printed in Old English hung in the storefront windows.

The paved street was old and crumbling, almost mimicking a dirt road. People were friendly and everyone walked. Does anyone even own cars around here? Mason wondered, looking around for horse-drawn carriages. Time had stopped in this peaceful small town. Just about the time Mason was convinced he had taken a turn into the Twilight Zone, he saw a 7-Eleven store at the end of Main Street next to a McDonald's and was reminded that he was indeed in the twenty-first century.

Sitting across the diner in a booth, Mason watched a Mexican family. They reminded him of his own family. The older brother was picking on the younger brother and annoying the parents, not unlike Mason's older brother constantly picking on him growing up. Mason looked down at the local newspaper and noticed the date, June 2, 2017. June second, Mason thought to himself. Our first date.

Redirecting his thought, he remembered the date she died, April 27, 2016. Then he thought about her other day, her birthday. March 18. Happy late birthday, Kel, he said to himself. He looked back at the family across the diner and was reminded of when he was in fifth grade, a grade that would forever change Mason. His thoughts drifted to when he was a ten-year-old boy, just finishing up fifth grade. He was at a neighbor's house for a birthday party.

"Come on, Mason, tag you're it," a boy said, tagging a ten-year-old Mason and running away with Mason in full chase. It was the first weekend of June and the Marquez family had the ceremonial "kick-off the summer" barbeque and pool party. It was touted as the party the neighborhood looked forward to every year and usually lived up to the hype. That year would be no different.

The memory of the party brought a smile across Mason's face. That is, until the waitress brought Mason abruptly back from the Marquezes'. "You gonna try the pie? Hello, anyone home?"

"Excuse me?" Mason asked the waitress, not hearing her question.

"The pie, you gonna try the pie?" she repeated.

"Oh yes, the clerk at the motel said it's the best in the state," Mason said.

At which the waitress pointed to a framed newspaper article on the wall, claiming, "Mabel's Cherry Pie—Best in State."

"Okay, I guess it must be. I'll take a slice, thanks," Mason said, seeing the shortness in the waitress's demeanor, as if she went through that line of questioning with every customer.

"You want it a la mode?" she asked.

"Yes, that'd be great," Mason replied.

Hardly acknowledging him, she walked away. As Mason stared out the window of the diner taking in the uniqueness and the beauty of the small town, he remembered the hustle and bustle of Chicago. Pondering whether or not he even wanted to go back to Chicago, he began thinking for the first time in his life about relocating.

"Here you go, sir," the waitress said, putting down the famous pie.

"Thanks," Mason said as he began to devour it, noting that it probably was the best cherry pie he had ever had.

When he got back to his motel room, he sat on his bed and turned on the television to watch the news. He looked at the attaché case sitting on the floor against the wall and said to himself, if I don't get this over with, this is going to be a miserable drive. Getting up, he retrieved the case and set it on the bed. Feeling confident that he could beat the case, he decided to examine the contents, knowing the demons it would conjure up. Taking a deep breath, he slowly loosened the straps and opened up the case. Looking inside, he noticed a white envelope with "Mason" written on it. Pulling it out, he recognized the writing as Kelly's. That doesn't make any sense, he thought. Opening the envelope, it contained a handwritten letter from Kelly.

My dearest Mason,

If you're reading this, I guess you were right about something happening to me. After you left for work I ran after you to tell you I love you and I saw you throw this bag in the dumpster. I guess my curious nature got the best of me, so I grabbed it after you left. I'm sorry to sneak a peek but it was killing me not to, I hope you understand. If everything in this bag is true, which I'm assuming they are by your behavior, you have an amazing gift. I can't imagine the strength it must take to keep that kind of information to yourself. I wish we could've talked about it, I would've understood and helped you in any way I could. At least I understand why you were so adamant about me not leaving the apartment. Anyway, let's hope there's a mistake, if not, there's nothing we could've done about it. Don't be afraid of your gift, find a way to use it for good. Know that I love you and hope to see you tonight.

Love, K

With tears slowly rolling down Mason's face, he set the letter down and closed his eyes and thought about Kelly. He wished he had told her about his gift. If he learned anything from his father, he learned the importance of a support system. Remembering Kelly made him remember how completely alone in the world he was. A sadness closed in around him. Round one went to the attaché case. As he laid down on the bed, he again drifted back to his fifth grade summer party.

"Dad! Watch this cannonball," Mason said, launching himself into the air and coming down with a splash that covered the front of his father's shirt and added the sweet taste of chlorine to his Pabst Blue Ribbon.

"Good one, Mase!" his father yelled back to him, shaking off the water. "Now come on, dinner's ready; we're going to eat," he continued. As everyone climbed out of the pool and started heading to the other side of the house where the barbeque and tables were set up, Mason lagged behind. With no one looking, Mason snuck one more cannonball before dinner.

"Mason! Come get your burger," his father called out. "Elaine, will you find Mason, tell him his dinner's ready, please."

"Mason!" she called out. Walking over to a group of boys he was previously playing with, she asked, "Have you guys seen Mason?"

"No Mrs. Rhimes," they answered.

She walked back to Patrick and nervously asked, "Pat? I can't find him. Where was the last time you saw him?"

"The last time I saw him, he climbed out of the pool," a concerned Patrick told her.

A panicked fear came over Elaine that only a mother could understand. "Oh God no!" she hoped.

Patrick put down his plate and the two of them hurried to the other side of the house. As they came up to the pool area, time slowed almost to a stop. The world moved in slow motion around Patrick and Elaine as they were horrified by what they saw. Elaine screamed an ear-piercing shriek.

"Mason!"

Then time sped up to light speed. Like a gazelle, Patrick ran to the edge of the pool and dove in headfirst. He grabbed his son, who was floating facedown.

As his father pounded Mason's chest and attempted CPR, Mason fell off his bed in his motel room and woke up sweating and breathing hard.

Mason had just relived the tragedy that befell him twenty-one years earlier. After gaining his composure and getting a drink of water, he sat down and again looked at the now opened case. Round two went to the case as well. He reached inside the case and pulled out the paramedic's report.

Attempted CPR for 22 minutes while en route to hospital—no response. Contacted Dr. Evanich at Elmbrook Memorial who pronounced death at 1744 hours. O'Connor and I ceased CPR efforts. At 1750 while en route patient became responsive – A/O (X4). Administered O2 100%, and started IV. With decedent's parents we completed transport to Elmbrook Memorial- code 1.

Mason remembered doing one more cannonball and when swimming to the edge of the pool underwater, knocking his head against the side of the pool. He never could open his eyes under water. The next thing he remembered he was in the ambulance going to the hospital. He would never forget the look on his parents' faces when he woke up.

"Mason? Mason! Oh my God, Mason! Are you all right?" his mother said, hugging him with a death grip.

"Move aside ma'am," the paramedic said, quickly moving Elaine to get a look at Mason. Then, looking at the driver, he said excitedly, "John, we got a miracle back here. Get this kid to the hospital; he's awake and responding."

Thinking about the scare he gave his parents crushed his spirits. It appeared the case was going to win round three. Knowing that the outcome could have been much worse, however, he began to feel slightly charged. Being older now, he could only imagine the pain of losing a child. He was thankful that he didn't put his parents through that experience. As a consolation, he thought, if the worse thing to happen to me is this stupid curse, I should be pretty thankful.

Indeed, for the first time in his life he looked at his gift as an "either or" situation. I'm either dead and my parents have to live with that, or I live and deal with this weird thing. I choose to live, he continued positively to himself. Besides, after the trip he just had with his father, he was even more thankful that he dodged that perilous fate twenty years earlier. Round three went to Mason.

Feeling lucky, he reached in and pulled out several newspaper clippings.

"Local boy beats the odds." "Miracle boy doing well." "Wonder boy survives drowning."

All of the headlines referred to a boy who survived a tragedy. Mason's thoughts turned to the parties held in his honor. The community was thankful that he was alive and well. The incident almost single-handedly pulled the town together. That summer tuned out to be a bittersweet time in Mason's life. The kindness and attention lasted all summer, but the start of sixth grade would be a tough life lesson for Mason to learn. Like Jesus riding into Galilee at the commencement of the Passion, the very people that were thankful he was alive would soon be the very ones that tortured him and ran him out of town.

The last article he pulled out of the case disturbed him. The headline read, "Local Fifth Grader Dead for 22 Minutes Lives to Tell About It."

This one struck a nerve with Mason. This one reminded him of the first time he used his "gift" back on August 25, 1996. As a ten-year-old, he had no idea what was going on or why dates came to him, nor did his parents.

"Come on Mason, we're going to be late," his mother called out.

"I'm coming, Mom."

"Now remember, your grandmother is frail, so you be nice," she warned while driving to his grandma's house.

"I will. After all, today is her birthday, right?" he asked.

"No, Mason, her birthday is in November. You know that, don't you?" she replied. "Why do you ask?" she curiously asked.

"You know when we saw her last week?"

"Yes, what about it?" his mother asked.

"When she hugged me, I saw 'AUGUST 25, 1996.' That's today, so I just thought it was her birthday," he said.

"No, now stop being silly. Come on, we're late."

"Hi Grandma!" Mason said, running up to his grandmother and hugging her.

"There's my little angel," she said, smiling with her arms outstretched. As they embraced, a jolt of electricity shocked them both.

"Ouch! My goodness, Mason, you're full of static electricity."

"Ow! Yeah, I got totally shocked," Mason said, laughing.

"AUGUST 25, 1996" resonated in Mason's head again as he felt the shock. He looked at his mother, who thought he had played a joke on his aging grandmother, and held his arms up as if saying, "I didn't do anything."

"Mason, go help your father with the groceries," his mother said, as if replying, "We'll talk about this later."

"But Mom, I—"

"Don't start. Now go help your father," she said, cutting him off midsentence. Looking at her mother, she said with a chuckle, "Sorry Mom, sometimes he has too much energy, literally, I guess."

"Oh Elaine, he's fine. He didn't do anything wrong. I may be old but still remember how kids are. Besides, he's still my angel," Elaine's mother said.

"Thanks," Elaine said while hugging her mother. "How are you feeling?" she continued.

"I'm old, that's how I feel."

"You know what I mean. How are you doing with Dad being gone?"

"It's been six months and I'm doing fine. Now come in and sit down," she said, disregarding her daughter's question. Elaine's father had succumbed to cancer six months earlier. Although Elaine was concerned about her mother, she knew her mom was a fighter.

"Hey Gracie!" Patrick said, coming into the kitchen carrying bags of groceries for dinner.

"Hi Patrick," Grace said, hugging him.

"Gracie, you're looking great. How are you doing?" he asked.

"Oh, I'm hanging in there. Where's Sean?" she asked.

"He's at a football camp and staying with a friend. It seems like sports are seven days a week now."

"That's okay, I know he's busy. He's always been so independent, not one for family functions I guess. So what's for dinner?" she asked as they walked outside to Patrick starting the barbeque.

"I'm going to barbeque some steaks and chicken. How's that sound?"

"Great. I'll start making a salad," she insisted.

While Patrick, Elaine, and Grace started making dinner, Mason played with Sophie, Grace's seven-year-old border collie.

As the evening began to wind down, Mason and his parents were preparing to leave.

"All right Mom, we'll pick you up tomorrow at 10:15 for breakfast," Elaine said as they were preparing their good-byes.

"Fine, honey. I'll be ready."

"Bye, Grandma," Mason said, giving her a hug. "Ow! I got shocked again," Mason said, laughing.

"You sure are full of electricity, Mason," Gracie said, shaking off the shock and laughing with Mason while giving him an odd look.

"Mason!" his mother started.

"I didn't do anything!" he exclaimed.

"Thank you guys for coming over. Patrick, the steaks were great," Grace said.

"Thanks. I think we all did a pretty good job. We'll see you tomorrow."

That was the last time anyone saw Grace alive. The next morning when they arrived to pick her up, she never answered the door. When they let themselves in, they found Grace lying peacefully and permanently asleep in her bed. Later that night when Elaine and Patrick were tucking Mason in for bedtime, she questioned Mason.

"Mason, when you saw Grandma yesterday you said there was a date in your head. What did you mean?"

"I don't know. Whenever I meet people I see a date in my head," he replied. "I think it's their birthday," he continued innocently.

Looking at Patrick, a puzzled Elaine questioned him further. "What do you mean a date for them?"

"When I touch people, I see a date for them. I'm not sure what it means; that's why I asked if it was Grandma's birthday."

"Do you see it with everyone?"

"Only people I touch," he answered.

Looking at Patrick, she said, "We need to get him to a doctor."

"We'll take him tomorrow."

Chapter 29

Doctor Evaluations
Tatum, New Mexico
June 2, 2017

The hotel room in Tatum, New Mexico, marked the first time in years Mason had thought about what happened to him. Mason reflected on the first time he remembered using his ability. As a child, he couldn't comprehend the concept or the finality of death. Death was a dark and unknown concept to him as a child. It wouldn't be until he was scrutinized for it before he truly recognized what the dates meant. And although he wasn't sure if the dates could be changed, he hadn't seen it happen. But he hoped by knowing, maybe he could change them.

Remembering the events brought back familiar feelings of uncertainty. This time was different; however, he wasn't a scared sixth grader any longer. As an adult, he found himself for the first time with a strong desire to understand what happened. He was pleasantly surprised that Kelly had retrieved the case that he feared so much. It brought some semblance of peace to him knowing that Kelly knew his situation. He was now becoming more and more intrigued with his past as he started to dig deeper into the case. In his quest to find his truth, he pulled out one of many doctor evaluations.

"Mason seems to believe that he knows when people are going to die. He believes something happened to him that originated from his accident. He was told by people that he was special because of the accident and I believe he began to believe that he was different. When the attention weaned from his accident, he began his fascination with dying. Perhaps guilt-driven. I believe he should grow out of this fascination with proper support from his family and continued therapy in dealing with the accident. My recommendation is family therapy to include both parents to reinforce the family support system."

"Idiots," Mason said to himself. Those doctors didn't have a clue what was going on, he thought. Then he thought of one doctor in particular, Dr. Stein, a psychotherapist who was getting frustrated with Mason.

"Look Mason, we've been through this for weeks. I'm going to be blunt; your fixation with death is an attention getter. The attention you received from your accident positively reinforced your ideas, but the fact is, it's not real. Furthermore, death is not something we joke about. It's time to move on to more productive thoughts now," Dr. Stein sternly told a ten-year-old Mason.

"I'm not making it up," a young Mason said exhaustedly.

"All right Mason, I was going to wait on this, but you leave me no choice. I have an idea. Are you willing to take a walk with me?" he asked Mason, confident that he was going to pull the trump card on Mason. Dr. Stein's intent was to call Mason's bluff, a move that could be therapeutically disastrous if it didn't go as Dr. Stein planned.

"Sure, where to?" Mason asked confidently.

"Here's what we'll do," the doctor explained. "We'll walk down to the terminal cancer wing of the hospital. It's on the fifth floor, and we'll meet the patients that are very sick, and you can actually see that death is no joke. These are real people who are probably going to die."

He masked his true intentions of essentially having Mason make predictions by explaining that he just wanted him to meet "real" sick people. Mason, however, knew what the doctor was doing and had his own plan to prove it to the doctor.

"Yes, that might be helpful in my therapy," Mason said, almost mocking the doctor, who was well aware of Mason's sarcasm.

"Mason, this is Mrs. Richardson," Dr. Stein introduced.

"Hi, nice to meet you," Mason said, shaking her hand. As he shook her hand and felt the short shock of electricity, "SEPTEMBER 18, 1996" came to him. As they walked away, Mason said to the doctor, "Next week, September 18."

"Excuse me, Mason?" Dr. Stein asked, knowing full well what Mason meant.

"That's her date. September 18, 1996," he said again.

"All right Mason, I'll write it down and we'll keep an eye on her. What about Mr. Miller?" he asked.

"October 30, 1996," Mason said.

They went down the entire wing, "meeting" each patient. Like a prosecutor and a defense attorney preparing their cases, Mason and Dr. Stein were both very confident that they were making their cases for Mason's sanity. In all, Mason made thirteen predictions, ranging from two days to eight months.

Four weeks after the predictions were made, Patrick Rhimes received a frantic call from Dr. Stein: "Could you, Elaine, and Mason be at my office tomorrow at 8 a.m.?"

"Sure. Is everything all right, doctor?"

"Yes, I just need to see you."

"Fine, we'll be there first thing in the morning," Patrick said, looking at Elaine and not knowing what was going on. The next morning, they rushed to Dr. Stein's office.

"Please, Elaine and Patrick, come in," a preoccupied Dr. Stein said, welcoming the Rhimeses the next morning.

"Hi Dr. Stein," Mason said, greeting a very serious doctor.

"Good morning Mason, come in," Dr. Stein said, ushering Mason and his parents into his office.

"Patrick, Elaine, I have to level with you. It's been a month, and eight of Mason's dates have come true, and frankly, it puzzles me," the visibly troubled doctor said.

"Surely it was luck or a coincidence," Patrick said to the doctor.

"I have no idea what it is," Dr. Stein said. "I would like to run a series of tests, call some experts in, and start documenting his abilities," he continued.

"No way!" Elaine said. "For crying out loud, he's ten years old and school just started. I'm not going to let you poke and prod him like a research project," she said adamantly.

"We can get some very important information from him, Elaine," Dr. Stein said.

"No, I'm with Elaine," Patrick said. "He's been through enough this summer. It's already getting out that he's made some predictions. Now some people are blaming him for people dying."

"But we might be able to explain—"

"No, we're done. As far as we're concerned, it was a coincidence," Patrick said, cutting off the doctor and getting up. "Thanks for your help, doctor, but I think we're done with this stuff."

Grabbing Mason's hand, Patrick rushed them out of the office to the car.

They stopped at the car. Before getting in, Patrick squatted down to look Mason in the eyes. "Mason, I'm not sure what happened in that office, but this is over."

"But Dad, I didn't make it—"

"It doesn't matter," his father said loudly. "It's over; we're not going to discuss this again. Keep this stuff to yourself. Don't tell anyone about this ever. You can really hurt people with this. Am I clear?"

"Yes, Dad," a dejected Mason replied while a nervous Elaine just looked on.

Back in the hotel room, Mason somberly put the removed items back into the case and closed it up. He realized that the only reason the memories that he had avoided over the years were painful was because he wanted people to know what he could do. It wasn't an ego thing; he simply wanted to help people. Unfortunately, society didn't really want that kind of help. The words of his mother eased his mind: "Embrace your gift and use it for good."

"I'll try; I'm not sure how," he said to himself as he drifted to sleep.

Mason was on the edge of a rolling pasture staring out over a grazing herd of sheep. There was not a cloud in the sky. Green grass, summer temperatures, and a light breeze accented the peaceful beautiful day. Suddenly, the sky turned gray. Massive white and gray clouds rolled in. The wind began to howl. The deep rumble of thunder accompanied by bright bursts of white lightning began to jump from cloud to cloud. The scattered raindrops quickly turned into a downpour.

Mason took cover from the torrential rains behind a rock outcropping. Lightning began to strike all around him. The cracking sound of thunder crushed his ears. The falling rain turned to golf-ball size hail, striking the ground around him with daunting force. Every pellet of hail that smashed into particles on the rocks around him reminded him of the fragile nature of his humanity. As quickly as the storm rolled in, everything stopped. He hesitated to look up, but knew he had to. He stood up and looked out over the field. Instead of the peaceful pasture he was in earlier, now it was dark and lifeless. He saw 384 dead sheep in the field.

A sad, nervous feeling came over him when he noticed Kelly standing in the field wearing a bright white linen dress. She waved for him to come toward her. He longed to see her. His heart began to beat with anticipation. He walked toward her and noticed Ray Reed and many other people that had died standing and looking at Mason with a blank gaze. When he arrived at Kelly, he asked, "What's going on, Kelly?"

"You need to help them," she replied.

"What do you mean?"

She pointed to the dead sheep and said, "Save them."

Mason looked out over the sheep where Kelly was pointing and questioned, "Save them? They're already dead." When he turned back to her she was gone, and in her place was the large white owl he was getting accustomed to seeing in his dreams. Stumbling backwards, he dared not make any sudden movements. Perched on a large boulder, the large white bird's mesmerizing gaze was locked onto Mason. It's piercing, deep-set red eyes, glowing white feathers, and razor-sharp black talons controlled Mason. In an apparent stalemate, the owl opened its small mouth, snarled, and screeched a loud shriek. Then it unfurled its enormous wingspan and flew away.

As the owl disappeared, he turned around and was startled again by a tall, dark-hooded shadow figure towering over him from behind. The faceless figure caused him to fall to the ground and knock his head.

"Whoa! What the hell?" he said to himself, abruptly sitting up in bed and emerging from his dream. He looked around, but his eyes weren't ready to focus. Not yet. Rubbing them helped rub away the confusion that was slowly subsiding. His breathing began to settle back to normal. After wiping sweat away from his brow, he was able to regain his bearings.

"If this is part of my 'gift,' I sure don't get it," he said to himself, trying to calm down.

Chapter 30

Strange Weather
Homa, Oklahoma
June 3, 2017

As Mason drove out of Tatum, New Mexico, he thought about his dreams. What's with the 384 dead sheep, the 384 dead fish, the 384 burnt houses, and the 384th floor of the building, and what is Kelly doing? he thought. Am I missing something, or are they just stupid dreams?

With the sun beating down on Mason, he drove mile after mile with undirected thought, thinking about his ability, his family, Kelly, and the meaning of it all. Why and how things and people were intertwined consumed his thoughts.

Is Kelly trying to tell me something? he asked himself. If she is, she needs to be clearer, he finally concluded. Bewildered, he turned his attention to the scenery and the enthralling hum of Blue Lightning's powerful Mustang motor.

A hot, dry, and cloudless sky reminded him of the beauty of the country not often seen in Chicago. No skyscrapers. No gangs or crime. No hustle and bustle. A graceful hawk with its wings expanded, effortlessly gliding overhead, helped guide his thoughts. This is exactly what I needed, he decided.

The scenery changed from the red rock outcroppings and spectacular cliffs of New Mexico into rolling hills of northern Texas, followed by the impressive Wichita Mountain range in southern Oklahoma. Crossing into Oklahoma, he remembered Irene's friend at the University of Oklahoma in Norman, but figured that wasn't part of his plans. After seven hours of driving, Mason came upon a small town where he would rest for the night.

"*Welcome to Homa, Oklahoma, Home of the 2005 3A Football State Champion, Homa Cowboys.*"

A small town that loves their high school football team, Mason thought. It reminded him of his high school days. If it wasn't for Al, his high school experience could have been horrible. Al was a good athlete and popular in high school. As high school politics dictated, the popular kids' friends were automatically popular. Although Mason never really bought into it, he was secretly thankful, especially after the tormented past he had experienced.

Eventually, Al had helped Mason get through some of his insecurities and come out of his shell. In return, Mason helped Al with his schoolwork. They were the kind of friends like his father and Ray; in fact, they, too, were more like brothers.

As he pulled into the Cottonwood Inn to get a room for the night, he noticed a man and his family trying to get bags out of his packed minivan a couple of parking spaces away.

"Richard, just unload it; we can reload it tomorrow," the man's wife said to him.

"I'm getting it. I just need you to hold this top bag and I'll pull out the bottom one," he ordered.

"It's too heavy; just pull it out," she said, getting more and more irritated.

"Will you just do it and quit arguing," he shot back at her. As the wife tried to help him unload the bag, their fourteen-year-old daughter and five-year-old boy looked over at Mason and caught him staring at their parents.

"Will you guys hurry up? You're making a scene and people are staring at us," the girl said to her parents. Mason abruptly looked away, as if he hadn't noticed their minor quarrelling. He knew he was busted.

"Can I give you a hand?" Mason asked, walking over to the couple.

"Thanks, but no, mister, we finally got it," the man answered.

"He would be out here all night before asking for help," the man's wife interjected sarcastically.

"Julia, I told you I had it," he said back to her. As they continued to argue, their young son stared at Mason and waved. Mason waved back, smiled, and excused himself. The couple's daughter, pleading with Mason, mouthed, "Take me with you." Mason smiled and mouthed back, "Sorry, you're on your own."

The town was similar to that of Tatum, New Mexico. Privately owned businesses with family names lined the main street and long oak tree branches reached out like nature's canopy over the road. Old decrepit lampposts lined the main street. Slightly crooked and protruding from the cracked sidewalk, they looked as if they were a hundred years old. Mason approached two elderly Indian gentlemen who were wearing faded blue jeans and boots, had long gray shoulder-length hair flowing out from under their cowboy hats, and were sitting on a bench outside of Kerry's Hardware store.

"Pardon me, guys. Is there a restaurant around?"

The two Indians stopped their conversation and turned to Mason. After examining him, one of the Indians spoke up. "Sure, best steakhouse in Oklahoma is around the corner at the next intersection. It's called the Apache Steakhouse; can't miss it."

"Great, thank you," Mason replied.

"No prob, mister. You not from around here?" he asked before Mason turned away.

"No, just passing through on my way up to Chicago."

"I'm Q and this is Sunny," the elder Indian said, introducing them.

Sunny then added, "Short for Sunukkuhkau and Qaletaqua."

"Q and Sunny are much easier to remember. I'm Mason; nice to meet you."

With one leg folded over the other and one arm outstretched along the back of the bench, Q calmly pointed out, "You know you're pretty far off of the beaten path, Mason?"

"Yes, I know. I'm trying to see a little of the country before I get back to the city."

"Kind of on your own vision quest, huh?"

"Yes, I guess you can say that," Mason replied.

"Well, good luck on your quest. Remember, the most important part is to see the signs. If you don't pay attention to them, you'll miss it," Sunny added.

"I'll miss it?" Mason questioned, remembering what the little girl, who wasn't really there, said at the pool.

"What he's trying to say is whatever you do, don't ignore the signs, even if they scare you," Q clarified.

Almost on cue, the familiar large white owl with red eyes that had come to plague Mason flew by and landed on a light post right next to them.

Sunny looked at Q and then back to Mason and said, "I hope that's not for you," pointing to the owl. Then the two Indians began to laugh loudly, as if it was a joke. Mason, not quite understanding the humor, questioned them. "Why, would that be a bad sign?"

The two Indians realized they were being rude and settled down. "We're sorry," Q said, "the owl is not a bad sign really, it usually has something to do with death."

"Don't think I've ever seen one like that, though," Sunny said curiously. All three of them looked at the owl, at which point it let out a screech and flew away. "See, no problem, he's gone. He's just looking for dinner, like you," Q said, not paying much attention to it.

"Yes, I guess that's right," Mason said, parting ways with the oddly smiling Indians.

"If you're really hungry, get the Big Geronimo," Sunny suggested. As Mason turned back around to thank the Indians again, he saw them whispering and pointing at him. When they saw Mason catch them talking about him, their pointing turned to a wave.

"Thanks. Have a good night, guys," Mason said, waving back skeptically.

The Apache Steakhouse restaurant was decorated with authentic Indian art and paintings. Like the other small town restaurants Mason visited, it had a gift shop in the front selling local Indian art. As Mason walked in, he saw the couple from the parking lot and their children eating.

They recognized Mason as well and waved.

"Good evening," Mason said, walking up to their table. "I see you survived the luggage dilemma."

"I had it under control the whole time, right, honey?" the man said.

"If you say so, Richard," his wife answered, shaking her head.

"By the way, I'm Richard, this is Julia, this is Michael, and our little angel Caley," Richard said, introducing his family to Mason.

"Nice to meet you. I'm Mason." As Mason accepted Richard's outstretched hand, the usual shock of static electricity hit Mason. "JUNE 4, 2017" flashed to Mason's mind upon touching Richard's hand.

"Hey, you've got an electrifying handshake," Richard said, laughing and shaking his hand.

"It must be the dry air," Mason replied. In sequence, "JULY 19, 2033" came to Mason when he shook Julia's hand, "OCTOBER 12, 2080" when he shook Michael's, and "NOVEMBER 1, 2069" when he shook Caley's hand.

"Would you like to join us for dinner?" Julia offered. As Mason thought about it for a minute, he thought about the dates, something he couldn't ignore any longer.

The dates came so fast, I couldn't get them all, Mason thought. Did one of them have a June 4? My God, that's tomorrow? What was the year? But which one was it? While Mason continued his internal interrogation of himself, Richard stood up and put his hand on Mason's shoulder. "Are you all right, Mason?" he asked, pulling up a chair for Mason. "Here, sit down; you look like you just saw a ghost."

"JUNE 4, 2017" flashed at Mason again, along with the familiar jolt of electricity when Richard touched him. Mason looked at Richard and could feel his appearance becoming increasingly pale.

"Here Mason, have some water. I think you're having a touch of heat stroke," Julia said.

"Thank you; that's better," Mason said after taking a drink and catching his breath. Looking at Richard's family and knowing that they could lose their father in one day saddened Mason. There's got to be a way to change it, Mason thought. I have to figure this out. Mason's color started to come back and the initial shock started to subside.

"You know, I really don't feel that great right now. Actually, I think I'm going to go lay down."

"We understand, Mason. If you need anything we're in room 384 at the inn," Richard offered.

"Room 384," Mason said exhaustedly, as if not surprised. "Thanks; you guys have a good night."

"You too, Mason," Julia said.

The walk back to the inn was heart wrenching. Richard was in room 384. Maybe that's what the dreams were about; Richard being in room 384 and his day tomorrow.

As dusk was setting in, Mason noticed a strange sight. Off in the distance, on the horizon, he saw a cloud bank moving toward the town. Squinting to get a better view he couldn't quite make out the cloud or fog bank, but it was moving rapidly toward the town. He stopped and looked around. People were walking about, doing their business, not noticing the strange front that was about to befall them. He found it odd that nobody seemed interested in the darkening sky.

While the storm front had blanketed the sky on the horizon, there was no sound or wind associated with it. Maybe it was just how dusk begins out here, Mason thought while watching the sky become darker. As he continued to walk, he kept watching the cloud bank getting closer. Stopping again, he looked around. A few people stopped, stood in the street, and began to watch the fast approaching storm front. Oklahoma is no stranger to tornados and strange weather, he knew, but this seemed different. A quiver ran up Mason's spine as the blur that he had been watching began to faintly come into focus. As the cloud got closer, Mason could tell that it was no cloud bank.

"Is that a swarm of locusts?" a man standing in the street next to Mason asked, while looking at the rapidly approaching haze.

"I've seen locusts in Chicago during the locust breeding years, and I can assure you, that's not locusts," Mason said while never taking his gaze off of the waving phenomenon in the sky.

"In fact, it looks like birds," Mason offered.

"If those are birds, either they're huge or there are a lot of them," the man said to Mason.

"I have a strange feeling, sir, that they're both," Mason replied.

"Yes, those are definitely birds, but my God, what kind of birds are that big?" Mason said under his breath.

"I don't know, but are they coming here?" asked a woman who was standing behind Mason.

"I don't know," Mason said, turning to the woman. "I hope not."

With the setting sun illuminating the oncoming birds like a spotlight, the multitude of large white birds was clearly in sight now. Their massive wingspans thrashed the cool evening air against a darkening sky. The main street quickly filled with people looking in amazement at the enormous flock of birds approaching the town. The awesome sight of thousands of white birds coming straight for them paralyzed them with fear and awe.

The white birds, with black talons dangling beneath them and red eyes, were being led by one that was significantly larger than the others. As the birds got closer, Mason tried to make out what kind of birds were they. There's no way those are owls, he thought. As the birds made their way over the town, their eyes were fixed straight ahead on their leader. Not one of them made a sound; the flapping of their gigantic wings didn't even generate any sound.

A truly impressive sight, Mason thought. Large, beautiful white birds that fly gracefully through the air and make no sound; my God, those are owls.

As the leader of the flock passed the end of the town he made a ninety-degree turn straight upward like an F-20 fighter jet. The following birds, with perfect austerity, split into two halves, each circling either right or left, and coming back, encircling the town. The lead bird flew back to the middle of the town and hovered above the following birds who were flying underneath in lines with military precision.

Without warning, the lead bird let out a loud ear-piercing screech. As if following a command, the thousands of following birds began to screech as well as they circled the town. People tried to cover their ears from the screeching. Chaos ensued. The owls began to descend with a vengeance on the people, attacking, slashing, and thrusting their razor-sharp talons into fleeing townspeople. People were running and screaming as the large birds were decimating the townspeople. The white feathers around their small, finely honed beaks turned cherry red from blood and matched their eyes.

Mason took cover in a building and watched the horror through a window. As he was watching, he made eye contact with the lead owl, who changed direction almost instantaneously and, with a loud screech, accelerated toward Mason. He ducked under the windowsill to hide when the bird came crashing through the window and landed on a desk. Mason sat under the window with broken glass covering him, in fear of the large bird. Like in Mason's dreams, he found himself staring eye to eye with the menacing owl. Its red eyes glared at Mason, and then it opened its wings, exposing an eight-foot wingspan. The white bird, covered in blood, started making a clicking sound as it stared at Mason. In the background, Mason could hear the cries and screams of people being slaughtered by the owls. It was pandemonium.

Yet Mason sat in a room in an apparent standoff with the large bird. The red piercing eyes of the owl stared straight through Mason; Mason just stared back in fear. The bird lowered its head and pointed its wings downward, snarled, and slouched down as if to prepare for attack.

With another ear-piercing screech, the bird leapt from its perch and flew right over the top of Mason's head as he dove for cover. The owl flew out of the same window from which it had entered, covering Mason in blood dripping from its wings. While lying flat on the floor, he noticed that the cries and screaming of the people had ceased.

While he lay there, he noticed blood on his arms that had dripped off of the owl's wings as it flew over Mason. With a deep sigh, Mason stood up and looked out the window. He saw dead people lying in the street. Off in the distance, he could see the dark cloud of birds getting smaller and smaller as they disappeared into the horizon.

As quickly as the birds came and decimated the people of the town, they had departed. Not knowing what to do next, he slowly turned away from the window, and standing directly behind him was Kelly. "Whoa!" Mason said, stumbling backwards and hitting his head on a light fixture mounted to the wall. Just then Mason woke up to a knocking on his hotel door.

"Mr. Rhimes? Mason?" a voice called from the other side of the door.

What the . . . Mason thought to himself as he sat up.

"Mason? You in there?" the voice called out again.

Gathering his senses, Mason replied, "Just a minute."

As Mason lumbered to the door he shook the confusion out of his head, not fully understanding where he was. He thrust open the door.

"Can I help you?" Mason asked abruptly.

"Good morning, or should I say afternoon, sleepyhead," an upbeat Richard said to Mason.

"Oh, hi, Richard. Sorry, I didn't recognize you."

"No prob. Just wanted to make sure you were all right. You left in kind of hurry last night."

"Thanks, I'm fine. I actually slept great."

"Well you must've needed it; it's past noon."

"No way!" Mason said, surprised. "I've got to get going."

"Well we're glad you're feeling better. We need to get going too. We're headed up to Colorado Springs. Where are you going?"

"Chicago for me. You know, back to the wind," Mason replied. As Richard held his hand out to bid farewell to Mason, Mason braced himself for the shock that would get more intense the closer the death date was. Not to be disappointed, "JUNE 4, 2017" came with the full electrical shock to Mason.

"Have a safe trip," Richard offered, shaking off the strange sensation.

"You too," Mason said, trying to recover from the shock.

Watching Richard and his family pull out of the parking lot, Mason hoped his feeling was wrong, like he always did, but so far, no one had proven him wrong.

After a quick lunch, Mason hit the road again with his mind racing about his latest dream.

Maybe it was about Richard; he was in room 384, Mason thought. Then why were there so many owls? And what's with Kelly again? So many symbols. What does it all mean? he wondered.

While driving out of town on the narrow two-lane county road, he noticed a vehicle pulled over on the shoulder and people walking around it. As he approached, he noticed it looked like Richard's minivan. Knowing what he knew about Richard on this day, Mason's heart rate sped up. Pulling up behind the minivan, he recognized it; it was indeed Richard's. Mason cautiously walked up to them.

"Hey guys, need some help?" Mason asked.

"Hi Mason," Julia said. "Boy, we just keep running into you."

"Yeah, crazy, huh," was all Mason could muster.

"Hi Mason," Richard said, walking out from the front of the vehicle. "Looks like we have a flat tire," he said, looking at the front driver-side tire.

"Can you fix it, Richard?" Julia asked, standing beside the minivan.

"Yes, it's just a flat tire."

"I can help with it," Mason offered.

"No Mason, we can get it," Richard said.

"Oh, I don't doubt that at all, Richard, but if we do it together it'll go faster," Mason said.

"Are you sure you have time?" Richard asked.

"Sure, we'll bang it out in no time," Mason assured him.

"All right, but if you need to get going, don't feel like you have to stay," Richard said.

"Deal," Mason said. "Now where's the tire iron? I'll start loosening the lug nuts while you find the spare."

Chapter 31

Innocence Lost
Homa, Oklahoma
June 4, 2017

"Come on, Jimmy, step on it," Bud McRing yelled to Jimmy from the backseat of the old beat-up white Ford F-150.

"I'm already going sixty-five; leave me alone."

"If you can't handle the speed, maybe you're not cut out to be a racer," Brendan said, sitting next to Jimmy in the front seat. "Here, take a drink," he continued as he passed a bottle of Jack Daniels to Jimmy.

"I'm already buzzed. I don't want anymore," Jimmy said.

"Don't be a pussy!" Mike yelled to Jimmy from the backseat next to Bud.

"Come on Jimmy, if you want to hang with us you better be able to party," Brendan said.

"Brendan, Dad's going to kill us if he finds out you let me drive, especially if he finds out I was drinking," Jimmy said.

"Look, he's not going to find out. Now take a drink and step on it."

As the speedometer pushed past eighty mph, the four teenage boys sped down the winding county road, taunting Brendan's fourteen-year-old brother Jimmy with booze and driving fast. Jimmy continued to drink the whiskey and drive fast. Coming over the crest of a hill, Jimmy could see something going on up ahead on the shoulder of the road.

"Brendan, what's that up ahead?"

"It's a car pulled over on the side of the road."

"Should I stop?"

"No dumbass, speed up and blow right by them," Bud interjected.

"Yeah Jimmy, see how close you can come to them," Mike laughed while backhanding Bud.

"Brendan, I don't like this," Jimmy said, starting to get concerned. "I think I'm going to puke."

"You're doing great; just keep your eyes on the road," his brother said.

"Quit swerving, Jimmy, you're going to make me sick too," Mike said.

"I can't help it," Jimmy yelled.

"Don't you dare puke," Bud ordered.

"Come on, see how close you can get," Mike prodded.

Between Bud yelling, Mike taunting, and Brendan talking, Jimmy was overloaded and began to stress out. While rapidly approaching the vehicle that was pulled off to the side of the road, Jimmy realized there were actually two vehicles pulled over. He could feel his mouth begin to salivate, the kind of salivation that precludes vomiting.

"Look at that idiot driving like a bat out of hell," Richard said to Julia from the back of the minivan as they unloaded luggage to find the spare tire. They watched the rapidly approaching white truck swerving back and forth across the road.

"Good God, they're all over the road; they're probably drunk," Julia said back.

"Get the kids and stand over there," Richard said, pointing to a tree on the other side of a ditch running parallel to the road, well out of the way.

"Dad, check this out," Michael called to his father from the ditch he was playing in.

"Michael, go with your mother and get away from the cars," Richard ordered, more seriously this time.

"Dad, come here. Look at this weird frog," Michael said, disregarding his father's request.

"Michael, I'm not going to tell you again. Get over there with your mother!" Richard shouted again.

"All right, just a second. I want to catch this guy."

"No Michael, now!" Richard yelled back.

While Richard argued with his son, the pickup truck was fast approaching Mason and Richard's vehicles.

"All right Jimmy, slow down a little and just go around them," Brendan instructed his younger brother.

"Come on Jimmy, speed up," Bud yelled to Jimmy, laughing.

"Yeah, come on Jimmy," Mike added, laughing as well.

"Knock it off!" Brendan finally shouted to Bud and Mike. "We've been drinking way too much to screw up."

"There must've been an accident," Jimmy said, looking at the vehicles and trying to see why the cars were pulled over. With all eyes in the truck focused on the people who looked like they were trying to fix a flat tire on the side of the road, the truck drifted into the oncoming lane of traffic. The next sound they heard would forever be burned into their brains.

They heard a loud screaming horn blast from a semitruck barreling down the road on a head-on collision course with the white pickup truck. The horn startled Jimmy, whose life flashed before his eyes as he stared directly into the chrome grill of the fast approaching semitruck.

"Jimmy, look out!" Brendan yelled while grabbing the steering wheel and yanking it to the right, grossly overcompensating. He changed the collision course from the semitruck to the front of the minivan where Mason was working on the lug nuts, oblivious to what was about to occur.

In a split second, Richard grabbed the back of Mason's collar and, in one swift motion, pulled him out of the road and threw him into the ditch on the side of the road. The racing, out-of-control pickup truck then locked up its brakes, but not before hitting Richard and sending him thirty feet in the air to his untimely death.

"Nooooo!" Mason yelled while Julia let out a horrified scream.

The smell of burning rubber coupled with the sound of shredding metal accompanied a plume of smoke that temporarily masked the destruction of the minivan. As the pickup truck smashed into the front end of the minivan, it rolled onto its side and slid to a stop some twenty feet up the road. The semitruck downshifted and began to jackknife as it, too, came to a screeching halt, stopping just short of the wreckage from the minivan.

Mason watched from the ditch as the events unraveled in slow motion. He looked over at Richard's children and watched as their innocence was torn from their young souls in a split second. No child should have to lose their father, let alone watch him die, he thought.

The two children watched in shock, not able to speak, not able to breathe. Julia tried to protect them, but it was too late. They just watched their father die, saving Mason. Mason knew that the finality of their father's death would not hit them for several days, at which point it would crush them.

"Mister, are you all right?" a scratchy man's voice said, approaching Mason.

Looking up to a large, older, burly white-haired man with a thick white beard, Mason replied, "Yes, I'm fine. What about Richard?"

"If you're talking about the man those punks hit, I'm sorry sir, but he's no longer with us," the large humble man said, helping Mason to his feet. "I've already called the police; they're on their way."

"Thank you. I'm Mason," he said while offering the truck driver his hand.

"I'm Roy, Roy Turner," he said, shaking Mason's hand, "and that's my rig."

"JANUARY 20, 2019" came to Mason's head as he shook Roy's hand.

"What about the people in the pickup?" Mason asked.

"Those little assholes are fine; drunk, but fine. I hope those son of a bitches rot in jail," Roy said, looking with disgust at the four teenagers crawling out of the pickup truck windows.

"Well Roy, I appreciate your help. That lady over there just lost her husband and her children just lost their father," Mason said, directing Roy's attention to Julia, Caley, and Michael huddled under a tree.

"I'd better check on them," Mason said, starting to walk over to them.

"I'll round up those punks for the police," Roy said.

"Are you guys all right?" Mason asked Julia and her children.

"We're okay. Is Richard . . .?" she cautiously asked, not being able to bring herself to finish her sentence.

"Julia, I'm so sorry," Mason said. "The police are on their way. In fact, I think that's them coming down the road." They looked up the road and could see a convoy of police cars, ambulances, and fire trucks coming toward them with their emergency lights and sirens blaring.

As the last vehicle of the convoy of police cars pulled away to go back toward town with Richard's family, Mason leaned against Blue Lightning and watched the tow truck pull the remains of the wreckage onto its flatbed. Mason replayed the events over and over in his head. Why? Why does this keep happening? he wondered. If I wasn't there, Richard wouldn't have had to save me and could still be alive. The horn from Roy Turner's semitruck blasted again, startling the hell out of Mason for a second time. When Mason looked up, Roy was waving out of the truck window to him.

"Good-bye," Mason replied, waving to Roy. With Roy's truck gone and the tow truck pulling out, Mason found himself alone. There was a peaceful, but numbing, silence. Torn between going back into town and helping Richard's family and hitting the road, he reflected on the long-term effects of the accident.

The lives of the boys who were acting like irresponsible kids would be changed forever, the newly widowed mother, her children, and their extended families' lives would be changed forever, and the peaceful trip back to Chicago had just taken a serious turn for Mason.

First Kelly, then Ray Reed, and now Richard. All three had some relationship with me and now they're all dead, Mason thought. Ray and Richard were only two weeks apart. His thoughts continued to race.

Who's next? Were there others I just didn't notice? What if my not dealing with it is actually causing it? Am I causing these people to die? If my negligence is causing this, I can't live with that, Mason concluded. His earlier coping mindset of withdrawal and not dealing with it was no longer an option.

Maybe it would go away. Maybe it would continue to happen over and over until he actually dealt with it. Either way, I've got to figure this thing out, Mason thought. He decided it was time to make the call.

"Hi Dad. It's me, Mason."

"Hi Mason, we were just wondering where you were."

"I'm in Homa, Oklahoma. It's a small town in southwest Oklahoma."

"How's the trip going?"

"It's fine. I was thinking about meeting Irene's friend in Norman. If she's around I would like to talk to her for a second."

"Yes, she's right here; I'll put her on. Have a safe trip and call later and let us know how you're doing."

"All right Dad, I will."

"Hello Mason," Irene said, taking the phone from Patrick.

"Hi Irene. I wanted to talk to you about your friend in Norman."

"Oh, he's waiting for your call and is really interested in talking to you."

"What? How did he know I'd call?"

"I talked to him yesterday and told him about you," Irene said.

"Yeah, but I said 'maybe'?" a puzzled Mason asked.

"I told him you weren't sure, so not to get too excited, but he assured me you'd call. I guess that's why he's a doctor."

"Maybe. Anyway, I just wanted to make sure it was all right," Mason said.

"He's already set up the guest room at his house, so plan on staying there."

"That's not necessary; I'll probably get a hotel."

"Well, Max and his wife are very nice, you'll like them. Call him, and good luck. Let us know how it goes."

"I will. Thanks, Irene. Take care."

Mason closed his cell phone and looked back at the accident scene. Broken glass, vehicle fluids, and fragments of metal still littered the side of the road. The nervousness of finally talking to someone who allegedly knew something about this ability crept up on him. Mason pulled out onto the country road and drove toward Norman.

He knew what he needed to do. Mason knew that he needed to understand more about his ability. He realized that part of his hesitation for learning about his ability was fear of finding out that he was, in fact, responsible for peoples' deaths, a cross he was not sure how to carry. In the end, he remembered what a college professor told him.

"To solve a problem you must understand it. If you solve the wrong problem, not only do you create additional problems, but you potentially make the original problem worse. It all begins with knowledge."

His vision quest just turned into a knowledge quest.

Chapter 32

Deadly Chatter
Washington, DC
June 4, 2017

A knock at Colonel Austin's open door broke his concentration on a report he was working up for the president.

"Come in, Brian. What can I do for you?" he said, putting his pen down and leaning back in his chair, giving Brian Dougherty his full attention.

"Sir, the NSA has picked up considerable chatter coming out of the Middle East."

The colonel sat up, took off his reading glasses, placed them on the large cherry wood desk, and said, "Close the door. What are we talking about?"

Brian walked up to the desk and handed Austin a piece of paper containing the transcript of some of the chatter. "Word is spreading like wildfire about a hit inside the US."

"Those son of a bitches. They're going to complicate our lives, aren't they?"

"It would appear so, sir."

Austin sat back in his chair and spun around and faced the window. He began to read the transcript. The gears in his head were spinning a mile a minute. Brian didn't want to break the colonel's concentration and allowed the colonel to sort through whatever decision-making matrix he was using. The colonel spun back around and asked, "Do we know if it's credible?"

"No, not yet."

"How soon until we know?"

"The problem we're running into is, like other extremist groups, they use the media to circulate misinformation to the masses. They hide behind chaos and confusion and utilize scare tactics. That's how they are able to survive. It's spreading so fast that either it's a bluff or they are very close. I mean, we're getting hits from all over Europe and South America about this."

The colonel thought for a minute and then said, "If it were limited to the Middle East, I'd be more apt to consider it a ploy. South American intel usually doesn't play that game."

"And Europe could be hit and miss on whether it's accurate," Brian added.

"What else do you have on this group?" the colonel asked.

"In a nutshell, Ahmed has his people convinced that he is the next great prophet. However, there is unrest growing because his followers are starting to question his ideologies. Which, by the way, is another reason why he must do something big, to squelch the masses. He knows that his gig is up as leader if he doesn't do something, and something big."

"I see, another jackass who needs to prove something."

"Exactly," Brian agreed. He walked over and sat in a chair in front of the desk and continued. "It started when Ahmed began requiring females of all ages report to his palace for 'sexual indoctrination' or 'special blessings' from Allah. That led to Ahmed and his brother holding sex parties and basically raping women at will. Reports indicate they are pedophiles, sexual deviants, and are reckless with their killing. Nobody will disagree with him for fear of being killed. That said, word has spread in their village, and the villagers are starting to demand answers."

"Can we use that to instill a revolution?" the colonel asked.

"Possibly. I mean, all the components are there. I'm not sure there are enough revolutionaries willing to overthrow this nut."

"That's not a problem, Brian; we'll supply the freedom fighters. The villagers will be amazed at how many people are actually in that village. Any way to get a U/C in there?"

"No way. It's too unstable. If we got an undercover op in there and they burn him, he'd be tortured and killed immediately. And if he didn't get burned, they'd force him to take part in some kind of rape, murder, or something else. If he refused, then they'd kill him."

"True. Besides, if they are planning something here, they'll be overcautious to newcomers. What about acquiring an asset?" the colonel asked, running the gamut of options used in the intelligence world.

"Again, possibly. I mean in a situation like that, I guarantee someone is ready to make the break; we just need to find them."

"There has to be an option, Brian, and we need to find it," the colonel said as he stood up.

Brian recognized the meeting was over and stood up as well. "We'll keep at it until we do, sir. I'll keep you informed."

"Thanks, Brian." The colonel swung his chair toward the window again and picked up where he left off, contemplating his next move.

Chapter 33

Journey of Death
Medora, Canada (North of the North Dakota Border)
June 4, 2017

The transporters unloaded supplies from a truck in the middle of the night and loaded them onto a ten-foot rubber raft at the edge of the Souris River.

"It's cold here, Hallid. I can't wait to get back to the homeland," Malik said, blowing into his hands.

"It's cold because it's night and we're by the river. During the day it's not so bad," Hallid said.

"I don't know how you live here, Hallid, it's too cold for me too," Arsal added.

"I do it for Allah. Besides, someone has to protect our route."

"You are a blessing, Hallid," Malik said as they finished packing the raft with numerous packages being smuggled into the US.

Looking at Malik and Arsal, Hallid gave them their final instructions. "Brothers, you know this mission is for Allah. Stick to the plan and deviate for nothing. If an infidel tries to stop you, you must kill them and hide the bodies. Travel only at night and sleep during the day. Keep the supplies hidden during the day, especially the main package. That package is more important than all of our lives combined."

"We will, Hallid, we understand." Using only their flashlights for light, all four men examined a map. Hallid showed them their route.

"Remember, follow the GPS route already loaded in your Garmin. You'll follow the Souris River until it bends westbound, then follow the Stanley River; it'll unload into the Missouri River. Take the Missouri until you get to Atchison, Kansas; it's just north of Kansas City. There, a driver will pick you up and get you to the final site. The coordinates are all loaded, all you have to do is follow them, but take the map in case there's a problem." Hallid handed Arsal the map.

"Contact me when you've made it to the Stanley and Missouri rivers and then at Atchison. At Atchison, I'll arrange for the transfer. My men will meet you and take the other packages and a driver will get you to where you need to go. Once the transfer is complete, your mission is done. We will give you directions when the time is right to come home. When you return to the homeland there will be a party in your honor. You and your families will be blessed by Ahmed himself."

With those words the transporters smiled and became very excited, shaking each other's hands.

"Relax my brothers; there will be plenty of time to celebrate later. Stay focused and stick to the plan," Hallid said.

"Of course, Hallid," they said, straightening up.

"May Allah protect you, brothers," Hallid said as they pushed the raft into the water.

"And with you, Hallid!" they said back.

About twenty feet off the shore they started the small outboard motor, and in the cover of night, dressed in black, their journey of death and destruction had begun.

Rabwah, Pakistan

Aleem was led to the pool area of the palace to wait for Ahmed. He sat at a glass table and watched as the servant men trimmed the bushes and cleaned the pool. Young women soaked and swam in skimpy swimsuits.

Their sole purpose in life seemed to be staying attractive for Ahmed, he thought. It was a proposition that made him nervous for his own young daughter. He felt sorry for them. They had no idea what was in store for them when they no longer served their purpose.

"General Aleem," Ahmed called out from behind Aleem, walking into the pool area with a smile on his face. "How are you this fine day?"

"Fine," Aleem replied as he turned and jumped out of his chair.

Ahmed gave Aleem a brief hug and they both sat in chaise lounges beside the pool. A servant brought them both *Khamr* and a fruit plate. Ahmed sipped the Khamr and continued to fill Aleem in on the update.

"Our sources report that the package is on its way."

"Ah, that is good news, Ahmed. When will it get to America?"

"It's already across the border and should be to our location in a couple of days," Ahmed replied with excitement.

"It's already in America? But how?" Aleem asked with disbelief.

"Yes, my cousin's route into America hasn't failed yet. Next week will be very exciting."

"Do you know the target yet?" Aleem asked.

"Soon it will be revealed to me." Ahmed stopped, looked around to make sure no one was within hearing distance, and then continued. "In the meantime, there is another matter that requires your expertise, Aleem."

Aleem leaned in toward Ahmed, as he could tell it was something important. He lowered his voice as well and asked, "Yes, what is it?"

"I need you to arrange for a martyr for me next week."

"Of course. Where do you need him?"

"America," Ahmed said as his smirk disappeared from his face.

"America?" Aleem confirmed. His thoughts began to race. He secretly hoped Ahmed had changed the plan. He hoped Ahmed would use a series of martyr attacks throughout the United States, timed in sequence like the airplane attacks in 9/11.

"Yes, is that a problem?"

"No, I'll need to see who is available. There are plenty of sleeper cells that can be activated, but they are not all Almazorian."

"Do what you need to do, Aleem, but I need a martyr next week to do our attack."

"You're right, Ahmed. We will have one. Do not worry."

"That's the spirit," Ahmed said. Then, removing his sunglasses, he looked into Aleem's eyes and advised him, "Because if we don't, you and your family will have to suffice."

With a deep breath and a drink of *Khamr*, Aleem swallowed and knew Ahmed was serious.

Chapter 34

A Mean Succotash
Norman, Oklahoma
June 4, 2017

With the top down on Blue Lightning, the low, spellbinding rumble of its engine, and another ginger-colored sunset inching its way across the vast Oklahoma sky, Mason pulled into the Meadow Ranch subdivision on the northeast side of Norman, Oklahoma. The security gates were still open from the previous car, so Mason shot through them. Marveling at the capacious houses in the neighborhood, he saw one colonial mansion after another. He finally found Dr. Hogan's house.

"4425 Meadow Drive, there it is. Geez, teachers here must do pretty good," Mason said under his breath as he pulled into the circular drive. There was a large white Greek goddess water fountain in a courtyard between the driveway and the house. Four large white columns accentuated the entryway of the large white colonial house. While sitting in Blue Lightning admiring the perfectly manicured landscaping, Mason didn't notice the large white entryway door fly open and a short white-haired man emerge and start heading toward Mason's car.

"Hello, Mason!" the man said excitedly, opening Mason's door to greet him.

"Whoa!" Mason said, surprised, as he turned around to see his door being opened.

"You are Mason, right?" the elderly man asked, sporting a white goatee, thin black-framed glasses, and an ivory cane, extending his right hand to Mason.

"Yes, yes, I'm Mason," he replied, shaking the man's hand.

"I'm Max Hogan and I am pleased to meet you finally. I've heard a lot about you."

"Thanks, nice to meet you too. I'm not sure what Irene has told you, but she might've embellished a little," Mason offered as he stepped out of the car.

"Oh, I've known Irene for years, and she usually doesn't embellish," Max said with a smile and continued. "Let's get your things and I'll show you to your room."

"Oh no, Dr. Hogan. I'll grab a hotel—"

"Nonsense. First of all, call me Max, and secondly, you're not staying in a hotel, and that's the end of it," Max said sternly.

"Really, I couldn't—" Mason started again.

"Nope, it's already done," Max assured Mason, cutting him off again.

Knowing again that Mason wasn't going to win this one anymore than he would with his father, he graciously agreed and followed Max into the spacious house.

"Here's your room, Mason. It's got a television, bathroom, whatever you need. Almeda's making dinner, so take a load off. There's a garden out back if you'd like to explore. Make yourself at home and we'll come and get you in about an hour," Max said, closing the door to Mason's room. A mix of old Indian art and antiques covered the walls of Mason's guest room. Pulling back the large flowing drapes revealed spectacular views of acreage and age-old mature landscaping. A beautiful sight, Mason thought.

Mason turned on the television and watched the news until a knock at Mason's bedroom door followed by the muffled sound of Max's voice broke his attention. "Mason, are you up?"

"Yes, I'll be right there," Mason said, turning off the television and opening the door.

"Dinner's ready if you are," Max said.

"Yes, I'm starving."

"Good. Almeda made enough to feed an army."

As they walked down the giant circular stairwell to the lower level of the house, Mason noticed the walls were lined with old antique paintings depicting scenes of Indians at war.

"These are interesting paintings," Mason said, pausing to examine them on the stairwell.

"Oh yes, those are Almeda's. She's native Keetoowah Indian."

"Keewatah? I've never heard of them," Mason said, mispronouncing her tribe.

"No, Kee-too-wah. They're a band of Cherokee Indian. Most people call them Keetoowah Cherokee Indian, but the true Keetoowah drop off the Cherokee in an attempt to separate and maintain their history," Max said. "Almeda is very active in the Indian affairs community and continues to try and preserve their culture."

"What's with the pyramids in this one?" Mason asked, pointing at one painting.

"That represents where our original roots are believed to have come from," Almeda said, walking into the hallway and answering before Max could. Mason and Max turned to see an elderly Indian women standing in the doorway between the dining room and the main hallway.

"It is believed that the Keetoowah were descendants of the Mayan Indians and moved north and eventually settled in what is now called Oklahoma," she continued.

"Ah, this is my Indian wife Almeda," Max said, introducing Almeda from halfway up the stairwell. "She also happens to be a professor of Indian history at the University of Oklahoma. Almeda, this is Mason," he continued.

"Nice to meet you," Mason said, walking down the rest of the stairs to greet Almeda.

"I am pleased to meet you, Mason," Almeda said, greeting him with a big hug. "I know Max has been very excited to talk to you."

"It's not that big of a deal, believe me," Mason said humbly.

"You have an honest spirit, Mason. Perhaps that is your gift?" she asked rhetorically.

"Now come on, let's eat. Almeda makes a mean Cherokee succotash," Max said, pulling a perplexed Mason into the dining room.

Mason devoured Almeda's succotash like it was his last meal.

"I've never had succotash before. That was awesome," Mason said to Max and Almeda.

"Thank you, Mason. I learned how to make it from my mother," Almeda said.

"The indigenous peoples are great cooks, Mason; they really know how to live off of the land," Max said.

"I don't know about that, Max. I love a good pizza any time," Almeda said. "And, there's always apple pie."

"You guys know how to hit the right buttons," Mason said.

"Good, you like apple pie?"

"You bet," Mason said.

"I'll get it so you two can talk," Almeda told Mason and Max as she cleared the table.

"Well Mason, we both know you're not here because of Almeda's succotash, so why don't you tell me about your gift," Max asked.

"I'm not sure it's a gift, but it's definitely weird, and I'm sorry if it's not what you expect," Mason offered.

"Mason, first of all, if it's nothing, then having a guest and meeting you was worth it enough. Secondly, people that use their abilities to do harm are bad, not necessarily the ability. In other words, for example, the Internet is not inherently bad, it's when people use it for bad that it becomes a dreadful tool. Or the adage 'guns don't kill people, people do.' It's like that with people that have special abilities; the ability is not bad, it's how the person uses it. Typically, a bad person will use their gift in bad ways, and good people will use it in good ways. Does that make sense to you?"

"Yes, I guess I never looked at it that way before."

"And finally, I'm not here to judge you. I'm here to help shed some light on your ability, because I have studied and helped many people that may have similar abilities. In other words, there are a lot of people with special abilities. I'm here to tell you, you're not alone."

"It sure seems like I am," Mason said.

"All right, here you go," Almeda said, interrupting the two with apple pie a la mode.

"Thank you, this looks great," Mason said.

"Trust me, Mason, you've never had anything this good," Max said, pointing to the pie.

"Mason, if you don't like it, that's fine. Max is a little biased," Almeda said.

"No Almeda, this *is* really good. Max is right," Mason said after taking a bite.

"Oh thank you, that's sweet of you to say," Almeda replied. "I'm going to finish cleaning up. Why don't you two go to the parlor so you can talk?"

"Great idea. Come on, Mason," Max said, getting up and leading Mason into the round-shaped parlor room.

Chapter 35

Dimensions All Around Us
Norman, Oklahoma
June 4, 2017

The sweet aroma of the apple pie and cinnamon erased the smell of musty books. Antique sconces lined the walls of the parlor and gave a low, intimate, indirect light. Rich mahogany wainscoting contrasted the green and white Persian carpet. They sat on adjacent soft brown leather sofas.

"Mason, I want you to be open and understand that this is a safe environment. With other people I've talked to, I know things can sound kind of crazy. I want you to know, there's nothing too crazy and nothing too insignificant. If I'm going to help you, you can't leave out details that you think aren't important. I have to know everything. Although, I'll admit I'm a little curious, but I really just want to help."

"All right," Mason replied with a deep breath, sitting back into the smooth leather. The sofa enveloped him as he sunk in. It was probably the most comfortable sofa he had ever sat on. Max leaned toward his desk and grabbed a notepad off of it. As he sat back, the sound of squeaking leather came from the sofa. It reminded Mason of the squeaking sound the owl made. Max put his reading glasses on and began to write.

With his head tilted down, Max looked up at Mason through the top of his glasses and began. "Now Irene said you have premonitions?" Max's voice was low and soothing. He made it easy to open up.

"They're not really premonitions," Mason said, searching for a proper explanation.

"Irene said you predicted Ray's death?"

Mason's fidgeting was a good indication to Max that he wasn't as comfortable as he looked. Mason corrected Max: "I knew the day he would die."

"Did you know how he was going to die?"

"No, I only knew the date." Mason sat up in the sofa and tried to explain his ability further. "Look, in a nutshell, when I meet people I see the day they will die. Sometimes they are associated with dreams and sometimes not. It's almost like the dreams tell me to pay attention to something more than normal."

Taken aback by what Mason said, Max stopped writing, removed his glasses, and focused on Mason. His mind raced. Does he know mine? he wondered. Do I want to know what it is? His heart rate increased. He would not be able to "un-hear" it. With one question, he could find out when he would die. Would knowing it change me? he thought. Sitting across from someone who knew a very intimate detail about him was chilling. As strange as it sounded, Max had no doubt that Mason was telling the truth. But before getting too ahead of himself, he needed to clarify some things with Mason.

"Mason, I believe you. Let's explore the details so that maybe we can figure out *why* you have this ability. What exactly do you mean? Do you see where or how they will die?"

"No, I only see the date," Mason said confidently.

"How do you see it?" Max continued with great interest.

"When I come in contact with someone, a date shows up in my head."

"Do you have to be in physical contact?"

"Yes, like if I shake someone's hand or if someone touches me."

"And you believe it's the day a person will die?"

"Yes."

Max hesitated and realized in all his interest he had stopped writing. He put his glasses back on and began writing feverishly. Mason tried to read what Max was writing but it was too hard to read cursive upside down. The writing made Mason nervous, although he was used to doctors doing that. They all seemed to react the same. Max, however, seemed to believe him.

Max looked up again and asked Mason, "How do you know that's what it is again?"

"Because I've tested it over and over and nobody has proven me wrong. It started with my grandmother, then my mom, then Kelly, and several others. I even tried to change Kelly's death, but it didn't work; she still died. So I don't know if I can change anyone's day or not. I guess that's partly why I'm here. I guess if I *can* change a person's day, but haven't because I don't understand it, I'd feel even worse."

"Interesting. I've never met anyone with that kind of gift. I'm sure that can be quite a burden to know when someone will die. How do you handle that kind of information?"

Mason thought for a minute. He remembered his father telling him to ignore it and it would eventually go away. His mother telling him to embrace it but be strong. His childhood friends tormenting him because of it. Then he recalled how he decided to handle it.

"I just learned to ignore it. I mean, most people don't die right away, so usually the dates are far enough in the future that I don't pay attention. It gets hard, though, when the dates are close, and even harder when it's someone I know. It got to the point where I wouldn't even recognize it. I realized that people don't want to know that kind of information." Mason looked at it like waking from a dream. So vivid and yet within seconds after waking up, we can't recall it.

"Irene said something about a shock and you told Ray something. What was that about?"

"The closer someone's day is, the stronger the shock is. It kind of forces me to pay attention. With Ray, the shock was pretty strong. During the shock, I think he saw something or knew something, or somehow it was transferred to him, and when it ended, he knew too. It happened with my mom also."

Max was intrigued by Mason's story. He had never heard of this before. He stretched his memory but couldn't think of anything related to this. People with premonitions or extrasensory perception tended to have similar experiences. This was different. This was almost supernatural. Max knew Mason was carrying a serious burden of information and didn't want to overload him on his first night. Mason was pretty sure Max didn't know what it was either. He watched as Max shook his head unconsciously while writing. He started to lose hope, knowing that Max didn't have the answers he had hoped for. If Max didn't know, nobody would. Despair slowly began to seep into Mason's head. He was afraid he had exhausted yet another possible avenue to answer why he had his ability.

"All right Mason, just a few more questions and we'll hang it up for tonight. Do you know your date?" Max asked.

"No, that seems to be the only one I don't know."

"Any idea why you think that is?"

"I have no idea. I've thought a lot about it. Maybe my death is not defined, maybe it's a curse, maybe I never die, I just don't know. I've actually considered suicide to see what would happen."

"We're all glad you didn't try that experiment. Now you've had this ability your entire life or as long as you can remember?"

"No, there was an accident when I was ten years old. I drowned in a pool and apparently was dead for twenty minutes. When I came to, I started seeing the dates of people."

Max perked up and became very interested. "That's when your ability started?"

"Yes."

"Do you remember what happened for those twenty minutes?"

"No, I just woke up and I was inside an ambulance."

Max started writing again, this time shaking his head up and down. His curious nature turned into mild excitement. He appeared to have an epiphany. Mason then sat up a little more. He tried again to see what Max was writing. He needed to know what Max was thinking.

"Doc, what are you thinking?" Mason asked, trying not to break Max's train of thought.

Max stopped writing and explained, "A lot of people have 'near-death experiences' where they see loved ones or angels on the other side. Do you remember seeing anyone or anything when you were unconscious?"

"No, nothing. I've tried, but I've always come up with nothing," Mason admitted.

"Oh, I wouldn't worry about that," Max assured him confidently. Max closed his notebook and removed his glasses, as if something finally made sense. He looked at Mason like he solved a puzzle, smiled, and said, "I think we can shed some light on this thing."

"Really, you think so?" Mason replied with anticipation. After twenty years of having no idea, it was killing Mason to know what Max had figured out. "What! What is it, doc?"

"All right Mason, follow me on this," Max said. "It may get a little deep, but just follow me."

"Okay, I'm listening," Mason replied, focusing intently on Max.

"You see, Mason, we are surrounded by many different dimensions. Theoretically, those dimensions have different properties than what we are accustomed to in our world. In fact, some theorists believe that when we die we move into another dimension with a new set of rules and limitations and are governed by a set of completely different principles and laws."

"Those dimensions are independent and anomalous to our world. Just as ours is to the other ones. However, because of the proximity between dimensions, occasionally brief interactions between dimensions occur. Sometimes when people have interactions or some kind of exchange with another dimension, the properties that govern that dimension, or those attributes or characteristics of that dimension, can stay with that person when they return into this world. In our world it manifests itself as a gift, but in that specific dimension it may be a common ability or common knowledge."

"Okay," Mason said, slowly trying to understand. "You're saying that I went into another dimension?"

"Possibly. We know that one of the more closely related dimensions is a spiritual or nonphysical dimension. In those types of dimensions, they don't have ears so they don't hear by sound vibrations bouncing off of air molecules. They don't have physical eyes, so they don't see by images reflecting off of the retina and traveling down an optic nerve. For that matter, they don't breathe our air, or smell our smells. They don't have any physical parts. What they do have is different and heightened mental or cognitive senses. Since our world also has a mental or cognitive realm, advanced mental ability can and does apply to our world, whereas our physical realm or ability won't help in a spiritual dimension. That is unless that dimension also has a physical component. Do you follow me?"

"Doc, you're right, that is some pretty deep stuff," Mason said, sitting back into the soft leather again. "Even if that were true, it still doesn't answer *why* I have it."

"I know it can sound pretty out there. But consider this: when someone sees a ghost or has a premonition, they are essentially validating or at least witnessing the existence of other dimensions or realms."

"And you think that happened to me?" Mason asked.

"Possibly, however, it's difficult to empirically prove. Most people can't pinpoint when the incidence occurred. In your situation, however, we know exactly when and what happened, we just don't know where you went."

"I don't know, Max, I'm not sure I buy all that stuff. Sounds kind of sci-fi to me."

"I know it can be difficult to wrap your head around, but it does explain some things in our world that we otherwise can't explain. Keep in mind, you're not the only one who's experienced this phenomenon."

"I mean, you're the only one that I'm aware of with this particular ability. But there are a lot of people with other very unique gifts as well. You say you see the date that a person dies. Some people see *how* a person will die, or *where* a person will die. Some people see heinous crimes through the eyes of the victim, while others see the crimes through the eyes of the perpetrator. Some people see images of future events, some see past events as if they are there. Some see people that are deceased, but can't communicate with them, while others are able to communicate with the deceased, but can't see them."

"What I'm trying to say, Mason, is nobody could possibly have all the abilities, psychic or otherwise, from the other dimensions. If they did, their mind would explode. That's why people have small parts or gifts. Usually, the special abilities aren't more than a person can handle. Yours is unique to you. A lot of people couldn't handle having the knowledge you possess."

"Why me, Max? I mean, why dump that on a ten-year-old kid, especially with no guidance?"

"Aha, now we're asking the right questions," Max said enthusiastically. "Again, from my experience, nobody has a special ability just for the sake of having it. There is always a purpose. We need to figure out what yours is," he continued.

"You realize, doc, if most people heard this conversation, they'd think we were crazy?" Mason said.

"Yes, I agree. However, a lot of people don't want to know things. People don't want to know what's inside a hot dog or how exactly they make hamburgers. In the same sense, a lot of people don't want to hear explanations for what they cannot understand. It's easier to remain oblivious, and many people feel like that when it comes to psychic abilities."

"I guess I never thought of it that way, but you're right. In the end, you can't blame them, can you?"

"No, that's why most people with special abilities keep it to themselves. Nobody wants to set themselves up to be ridiculed and mocked. It's a carefully walked line with most of us."

"Us?" Mason questioned. "Do you have this stuff also?"

"You are sharp, Mason. I, too, have an ability."

"What is it?" Mason asked.

Max tried in vain to explain they were there to talk about Mason. But he knew Mason wasn't going to let him off that easy. As expected, Mason jumped right in.

"No way," Mason replied. "After all I just told you, you can't not tell me."

Knowing Mason was right and that he wasn't going to let it go, Max gave in.

"All right, it's only fair. I'll tell you and you'll see how closely related our gifts are. I see future events, but I don't understand them. I don't know where and when the events will unfold, I just know how they will happen. I knew of an airplane crash, but it wasn't until after I saw the news that I realized it was in Russia. I'm sure my counterpart is out there who knew some tragedy was going to happen, but not the how."

"Max, what's the point?" Mason asked, puzzled.

"The point is, if all of us that have psychic abilities came together, there would be a greater served purpose."

"Like the Super Friends," Mason said sarcastically.

"Sort of," chuckled Max. "The difference is superhuman strength isn't real, however, psychic abilities are very real. Remember, we use less than ten percent of our brains; that's a lot of untapped potential."

Chapter 36

When the Owl Sings
Norman, Oklahoma
June 4, 2017

Max and Mason sat in the parlor and continued their discussion on people with special abilities. It was the first time Mason could remember that he was at ease talking about his uniqueness. Max had a way of calming Mason to the point where he wanted to talk about it and didn't realize it. Every time something made sense, another weight came off of Mason's back. Max knew they were in a good place, so he continued learning about Mason's ability.

"Now Mason, is there anything else that you can think of?"

Mason thought for a minute and said, "The only other things, maybe, are my bizarre dreams."

"Dreams, of course; Irene mentioned that. It is quite common for people with psychic abilities to have very vivid dreams," Max explained. "What can you tell me about them?"

Just then, Almeda came in and sat down on the sofa next to Max.

"Oh, should I leave?" Almeda asked, realizing that they were in a deep discussion.

"No Almeda, it's okay," Mason said. "I don't mind, I'm just thinking," he continued.

"We're talking about his dreams, Almeda," Max said.

"Okay, you guys do your thing. I'm just here to watch," she replied.

"Mason, you were saying," Max said.

"Yes, I don't know. They're usually pretty strange. They usually deal with death. I know, hard to believe, right?" Mason said sarcastically, as if everything about him dealt with death.

"Sometimes death just symbolizes an end to something," Max said.

"That's what Irene said," Mason replied. "But she didn't know my past. They seem to be very specific now," he continued.

"What do you mean, Mason?"

"For example, the number 384 keeps showing up in my dreams. In the last town I was in, a guy I met at a restaurant was staying in room number 384 at the motel. His death day was today. When I was driving out of town I saw him pulled over to the side of the road and I pulled over to help him. I was helping him change a tire when the next thing I knew, he pulled me out of the road and was hit and killed by a truck. So I think the dream had something to do with him being in room 384."

"So it's always just the number 384?" Max asked.

"Well, no. There's usually 384 dead something."

"What do you mean 'dead something'?"

"It's either 384 dead fish, 384 dead people, 384 burned houses; it's always 384 something."

Max looked at Almeda with a somewhat baffled look on his face. "Your dream definitely wants you to pay attention to the number 384, but 384 what, is the question. Are there any other commonalities between your dreams?" Max continued to prod.

"No, it's usually nice, storm rolls in, storm rolls out, and there's 384 dead something."

"You know, the dream may be easier than we think."

"What do you mean?" Mason asked Max.

"It very well may be telling you that 384 people are going to die."

"But what good is that? I can't change it."

"How do you know you can't, Mason?"

"Because I've tried," Mason said sadly. "I tried to change my fiancée's day and she still ended up dying by a fluke stray bullet. I've tried to warn people, but they always end up dying. If there is anything I've learned from this thing, it's that you can't change your death day," he continued.

"Okay, Mason, let's go with that; if you can't change it, why the warning?" Max probed.

"I don't know, I just don't know. Maybe it's a wisdom thing."

"What do you mean?" Max asked.

"Maybe it's trying to get me accustomed to the death thing. There's always this damned owl in the dream staring at me. In fact, in the last one a flock of owls attacked the town I was in. But before the owl attacks me I wake up. Owls mean wisdom, so maybe it's a wisdom thing."

When Mason said "owl," Almeda looked up sharply at Mason and then curiously at Max, as if he should know something. Max picked up on Almeda's body language immediately. He knew Almeda had something to say. She showed too much interest at what Mason said.

"Quite possibly," Max said. "But I'm not convinced. Almeda, what do you think?"

"Are the owls in all of your dreams?" Almeda asked.

"Yes, just about all of them. But they're not nice wise looking owls, they're scary as hell."

"We have to delve more into the owl symbology," Max said. "The general perception is 'the wise old owl.' I can make some calls tomorrow and maybe get a better idea," Max continued.

"Excuse me, I know this isn't my thing," Almeda interjected, "but I know a few things about owls."

"By all means, what about them, Almeda?" Max asked.

"Owls are an ancient symbol. Some cultures associate them with magic or as a sorcerer's bird. Cultures around the world associate the owl with death or illness. The Irish believe the owl is the sign of the underworld. In ancient Italy, the owls are associated with the god of darkness. In the ancient Aztec culture, one of the evil gods wore a screech owl on his head. Generally speaking, it's only been later in the United States and England that the owls represent wisdom. In fact, a group of owls are called a parliament. Everywhere else in the world they represent death, illness, curses, or some kind of evil."

Max and Mason stared in amazement at the amount of information Almeda had.

"Guys?" she asked, breaking their stares.

"Oh, sorry Almeda, it's just that I find it fascinating," Max said. "But I have to ask, how do you know that?"

Looking back at a surprised Mason, she continued. "I've studied ancient Mayan and ancient Mexican civilization for years, and in those cultures, the owl is the messenger of the god of death. It is believed to be the only bird that can fly between our world and the underworld. The Mayans had a belief that said, 'When the owl sings, the Indian dies.' That's why people were scared of the owl; if they heard its call they believed they would die. Essentially, they believed the owls are the keepers of the dead."

"I always thought they just went 'whooo,' but I've heard them screech," Mason said. "It's pretty creepy."

"That's right, Mason, owls have a very terrifying cry, and although they typically come out at night, some roam by day. They have also been known to attack people."

"Okay, so the owl from hell is plaguing my dreams," Mason said. "And this is the part that will surely convince you I'm nuts. I've seen the white owl in real life."

"Are you sure it's the same one?" Almeda asked.

"Yes, trust me; you see this thing once, you don't forget it. I saw it when I was a kid before another kid died, the night before Kelly died, and in Arizona before Ray died. In fact, I saw it last night, and this afternoon Richard died."

"Did you have them in your dreams before all of those occasions?" Max asked.

"Yes. They were very vivid dreams that always dealt in death."

"It sounds like your dreams may foretell that someone near to you will die," Max replied.

"Yes, perhaps, but why?" Mason asked.

"That's the million dollar question. We find that answer and we understand your gift," Max replied.

"The problem is, how do we find that out?" Mason continued.

"It's getting late, Mason; let's sleep on it," Max said. "I have an idea we can try tomorrow," he continued, looking at Almeda as if he were up to something.

"That's great. I'm pretty wiped," Mason said.

"All right then, we'll hit it tomorrow," Max replied as they all left the parlor.

"Good night, guys," Mason said, walking up the circular staircase.

"Good night, Mason," Almeda said.

After retiring for the night, Max and Almeda sat in bed and continued to discuss Mason's profound ability. The low light given off by the nightstand light dimly lit the room.

"What do you make of it, Max?" Almeda asked.

"I'm not completely sure. I mean, obviously he has a gift. He knows when people are going to die. But, I think there's more. Everyone that I've helped has always had a purpose. There are no gifts that are mere novelties. We have to figure out why he is being given additional information outside of his natural ability."

"Unless you don't have his ability pegged yet?" Almeda questioned.

"Of course, Almeda," Max said. "You could be right; there may be more to it than we know yet."

"Dare I ask what you want to try tomorrow?" Almeda asked with raised eyebrows.

"You'll see." Max gave Almeda a mischievous smile and rolled over. "Good night, Almeda."

Chapter 37

The Mind Warp
Norman, Oklahoma
June 5, 2017

The smell of bacon, eggs, and percolating coffee filled the house first thing in the morning. Max was excited after learning about Mason's ability from the night before and had plans to figure it out once and for all. But it would take risk. It would take courage. It would take complete submission by Mason. Max wasn't sure he'd go for that. He wasn't sure Almeda would either. He also knew there was no other way.

"Ah, good morning, Mason. I hope you slept well," Max said, greeting Mason as he walked into the kitchen.

"I slept awesome. Thanks."

"Good. Have a seat, Mason," Almeda said, pulling out a chair at the kitchen table for him. "Would you like coffee or orange juice?"

"OJ would be great, thank you."

Max carefully tried to explain to Mason his plan to extract more information about his ability.

"Well Mason, I have an idea after breakfast I would like to try."

"Is it going to hurt?" Mason replied with a sigh.

"No, no, nothing like that. What I'd like to do is hypnotize you and regress you back to the day you drowned. From there we can see what actually happened to you on that frightful day."

As expected, Mason was not ready for that. "No way. There is no way I'm going to relive that miserable experience."

In Max's calming monotone voice he explained, "You said you didn't remember anything after hitting your head. The next thing you knew, you were in an ambulance, right?"

Mason's stomach fell to the floor; he knew nothing was free. This was going to be a painful experience. He was smart enough to know if he wanted the information, it would cost him some emotional pain. He knew deep inside that ultimately he would end up going through that miserable experience. But he fought nonetheless to see if there was any other alternative, any other way out.

"Yes, but I don't want to remember drowning."

"You won't remember anything from the hypnosis, Mason," Max assured. "Mason, look, there is a surefire way to find out what happened to you. But we have to go back to that day. I can't guarantee to you that it won't hurt or that it won't bring back some painful memories, but at least we will know what happened."

Almeda knew this was serious. Knowing that he only did the hypnosis in extreme cases, she was more than a little nervous about it. "Are you sure there's no other way?" she asked.

Max shook his head and sipped his coffee. "Number one, the memory has been repressed for twenty years, and number two, if he did transcend into another dimension, there's no other way to get to it."

Mason could see the concern on Almeda's face and knew Max was serious about it. But, in light of the information about the owl from last night, what was the alternative? Not do it and possibly never find out? Mason played "point-counterpoint" in his head but couldn't find any reason not to do it, other than being scared of the obvious—finding out what happened. He was getting closer to submitting.

"What is the worst thing that can happen, Max?" Mason asked, as if maybe it was so dangerous Max would decide not to do it.

"Well, I have to be honest, there are some risks. Usually it goes fine; I've done this many times."

"But . . .?" Mason interjected, prompting Max to give him the rest of the details.

Max took another sip of coffee, as if trying to buy time before dropping the bomb on Mason. He considered how exactly to tell Mason the ultimate consequence. There is no other way then to just tell him, he concluded.

"If while you are under you could have a bad reaction and basically stay under indefinitely."

"What do you mean indefinitely? Like a coma?" Mason was surprised that the doctor was so casual about it.

"Yes, precisely. If while you are under you actually cross over to the other side and something was to happen to you, you could possibly stay on that side."

"What do you mean 'stay on that side'? Like I die?" Mason asked, growing more concerned.

"Yes, technically. But more than likely, you would just stay in a vegetative state," Max said hesitantly.

"Technically! I either die or I'm a vegetable. Are you kidding me?" Mason cried.

"Here you go, Mason, have some eggs," Almeda said, placing a plate in front of him, thinking comfort food would calm him down.

"Thank you, Almeda; hopefully this isn't my last meal," Mason said half seriously.

"I understand your concern, Mason. Believe me, I don't take this lightly. In a way, I'm kind of glad you see the seriousness of this technique. It's important to understand that the problems arise when the patient fights the doctor. I will need your complete submission if this is to work. People that say they can't be hypnotized, to a degree, are right. Without your assistance and cooperation, you probably couldn't be. The bottom line, Mason, is if we do it, you have to agree to be compliant and you have to trust me."

"These eggs are unbelievable, Almeda. Are you sure you don't run a restaurant?" Mason said, before making up his mind. Maybe I'm supposed to find this out, Mason thought. Maybe this is all part of whatever it is. Mason's internal thoughts came full circle and started to not make any sense. However, the decision became more clear. "Max, I didn't come this far to walk away now. If you believe this will help, let's do it," Mason concluded.

"Are you sure about this, Mason?" Almeda asked.

"If the last thing I have in this world is your cooking, Almeda, I'm okay with that," Mason said, lightening up the tone. "Besides, I want to know what happened to me."

"All right, Mason, I'm going to need to get some more information from you specifically about that day. Let's hit the parlor," Max said eagerly.

They retreated to the parlor where Max pulled closed the drapes, instantly darkening the room. Mason sat on the familiar brown sofa and sank right in. Comfortable but nervous, Mason made small talk in an attempt to calm his breathing.

"You have done this before, right, doc?" Mason asked, trying to reassure himself that he made the right choice.

"You'll be fine, Mason. I'm just going to talk to your subconscious. You'll be totally relaxed but not even fully asleep. Go ahead and relax on the sofa; I'll be right back," Max said, going to retrieve his notebook and a video recorder.

"Okay Mason, now I want you to lie down on the sofa and relax," Max said, handing him a pillow and pulling up a chair next to the sofa. He dropped a crystal from a string in front of Mason's face. "Almeda is sitting right there and I'm going to videotape this session. Is that okay?" he asked Mason.

"Yes, fine," Mason responded.

"All right; I'm dimming the lights and turning on the mechanical metronome. I want you to relax every muscle in your body. Take some deep breaths and focus on the rhythmic sound of the metronome."

As Mason stared at the teardrop shaped crystal and listened to the slow, constant ticking sound of the metronome, he felt himself relaxing. Max's low monotone voice ushered in a serene state of mind for Mason.

"Focus on the prisms inside the crystal, Mason. Follow it from side to side, focusing on the prisms that go deeper inside the crystal. Relax and concentrate on the crystal and listen to my voice. Your eyes are starting to get tired. Close your eyes and focus your thoughts inward, just like the crystal. See the peaceful blackness and go to it. You are now completely relaxed. Can you hear my voice, Mason?"

"Yes," Mason replied, peacefully resting with his eyes closed.

"Good; at any time during this session, Mason, if you hear me say the word 'fire,' I want you to wake up instantly. Do you understand?"

"Yes."

"Very good. Now let's get started. I want you to go back two weeks ago when you were in Arizona. Are you there?"

"Yes"

"What are you doing?"

"Laying by the pool."

"Good. Now I want you to go back six months. Are you there?"

"Yes."

"What are you doing?"

"Writing an article?"

"What are you feeling?"

"Sadness."

"Why?"

"Kelly died and I didn't tell her the things I wanted to tell her."

"You know you didn't cause her death, right?"

"Yes, I know."

"Good, Mason; you're doing great. Now let's go a little further back. Do you remember being a senior in high school?"

"Yes."

"Good; go back to your senior year in high school. Are you there?"

"Yes."

"Good. How do you feel?"

"Fine. Al and I are going to a see the White Sox game with my dad."

"Are you happy?"

"Yes."

"Is Al your friend?"

"Yes, best friend."

"Good, Mason; I want you to go further back to fourth grade. Are you there?"

"Yes."

"What are you doing?"

"Playing dragon and tiger with my Dad."

"Are you having fun?"

"Yes," Mason said, starting to laugh.

"Do you love your mother and father?"

"Yes, very much," Mason said smiling.

Max looking over to Almeda and smiled, as if telling her, "So far so good, but get ready." She just nodded her head in agreement and held her hands together.

"Good, Mason. I want you to go to the morning of June 1, 1996— right after you finished fifth grade. Are you there?"

"Yes."

"I want you to go to when you arrive at the neighborhood party. Are you there?"

"Yes."

"How do you feel?"

"Good; we're having fun."

"Good, Mason. I want you to go a couple of hours later when you were swimming in the pool with your friends. Are you there?"

"Yes."

"How do you feel?"

"Good."

"What are you doing in the pool?"

"Playing tag."

"Is it fun?"

"Yes."

"Can you describe what happened to you in the pool when you got hurt?"

"My dad told everyone to get out of the pool for dinner. But I didn't want to; I wanted to keep playing. I climbed out of the pool but wanted to do one more cannonball. Nobody is looking; I'm going to jump back into the pool. The water is cold. I'm swimming underwater towards the wall as fast as I can so I don't get in trouble. *Ouch!*" Mason yelled, taking his hands to his head and startling Max and Almeda.

"Are you okay, Mason?"

"No, I can't see. I'm . . . drinking . . . too much water!" Mason said, coughing and acting like he was swallowing water. His breathing began to increase and he started tossing his head from side to side. He was going into distress. His body began to convulse as if he were drowning.

"Mason, what's going on?" Max asked, trying to stop him from falling off of the sofa. Almeda's eyes grew large. She covered her mouth with her hands. She was overcome with fear.

"Mason . . . Mason, talk to me; what's going on?" Max said, trying to remain calm.

Mason called out in fragmented words: "Can't talk . . . can't see . . . can't breathe . . . Mommy? Mommy, I'm scared! Mom—" He then went completely limp.

"Oh God! Mason, wake up!" Almeda yelled.

"Almeda!" Max scolded. He put his hand up to tell her not to talk and refocused on Mason.

"Mason, when you hear the word 'fire,' you will wake up. Mason, fire. Mason, fire," Max repeated. "It's not working. He's stuck," Max said, trying to remain calm.

"Max, what's happening?" Almeda asked, fully aware of what was happening.

"Almeda, calm down," Max replied. "Sometimes this happens on very intense experiences."

"Mason, fire," Max said again, calmly. "Fire. He's still not responding."

"He's not breathing, Max. Do CPR!" Almeda cried.

"Hang on, Almeda, he's still breathing. It's shallow and I have a weak pulse, but he's still with us."

"Mason, are you there? Can you hear me? I really need you to answer me, Mason. Come on, buddy, I know you can hear me. Let me know you're okay," Max continued.

"I'm fine," Mason said with a faint whisper.

Looking back at Almeda with hope in his face, Max asked again, "Mason, are you okay?"

"Yes." Mason's eyes remained closed and his breathing was weak. He lay perfectly still on the sofa. Calm. Peaceful. Alive.

"Mason, I need you to take a few deep breaths for me and then keep breathing."

"Okay," Mason said. With that, Mason's breathing started to get more normal. With a sigh of relief, Max put his hand on Almeda's knee, acknowledging that Mason was out of the woods and back with them.

"Are you back with us now, Mason?" Max asked.

"Yes, I'm fine," Mason said.

"Good, Mason, good job. That was close. Welcome back, Mason."

"Back where?" he said to Max, catching him off guard. Looking first at Almeda, Max looked again at Mason, who still had his eyes closed.

"Mason, are you all right?"

"Yes."

"Can you open your eyes?"

"Yes." Mason turned his head to the side and opened his eyes, revealing blood-red pupils staring at Max and Almeda.

"Oh God!" Almeda said as she put her hands over her mouth.

Realizing that Mason was still under, Max began to work with Mason again. "Go ahead and close your eyes, Mason."

Mason turned his head back and closed his eyes "Okay." Max looked at Almeda, who was visibly scared, and searched for his composure. He wiped the sweat that began to pour down from his forehead.

"Okay, good, Mason. Can you tell me where you are, Mason?"

"I'm at a feast."

"Is it the neighborhood party?"

"No, it's a feast like Thanksgiving."

"Why do you think it's Thanksgiving, Mason?"

"Because all the Indians are here," Mason said. A shocked Max looked over at a now petrified Almeda.

"Oh God, no," Almeda said under her breath with her hands still over her mouth, shaking her head.

Max was walking on uncharted territory now. He wasn't completely sure where Mason was. He could feel his own heart pounding. The room became like a sauna. He tried to calm his breathing; he knew he had to remain in control if he was to help Mason.

"Mason, are the Indians treating you nicely?" Max continued.

"Yes, they are really nice."

"Mason, is there anyone there that you know?"

"Yes, Ah Puch. He said we have a secret now."

"How do you know him?"

"He saved me."

"Mason, did Ah Puch give you anything or say anything special to you?"

"Yes, he said I'm special now and I have a present, but I can't see it; it's inside me."

"Mason, what does Ah Puch look like?"

"He's a really big Indian and he has a pet owl; it's really cool. He said he is my friend now and so is his pet owl."

"Mason, can you describe what the owl looks like?"

"Yes, he is huge and beautiful. He is white and has red eyes. He is a friendly owl."

"Mason, can—" just then Almeda tapped Max, interrupting him and signaling him to end it now.

"Yes, okay," Max mouthed to her.

"Mason, I have one more question for you. Did Ah Puch tell you what to do with your special present?"

"He said he will send his messenger for me when he needs me."

"Good, Mason. I want you now to go to when you were in college at Northwestern, okay?"

"Yes. Can I say good-bye to Ah Puch?"

"Yes, of course," Max said, again looking at Almeda nervously.

"Good-bye Ah Puch. Okay, I'll wait for you."

"Mason, are you at Northwestern University now?"

"Yes." Mason's demeanor changed instantly to that of an adult.

"Good, Mason. Now I want you to come back to today. I want you stay relaxed. I'm going to count backwards from five and when I hit the number one, I want you to wake up, okay?"

"Okay."

"Five, four, three, two, one. Wake up, Mason." With that, Mason opened his eyes and looked around. His eyes were normal again and he seemed relaxed.

"Well, are we going to do this or not, Max?" Mason said.

Max and Almeda looked at each other and smiled. They each breathed a sigh of relief.

"What? What's the deal?" Mason asked, sitting up on the sofa.

"Mason, you've been under for about thirty minutes," Almeda said.

"No way!"

"Way!" Max said. "And we got our answers."

"Seriously?" Mason questioned. "I need a drink."

"Here you sit. I'll be right back," Almeda offered.

"Well Mason, the good news is we know where you got your gift. The bad news is, we're not sure what you're supposed to do with it. However, it would appear that you're being called upon."

"What do you mean?" Mason asked.

"When you drowned, you crossed over into a different realm. While you were there, you were given this gift by Ah Puch, who told you he would call you when he needed you. Apparently, he's calling on you."

Almeda then entered the parlor and handed Mason a glass of water with one hand and held a large book in the other. She sat down and put the large book on her lap.

"What do you have there, Almeda?" Max asked.

"A book on Mayan gods. Ah Puch is the god of death in Mayan mythology. The Mayans believed he was a very powerful god who brought death to whomever he decided needed it."

"Needed it? Who would need death?" Mason asked.

"Anyone who needed their spirit cleansed," she replied.

"Right, of course," Mason said sarcastically. "You need cleansing, so get killed? Makes perfect sense."

Almeda paged through the index. "Ah, here he is." She began to read from the book:

"Ah Puch is the God of Death. Accompanied by his owl messenger, Ah Puch is believed to be keeper of the souls. He determines whether souls go to the netherworld for punishment or whether they can enter the paradise world. Typically, he is associated with destroying morally corrupt civilizations in order to bring balance back to the world. It is said that he will come back whenever the world needs to be cleansed of its immoral element. He will claim the evil souls and remove them from our world. The legend says that before he comes, he will warn the evil culture and give them a chance to atone for their evil practices. They will be warned through innocent blood by a pure soul. If they do not change, they will be destroyed. His feast day is June 1."

"That's just legend, right?" Mason asked, hoping it was.

"Mason, while you were under, you said you met Ah Puch and that he gave you a present," Max said.

"Mason, the Mayan civilization disappeared overnight. Sodom and Gomorrah disappeared overnight, as did many other immoral civilizations throughout history," Almeda said.

"Even if it were true, all they have to do is repent and they're saved, right?" Mason asked.

"Not exactly. Listen to this." Almeda continued to read:

"The reason Ah Puch is so feared is because of how they must prove to him they are repentant."

"There's always a kicker," Mason said.

"Yes, and with Ah Puch there is as well. With the Mayans, it was believed that in order for them to be saved, the tribal king was to sacrifice himself for his people. This outraged the king, who ordered all owls be hunted and killed, believing that if the owls were dead, Ah Puch could not carry out his commands.

"What the king failed to accept is number one, owls are very hard to hunt, and number two, the owls that destroyed their culture were not of this world."

"So the king's ego or pride was the reason the entire civilization was wiped out?" Mason asked.

"It's probably more that the king allowed the corruption, and the only way to get the people to believe what they were doing was wrong was to have him publicly sacrifice himself," Almeda added. "Remember, they believed in human sacrifice for a lot of things."

"Mason, your accident happened on June 1, Ah Puch's feast day, right?" Max asked rhetorically.

"Yes, but Max, come on," Mason said in disbelief.

"Well, it all makes sense. As a ten-year-old, you were probably considered innocent and pure," Max explained. "You were obviously given this gift to use at some point."

"But how does he know when I'd use it?" Mason asked.

"I don't know; my guess is that he gives it to someone different in every generation and if he needs them, he calls them. In other words, every generation may have someone like you. When you eventually die, someone else will get it," Max continued.

"And how exactly am I to inform a civilization that they're in grave danger?" Mason questioned.

"I'm afraid that's as far as I think I can take you, Mason. You will need to figure out how to use it. All we know for sure is that the owl is calling you. I wish I could help, but I think it's up to you now," Max said softly.

"I think I get it. The problem is, I don't understand what *it* is."

"Mason, when the time comes, you'll know it," Almeda said, consoling Mason.

"I know it's a lot of information, Mason," Max said. "But we're closer than we were yesterday."

"You both will never know how much you've helped me. I've struggled with this my entire life, and finally I have some answers. Unfortunately, but as expected, it also raises new questions. At least now I know what to look for, I think," Mason said, knowing that he had no idea what to look for.

"I'm sure it will all make sense some day," Max said, encouraging Mason.

Chapter 38

Done with Small Towns
Greenfield Ranch, Oklahoma
June 5, 2017

Later in the afternoon, Mason was ready to continue his trip to Chicago. He loaded his bag and said good-byes. As Mason drove out of the Hogans' driveway, Max and Almeda watched him. Max had a strong feeling of discontent about Mason's ability. Death was nothing to take lightly. He knew there was more to Mason's purpose, though he was content leading him in the right direction.

"Max, do you think he'll figure it out?" Almeda asked.

"I hope so, because what I saw in his future didn't look so promising for a lot of people," Max said with concern emanating from his face. They watched as Mason's car got smaller and eventually disappeared into the horizon.

Mason drove northeast out of Norman. He couldn't get his mind off of his stay with Dr. Hogan. He realized that the only person who would believe his crazy story was Al. Everyone else would think he was nuts. In the end, he thought, he really wouldn't need to explain it to anyone. The only thing he knew for certain was that there was now a sense of urgency to get home.

"Enough of the small town experience," he uttered. "Give me a Holiday Inn with a pool and cable and I'm good."

As the miles passed under a scattered sky and dry Oklahoma heat, it seemed Mason's drive took him further and further from civilization. He drove for hours and contemplated his trip.

My dad's a partier and his best friend died, I still have nightmares, a guy died saving my life, I've been hypnotized, and the whole god of death thing; what a trip, he thought. My God, what could possibly be next?

Then it happened. *Bang! Clunk! Clunk!* Mason's car made a horrible sound and smoke started pouring out from under the vehicle. Mason pulled the car off the two-lane road and onto the shoulder. He looked around for any sign of life, but saw none. Then, looking up to the heavens, he shouted, "Are you kidding me? There is no way that just happened. Wait, of course it did. Because I'm in the middle of freaking nowhere!" He banged his fist on the steering wheel. Pulling out the map and trying to get his bearings, the only determination he made was that he was completely lost.

After an hour of walking aimlessly and with nobody in sight, he spotted what looked like a long dirt driveway or possibly a dirt road. As night was quickly approaching, he had no choice but to follow it. While walking on the dirt road he saw nothing representing signs of life. No old farmhouses, hay stacks, nothing. For God's sake, he thought, does anyone live out here?

Then he heard a noise. In the distance, rapidly approaching him from behind, he saw a vehicle speeding down the dirt road toward him. The dirt cloud behind the vehicle rose up and followed the vehicle closely. Looking up to the heavens as if God himself answered his plea, Mason mumbled, "Please let this be a nice person." As the pickup truck now in plain view grew closer, it slowed down and stopped next to a waving Mason.

"Evening, mister, is that your car back on 94?" the female's voice said, coming from the inside of the truck.

Walking up to the rolled-down passenger-side window, Mason observed a tomboy-like brunette wearing a cowboy hat, blue jeans, and work gloves. She looked as if she just stepped off of the range. The hat was shielding her face so he couldn't make out her eyes. At this point, he was just happy to have a live person.

"If you're referring to a blue Mustang on whatever that main road is, yes, it's mine and it broke down."

"Where are you heading to?"

"Chicago," he hesitantly said, expecting her to inform him that he was lost.

"I think you're lost. You know you're a long way from the interstate," she said, right on cue.

"Yes, thank you, I just figured that out," he said, as if at his wits' end. "Would you be able to give me a ride to the nearest town where I can get a tow truck to pick up the car?" Mason asked.

"Um, sure," she said, nervously looking around.

Recognizing her hesitation, he realized the situation. He tried to make her more comfortable about giving a stranger a ride. "My name is Mason. Look, I know you're not supposed to pick up strangers and I understand. I mean, you don't know me; I could be a psychopath, a serial killer, or just a plain weirdo. But I assure you, I just need a ride, no trouble."

"Oh, I'm not afraid of you, Mason; you don't look like a psycho. I'm just deciding where to take you; we're really not by anything close."

"Well, where are you going?" he asked cautiously, not to cross any boundaries.

"Um, I'm going to my town, I guess."

"Now that was really convincing," Mason said.

"No, I'm just thinking if it would be better to take you to a bigger town."

"It's going to get dark soon. Does your town have a mechanic, restaurant, and a motel?" Mason said, now overtly mocking her.

"Yes smart-ass, get in," she said smiling, appreciating the mental jabs. As he opened the passenger door, the dome light came on, illuminating her face. Mason then realized how attractive she was. Taken aback, he had not noticed that he had stopped halfway into the truck and was staring at her.

She broke his stare: "It's a better ride inside with the door closed, but it's your choice."

"Yes, sorry." Mason said, blinking his way back from embarrassment. He slammed the door and the rickety old truck started moving. Squeaking and bouncing, it felt like they hit every groove in the road. It beats walking and at least I can get my car fixed, he thought.

"Thanks a lot, Ms. . . . um," he started saying.

"Oh, Claire, Claire Burnhardt," she said.

"Thanks a lot, Claire. I really appreciate this."

"Don't mention it; it's on my way."

"I was checking my map and am really lost. Am I still in Oklahoma?" Mason asked.

"Yes, there was an eastbound turn about two hours ago that would have put you on the main interstate and run you up through Missouri. You just missed it. They need to fix the signs, they're not very clear. If you blink, you miss it."

"Yeah, I didn't even see it. Where does the main road that I'm on go?"

"About sixty miles up you'll hit the Kansas border and about another forty and you'll hit a main artery that'll get you to a highway. Nearest town is probably Idledale, an hour back where you came from."

"Good God, I have no idea how I ended up here. I'm driving back from Arizona and thought I'd hit the small towns on the way instead of taking the main interstates. You know, see the country. But man, I'm not even close," Mason explained.

"Well, about another ten miles or so we have a little town. We'll get you set up there."

"Thanks. I just hope someone can fix my car."

"Frank's Auto will be able to fix you up, no problem."

Chapter 39

No Floaters
Souris River, North Dakota
June 5, 2017

"Malik, wake up," Arsal whispered as he tapped his partner on the leg.

"What! What is it?" Malik said, coming out of a deep sleep.

"I hear something."

"Kill the motor, quickly," Malik said. The low hum of the outboard engine went silent. The two transporters sat drifting slowly down the Souris River. The only light emanating from the partial moon was blocked by an overcast sky. With the blackness closed in around them, only the LED readout from the Garmin GPS offered any light.

"Hear that?" Arsal whispered.

"I don't hear anything," Malik replied. "Wait; yes, there are voices."

"I told you. What do we do?" Arsal asked.

"Shh, they are getting closer."

The voices could be clearly made out now.

"Come on guys, they aren't going to tap themselves," a voice said, followed by the sound of an opening beer can.

"Yeah, that's what Rene said last night. Booyah!" another voice said, followed by laughter from several men.

"Shit, Malik, someone is out here fishing, but where are they?"

"I don't know. I can't see; just be quiet." They sat in the boat hoping to drift by without being seen, but a two-hundred-watt floodlight wasn't going to let that happen.

"Hey, what have we here?" a voice said as Arsal and Malik threw their arms up to block the blinding light being shined directly into their eyes.

"Hello, we are out looking for fishing," Malik said in his broken English.

"Looking for fishing? Are you retarded?" a large red-haired man said, mocking Malik's English.

"Besides, where are your poles?" another one pointed out.

"We haven't opened them yet."

"Where are you two from, and what the hell are you doing out fishing at three o'clock in the morning?" the red-haired man asked as he spit tobacco juice into the water.

"We are visiting from Baghdad," Malik said. "Now we must be on our way. Good day."

"Oh, I don't think you're going anywhere," one of the men said, putting his foot on the raft's bow, stopping the raft from moving.

"What's in the box, Mohamed?" the large red-haired man said while he wiped tobacco spit from his thick beard.

Malik looked at a concerned Arsal and said, "We don't want trouble."

"Sorry, raghead, but you got it whether you want it or not. You wouldn't happen to be smuggling drugs into our country, now would you?"

"No, of course not," Malik answered.

"Good, because I'd hate to see someone cutting in on my business," he said, turning to the other three men and smiling. "Now, I'm only going to ask you once more. What's in the box?"

Malik's demeanor turned serious. He calmly said to the drug runners, "Take your drugs and leave, and we'll let you live."

"Hey Red, I think they're comedians," one of the men in the boat said.

"Or they're just stupid," another one said.

"They obviously can't see who has the weapons," Red said, holding up his rifle.

Malik looked at Arsal as if speaking the same language. There was no alternative. While the drug runners were laughing, Malik and Arsal pulled their 9mm handguns out of their waistbands and in one decisive move opened fired on the four men in the boat. All four were killed before they knew what hit them.

"Malik, what do we do with the bodies?"

"Stab them so we don't have any floaters; we want them to sink. Then we'll shoot out the bottom of the boat and sink it."

Chapter 40

Twilight Zone
Greenfield Ranch, Oklahoma
June 5, 2017

Claire and Mason drove through the rolling pastures and in and out of wooded areas as twilight was setting in. Watching the orange Oklahoma sky lose its last bit of color was a spectacular sight. Mason noticed a huge owl fly out in the distance. An owl, imagine that.

"What was what?" Claire asked, looking out in the distance.

"Looked like an owl."

"Yes, probably," Claire said nonchalantly. "There are lots of them out here."

"I'm sure there are." Mason said under his breath, shaking his head, "I must be losing my mind."

"What's that about losing your mind?" Claire asked.

"Oh nothing, I just think they're interesting."

"They're very pretty birds. Very intense looking. I've seen them carry off small dogs. Very powerful," Claire added.

With darkness almost completely set in, they entered the dimly lit town. Mason could barely make out the buildings. The roads were dirt and the buildings were old. Right out of the old Wild West, Mason thought to himself. "What's the deal with the lights; you guys don't pay your electric bill?"

"No, we're just pretty far out there and it's an old town. Here we are; Frank's Auto."

Claire honked the horn as they got out of the truck.

"How you doing, Claire?" a tall, slender, elderly man said, coming through the front door of the house. He walked over to Claire and hugged her.

She introduced Mason and explained that his car broke down. Frank looked at Mason curiously. They didn't get many visitors in town. His shop consisted of a detached two-car garage. Mason didn't care, as long as he could fix his car.

"What happened to your car?" Frank asked very pointedly.

"I don't know. I was driving along and it made a clunk sound and smoke started pouring out from under the car."

"Huh, strange. I'll tow it in and take a look at it in the morning." Mason got the impression Frank didn't believe him, but he'd see it eventually.

"Let's go, Mason. Thanks, Frank, see you later," Claire said, jumping back into the truck. "On to Marcie's Motel."

"There's a restaurant next to the motel if you're hungry," Claire said.

"That would be great. You can join me if you're not busy," Mason said.

"Thanks, but I can't."

Realizing the awkwardness of what he said, Mason fumbled through, trying to clarify it. "No, no, I didn't mean, um, you know, that. I meant, you know, just to say thanks," Mason's words finally stumbled out.

"I know, Mason. That's nice of you, but I play cards with my grandfather on Monday nights," Claire said, mildly flattered.

"I usually just eat my feet on Monday nights," Mason said, embarrassed.

"It's all right, Mason," Claire said, cutting him off. "Maybe I can meet you for breakfast, unless you eat your feet then too."

"No, I try to actually eat food in the mornings," Mason replied, a bit surprised she even countered.

"Definitely has that small-town feel," Mason said, changing the topic. "By the way, what's the name of this town anyway?"

"Greenfield Ranch. Settled by the Greenfields some 150 years ago. Made their living raising cattle and passed it down from generation to generation. Mitch Greenfield still technically owns the land. You know that long ten-mile stretch of dirt road off of 94 that I picked you up on?"

"Yes."

"That's all part of this town."

"That's pretty big. I bet it's quiet around here," Mason commented.

"At night it's pitch black. You can see just about every single star," Claire said.

"In Chicago, you never really see night. It's pretty bright all the time. Until you see this, you really don't realize what you're missing," Mason said as he stared up at the night sky.

"Here we are, Marcie's. She's a friend of mine; don't let her scare you."

"What?" Mason asked. "Why? Hey, why would she scare me?" he continued, with Claire dismissing him completely.

They entered the large two-story house through the front door. "Hey Marcie!" Claire called out from the front desk in the living room.

"This kind of looks like someone's house?" Mason asked Claire.

"Coming, just a minute," a voice called out from upstairs.

"It is; it's Marcie's house."

"Oh, I see."

"We don't get a lot of visitors here, Mason, so there's no need for a Holiday Inn," Claire explained.

"It's fine, I was just, you know, um, noticing."

"Hey, Claire," a middle-aged women said, coming down the stairwell with her arms full of towels. "Oh my, why didn't you tell me we had company?" she said, looking over Mason as if he were for sale and smiling.

"Marcie, stop ogling. This is Mason. Mason, Marcie. You'll have to excuse her, manners aren't her thing," Claire said.

"It's all right. Hi, nice to meet you," Mason said, stretching out his hand and then waving as he noticed Marcie's hands were full.

"Nice to meet you too, Mason. Let me put these down."

"Mason needs a room tonight; his car broke down over on 94. Frank's on his way to tow it in and fix it."

"Oh, no problem. I have the perfect room for you."

"Thanks, anything would be fine."

"Not picky, are you, Mason?" Marcie asked, looking up as if he were talking about her.

"Excuse me?" Mason said, not sure where she was going.

"Not picky about the room, are you? What did you think I meant?" Marcie said with a devious smile.

"Marcie, he needs his own room, he's not sharing yours," Claire said, joking with Marcie.

"Oh all right. If you change your mind, I'm down the hall," Marcie said to Mason with a wink.

"I'll keep that in mind," Mason said, making a mental note of where not to wander off.

"Your room's up the stairs, first door on the right," she said, as if disappointed.

"Thank you. I'm just guessing that I don't need a key, right?" he asked.

When Claire and Marcie stopped laughing, Marcie said, "No, we don't have keys."

"No problem, since I have no luggage until my car gets back. Maybe I can go to Dave's Diner and eat," Mason said laughing, trying to be funny pointing out that all the businesses seemed to start with people's names. Noticing he was the only one laughing, and feeling slightly embarrassed again, he stopped and cleared his throat. "Or you can just direct me to some Tabasco for my other foot."

Marcie then awkwardly spoke up, "Claire's Café is right next door."

"Claire's Café?" Mason said, looking over at a smiling Claire who appeared to be enjoying the rectal exam they were putting him through.

"I wonder if they have burgers?" he said, smiling back at her.

"I don't know if they know how to make hamburgers out in this small town," Claire said sarcastically. "I think you only get those in the big city. Isn't that right, Marcie?"

"I don't know, Claire, I've never been to a big city before."

"Nice, okay! You've made your point. I'm sorry, I didn't mean it like that," Mason said.

With that, Marcie and Claire laughed while Mason shook his head.

"We're just messing with you, Mason," Claire said. "Of course they have burgers. Come on, I'll take you over," she said, ushering him to the door.

"Great, for a minute you freaked me out. Claire's Café, that was good," Mason said as they walked, relieved that he didn't insult Claire.

"That part we weren't messing with you, it is Claire's Café," Claire said and continued, "and I'll go ahead and spare you the humiliation, since you have no more feet to put in your mouth. Yes, it's mine."

"You know I didn't mean anything—" Mason started, but again was cut off at the knees.

"Mason, are you always this uptight?"

"No, just hungry and tired."

"Well I'll fix the first part of that, but you're on your own for the second part," Claire said as they walked up the front wooden steps to the porch of Claire's Café. Continuing her sarcastic attack on Mason, she said, "Oh my God, a business where the owner doesn't live upstairs, no way!"

"Funny," Mason said, noticing Claire's jovial nature. As they walked into the diner, Mason noticed the quaint little restaurant was much larger inside than it looked from the outside. A large room with antiques and old pictures lined the walls, embroidered tablecloths covered the tables, and small chandeliers hung from the ceiling. A half wall and counter bar separated the dining room from the kitchen grill. Along one side of the restaurant by the windows was a series of booths. A sparse population of patrons sat eating their dinners as if out of an old John Wayne Western movie.

"Hi Natalie!" Claire called out as she walked in.

"Hi Claire. Looks like you found a stray?" Natalie said from behind the counter.

"This is Mason; Mason, Natalie."

Mason gave the obligatory wave.

"Here Mason, have a seat," Claire said, climbing into a booth along the windows and pulling off her hat, exposing her shoulder-length dark black hair.

"Thanks, this is really nice," Mason said as if pleasantly surprised. "Did you decorate the place?" he asked.

"Yes, Natalie and I did. Natalie's my cousin."

"It looks great," Mason said, looking around. He noticed the few patrons that were in there had stopped eating and were staring at Mason. Feeling like he was an exhibit at the zoo, he leaned into the table and whispered to Claire, "Why is everyone staring at me?"

"Maybe they like you. Marcie sure did," she said with a grin.

"I don't think that's it," he replied.

"It's nothing. I told you we don't get many visitors."

"It's kind of creeping me out," he said without moving his mouth as he gave a fake smile to an elderly couple staring at him with blank expressions on their faces.

"All right!" Claire said in a loud voice, turning her attention to the room. "This is Mason; his car broke down and Frank is going to fix it. So stop staring, thank you." With that, everyone went back to their business as if time had restarted.

"Thanks Claire, you really know how to handle people," Mason said, finally getting a closer look at Claire's brown eyes.

"It's a small town, everyone knows everyone."

"I don't know if that's good or bad," Mason said. Studying Claire's face in the well-lit room, Mason commented, "You know, you've got great eyes."

"Thank you, Mason, that's nice of you to say," she said while looking down, a little embarrassed.

"Sorry, I didn't mean it in a weird way. I'm just saying, you have great eyes," Mason said, his voice trailing off, trying not to embarrass himself again.

"Let me get you dinner started. You want a burger?" Claire asked to change the subject.

"Yes; cheeseburger, fries, and a Coke would be great."

"I'll get Murph right on it. I'll be right back."

As Claire walked away, Mason watched her talk to Natalie and Murph, the large Indian cook. Claire reminded him of Kelly. Wherever she was, she lit up the room with her smile. Both were smart and witty. But the closer, they both had great eyes. A smile crept across his face with the thought of the likeness between the two. Intrigued by Claire, Mason didn't notice the tall slender gentleman walk up to his table.

"Pretty, isn't she?" the man said as he interrupted Mason's thoughts.

"Excuse me," Mason said, redirecting his attention and acting as if he wasn't staring at Claire.

"Claire—she's pretty, isn't she?" he asked again in a slow, deep, thick Southern drawl.

"Um, sure. I really hadn't noticed," Mason replied, knowing he was completely busted.

The elderly man removed his cutter-shaped cowboy hat and ran his hand through his long black and gray hair, as if it had been a long day. He was in no mood for games. His thick mustache, wrinkled face, and raspy voice reeked of a life full of experience.

"Right, well you must be Mason. I'm Joe; I'm the mayor of this town."

"Pleased to meet you," Mason said, trying to get up out of the booth.

"No, no, stay seated," Joe insisted, placing his hand on Mason's shoulder. "We don't get many visitors here, so I thought I'd personally come and welcome you to Greenfield Ranch," Joe continued.

"Have a good evening, Mason," Joe said with a smug smile and walked over to Claire and gave her a hug. Mason watched them talking. Claire's facial expression went from smiling and happy to serious and somber in an instant. There was definitely some hostility between the two. Just then, they both looked over at Mason and caught him looking at them. Mason immediately turned his attention to the chandelier, but knew it was too late. When he looked back Joe was walking away and gave Mason another fake smile and waved good-bye. Claire walked back over and sat back down in the booth with Mason.

"Everything all right, Claire?"

"Yes, it's fine. The mayor just bugs me sometimes," she said, visibly irritated.

"I take it there's a little history between you two?" Mason asked.

"Maybe. Is there a Mrs. Mason in Chicago?" Claire asked very succinctly.

"Now that's what I call a redirect," Mason said. "Don't you have to play cards tonight?"

"I told the mayor I wasn't coming."

"I thought you were playing with your grandf—. Oh, I get it. The mayor is your grandfather."

"You got it. A bunch of us play poker on Monday nights. It's not a big deal if I miss it."

"I'll be fine if you want to go; you don't have to babysit me," Mason said.

"You want to get rid of me that bad, huh?"

"No, not at all. I just don't want to throw a wrench in your plans."

"I appreciate it, but if you don't mind I'd rather stay and talk."

"Awesome. I mean, that's fine," Mason said, trying to hide his already blown excitement.

"Now how about Mrs. Mason?"

Feeling a little like he was being interviewed, Mason answered Claire's questions. "No, no wife, no kids, no girlfriend. No strings to speak of," Mason told her, trying to minimize his situation, but not being that far off.

"What kind of work do you do?"

"I write for the *Chicago Sun* newspaper."

"So you're a writer? What do you write about?"

"Mostly whatever the boss tells me to cover."

"That's kind of interesting."

"It's really not a big deal, believe me," Mason said, downplaying his profession.

"A writer in this town would be terribly bored. Never really anything going on here," she explained. "You know, small town politics, that's about it."

"I don't know small town politics, but I understand big town politics and I want nothing to do with them," Mason said, reflecting on his piece on corruption.

"Sounds like its personal?" Claire asked.

"No, I just don't like big city politics."

"Fair enough," Claire conceded.

"So if you don't live upstairs, do you live in the kitchen?" Mason asked.

"Yes, in the meat freezer!" she replied. "No, I'm down the street about a mile. We try to keep everyone spread out. No need to be packed in when we have as much land as we do."

"So everyone has some acreage out here?"

"Yes, most everyone has about ten acres or more."

"Wow, that's great. In Chicago, you're lucky if you can afford a two-bedroom, 800-square-foot condo."

"Here you go Mason, one cheeseburger and fries; enjoy," Natalie said as she dropped off his order.

"Thanks, Natalie, looks great. Are you going to eat, Claire? Because I'll wait," Mason said, stopping himself from biting his burger, trying not to be rude.

"No, go ahead. I'll have a piece of pie with you for dessert."

"What small town wouldn't be complete without pie?" Mason said sarcastically.

"What? We have great apple pie," Claire said.

"Oh, I don't doubt it," Mason reassured her.

"So what's got your grandfather's feathers ruffled anyway?" Mason asked as he bit into his burger.

"Oh, he just has a lot on his mind I guess," she said.

Mason stopped chewing, looked around at the seven elderly people in the restaurant, looked out the window to see a few people meandering down the street, and said mockingly, "I can understand that; this place is a heart attack waiting to happen." Claire finally smiled. "There she is; she's back. Where have you been? I thought you were on an extended break," he continued.

"Sorry, he just gets to me sometimes. My dad died when I was a kid and my grandfather basically raised me. Sometimes he needs to figure out that I can take care of myself."

"Did he warn you about me?"

"No, we were just talking," she said after a long pause.

"Come on, your silence has already answered it," Mason said, prodding her.

"He said to keep an eye on you; he doesn't trust you."

"I'm a stranger, you're a beautiful—. I mean, you're like his daughter, he's just worried about you. Can't blame him for that. Hell, I'm the stranger and I'm worried about you!" Mason said, smiling.

"Have you ever thought, maybe you're the one who should be worried?" Claire said, trying to be serious.

"No, no, I didn't think of that until right now. Thanks for making sure I won't sleep tonight," he said somberly.

"If I were you I wouldn't go to sleep with Marcie on the loose," Claire said with a laugh. "I think she likes you."

"I'm thinking she's not my type, or I'm not her type, or both."

"If you're breathing, you're her type," Claire said.

"Great. Make sure you check on me tomorrow in case I don't make it," he teased.

Chapter 41

A Nice Easy Fix
Greenfield Ranch, Oklahoma
June 5, 2017

After leaving the café, Joe pulled into Frank's shop that was attached to his house. Frank was under Mason's Mustang trying to assess the damage and heard Joe pull up.

"Evening, Joe," Frank said, coming out from under the car.

"Hi, Frank. What's the deal with the car?"

"Well, I won't know for sure until tomorrow, but it looks like a transmission problem," Frank guessed.

"Oh, great, a nice easy fix. Think you'll be able to repair it?" Joe asked.

"Haven't done work on a '65 Mustang in probably thirty years, let alone a transmission. I've got to find parts, which won't be easy, and it certainly won't be fast," Frank told him.

"I wonder if it wouldn't be better to tow it back to Neil's place in Idledale and let them handle it," Joe suggested.

"Not a bad idea. It would sure make my life easier. I'll call Neil in the morning and see what they can do," Frank said.

"Good. In the meantime, let's have Jessica run his registration and do a background on Mr. Mason. Let's find out who exactly is in our town."

"Will do, Joe. Have a good night."

"Talk to you later, Frank," Joe said, climbing back into his car.

It was past closing time at the café and Claire and Mason were the last two people in the restaurant. The chairs were turned upside down on the tables, the lights in the kitchen were off, and Natalie and Murph had just left. The awkward silence of them being alone had set in.

"Mason, I hate to be a party pooper, but I should probably get going," Claire said as she finished her tea.

"Yeah, I guess it's getting late. Maybe Marcie will already be asleep," Mason hoped.

"Unlikely; she'll be waiting for you," Claire said, bursting his bubble.

"Well, it was really nice meeting you. Thanks for picking me up," Mason said, walking to the door with Claire.

"It was nice meeting you too, Mason," Claire said as she turned and shook Mason's hand.

"JUNE 16, 2017" flashed into Mason's mind. Enthralled by Claire's eyes, he almost missed it, although the shock made that difficult to do.

"You're full of electricity, aren't you?" Claire said, rubbing her hand.

"I guess so," Mason replied, trying to write it off and remember her date. Wait, was hers the sixteenth or was that Frank's or Joe's? What was the year? He couldn't remember; they were too close together. Whatever it was, it was close.

Mason walked down the street to Frank's to get his suitcase out of his car. He couldn't get Claire out of his mind. She reminded him so much of Kelly. As he walked up to Frank's place he saw Frank standing there, waiting for him.

"Howdy, Mason."

"Hi, Frank."

"Well, I got a look at the Mustang. Might be a transmission problem."

"Transmission. The car's got 60,000 miles on it?" Mason replied, as if not believing him.

"If it's been sitting long, maybe it rusted through. I don't know yet. I'll know more tomorrow when I can get it up on the lift."

"Thanks, Frank."

The walk back to Marcie's Motel with his luggage draped over his shoulder was relaxing. Mason noticed the calm, cool Oklahoma night air and the peaceful sound of crickets. He hadn't noticed that he was alone in the small town until he heard an owl make a "whoo" sound.

Stopping and looking up, he saw the familiar white owl perched on the corner of a building, as if keeping watch. After watching it turn its head back and forth for a few seconds, it opened up its massive wingspan and leapt from its perch, not making a sound. Amazing, he thought as he watched it disappear into the night.

For a few brief moments, his mind shifted from Claire and his car to a place of peace and solitude. He continued to walk down toward Marcie's house, and then he heard a strange sound permeating the night. It sounded like a party.

Following the sound, he walked along the side of a building to the backside. He continued walking out through the grass behind the buildings and into a dark, wooded area. The further he walked into the woods, the louder the sounds became. He could now see a light shining through the trees. The distant sounds of music were now clear. Drums? Like tribal drums, probably some Indian ritual, he thought. Not wanting to be seen, he snuck up on the light and sounds.

As he peered through the trees, his heart began to race. The pit in his stomach instantly morphed into a boulder. He couldn't believe his eyes. He saw what appeared to be an ancient city across a clearing. A large pyramid-shaped stone structure that was flat on top was located in the middle of the city. Smaller stone huts lined the main dirt roads. What was an ancient city doing in the middle of the woods?

Behind the large pyramid-shaped structure, he witnessed thousands of Indians dancing around a huge bonfire and drinking. He heard a loud voice, but could not make out what was being said. Looking up to the top of the pyramid structure he saw a large Indian wearing a full Indian headdress and paint on his face, and with a large white owl by his side. When the large Indian raised his staff, the enormous owl stretched out its wings and screeched. Thousands of owls appeared out of nowhere and descended on the Indians, tearing them apart with their sharp black talons.

The cries and screams of the people were deafening. Mason watched as the people were being slaughtered. Terrified, he stayed low and hid until the carnage ceased. When not a soul was moving, the large Indian cried out something in an Indian language and the owls left.

With that, the large Indian disappeared. Mason sat barely able to breathe and surveyed the scene of corpses. He saw a young Indian boy walk up to the front side of the large pyramid structure. The boy looked up at the steep stairs that led up to the top. He stopped, looked around, and then proceeded to walk around it. As the boy approached the backside of the structure, Mason watched him drop to his knees and vomit as he took in the massacred dead bodies. The Indian boy then sharply looked in Mason's direction, as if he had seen Mason.

Paralyzed, Mason didn't make a move. The Indian boy squinted and moved his head as if he knew Mason was hiding in the brush. Finally, the Indian boy ran and hid in a small hut. With the Indian boy hiding in a hut, Mason took the opportunity and jumped up and turned to run back to the motel.

As he turned around, Mason slammed into the large Indian who originally stood on top of the pyramid and was now standing behind him. Mason fell to the ground. The Indian stood and stared at him while the menacing owl perched on a branch above him snarled. The more Mason tried not to breathe, the more he needed to.

The Indian reached down and grabbed Mason's arm. It burned, but Mason dared not break from the intense stare of the Indian. The Indian looked into Mason's eyes and said, "Tunkuruchu k'aay Masewal Kimil!" With that, the Indian and the owl disappeared. Mason lay back on the ground, tried to catch his breath, and rubbed his burned arm. A series of loud booms shook his ears. Jumping up, Mason woke up, falling onto the floor of his bedroom.

"Mason, are you ever coming out?" the voice banging on his bedroom door yelled.

"What?" Mason said to himself as he rolled on the floor. He looked around. Where's the jungle? "Good God, what the hell was that?" he continued as he gathered his senses.

"Hey Mason, are you up?" the woman's voice said again.

"Yes, just a minute," he replied, sitting up and noticing he was sweating profusely. After throwing on a shirt and shorts, he answered the door.

"Yes, oh, hi Claire," he said, fixing his hair.

"You missed breakfast and are about to miss lunch, so I thought I'd check on you. You know, make sure Marcie didn't get you."

"What time is it?"

"Twelve thirty in the afternoon. Are you sweating?"

"Yes, I had quite the dream."

"Must've been intense. You were saying something in your sleep, but I couldn't make it out through the door; sounded crazy."

"You heard that?" he asked

"Yes, it was pretty loud. I thought for sure you were talking to someone or had the television on. Hey, what's the matter with your arm?" she asked, drawing attention to the bright red scratch marks on his arm.

"I don't know. I must've knocked my arm when I was sleeping."

"Kind of looks like a burn; we should get it looked at."

"No, I'm fine," Mason said, rubbing his forearm and trying to gather his senses. "It's nothing," he continued. "I'll get cleaned up and be over in a little bit."

"Okay. Are you all right?"

"Yes, yes, I'll see you in a while," Mason said while closing his door, too preoccupied to realize he impolitely shuffled Claire away.

Chapter 42

It's All Bad News
Greenfield Ranch, Oklahoma
June 6, 2017

Joe sat in his office typing away on his computer. Being a morning person, he liked to get in the office before anyone else. It gave him time to get work done with no interruptions. Although the ringing desk phone broke his concentration, he hoped for good news.

"Hello?" Joe said, answering the office phone.

"This is Frank," the voice on the other end of the telephone said.

"Good morning, Frank. What's the word on the Mustang?"

"Well, the bad news is it needs a new transmission. The other bad news is Neil's out of town for another week and they can't get to it."

"Is there any good news, Frank?"

"No, the other bad news is I can't get another transmission in for about four days."

"Well, thanks for all that bad news, Frank. Would you like to give me any more while you're at it?" Joe asked with a sigh.

"Well, now that you mention it, Jessica called about our guest."

"Great. What did she say?"

"Turns out Mason is a Pulitzer Prize winning reporter for the *Chicago Sun*."

"Really? Just what we need. Thanks Frank, good work. I'm not going to ask you for anything else because it's all bad."

"Sorry Joe, hate to be the bearer of bad news. But it is what it is."

"It's not your fault, Frank. Let's just not give Mr. Rhimes anything to write about from here, okay?"

"Got it. What should I do about the parts? It'll be pretty expensive, and I'm guessing he's not carrying cash."

"Let's get it ordered and hope he can drum up the money. Either way, that's the only way he's leaving, so let's get it done."

"All right, I'll get on it. See you later," Frank said as he hung up the phone and noticed Mason walk into his office.

"Hey, I was just about to come see you, Mason," Frank said.

"Well, how does it look?" Mason was optimistic that it wasn't as bad as it sounded, although Frank was about to squash that hope. He was a straight shooter and didn't sugarcoat many things. "Your transmission is shot," he informed Mason.

Mason's heart missed a beat. "What? Did it rust through, like you thought?"

"No, actually there's a clean break, almost like it was purposefully cut off." Frank's passive accusation was noticed by Mason. However, Mason was getting accustomed to the underlying mistrust that the town offered.

"How the hell does that happen?" Mason asked, knowing that Frank didn't trust that he *didn't* do it. *Why would they think I wanted to be here?* was all Mason could think.

"You got me; you must have hit a pothole, or something else is going on." Now that was pretty overt, Mason thought, but continued the banter nonetheless.

"I don't remember hitting anything," Mason said, reflecting on his drive. "Can you fix it?"

"Yes and no. Yes I can fix it, but it'll take four days to get all the parts." Mason didn't care that Frank didn't trust him, he had nothing to hide. Mason was more concerned with what to do for the next few days. Maybe catch up on some reading?

"Okay, well, I guess I'll just hang out for a few days."

"There's one more small issue, Mason. I'm guessing you're not carrying $2,000 cash on you either."

"Uh yes, you're guessing right. You take Visa, right?"

"No, actually nobody in this town takes Visa."

"What, are you kidding me?" Mason said, surprised. It has to be because I'm a newcomer, he thought.

"Wish I was, son, but no, nobody takes any credit cards. We're a cash only town."

"Is a check considered cash?"

"No, only cash is considered cash. Sorry, it's our town's policy."

Mason started contemplating where he would get money to use. He wasn't sure he wasn't being scammed. Now the distrust was mutual. Unfortunately, they had the leverage—and his car. Mason accepted his checkmate position. Unless Mason knew how to fix a transmission, it didn't matter whether he was being scammed or not, it was going to cost him $2,000 to get out of there.

"Okay, then were does everyone get their cash?"

"Occasionally, we'll drive over to Idledale and use their bank. That's where our post office is as well. People from town make the trip pretty regularly; you can probably catch a ride."

Mason felt as if he was being taken advantage of, but under the circumstances, there wasn't much he could do about it. He was questioning his decision to see the countryside more and more.

Chapter 43

The Painting
Greenfield Ranch, Oklahoma
June 6, 2017

Mason waved at Claire as he walked into the café for lunch. The busy lunch crowd all looked at Mason simultaneously, as if he was from another planet.

"Hi, Mason. Have a seat, I'll be right over," she said, gathering up some plates and running them out to her customers.

"Hi, you look a little more alive now," Claire said, complimenting Mason.

"Yes, I feel better. You look busy," Mason said, looking around the café.

"Lunch rush; it's our busiest time of the day. But it's winding down so I can talk in a few minutes. First, let me get your order in. I'll be right back," Claire said, hurrying off to the kitchen.

When she came back she crawled into Mason's booth and breathed a sigh of relief.

"All right. God, it feels good to sit down."

"I feel like I should be driving or doing something," Mason said.

"By the sound of it, you're going to be here for a few days," Claire said.

"I guess word travels fast in this town?"

"Welcome to my world," Claire said, rolling her eyes.

"Hey, speaking of your world, what's with no one taking Visa?"

"Oh yes, that. Well, the town decided long ago not to accept any credit. Everything in this town is paid for in full. Nobody in this town has any debt."

"You're kidding me. Where do you keep your money? You have to have a bank."

"Oh, we do. Everyone has a safe deposit box with their money in it. We keep tabs, and at the end of every month everyone settles up."

"That makes no sense. If you want to buy a new car and it costs $20,000, how do you pay for it?"

"I take it out of my box and pay for it."

"People have that kind of money lying around?"

"Some do, I guess. Mostly people drive into Idledale and use their banks for a large purchase. Nobody knows how much money anyone else has, and nobody cares how much anyone has. We don't live for the money or the wealth, Mason; we live here for the quality of life."

"Aren't you afraid of thieves?"

"We have a pretty good police force here. We've never, as long as I've been here, had a problem."

"How can that be? I haven't seen a cop yet," Mason said.

"Then they're doing their job, because trust me, you have seen them; you just didn't know it. Not all cops wear uniforms. We know who they are and that's what is important," she answered.

"Interesting. So what happens if you run out of money? It's not like you can go get a loan, right?"

"Correct again. It just depends on the situation. If someone uses all their money paying medical bills, the town will help them out. If they are merely reckless, they may be forced to leave the town completely. Mason, it is a very peaceful town; we don't have many problems."

"Sounds more like a club or a commune. If you don't fit in, you're gone," Mason suggested as Natalie brought Mason's lunch to him.

"Here you go, Mason. Enjoy."

"Thank you, Natalie; looks good," Mason complimented.

"I take it Frank told you about going to Idledale to get cash?" Claire asked.

"Yes. In fact, I can't pay for this until I get some money," he said, inhaling his lunch.

"It's okay; we've kept track of your tab."

"That's good, because I sure haven't."

"Well, I might just have you washing dishes," she said with a smile and continued. "Actually, I'm going Idledale tomorrow; you can come with me."

"That would be great, thanks. You know, don't feel like you have to entertain me. I mean I can wander around on my own. I'm sure you'd rather hang out with friends or someone else?"

Claire leaned across the table and whispered to Mason. "I don't know if you've noticed, but there's not a lot of people here to hang out with."

"All right, I'm just giving you an out if you want it."

Joe Burnhardt walked in and headed over to Mason and Claire's booth. Pulling up a chair from a table and sitting at the end of the booth, he greeted them.

"Hello, guys."

"Hello, sir," Mason said.

"What's with the formality? Please, Mason, call me Joe. Well, looks like you'll be staying with us a couple of days, Mason."

"Yes, I'm sorry about that. I really didn't mean to invade your town. I'll be sure to lay low."

"Ah, it's not a problem, Mason. I'm sure Claire has told you, we are very leery of newcomers. You see, we just want to be safe."

"No, I understand," Mason reassured the mayor.

"Well, just wanted to stop by and apologize if I was short last night," Joe said, standing up and putting the chair back at the adjacent table. Putting his hand on Mason's shoulder, he said, "Enjoy your stay, Mason."

"I will. Thank you, Joe," Mason said, fighting back the shock he felt when "JUNE 16, 2017" flashed in his mind. Mason thought, June 16? No, that was Claire's. I'm getting them mixed up, he thought as frustration took over. I've got to figure this out. I can't let this happen again like it did with Kelly.

"See, he's not so bad," Claire said, breaking Mason's thoughts.

"So now your grandfather's all nice to me? You must've given him a piece of your mind."

"Let's just say we had a little talk about his manners."

"I see; must've been some talk."

"It was. I'll let you eat. I've got some work to finish up."

"Sure, thanks. I'll be wandering around town."

When Mason finished eating his lunch, he meandered out to check out the small town. The storefronts still had posts on which to tie horses. A peaceful town with no traffic lights, large oak trees, and antique everything. Time forgot to include Greenfield Ranch as it made its pass through the years. As Mason walked past "The Grocery," he could see a handful of customers walking inside the small store. It wasn't like the mega stores they have in Chicago. Curious, Mason entered the store.

"Can I help, sir?" a young twenty-something man asked Mason as he walked in.

"No, I'm just looking around."

"All right. If you need anything, I'll be at the counter."

"Thank you. Actually, on second thought, do you carry any kind of souvenirs?" Mason asked.

"No, not really. We really don't get too many visitors. You might want to check the Indian Art Boutique down on the corner; they have some pretty nice stuff."

"Thanks, I'll try them. I don't suppose you carry Red Bull, do you?" Mason asked.

"What is it? I might be able to find it."

"That's all right; could I just use the restroom?"

"Um . . ."

"You do have a restroom, don't you?"Mason asked, recognizing the clerk's hesitation.

"Yes, sure, sorry. I was thinking of something else," the young clerk said. "Just go through the double swinging doors and make a quick right; you'll see it."

"Great. Thanks. Through the double doors and make a right."

"Yes, be sure to make a right, don't go straight," the clerk reiterated.

"Got it," Mason said, thinking it was odd that he specifically made sure he didn't go straight. What was straight? he wondered. Mason walked through the double doors and could see a small warehouse area, the open restroom door to the right, and another door leading somewhere else straight back. While pondering whether or not to peek through the door that went straight back, it flew open and a large rotund man emerged, yelling into his cell phone. His red, round cheeks and scowl made Mason feel sorry for whoever was on the other end of the phone. His hair on one side of his head was draped over the top and vaguely masked his balding head. His mouth was moving so fast that spit was blanketing his thick black mustache.

"I don't care! That's not what the memo said, get it right," he said as he hung up and nearly ran Mason over.

"Are you lost?" the man bellowed to Mason.

"No, I was just looking for the restroom," Mason nervously replied.

"Bathroom's over there," he said, pointing to the open bathroom door.

"Oh, of course," Mason said, looking at the bathroom and then back at the man and trying to see behind him into the other room. The man noticed that the door he had just come through was still half open. Reaching back behind him he closed it, but not before Mason had noticed it was some sort of warehouse, much newer than the rest of the store.

"Now if you'll excuse me, I'm busy," the man said as he rushed through the double doors into the main grocery.

As Mason came out from the rest room, he again noticed that the people in the store had stopped to watch him. In fact, they were almost waiting for him.

"I'll just take a Coke," Mason said, walking up to the counter. Just then, the mayor came out from an office talking to the large man who almost ran Mason over a few minutes earlier. When they saw Mason, they stopped talking and waited for Mason to complete his purchase. Awkwardly, Mason took his change and walked out of the store, passing Joe.

"Good day, Joe," he said.

"Have a nice day, Mason," Joe said with an insincere smile.

Before the door closed, Mason could hear the other gentleman ask Joe, "Who the hell is that guy, and what's he doing here?"

Mason walked over to a bench and sat down to drink his Coke and ponder the paranoid nature of the town. A quarter-mile look in either direction down the main dirt road rendered old small buildings or shops with a sparsely populated hillside in the background made up of old ranch houses and fences. Must be where Claire lives, he thought. After making small talk with a few locals, Mason finished his Coke and continued his walk through the town. He wandered in and out of antique stores to get out of the unseasonably warm temperatures. He walked into the Indian art store and was met by an elderly Indian woman.

"Hello, can I help you?" she said, walking up to Mason.

"Oh no, I'm just looking around," Mason said. "But you have some really nice paintings," he continued.

"Thank you, I paint them myself."

"You're really good."

"Thank you."

"Are you Keetoowah Cherokee Indian?"

"No, Apache. How do you know the Keetoowah?"

"Oh, a friend of mine told me about them."

"I see. Not many of them left; however, they have a long history in these parts. Many tribal doctors were Keetoowah."

"Interesting," Mason said, looking around the store at the paintings.

"Perhaps I have one that might interest you," she said, directing Mason to the back of the store. The back wall was covered in hanging Indian blankets. Moving aside several of the blankets, she removed the last one and exposed a hidden painting hanging on the wall. Mason was completely shocked as the woman pulled the blanket back, revealing a canvas painting. Stunned, he asked, "What, are you kidding me?"

Looking back at Mason, her eyes grew large and intense. She replied, "No Mason, I just thought you'd like it. Why do you ask?"

"How do you know my name?" he questioned.

Smiling, she told him, "It's a small town; word travels fast."

Realizing he was blowing things out of proportion, he said, "Of course. Sorry. I've just had some weird things happen lately." Walking closer to the painting, Mason examined the old ancient city being ravished by owls, with the silhouette of a man in the foreground walking away from it, as if she painted it right out of his dreams.

"When did you paint this?"

"Years ago. I almost threw it away, but my husband made me keep it. You seem intrigued by it."

"If you only knew the half of it," Mason said, shaking his head in disbelief. "I guess I'll take it. I'm going to Idledale tomorrow to get some money; can I pick it up then?"

"Of course. I'll have it ready for you."

"Thank you," Mason said, looking at the other artwork as she escorted him to the front of the store. Before walking out of the store, he stopped and turned to the Indian woman and asked, "Just out of curiosity, do you know what the painting means?"

"No, Mason, only you know what it means."

"Excuse me?"

Walking up to Mason, her tone changed. Looking him intensely in the eyes, she told him, "You are the man in the painting, Mason. Only you and Ah Puch know its true meaning."

"How do you know that? How do you know who Ah Puch . . .? How can that possibly be?"

She grabbed his hand. Mason experienced an unusually intense shock, stronger than he'd ever felt before. She said in a deep tone, "It's time for you to believe, Mason; he counts on you. Do not let him down." Breaking free from her grasp and trying to catch his breath, he realized he could not see her death day. "How did you block your . . .?" he started to question, but with his mind racing, he could not finish.

"Go Mason, watch for the signs," she said as she ushered him out the door and changed her "Open" sign to "Closed." Mason stood for a moment and tried to focus. His head still reeled from the shock. He needed a minute before he began to stumble back to Marcie's. Confused, he looked back at the shop, deeply perplexed by the elderly woman standing in the window intently watching him. He thought to himself, I've never not been able to see someone's death day. But somehow she blocked me from seeing it. Like she knew I was able to see it, which means she knows more than she led onto. I've got to go back to the shop.

Looking back at the shop, the woman was gone and the shop looked vacant. He continued his internal arguing. No, I'll talk to her tomorrow. I gotta get some rest; those things are going to kill me, he continued. The shocks were both physically and emotionally draining.

Chapter 44

Miram
Greenfield Ranch, Oklahoma
June 7, 2017

Sitting in a booth in the café, Mason noticing four men he hadn't seen or met before sitting in a booth across from him, looking over some paperwork and talking. When they noticed Mason looking at them, they stopped talking, got up, and left the café. Natalie grabbed a newspaper off the counter and got Mason's Coke. She dropped them off at his table and informed him his order would be right up. He now understood what it meant to be a regular. Mildly amused, he liked it.

"Thanks," Mason replied as he began flipping through the *USA Today* newspaper.

"*Terrorist group threatens U. S. again,*" ran across the top of page three. Reading the article and shaking his head, Mason didn't notice Claire walk in.

"Anything interesting?" she questioned, walking up to Mason's booth.

"Oh, hi Claire. No. Same old BS; economy sucks, Yankees are going to win it all, and another group of terrorists want to blow us up."

"Things don't seem to change much, do they?" she said, climbing into the booth. She continued, "You're a writer; don't you guys get bored reporting on the same stuff all the time?"

"Sure, with mundane stuff, but when you do investigative writing it's different. It's kind of like putting together a puzzle. You get a tip or an idea, you research it, it leads to other information, that leads to even more information, and the next thing you know, you've exposed or uncovered something that would otherwise still be covered up."

Claire watched as Mason talked about his chosen profession. He was passionate about it. She admired that. She was once like that. He was honest and his intentions were noble, even if slightly misguided. She knew about the bad things in the world. She remembered why she chose the simple life here with her grandfather. There was a time when she was passionate about wanting to do good in the world. What had happened—did the world beat her down? Maybe; she was content with the simple life, however. She had enough of the rat race. That was someone else's fight now. Although it was pleasant to see someone still fighting it.

"Sometimes it seems that reporters will do anything for a story, though," she said.

"Yes, some will, and I can't stand them. There's enough legitimate work out there to investigate rather than to actually have to manufacture it or stoop to some petty level, just to make a name for yourself. Too many innocent people end up getting hurt." Mason realized he was venting. "Sorry."

Claire figured there was more to Mason's story than he led on and said, "You sound like you have experience with that?"

"Let's just say I've met people that have done some pretty unscrupulous things for a story. Like putting a child through hell and using them to make a name for themselves."

"I guess using children is about as sleazy as it gets," Claire agreed.

"Here you go, Mason," Natalie said, dropping off his breakfast.

"Saved by the omelet," Mason said, lightening up their discussion.

Claire agreed. "Yes, that was getting a little deep. How was your tour of our town yesterday?"

"It was cool. You have a nice little town here. What do you know about the Indian art store down the street?"

"What do you mean? It's been there forever, and Miram's painted for as long as I can remember. Why do you ask?"

"No reason. I went in and she talked me into buying an interesting painting; that's all."

"I've only known you a couple of days, but I can tell there's more to it than that," Claire said and cautiously continued, "and you mean *he*, right?"

"What do you mean?" Mason asked while devouring his breakfast.

"You mean *he* talked you into buying a painting, right?"

"No, I meant *she* talked me into it. The old Indian woman who runs the store."

Looking at Mason curiously, Claire informed him, "There is no woman that runs that store. Miram is a man."

"Okay, I guess I'm on crack," Mason said with a heavy dose of sarcasm. "I'm telling you, there was an old Indian woman that showed me a painting that was practically right out of one of my dreams. So I told her I'd buy it and pick it up today."

"I don't know what to tell you. Miram has run that shop forever," Claire hesitantly informed Mason, wondering what his angle was.

"Well, I'm not making it up. Maybe Miram has a lady friend that you don't know about."

"No, he's kind of a recluse," she rebutted.

Putting his fork down and finishing his Coke, Mason was confident he would show Claire up. "Well, it's simple enough; you can come with me to pick it up," Mason said.

"All right. I will if that makes *you* feel better." Claire was going to call him out on this one. She didn't know what he was up to, but she was going to find out. She knew there was more to Mason then he showed, and she was going to find out what it was.

"Oh, it's not for me, trust me," he said confidently. "You'll see."

Jokingly, Claire said, "Yes, I guess we'll see; and by the way, remember, crack kills."

"Oh, you're funny. Were you a comedian in a previous life?" Mason replied, finishing his breakfast. "Lead the way, it's your funeral," he said as they slid out of the booth. He thought to himself, that's not funny; I need to figure out a way to change her date. The small reprieve from the stress of knowing Claire may be dead in a matter of days was still eating away at him. He wasn't sure what he learned from Kelly and Ray's deaths, but it had to teach him something. There had to be something he could do. His sadness was endearing. Claire took it as humility; maybe it was.

"Good God, Murph, tell them to get a room," Natalie said while they stood behind the counter and watched as the smiling, flirtatious banter went back and forth between them.

Claire gave Mason the unofficial tour while they walked down Main Street.

"That's the post office over there," Claire said, pointing across the street to an old brick building with a worn out sign hanging crooked by the front door. Walking by a small ice cream shop, Mason commented on the character of the buildings. "You know, in Chicago, people are salvaging bricks from old buildings like these and using them on new buildings. You just can't get good antiqued bricks like this anymore."

"I guess like styles, everything comes full circle."

Another building, one of the only two-story structures in the town, was the city library. Like in most cities, the library was probably the most modern looking building.

"I'm assuming you have the Internet there?" Mason asked.

"Yes, we have Wi-Fi and it usually works. The library is open twenty-four hours. Kind of nice when you can't sleep; you just go in and grab a book."

"You just leave the doors unlocked?"

"Yes Mason, look around," she replied, as if saying, When is he going to believe me?

"Well, there's the Indian art store," Claire said as they approached the small wooden building with a large totem pole in front. "Are you ready?"

"As ready as I'm going to be," Mason said as they walked up the steps and entered the small store. It was quiet and very clean. Antique lights and old art filled the small room.

"Hello? Miram?" Claire called out.

A small elderly Indian man walked slowly out from a back room holding a painting in his hands. His eyes squinted behind his glasses as a wrinkled smile crept across his face. "Hello Claire, it's nice to see you," he said.

"Miram, this is Mason."

"Pleased to meet you, Mason," he said, still holding the painting.

"Nice to meet you, Miram," Mason said with a half wave.

"For what do I owe the pleasure of this visit, Claire?" Miram asked.

"Well, I'll let Mason explain," Claire said, completely punting to Mason.

"Sure," Mason said, caught off guard. "I was in yesterday and a woman showed me a painting and I said I'd pick it up today?"

After chuckling and looking at Claire, he said, "I'm afraid that's not possible, Mr. Mason. I was not open yesterday. I was at home not feeling well."

With a grin now creeping across Claire's face, she tried to maintain her composure as she said, "Well Miram, it appears Mason was mistaken."

"Yes, I'm sorry. Perhaps I can show you something now?" Miram offered.

"No, I'm telling you, I was in here yesterday and a woman showed me a painting that I agreed to buy."

"Mason," Claire said, trying to help him save face, "it's okay. Why don't we get going?"

"No, no, I don't know what you guys are up to, but I was in here," Mason said a little more adamantly.

Claire again tried to deescalate Mason's tone. "Mason, let's take it easy. I think it's time for us to go. Come on," she said, grabbing Mason's arm and pulling him toward the door.

"Wait!" Mason said, stopping. "I'll show you the painting," he said, breaking Claire's hold on his arm and walking to the back of the store. Miram and Claire followed behind.

Trying to minimize any further embarrassment, Claire called out, pleading with him, "Mason, come on." As Claire reached to grab Mason again, Miram put his hand on hers, pushing it down and blocking her from grabbing him. "It's okay, Claire, let him be," he said quietly.

She just mouthed "Sorry" to Miram and they followed Mason to the back of the store.

Picking through the hanging blankets, Mason said, "It's back here somewhere, hold on."

Claire and Miram stood and watched as Mason frantically pushed blankets around. Finally, getting to the end of a row of blankets, Mason's face lit up. "Here! Here it is," he said, pulling down the blanket hanging in front of it and dropping it on the floor.

Hanging on the wall was the painting that he had seen the previous day. Looking back at Claire, he advised her, "See, I'm not crazy." A look at Miram revealed an expressionless face, just staring at the picture.

"How did you know about that?" Miram asked Mason.

"I told you, a woman yesterday showed it to me."

"Come on Miram, this is a lucky guess, right?" Claire asked.

"I don't know, Claire." Turning to Mason, he asked, "What did the woman look like, Mason?"

"I don't know, an older Indian woman."

"Come here, Mason," Miram said, walking to the back office. Picking up a picture off his desk, he showed it to Mason. "It was not her, was it?"

"Yes, that's her," Mason said excitedly, recognizing the smiling woman in the picture.

After turning to Claire to show her the picture, Miram turned back to Mason and told him softly, "This is my wife Amona, and she's been dead for nine years. So if this is some kind of joke, it's time to stop."

Mason looked at the picture, speechless. Confusion set in. His mind raced with thoughts. What are they talking about? This doesn't make any sense. She was here, he said over and over in his mind. He looked at Miram, who was not joking, and at Claire, who gave him a sad look. He could tell she felt pity for him because she thought she was right. What she thought was embarrassment on Mason's part was mere bewilderment.

"Look, she was here, and she told me, um, about the painting."

Recognizing the hiccup in Mason's speech, Claire jumped in. "She told you what?"

"Um, about the painting," he said, trying to cover his steps and not tell them that she actually said he was the man in the painting.

"That's not what you were going to say," she said, trying to get more out of him.

"Mason, what did she say to you exactly?" Miram asked.

Feeling like he was being interrogated, Mason said, "All right, I asked her what the painting meant and she said that I'd know what it was. But I don't have a clue. I have no idea what she's talking about."

"And that's all?" Miram asked slowly, removing his glasses.

"Yes, that's it. Then she pushed me out of the store."

Looking skeptically at Mason, Claire was not sure what he was up to.

"This is crazy, guys. Miram, don't tell me that you believe Mason talked to Amona?"

"Claire, I'm not making it up!" he pleaded.

"Claire, spirits visit our world all the time. For whatever reason, she had to tell Mason something, and I believe it was meant for him and only him," Miram said with his old, quiet voice. Walking back onto the floor, Miram pulled the picture down and the three of them looked at it.

An ancient city was surrounded by lush rain forest. In the middle of the city was a large stone pyramid structure. Behind the pyramid, Indians were being ravished by owls, and in the foreground the silhouette of a man was walking away from the carnage with his head hanging down.

"Take it, Mason. Obviously it was meant for you," Miram said, placing it inside a bag and handing it to Mason. "Amona painted it right before she died and almost threw it out. It scared her, but I kept it, because it always reminded me of her. Now I understand it has a different purpose."

Puzzled, Mason reluctantly accepted the painting. "Thank you, Miram."

Walking out of the store with the painting, Mason and Claire walked back to Marcie's without saying a word. Mason couldn't get his mind off of the exchange between Amona and himself the previous day. He figured that he couldn't see her death day because she was already dead. This is nuts, he thought. He knew he couldn't tell Claire or Miram, but it made sense now. I still don't know about the painting and the dreams, he thought. What was it all about? he wondered. I have to figure this out, he told himself. Claire may be the next victim of this ability.

Arriving back at Marcie's, they stopped out front and Claire broke the silence. "Look Mason, I'm not sure what you did, but I'm not stupid. I know you worked me. I don't know how or even why, but I don't appreciate being lied to or being made to look like an ass."

"Claire, I never meant—"

"Save it, Mason!" Claire said, cutting Mason off and visibly annoyed now. "You don't owe me anything; it doesn't matter. I'll call you tomorrow when I'm ready to go into Idledale."

"Claire!" Mason called out, but she was already walking away. Mason turned around to see a smiling Marcie standing in the doorway.

"I told you, Mason, be careful."

Chapter 45

Joe's Visit
Greenfield Ranch, Oklahoma
June 7, 2017

Later that evening, trying to forget about the earlier events, Claire sipped a chai tea on her sofa in her living room and tried to read a book. She couldn't get her mind off of what Mason had done to her earlier in the day. She pondered what his motives could possibly be to want to trick her. A knock at her front door interrupted her internal discord. She took a sip of tea, pulled her robe tight, and opened the door.

"Hi gramps, come on in." She knew it would be a matter of time before her grandfather would be there. He had the pulse of everything in the town. His worn-out cowboy boots made a distinct clicking sound on her hardwood floors as he walked into her living room. He removed his hat and looked at Claire for a second before speaking.

"Thanks Claire. I hope I'm not interrupting anything?"

"No, just reading," she said as she sat back on her sofa.

Joe sat on an adjacent sofa and could see she wasn't her jovial self. Unfortunately, he was there to talk about the exact thing that made her despondent in the first place. A conversation he didn't want to have but needed to.

"Good. I wanted to talk to you about today."

Expecting the visit, she replied, "I wondered how long it would take to get to you."

"Is everything all right?" Joe asked. It was almost a rhetorical question; he could tell she was visibly upset and definitely not all right. He hadn't seen her this shaken in a long time. "Why don't you tell me what happened?"

She had rehearsed the story in her head a hundred times, and every time it made no sense. She gathered her thoughts one more time and distilled them into a brief statement summarizing what happened: "Mason pulled some game at Miram's place and I guess I lost my temper when he wouldn't stop." She knew if she told him the whole story about Amona and the picture, she would look like a complete fool.

"Miram says he had nothing to do with it, Claire. Whatever Mason did, he did on his own."

Claire concluded there was only one logical explanation. Mason got in there somehow and was able to look around; that was it. The door was probably unlocked. She just wasn't sure why after he pulled it, he wouldn't come clean.

"Well he is a reporter, who knows; maybe he has something up his sleeve. At any rate, we should keep an eye on him," Joe said.

Claire became animated and her competitive spirit came back to her. She sat up on the sofa and, as if trying to convince herself, she explained, "I know, it's just that usually I can tell when someone's feeding me a line of BS, but with Mason I didn't see it coming. I knew he was lying to me, but none of the physiologic signals were there. His pupils didn't dilate, he didn't fidget, his eye movements were completely consistent, his respirations were shallow, and his body movements were totally convincing. I'm just not sure how he did it." He could be a sociopath, she thought, which would be hard to see in such a short time frame.

"Well, don't beat yourself up about it. He got lucky, and that's exactly why we don't underestimate anybody." Joe stood up as he could see Claire was back from her funk. He put his cowboy hat back on and walked to the door. Claire followed.

"Yes, but I don't believe in luck. I'm usually good at picking out the scammers."

"Your emotions aren't clouding your vision, are they?" her grandfather said, pointing out the obvious.

"No, not at all!" Claire said with conviction and complete denial. Her own physiologic response to the question, however, made her examine that possibility further.

"Look, he may have pulled one over on me this time, but that's not going to happen again," she assured him. Her competitive nature took this as a jab.

"That's the spirit, Claire," Joe said, examining Claire's behavior and knowing that emotions may very well have compromised her sense of judgment. "We'll keep an eye on him; if he's up to something, it'll come out. It always does," he continued.

"All right. Thanks, Gramps." She gave him a hug before he left the house. Although she dreaded the visit, it reignited something in her that had been gone a long time: passion.

Standing in the doorway watching Joe drive away, Claire said to herself, "What are you up to, Mr. Mason? Whatever it is, I'm going to find out."

Claire took being made a fool of as a personal wakeup call, and as a challenge. Deep down she had a glimmer of respect for Mason. Not many people could actually pull off what he did. Her guard was typically heightened and her defenses usually too strong to break down. The challenge was almost endearing to her. Indeed, emotions played a part in her being tricked, she concluded as she returned to her chai tea. Her training and experience, however, were going to usher in the next round.

Chapter 46

Claire's Day
Greenfield Ranch, Oklahoma
June 8, 2017

"Hi, Mason, how's breakfast?" Claire said, walking up to Mason reading the paper in his usual booth. She was far more cheerful than Mason expected.

"Hi Claire," Mason said, looking up. "Look, about yesterday—"

"It's all right, Mason," Claire said, cutting him off midsentence. "I came to apologize; I was out of line and I'm sorry for freaking out on you."

"It's fine, believe me; I'm used to it." Mason wasn't sure what prompted the 180-degree turnaround, but he was glad it didn't linger on. It also still didn't answer the question of "why." Claire's death day was rapidly approaching, and he needed to figure out how to stop it. Fighting with Claire was not productive; if he was to stop this train, he needed her to cooperate, not fight him on it.

"What do you mean?" Claire asked inquisitively. Her senses were in full gear. She was paying attention now more than ever.

"Let's just say people don't always understand me."

"Interesting. Any reason why?" Claire asked, trying to get more information for her private counterassault later on.

"That's a story for another time. Suffice it to say that what happened yesterday with you has happened before."

"Really, the same talking-to-ghosts thing?"

Recognizing the mild sarcasm that usually accompanied the discussion of his unique ability, Mason knew that the line of questioning would probably continue until he gave her something.

"No, not exactly, Claire, but similarly weird. I've had some strange things happen to me and there just aren't a lot of answers."

Claire was torn between wanting to get information for her personal defenses and genuinely wanting to help. She recognized herself being sucked in again. He's good, she thought. But not this time, she continued. Much wiser than she was yesterday, she cautiously played along.

"Mason, talk to me," she said. "I'm a good listener," especially when I need information, she finished saying to herself.

"Maybe later when I figure some things out," Mason said, becoming somewhat despondent. The things he was trying to figure out dealt with Claire dying.

"In fact, Claire, give me your hand," he said in a very candid manner.

"Why?" she said shyly.

"Just let me see your hand, please," Mason said again, reassuring her it wasn't a come on.

"All right. Relax, Mason, you're starting to stress me out," she said as she lifted her hand across the table. When Mason grabbed it they both felt a shock. "JUNE 16, 2017" flashed to Mason's mind.

"No way," he said under his breath. His fear was confirmed yet again. Claire's death day was in fact next week. Can Joe have the same one? He thought he had been mixing them up. Mason second-guessed himself and had hoped he was wrong, but something he was starting to get used to was not reading into it. It is what it is, he thought.

Pulling her hand back and rubbing the shock out of it, Claire said, "No way to what?"

"Huh?" Mason said, not hearing a word Claire said and being too preoccupied to focus.

"Hello, Mason?" Claire tried to say.

Breaking his thought, he came back. "What, Claire, did you say something?"

"Yes, what was that?" she asked.

"What?"

"The 'I want to hold your hand' thing?"

"Oh, nothing," Mason said. "But I have to get going; I have some stuff to do," Mason continued, as if on a mission.

Hesitantly and trying to get Mason to focus on her by trying to look into his glazed eyes, Claire asked, "Do you still want to go to Idledale with me?"

"Yes, give me a half hour, okay?" Mason said.

"Sure, I was thinking more like two hours, but thirty minutes is okay."

"Great, see you in a while. Thanks for the breakfast," he said, heading for the door.

Claire just sat in the booth in dismay at what just happened. Natalie walked up and asked, "Did Mason just blow you off?"

"No, I don't think so. I think he's got something on his mind," a puzzled Claire said.

"It looked like he did, I just wasn't sure. I mean, it's none of my business, I just—"

"Natalie, I know! Go back to work," Claire barked at her. "And I'm leaving for the rest of the day; be sure to lock up," she continued as she left to go home and change.

Chapter 47

Thunder and Lightning
Greenfield Ranch, Oklahoma
June 8, 2017

Mason went back to his room to think about Claire's death day being on the same day as Joe's. "There's no way it's a coincidence; they're going to be in a car accident or something," he thought out loud. "I've got to figure this out; I have to keep them separated on that day," he continued. Pulling out a notepad, he wrote down Claire and Joe's day, June 16, 2017. While sitting on the edge of the bed thinking about the day and knowing it was in another eight days, Mason's mind raced.

A knock at the door shattered his thoughts. "Yes, can I help you?" Mason said, opening the door.

"Hi Mason," Marcie said, her hands full with towels and sheets.

"Oh, hi Marcie, come on in."

"Hi, Mason. I didn't mean to disturb you."

"No, it's fine. I'm just getting ready to go to Ideldale with Claire. I've never heard of a town that didn't accept Visa, but apparently this one doesn't," Mason seemed to say to himself, like he still couldn't believe it.

"I'm just going to change out the linens and I'll leave you alone. Unless you don't want to be alone," she said with the usual sultry grin, showing her crooked smile.

"Um, no, it's, um, well, I have to get going to meet Claire," Mason stuttered as he nervously left the room.

"Okay, but if you need anything, let me know," she said to a hurried Mason.

As Mason shuffled out of the front doors of Marcie's house he was stopped in his tracks.

"What is that?" he asked Claire, who was waiting in Marcie's driveway.

"Maybe they don't have these in Chicago, but out here we call them horses. You have heard of them, haven't you?" she asked.

"Yes, I think I saw one in a zoo once," he replied. As he walked closer, he appreciated their strength and beauty. They were large and magnificent creatures. In his amazement, all he could muster was, "Are we taking them into Idledale?"

"No, that would take a couple of days, unless you want to. We would just have to camp overnight?"

"No, I'm not much of a camper," he said, never taking his gaze off of them.

She could tell he had never been so close to a horse. The rookies all had the same endearing response. One she hadn't seen in years. It was a nice reminder of how lucky she was.

"They're beautiful, and seeing that there are two, I'm assuming one is for me?" Mason asked hesitantly.

"Oh, you are sharp," Claire mocked.

"Are we taking them anywhere in particular?"

"Do you fish?" she asked.

"Fish?" Mason pondered. "I go to fish fries on Fridays during lent. Does that count?"

"Yes, close enough," she said with a smile.

"I've never fished a day in my life," Mason reluctantly admitted, "and while I'm decrying any semblance of masculinity that I once had, I have to admit that I've never ridden a horse either."

"Well, should make for an interesting day, I suppose. Come on, load up; it'll be fun."

"It sounds like it'll be painful."

"Most things that are fun usually are, Mason."

Mason looked at Claire in her cowboy hat, sunglasses, blue jeans, and boots sitting in the saddle on top of her massive white and black horse. He knew that he really didn't have a say in the matter, nor did he want one. As Mason mounted up onto the large brown horse next to Claire, he was pleasantly surprised that Claire still wanted to see him.

"So what's this guy's name?" Mason asked.

"You're on Thunder, and my girl is Lightning," Claire said while patting her horse. "You ready to roll, Mason?"

"Where are we rolling to?"

"I didn't really feel like going to Idledale today. So I thought we'd go fishing at Chapman Lake. It's a couple of miles south of here."

"Sounds good; just remember, I've never been on a horse, so take it easy on me."

"No problem. Can I give you a tip?"

"Yes, that would be great. What do I do?"

Claire looked over and smiled at Mason, then hunched over into a racing position, kicked Lightning, took off like a bat out of hell, and yelled, "Hang on!"

"Oh shit!" Mason yelled as Thunder took off after Lightning. "Thanks a lot!"

As Claire raced down the dirt main street feeding Mason a cloud of dust, Mason held on for dear life.

Natalie and Murph stood in the picture window of Claire's Café and watched as Claire and Mason rapidly approached on their horses.

"Poor Mason. He has no idea what he's in for, does he?" Natalie said to Murph, shaking her head.

"That boy's gonna hurt tomorrow," Murph said with utter amazement as he watched Mason's look of sheer terror blaze past them while trying to keep up with Lightning.

"Unless she kills him today," Natalie said, following the dust cloud down the street.

Chapter 48

A New Safe Place
Greenfield Ranch, Oklahoma
June 8, 2017

"This is nice out here, Claire. Very peaceful," Mason commented as they trotted through the woods. The trees were full and leaves were bright green. The sounds of insects were a peaceful substitution for the sounds of engines and car horns.

"I love it. Not sure I could ever live where I couldn't have my horses."

"I can see why; they're awesome. Then again, my ass doesn't think so right now."

"You're a quick learner, Mason; you're doing pretty good on old Thunder."

"Trust me, it's all him, not me."

"Either way, not bad for your first ride."

"Thanks, I had a good teacher. Hey, is that the lake?" Mason said, pointing off in the distance.

"Yes, that's it."

With that, Mason and Thunder took off, leaving Claire and Lightning behind. Claire smiled and watched Mason rise out of the saddle, hunch over into a racing position, and make a mad dash for the lake. Aerodynamically cutting through the air like a bullet, Mason felt like he was winning the Kentucky Derby. He had never experienced anything like it in his life. At peace with nature and the universe, nothing was smoother or faster than Thunder at that moment in time.

Claire fought her competitive spirit to race him to the lake. She didn't want to ruin Mason's moment. Instead, she followed Mason and let him feel the exhilaration of horse racing. She admired his playful nature and was reminded of her first ride when she was eight years old, one of the last and fondest memories she had with her father. Inside she was touched that she was there for Mason's first ride.

"Whoa, Thunder," Mason said, pulling back on the reins as he arrived at the water's edge, followed closely by Claire and Lightning.

"Nice, Mason. You sure you haven't ridden before?" Claire asked sarcastically, knowing she could have blown him away if she wanted.

"No, this is my first time."

"You must be a natural," she continued as she stroked his ego and dismounted.

"Well, you know, I do work out," Mason said, as if trying not to brag.

"Oh, I'm sure you do. I can tell," she said.

"Really, I do. I mean, obviously not all the time, but you know," Mason said, trying to retract his cocky statement. He dismounted Thunder and stretched. He could feel the aches starting to set in. He knew tomorrow would hurt. But it was worth it.

"Okay, Richard Simmons, help me with the gear," Claire chuckled.

"What? You know I'm not gay, right?" Mason said, surprised.

"Oh sure, if you say so."

"No really, I'm not."

"Why, you have a problem with that?" she teased.

"No, it's just not my thing, that's all. If you are, it's—"

"I'm not," she said, cutting him off and thrusting a canvas pack into his chest.

"Good God, what are we fishing for, sharks?" Mason said, commenting on the size and weight of the pack.

"You plan on eating, don't you?" Claire asked.

"I guess."

"I packed a lunch and some drinks."

"Nice, you're pretty prepared. What do you want me to do?" Mason asked, trying to help.

"Here, assemble this fishing pole and I'll get your line ready."

As they unpacked the gear and got their fishing poles ready, Mason couldn't help but think about Claire's death day. He struggled with whether or not to tell her. He liked her, although he knew he would be leaving soon. He knew he made a mistake not telling Kelly, but he didn't want to hurt anyone, especially Claire. He stared out over the still peaceful water, wondering again why every time he started to like someone, they had to die. A morbid proposition, he thought. Maybe if I leave, she won't have to? Would Richard have died if I wasn't there? he thought. How would I have known? He had to figure out how to change Claire's date, period.

"It's beautiful, isn't it?" Claire asked, walking up behind Mason, breaking his thoughts.

"Yes, it's awesome," Mason said, regrouping his thoughts. "I could sit out here for hours and think," he continued.

"Funny you say that. I love to come down here and chill out. You know, like my safe place."

"It's a great safe place to have. In fact, I may need to replace mine with this," Mason said, looking over the water and surrounding woods.

"I'll share it with you, but you have to keep it between us," Claire said as she moved in front of Mason, blocking his view of the lake. Standing dangerously close, Mason lifted Claire's sunglasses and moved them to the top of her head, exposing her big brown eyes staring back at him. He looked past her high cheekbones at her full black eyebrows and into her chocolate-colored eyes.

She reached for his hands. As they touched, their fingers instinctively intertwined. With one harmonious conversion, they kissed. As their lips met, time came to a complete standstill. An energy pulsated through their bodies, fusing their souls together as one. The longer they kissed, the harder it would be to separate their souls back into two. For a brief moment in time, they knew each other their entire lives. Together, they transcended to a higher place, if only temporarily. Until a vociferous electrifying shock brought them back abruptly, nearly knocking them to the ground.

"JUNE 16, 2017" registered a painful reminder again in Mason's mind.

"Wow, that was pretty intense," Claire said, breaking her contact with Mason and trying to catch her breath from the shock.

"Yes, I'd say so," Mason said, shaking off the shock. "It must be the dry air."

"I've lived here a long time, Mason; it's not the air."

"Then it must be your electrifying personality," he said, trying to cover up the real reason.

"I don't know about that. There's something about you. I just can't put my finger on it."

"It's probably nothing," Mason said, discounting it.

"Oh, it's something," Claire said. "I suppose we could try it again just to make sure," she continued playfully, moving back into, and intentionally violating, Mason's personal space bubble. Mason hesitated because he didn't want to shock her again. Torn between a central nervous system shock and a heartache, Mason looked into Claire's eyes. He was powerless. Mason's hesitation was charming to Claire, as if to not look too anxious, which drew Claire in even more. As endorphins rushed through his system, his heartbeat began to do the tango. He succumbed to the mounting tension and embraced Claire, trying to absorb the electrical pulse shooting through his chest as they kissed. Although "JUNE 16, 2017" flashed to Mason, he didn't even notice it.

A few hours earlier, they were strangers going fishing to get away. Now they were something different. Fate would bring them together for some other purpose. The thing about fate, however, is only she knows what she wants.

"If I knew fishing was like this, I would've taken it up a long time ago," Mason said, breaking away from Claire.

"Believe me; not all fishing is like this. In fact, this is one of the best fishing trips I've been on since I can remember, and we haven't even fished yet."

"Me too. Of course, this is also the only fishing trip I've ever been on, but it's still the best."

"Not to sound cliché, but I still felt something," Claire said.

"Are you all right?" Mason nervously asked.

"Yes, are you?"

"Yes, I think I felt the same thing; maybe we have a connection."

"Now that's cliché."

"Yeah, on that note, maybe we should fish," Mason said, trying to save face.

"Good call," Claire said, allowing him some wiggle room. "I brought sandwiches if you want to eat first," she continued.

"That sounds great; kissing you really wore me down," Mason said, as if blaming Claire.

"Don't make me kiss you again. I'll really make it hurt this time," Claire said with a smile and leaning in to kiss Mason one more time. Like static electricity being discharged, the shock, although present, was much less than the other two times.

"For the record, that didn't hurt," a smiling Mason said.

"Hmm, I guess I'll need to work on that," Claire said as she unpacked the sandwiches.

Chapter 49

Path to Conversion
Stanley River, North Dakota
June 8, 2017

Drifting on the Stanley River, Malik turned on his cell phone and called back to Rabwah to give his superiors an update. "Hallid, we have made it to the Stanley River," Malik said into his cell phone.

"Good, Malik. Any problems?" the voice on the other end said.

"Yes, we had a problem. We ran into four men smuggling drugs into the country. We tried to let them go, but they refused to listen."

"Did you kill them?"

"Yes, just like you said to. Then we disposed of the bodies and sank the boat."

"That's four infidels you killed. Good work. Your training in the Iranian Revolutionary Guard has already paid off."

"Thank you, Hallid."

"Be sure to study the map in case any other problems arise. This package must get to the transfer point, at all costs."

"I understand; we are still on schedule. I'll be in contact when we get to the Missouri River." As day broke, they pulled the raft to the edge of the river, camouflaged it, and took turns sleeping while the other kept watch.

Rabwah, Pakistan

Through the window of his study, Ahmed saw Macmul's limousine pull up in the circular drive of the palace. He hurried out the front doors to meet his brother in the driveway. "Ah, Macmul," he said, greeting him with a hug. "Good news; the package is getting closer."

The two walked into the palace and directly to the pool area, where most of their meetings took place. Scantily clad servant girls brought them food and drink. Macmul looked at them as if they were property. He could hardly wait for the meeting to be over so he could get on with his indoctrination training of the girls. He engaged Ahmed.

"That is indeed good news, Ahmed." Cutting to the chase, he continued, "When do we strike?"

"Patience, my brother. Remember, we only get one chance to cripple them. Once they are down, we'll have the leverage to subvert them."

Macmul tilted his head down, looked at Ahmed out of the top of his dark sunglasses, and clarified, "You mean *convert* them, right?"

Ahmed quickly and decorously corrected himself with a deceitful grin. "Yes, of course, *convert* them. I get so excited."

A skeptical Macmul shrugged off the Freudian slip. "Me too, brother."

Ahmed shifted their focus. "I just met with one of al-Qaida's generals. He has assured me that they too will join the effort if we can prove to them we are serious."

"Can we trust them?" Macmul asked. "They have always mocked us."

"I'm not sure yet, but it won't matter because they have no idea what the target is. And they won't know until we have already proven that it was us. There is no way they can take credit for it. Nobody knows but us," Ahmed continued, hardly able to contain his excitement.

"Do you know the target, Ahmed?"

"All in good time, my brother. Allah will reveal it to me when he's ready."

"Hopefully 'Allah' does not toy with us," Macmul said, knowing that they both knew that "Allah" was a someone.

"I wouldn't worry about that, Macmul," he assured. Macmul knew Ahmed knew something, but wasn't giving it up. He'd known Ahmed his entire life. This was different and more real than any of his many grandiose ideas. Whatever it was, Macmul trusted his brother.

"Now, isn't there a wedding this weekend?" Ahmed asked.

"Yes, one of the Blacksmiths."

"Good, bring me the bride. I must make sure Allah seals her with his blessing before she takes her vow."

"Ahmed, is this a new rite for us?"

"All right, all right," Ahmed said, waving his arm as if he had made a mistake. "I'm sorry brother, I meant *we* must make sure she is blessed," he said, smiling sarcastically followed by a devious laugh.

"With pleasure. All praise Allah!" Macmul said, leaving the palace.

Chapter 50

Strangers No More
Greenfield Ranch, Oklahoma
June 8, 2017

"We should probably start heading back; it's going to get dark soon," Claire said, walking toward a serene Mason sitting on a log at the edge of the water.

"Already? I think I'm finally in my zone."

"It's all right, Mason, some days they just don't bite," Claire said, comforting Mason.

"Maybe they're scared of me."

"Yes, maybe they're afraid you'll shock them."

"Funny."

Just then, Mason stood up. "Did you see that?"

Looking out over the water at Mason's bobber, they watched it bob around.

"You're getting a bite, Mason."

Mason clenched his fishing pole tightly and intently watched the bobber.

"What do I do?" Mason asked.

"Hold tight, he's just checking it out right now. Wait until he takes the bait, then pull back."

They watched as the bobber plunged under the water and the line became taut.

"Pull, Mason, you got one!" Claire yelled as Mason pulled back on the rod and began to reel the fish in.

"This guy's a fighter, I can tell," Mason said, struggling with the rod.

"You're doing great. Keep reeling him in; I'll get the net." Claire waded out a few feet into the water and could see the fish flipping under the water. Bending down and trying to follow it, she called out to Mason, "A little more, Mason, I almost got it." Then with one swoop of the net, Claire scooped up the fish.

"Got it! Come here, check it out! She's a beauty!" she called out to Mason.

Mason dropped his pole and ran into the water to see his first catch. "Awesome, that's the first fish I've ever caught. What kind is it?" he asked.

"It's a rainbow trout. Nice job," she said, giving Mason a high five. She dipped the net back into the water to let the fish get water.

Mason asked, "Now what do we do?"

Not having any intention of keeping it, Claire carefully explained to Mason, "Well, we could take it with us, but we have to clean it."

"What do you mean clean it?"

"We have to gut it."

"You mean cut out its guts?"

"Yes."

"That's disgusting; do we have to?"

"If you want to keep it we will have to. Or we could catch and release?" Claire asked, knowing exactly what the answer would be.

"Do people do that?"

"Oh yes, that's what I usually do," Claire said. "But it's your catch, you decide. A lot of people like to fish but don't actually want to kill them, so they let it go," she continued.

"Yes, it's getting late; let's just let it go," Mason decided.

"Good choice," Claire reassured. "Now, hold the fish in one hand and with the other carefully remove the hook," she explained.

Mason backed the hook out of the fish's mouth, set the ten-inch fish into the water, and watched as it swam away.

"That was really cool; I can't believe I've never done this before," Mason said.

"We really should get going. It's definitely going to get dark soon," Claire said, looking up at the setting sun.

"Yes, of course," Mason agreed. "By the way, you ever catch one that big?" he continued.

Not wanting to burst his bubble or shatter his ego, Claire just smiled and offered, "I don't know; that was pretty good size."

"It was probably almost two feet, right?" Mason asked.

"Yes, probably pretty close," Claire said, rolling her eyes.

The ride back was a quiet one. It was the impending internal conflict of knowing that they would eventually part ways. They both knew how things would play out. What they didn't know was the only commonality between their versions of what would happen was that they would both go their separate ways. They both, however, had very different versions of how that actually would play out. Mason's car would get fixed and he would leave in a few days. Their lives couldn't be more diametrically opposed; and yet, as fate would have it, there they were. As they approached the town, Mason felt compelled to tell Claire the dismal news about her forthcoming doom.

"Claire, hang on. Before we go into town I think I need to tell you something."

Sensing where Mason was going, Claire cut him off before he could get sentimental on her. "Mason, we had a great time. Let's not complicate it. We both know the deal; let's not overanalyze things."

"No, you don't understand. There's—"

"Mason! I get it. I like you too, but it's complicated," Claire said, cutting Mason off.

"What? That's not what I mean. I mean, yes, but no. I—"

Cutting Mason off again, Claire leaned across her horse and kissed Mason again and smiled. "Last one to the restaurant does a shot!" she said, kicking Lightning and taking off, completely ignoring Mason.

"Oh God, not again," Mason said in hot pursuit.

They trotted down Main Street toward the café. Mason was beyond sore but had one of the best days of his life. He definitely didn't regret checking out the small towns now. They made it back to Claire's café, tied the horses to the post outside the front door, and went inside. The soft cushion in the booth was a welcome relief to Mason's rear. Sitting in the booth, acutely in tune with muscles in his legs he never knew he had, Mason was thankful the horse riding was over.

"I've never been this sore in my life."

"Wait until tomorrow; it'll be worse," Claire said.

"I can't wait."

"Here, the tequila will help you not notice it," Claire said, handing Mason a shot glass.

"I'm not much of a tequila drinker, but bottoms up," Mason said, wincing as the tequila burned his esophagus.

Frank walked into the restaurant and over to their booth.

"Hey, there you are. I've been looking for you, Mason."

"Oh, hi, Frank. I've just been getting worked over by Claire and her horses."

"Claire took you out on her horses, did she?" Frank said, looking at Claire, surprised. "That's mighty nice of her," he continued, as if there was some kind of inside joke in there somewhere. Claire just looked down, as if she was being passively scolded.

"Yes, I'm already sore."

"What can we do for you, Frank?" Claire interjected with a serious tone.

"Of course," Frank said, realizing he was being rude. "I just wanted to let Mason know I've started working on his transmission, but I'm waiting on a few more parts. I should receive them this weekend. I hope to have it wrapped up a couple of days after that."

"Great. Thanks, Frank," Mason replied.

"No problem. I'll let you get back to your dinner. Have a good night," Frank said, extending his hand to Mason.

"I'll talk to you later," Mason said, shaking Frank's hand. "JUNE 16, 2017" flashed in Mason's mind accompanied with the all too familiar shock.

"Quite the handshake you have there, Mason," Frank said, shaking off the shock he felt from Mason.

"I get that sometimes," Mason replied, then looked at Claire, hoping she didn't pick up Frank's comment. Too late. Claire looked back at him curiously.

"Good-bye, Frank," Claire said, visibly annoyed by the interruption. Turning her attention back to Mason, she asked, "What's with everyone getting shocked by you?"

Looking at Claire as if she completely insulted him, he asked, "What did you say?"

"What? I didn't mean anything by it."

"No, it's all right, but what did you say?"

"It just seems that every time you shake someone's hand, you shock them."

Recognizing the profound observation that Claire made and thinking about what she said, Mason looked at her while his mind went a mile a minute. Mason now thought about Frank's death day. He has the same day as Claire and as Joe, Mason thought to himself. No way, something is getting mixed up, he continued to think.

"Do you two need anything else?" Natalie said, walking up to their booth.

"No, we're fine. Thank you, Natalie," Claire said.

As Natalie started to walk away, Mason stopped her. "Wait, Natalie!"

"Yes, Mason."

"I just want to thank you for everything you've done for me," he said, stalling and trying to figure out a way to shake her hand.

"Okay, you're welcome, Mason. Do you need anything else?"

"No, but thank you," he said, standing up and outstretching his hand to her.

Hesitantly, she shook his hand and they both experienced a shock. "JUNE 16, 2017" flashed in Mason's mind.

"Ouch! You shocked me," Natalie said, releasing his hand.

"Sorry, static electricity," he said, looking at Claire with a scared look on his face.

"Anything else?" Natalie asked.

"No, thanks," Mason said.

"Mason, are you all right?" Claire asked.

Mason climbed back into the booth and replied, "Yes, yes, I'm fine." Mason looked down, overwhelmed with yet another death day, trying to process the information.

"See, I told you, you keep shocking people."

"Yes, pretty strange," he said with his voice trailing off.

"Anything you want to tell me, Mason?"

Wrestling with whether to tell her or not, he realized he needed to see the extent of what was happening.

"No, just a weird coincidence," he offered.

Not buying it, Claire recognized the oddness of his situation and knew there was more to it. Rather than press him, she decided she would get more information later.

"Well, it's been a fun day, but I have to get Lightning and Thunder home," Claire said.

"I'm pretty beat too. Can I give you a hand with the horses?" Mason offered.

"No, I got it. Go get some rest; you're looking a little tired."

"Yes, and sore. Thanks for everything; I had a really great time today."

"Me too," Claire said as they walked out to the horses and stopped.

"I'll see you tomorrow," Claire said, moving in and giving Mason a good-night kiss, then riding off on Lightning with Thunder in tow.

When Mason got back to his room he laid down, tired, sore, confused, and saddened. He closed his eyes and wrestled with Claire's death day. As he faded from consciousness he found himself face to face with the all-too-familiar tribal Indian leader standing in a lush tropical forest.

"Who are you?" Mason asked.

"I am one of many who are part of the lineage."

"Lineage? Lineage to what?" Mason asked.

"To Ah Puch, of course. You still haven't figured this out, have you Mason?"

"How do you know my name?"

"We are brothers, Mason."

"Brothers?"

"I am Ma'xu and I, like you, have been given a gift from Ah Puch."

"So you know the same thing I do?"

"No, Ah Puch gives you what you need."

"What did he give you, Ma'xu?"

"I received a gift that I needed, just like you received one that you need."

"I don't see why I need this thing. It causes a lot of pain."

"In my time, physical ability was more important than the ability of the mind. Today it is not so. Happiness is not always good, wisdom is gained through sorrow, and knowledge is gained through wisdom. Your wisdom must accompany knowledge."

"Why are you telling me this?" Mason questioned.

"Because Ah Puch has a special purpose for you."

"And I'm sure it involves people dying, right?" Mason asked.

"I do not know what that purpose is. It is for you and only you to know."

"What exactly happens when my purpose is fulfilled? Will Ah Puch then have no use for me?"

"You have little faith in the goodness of Ah Puch. If you serve him well, you will be rewarded."

"With what? I'm not sure I can handle any more of his gifts."

"I do not know; it is between you and him, nobody else."

"Do I have a choice?"

"Yes, but it is a great honor to find favor with the gods. To deny them will surely end in your death."

"What about— Hey, where are you going?" Mason asked as Ma'xu began to fade away.

"Embrace your gift," the Indian said as he disappeared.

Mason woke up sweating and sucked in a deep breath, as if he had stopped breathing. Looking around and then at the alarm clock on the end table next to his bed, he saw it was 12:38 a.m. What the heck was that? he wondered. I got to get some air. Mason got up and went outside to try and process his dream.

Chapter 51

Claire's Past
Greenfield Ranch, Oklahoma
June 9, 2017

Troubled by his dream, Mason walked down the dimly lit main street to clear his head. This dream was too real. What did Ma'xu mean? The midnight air was cool and dry. Taken in by the quietness, he was intrigued by the peaceful, serene feeling of a midnight walk. It was something that he never had in Chicago. He approached Sid's Bar and could see four people standing outside of the main door talking. While approaching them, he could start to make out their voices.

"Look, I don't care. I don't trust him; he's still a reporter," he heard a man's voice say. Realizing they were talking about him, Mason quickly hid on the side of the building and began to eavesdrop before they saw him coming.

He now could make out Claire's voice saying, "All I did was take him fishing; it's not a big deal, Joe."

"All you were supposed to do is keep an eye on him, nothing more."

"And that's what I did."

"Are you sure that's all it was?" a man whose voice Mason couldn't recognize questioned her.

"And how exactly would you like me to do it, keep him in the café all day?" she shot back. "He wants to get out and see the town; that's what people do when they go to a new town. So why don't I let him just wander around unaccompanied?" she continued.

"It sounds like that's what you did," the unrecognized man said.

"What the hell is that supposed to mean, Jake?"

"I'm just saying whatever happened at Miram's could've been avoided had you been with him."

"It was the middle of the day; everyone should've been watching him," she replied.

"Jake, relax. Claire's right; we all should've been a little more cognizant of what he's doing. If Claire sticks to him like a magnet, he may get suspicious," said a third man's voice that Mason recognized from the grocery. "Look, tell Frank to move his ass on getting his car ready or I'll have him selling bibles in the Ukraine," the man scolded.

"His car will be done in a couple days and he's gone," Joe reassured the man.

Mason had heard all he needed to hear and stepped out from the side of the building as if just walking up on them. Claire, being the first to recognize him, spoke up first to alert the other three that he was there.

"Hi, Mason, you're out late," she said as the other three turned around to see him. Looking disappointed in her, he didn't want to blow his newly gained information and didn't lead on that he knew she was babysitting him.

"Yes, I couldn't sleep so I thought I'd take a walk, maybe get a drink," he said, looking at the antiqued script on the bar windows.

"Hi, Mason," Joe said. "This is Rod Thompson; I believe you two met the other day. He runs the town grocery store, and this is Jake Nolan, this is his bar."

"Nice to meet you guys," Mason said holding up his hand with a half wave. Their demeanor and tone changed the minute they saw Mason. He knew they were putting on a show.

"Nice to meet you, Mason. Come on in, we'll get you squared away," Jake said, walking to the door, while Rod just looked at Mason with an odd glare.

"You want some company?" Claire added.

"No, it's all right," Mason said. "Don't let me interrupt you."

"Oh, I think we're done," Claire said with raised eyebrows to Joe.

"Have a good evening," Joe said with a completely disingenuous smile.

"I'll see you guys tomorrow," she continued as she ushered Mason into the bar. They weaved their way through the tables, across the oak hardwood floor, and made their way up the long dark mahogany wood bar. A finely polished sheen on the bar top reflected the blue and red neon Coors beer sign hanging behind the bar. The long rectangular mirror mounted to the wall behind the bar gave the illusion of the bar being much larger than it really was. The gold gilding around the edges of the mirror glistened as light made it through the slowly rotating ceiling fans. The dark wood shelves on both sides of the mirror housed multitudes of different liquors. If not for the red vinyl bar stools, Mason would have thought he was in the 1800s.

"What'll it be, Claire?" the elderly bartender asked.

"Two Jameson and Cokes, please. Sid, this is Mason; Mason, this is Sid."

"Nice to meet you, Mason," Sid said from behind the perfectly preserved antique bar.

"Nice to meet you, Sid."

"So this is Sid's Bar, but Jake owns it?" Mason asked Claire.

"It used to be Sid's. Jake is his son, so he passed it over to Jake a couple of years ago, but still helps run it."

"Ah, I see."

The tarnished brass light fixtures mounted on the bird's-eye maple wood walls kept the bar dimly lit. If it were any brighter, he was sure Claire would see his disappointment. An elderly couple slow-danced in the corner of the bar to an old Western song bellowing out from the jukebox. For a moment, Mason forgot the he was in the twenty-first century. The low rumble of the forty plus patrons seated at the tables and booths allowed

Mason to blend into the rich atmosphere of the Old West. Mason watched the three men walk away through the large picture window. Joe looked back and locked eyes with Mason through the glass. After they mutually broke their stare, Mason and Claire sat at the bar to figure out what each had heard.

"Is Rod always that friendly?" Mason asked.

"No, he's always like that. Him and my grandfather go way back. Rod's wife died twenty years ago and he's never been the same since. He always seems despondent, and that's with the people he knows. Don't worry about him; he just takes a while to get used to. What are you doing out so late?"

"I couldn't sleep so I thought I would go for a walk. You guys don't have a curfew, do you?" he asked sarcastically. He tried to keep his building anger under control, but his racing heartbeat and short breaths were making it hard to do. Claire saw it. He heard too much. She needed to do damage control.

"No, but I'm sensing something's bothering you. Are you all right?"

"Yes, I'm fine. Just have a lot on my mind."

"Anything I can help you with?" Claire offered.

"I don't know. Can I trust you?" he asked, putting her on the spot.

"Of course you can," she said, putting her hand on his arm, reassuring him.

"Are you sure I can totally trust you?" Mason asked again.

"All right, Mason, what's going on?" Claire asked.

"I don't know; why don't you tell me?" Mason's eyes were intent on her, waiting for an answer.

"What do you mean, Mason?"

"Oh I don't know, why don't you start with your new babysitting job."

"My what?"

"Don't give me that crap, you know exactly what I'm talking about," he said, his voice elevated. Claire had nothing. She had to give in.

"I get it, you heard us talking out front."

"Yes."

"How much did you hear?"

"Does it matter? Does it change anything? The fact is that you lied to me and your paranoid freak-show little town wants you to babysit me," Mason said, now visibly angry.

"Calm down, it's not what you think."

The Jameson soothed his nerves slightly. "Well then, what exactly is it? What am I missing?" he argued.

"They're just covering their bases. Maybe they are a little paranoid, but I offered to keep an eye on you. And it doesn't change the fact that I'm having a nice time with you. You have to remember, there is a 'good ole boy' mentality here. After you leave, I still have to live with it. If me hanging out with you satisfies their keeping an eye on you, then so be it. I didn't think it was a big deal. I'm sorry you found out that way. I should have told you, but what was I going to say, 'Hi Mason, the town wants me to keep an eye on you and I kind of like you, so I said sure'?"

After a long pause, Mason replied, "Yes, that's exactly what you say."

"All right, it sounded better here than it did in my mind," Claire said. "At any rate, the little scam you pulled at Miram's didn't help anything."

"The little scam?" Mason said, shaking his head. "I should've known you didn't believe me. You were just appeasing me. So am I still to believe that you were sorry for whatever you were sorry for? How can I believe anything from you?" he said. His disappointment and frustration was coming to a head. It seemed they both had secrets.

"All right, Mason, I'll level with you. Yes, I believe you got in there and looked around and then tried to make me believe that you talked to a ghost. I'm not sure what kind of attention you need or what you're trying to prove, but rather than argue and be mean, I chose to avoid it. Outside of me seeing the ghost, I'm not likely to believe it. Now since I leveled with you, the least you could do is level with me. How did you do it?"

"You expect me to level with you after telling me unless you see it, you're not going to believe me. You've already set me up to look like I'm lying to you. All right, I'll level with you. There was a lady that showed me the picture. The lady was the same one from the picture. If she's dead, then I talked to a dead person. That's it. You can conjure up all sorts of conspiracy theories if you want, but don't ask for the truth and when I give it to you, tell me I'm lying."

"You have to admit, Mason, it's kind of hard to believe."

"Trust me, I know how it sounds. But what the hell happened to you that you can't see honesty when it's right in front of you?"

"People aren't always honest and upfront, Mason. Certainly you can understand that."

Claire's words coupled with another Jameson calmed Mason down. He reflected about the things that happened in Chicago with the story; he couldn't trust anyone. Mason retracted a little. "You're right. I've seen it plenty in Chicago. And it's me who should apologize. I'm sorry for giving you crap about it. I know you're just being safe; I'd probably do the same thing," he conceded.

"It's okay, Mason. I'm sorry for questioning you, but I'm not used to being that upfront with people."

"My friend Al and I have a truth test that we do in Chicago when we have an issue. Maybe we make that same deal?"

"All right, what do you propose?" Claire asked cautiously.

"Sid!" Mason called out.

"Yes sir?"

"Two shots of Jameson please."

Throwing a white bar towel over his left shoulder, he nodded his head in agreement. "Coming right up."

"Remember when you were a kid and you made blood pacts?"

"Yes," Claire hesitantly agreed. "We're not going to prick our fingers, are we?" she asked.

"No; Al and I decided in college that pricking our fingers hurt too much, so now we do it over shots of Jameson Irish whiskey. You see, Claire, whenever we have an issue on whether we can believe or trust each other, we do it over a shot of Jameson. Neither one of us would ever disrespect the Jameson name by lying over it."

"Okay, I guess it's a shot of Jameson then," Claire agreed.

They toasted their shot glasses and drank their shots and ordered two more. They figured they had a lot of truth to talk about.

"All right, now that we have figured that out, I can assure you, Claire, that I didn't pull a scam on you."

"I'm not going to lie to you, Mason. I don't understand it, but I will try."

"Awesome, that's all I want you to do," Mason said, being more hopeful. "See, anything can be resolved over a Jameson."

"How about a hangover?"

"No, I'm afraid only a Red Bull will cure that."

"Really?"

"Yes, works every time," Mason reassured.

"I'll keep that in mind. So what's going on with not being able to sleep?"

"It's not a big deal; I just have strange dreams sometimes."

"Are they dreams or nightmares?"

"Both. I mean, they usually start as dreams and end up as nightmares. So I'm not sure what they are."

"Interesting; have you ever talked to someone about them?"

"You mean like a shrink?" Mason asked. "Yes, I have. In fact, very recently," he continued.

"What do you mean?"

"I'll give you the abridged version. My dad's girlfriend knows a shrink at the University of Oklahoma. So since it was on my way back to Chicago, I stopped by and saw him."

"What did he say?"

"Nothing really. I mean it was interesting, but in the end I just need to get used to them."

"You don't have a type of psychosis, do you?"

"If I told you the unabridged version, you'd probably think so; but no, I don't. And how exactly do you know about psychosis? You're not crazy, are you?"

"No, I studied criminal behavior in school."

"In college?" Mason asked, somewhat surprised.

"Yes, in college. You know, we are allowed to travel and do other things."

"Sorry, I'm an ass. I've known you for three days now and I really don't know much about you." Mason had come down from his bout of anger. Claire had a way of putting him at ease. The same way his mother did. The same way Kelly did. In the end, Claire was probably someone he could confide in about his ability. It would have to be soon; time was not on their side.

"Tell me about you," Mason said.

"Really, there's not much to tell. I was born and raised here, went to Creighton University in Omaha, then moved to D.C. and did some graduate work at Georgetown. Evaluated and counseled criminals, and eventually moved back."

"Yeah, something tells me you're leaving something out," Mason said, probing for more information.

"What? That's it, really," Claire said as if she was trying to convince herself as well as Mason. There was more to her story. She found herself in a precarious situation; she had to give a little to get a little. And she needed to build his trust and she needed to know more about Mason. If she was to get more, she'd need to lay a foundation now. Sitting up on her bar stool, she was ready. She finished her liquid courage and jumped in.

"So what was your degree in?" Mason asked, not letting her off that easy.

"My undergraduate is in psychology and criminal justice."

Mason got the feeling she wasn't going to volunteer much. He had to direct his questions carefully. "And your graduate?" Mason continued.

"Clinical psychology," she said hesitantly.

He knew it, she was very smart. How smart, though? "Dare I ask, your doctorate?" Mason said, completely probing.

"Well . . . yes, I did a PhD in the neuropsychology of criminal behavior."

That one surprised him. "You have a PhD in neuropsychology?"

"Yes."

"I don't even know what that means!" Mason said, astonished.

"It's along the lines of the study of the brain, and I applied it to criminal behavior."

"Like, criminal profiling?" Mason asked.

"Yes, there's some of that," she replied. "But it's also sleep disorders, dream analysis, and psychosis, all of which deal with the brain. That's why I asked about the dream?"

It was starting to make sense. She was pretty sharp. Too sharp to be in this town. What was she running from? What are we all running from? "You said you counseled criminals?"

"Yes, I did a stint working for the State of Maryland Department of Human Services working with criminals." She had learned through her work to just answer questions and not give too much extra information. Mason wasn't going to let her off with yes and no answers. She didn't mind it. Mason was someone she could talk to. Was it the Jameson or was it the company? She wasn't sure as they ordered another round.

"Did you like it; the counseling, I mean?" Mason clarified after watching Claire take a swig of Jameson.

"Some of it, but after reading their cases and getting involved with them, it was difficult to have empathy for them. I quickly realized that most of them didn't want help; they just wanted to get through the court-ordered therapy and get back to committing crimes. Essentially, they were playing the system and playing me, and I got sick of it." That was the most she had talked about her life in years. It was definitely the Jameson.

"So that's when you quit?" Mason asked.

She was on a roll. It felt surprisingly good to talk about it. She opened up.

"No, I quit after meeting Rulon Woodly."

"Who was he?"

There was no more thinking about the answers or the consequences of her answers. Without hesitation, she told Mason the story.

"He was a juvenile sex offender. I met him when he was seventeen. He was six foot three and about 280 pounds. He had been sexually assaulting boys and girls in his neighborhood, basically anyone he could get a hold of. When I began to counsel him, he played along for the first month because he liked me. Then the honeymoon period was over." Claire hesitated and looked down at the floor. It was an obviously painful memory for her. But she wanted to talk. She felt compelled to continue. The memory had been repressed for so long, she almost forgot about it. It was time to get it out. She continued.

"Rulon and I were in a classroom. I was trying to get him to understand the anger escalation cycle. I was at the board writing out the cycle and I turned around to ask him a question. When I looked at him, his eyes were glossed over, his mouth was open, and he looked catatonic. He was just staring at me. I asked if he was all right and he smiled and said 'Oh, I'm fine, Claire.' I recognized that something was up and I slowly started moving to the opposite side of the room where there was a panic button on the wall. I'll never forget his crazed stare. He was almost drooling. He stood up and said, 'Claire, we both know what's up. You fight and I'll kill you.'"

"My God, weren't there guards?" Mason was completely engaged, listening to her every word.

"The guards were there almost immediately after I hit the button. Rulon didn't make it four feet before they took him down and tazed the hell out of him. I stood there and watched them handcuff him and drag him back to his cell. His psychotic eyes never left me. The next day my boss said that Rulon filed a complaint and that he did nothing wrong. He was going to the board to write something about the cycle and I freaked out. I told my boss what Rulon said to me and he said even if he did, crazy people say stuff like that all the time. I was ordered to get therapy and the guards were disciplined for using excessive force."

Mason couldn't believe her experience, although he did know what it was like to have his life threatened. This was different; psychotic people are a whole different animal. Their logic may be flawed, their purpose may be misguided, but worst of all, they can't change their behavior on their own.

His earlier thoughts of why Claire would live back there instead of in the real world were starting to look more clear. Claire saw the very system she was a part of turn against her. She saw firsthand how dysfunctional the system had become. Mason thought her story was over, until she continued.

"I went to Rulon's cell and asked him through the bars why he lied. He said, 'Look Claire, I'm seventeen. I turn eighteen in two months and I'm out of here with a clean slate. Then we'll be able to spend some quality time together without the guards.' I told him if I ever saw him again I'd kill him. He just smiled and said, 'I suggest you sleep with the lights on, because you and me are going to happen whether you like it or not.' I said we'd see about that. As I walked away from his cell I could hear him whispering, 'Two months, Claire.'"

"Did you turn him in?"

"Yes, I filed a formal complaint all right."

"What did they do?"

"Turns out, he filed a complaint that I went to his cell to harass and threaten him. When they questioned me about it, I told them what happened and what was said. They focused in on the fact that I said I would kill him. So they put me on leave, and again ordered me in therapy. That's when I realized that the system is all BS. I didn't need the headache, so I quit."

"That's unbelievable. I don't blame you for leaving; I sure would have."

Trying to lighten her mood, she sat straight up and gave a forced smile. The kind that reassured her that she did the right thing.

"So, here I am. This is a very safe town, so I'll stay here until I want to do something different."

"I could think of worse places to be, that's for sure." Mason was satisfied. Claire opened up and that went a long way with him. Tomorrow he would do the same. They had a psychological contract now that meant they could trust one another.

"We need to drive into Ideldale tomorrow. Is that all right?" Claire said, finishing her drink.

"Yes, I'm sure Joe and everyone else wants to make sure I'm going to pay for my stuff, right?" Mason asked.

Claire smiled and agreed, "Yes, that's part of it." Mason knew that would be the perfect chance to fill her in. He hoped she would trust him as well.

"I wonder what would happen to me if I couldn't pay; would they flog me?" Mason asked curiously.

"No, probably put you to work, unless you prefer the flogging. I'm sure they would make a concession for you."

"I'm sure Joe would," Mason said, not really joking. "I guess I'm going to head back to Marcie's and see if I can actually get some sleep. Hopefully she's not waiting up."

As Mason walked back to Marcie's, he thought more about Claire. He hoped she was being straight with him, because tomorrow was a big deal for him. He was ready to tell her. He wished the topic wasn't so serious or dark, but she had to know. She was smart and might be able to help him figure out a way to stop it. It was going to be a conversation he was not looking forward to, but it was time.

Chapter 52

The Unabridged Version
Greenfield Ranch, Oklahoma
June 9, 2017

"How are you feeling?" Claire asked, joining Mason in a booth at the café with a cup of coffee.

"I feel great; Jameson has a way of making me sleep pretty solid. How about you?" Mason said, folding up the newspaper.

"I'm okay; I think *he* made me sleep well, too," Claire's said with a smile.

"You're not in a good mood just because you're getting paid today, are you?" Mason said, noticing Claire's pleasant mood.

"No, no reason; I'm fine."

"See, Jameson's good for you."

"I don't know about that, but I had a fun time with you last night," she said. "I haven't talked about that stuff in a long time. It was good to get it out."

"I guess I needed to vent as well," Mason admitted.

"There aren't many people here to just go and talk to."

"What about Jake? He seems pretty interested in you."

"Jake? No, we've been friends for a long time, but it's like a brother-sister thing. He's just looking out for me. That's the drawback to small towns—everyone knows everyone. Makes it hard to get involved."

"I get it. That would be tough. I'm not sure if it's good or bad that I'm not from here. On the one hand, I'm not from here so I get to hang out with you. On the other hand, I'm not from here so I'll be leaving."

"Kind of sucks that we have totally different lives," Claire said somberly.

"In the meantime, I guess we have fun until that time comes, right?" Mason said, trying to find something positive.

"Yes, great point. Your breakfast is ready. I'll get it, finish up some paperwork, and we'll head out."

Driving out of Greenfield Ranch during the day gave Mason a chance to see the scenery better than when he came in. It had more forest than he remembered from four days earlier. Looking out over a rolling pasture, Mason saw an old compound with ranch-style houses and buildings surrounded by a thicket of trees.

"What are those old buildings?" Mason asked, pointing in the distance out his window.

"That's the original Greenfield Ranch, from the first settlers."

"Anyone live there now?"

"No, those structures are all run-down. No one has lived in those for a hundred years." As they drove by the complex, Mason thought he saw something move by one of the buildings. Rubbernecking, he tried to see more, but it was too far away.

"What are you doing?"

"I thought I saw something at that complex," Mason said, turning back around to face frontward.

"Probably a deer or some kind of animal."

"Maybe," Mason said, slightly puzzled. Didn't look like a deer, he thought. Deer don't sparkle.

"So no more dreams last night?" Claire asked, bringing him back into the truck.

"No, slept like a log. You?"

"I usually sleep pretty good out here."

"I bet; I know I sure would," Mason said.

"So Mason, you said the other night if you gave me the unabridged version of your life I'd think you have some kind of psychosis. Well, we've got an hour and nothing to do. How about it—will you give me the detailed version?"

"I'm not sure you're ready for it; it's pretty deep," he said, though he knew he was going to give it to her.

"I can handle some pretty deep stuff, trust me. Come on, you have nothing to lose. What, do you see dead people?" she asked somewhat carelessly.

"Not exactly. Look, I'll tell you because I've been wanting to, I just wasn't ready, but I'm not completely sure how to tell you."

"Start by just saying it, then we'll discuss it."

"All right, here it goes; you're going to die."

In a very anti-climatic tone, Claire replied, "That's it? I know that, Mason; we all are."

"Yes, but we're not all going to on Friday."

"What Friday?"

"This next Friday, June 17."

Not terribly surprised, Claire played along, not knowing where he was going with it. She learned from Miram's place not to show her cards too early. "And you know this because?"

"Because I see the date that people die when I come in contact with them. That's why you get shocked, see." Mason reached over and touched the skin on her arm and they both received a shock.

"Ouch!" Claire said after getting shocked.

"The closer the date, the stronger the shock," he continued.

"So you're telling me that I have seven days left to live?"

"Yes, I think so."

"What do you mean, you think so?" Claire asked, still not very convinced, knowing there was some explanation coming. "I mean, you either know or you don't, right?"

"Yes and no. I've never been wrong, but I've also never had this dilemma before."

"And what dilemma is that?"

"I know how this sounds, believe me, but Joe, Frank, you, and Natalie all have the same day. So either you all die on Friday or there is something going on with my ability."

"So now we're all going to die?"

"Yes."

Mason expected some questions, but hoped they would be more constructive. He wasn't sure how Claire would take it. There was a part of him that hoped she would simply believe him. But another part of him knew she was too smart to just go all in. He was also no fool. He knew how it sounded. He trusted that she would come around eventually.

"Do you realize what Joe would do if he knew you thought that?" Claire asked, still not completely believing Mason.

"Yes, that's why I haven't said anything."

"Mason, you have to keep that between us for your own safety." Claire hoped Mason was interpreting something wrong. They had been through enough in the last few days for her to believe he wasn't trying to scam anyone.

"Fine. But what can we do?"

"How exactly did you say we were going to die?" Claire asked, keeping her composure and probing for information.

"I didn't say how." Mason's large exhaled breath showed the beginning of his frustration. Claire recognized it, but wouldn't back off.

"So you haven't decided yet how we're all going to die?"

"No Claire, I don't decide how someone dies; I only know the date."

"Any idea how we would find that out, Mason?" Mason picked up on her subtle patronizing comments and looked out the window. He pondered his words carefully. He had to convince her, like everyone else he'd ever tried to tell. How was he supposed to do that? His timing may have been ill conceived. I've got to keep trying, he concluded.

"I don't know; there's probably someone, but I don't know how to get a hold of them," Mason told her. "Claire, you really need to believe me on this. I've said it a hundred times; I know how it sounds. Do you really think I'd set myself up like this?" Mason's calm but serious tone resonated with Claire. She was at least willing to hear him out.

"All right Mason, I appreciate you opening up and trusting me enough to tell me that. Any ideas on how to stop it?"

"No, I've been beating myself up, trying to figure it out."

"Didn't you say you talked to a doctor in Norman, Oklahoma?" Claire asked.

"Yes, Dr. Hogan at the University of Oklahoma. I was just thinking about him; he might be able to contact some other people. He's one of the few people that understand this thing."

"Is he a specialist?"

"You could say that, I guess. I don't know anyone else who deals with this kind of phenomenon."

"Interesting. Dr. Hogan," she said as she made a mental note.

"Claire, are you okay?"

"Yes, I'm fine; why?"

"Why? Because you just found out that you're going to die in seven days, and you're fine?"

Claire's thoughts began to race. I can't believe how comfortable he is with this, she thought. Of course, he's been dealing with it his entire life. I really hope he's not psycho; I'm out on a limb here.

"Claire, the fact that you're okay with this tells me you may not fully understand your fate, you may be in a state of denial, or you simply don't believe me."

"Mason, give me a break; I'm just trying to take it all in. If what you're saying is true, then I've got some things to think about. Just remember, let's not alarm anyone. We'll talk about this later, okay?" Claire needed to process the information. It's obviously not true, but what's his endgame? she wondered. Who do I involve in this? She decided to see how it played out.

They entered the Idledale city limits. It was a small town that was a thriving metropolis compared to Greenfield Ranch.

"Wow, is that a McDonald's?" Mason commented.

"Yes, this is our big city," Claire said, pulling into a parking space and trying to maintain her composure. "We can walk from here."

The small downtown business district had an outdoor mall, banks, businesses, restaurants, and life. Cars drove by, people walked up and down the mall, busses drove their routes, police officers walked their beats, and an overall sense of a community was in the air. As they walked down the sidewalk toward the bank, Mason noticed a scattered sky, a slight breeze, and the smell of lilac blossoms in the air—new to him, but just another beautiful Oklahoma summer day to the locals.

Mason noticed that Claire was somehow different. His fear was being realized. When people know their death date their innocence disappears, their outlook becomes pessimistic, and, most importantly, their hope vanished. People definitely change. At that point, he questioned whether he had done the right thing by telling her. He now was somewhat thankful that he never told Kelly. To see Kelly's optimism and spirit disappear would've crushed him. No one likes to be the bearer of bad news. They stopped in front of the bank. The news was finally starting to hit Claire. Whether Mason was right or wrong didn't matter as much as it made her consider her own finite life span.

"Here's the bank; they'll cash a check for you. I'll wait here," Claire said as she watched Mason disappear into the bank.

Claire sat on a bench outside the main door and pondered her next move. Her thoughts ran the gamut of emotions. He's so wrong, he's probably crazy, she decided. But what if he's right? Then I have seven days left to live. I should've done more with my life. What if he's wrong? Then I get to live. Who is he to drop that on me or anyone? Do I tell Joe? Do I let him leave before next Friday? What the hell am I supposed to do now?

As she sat thinking and not noticing life go by, an approaching ambulance got her attention. With its lights on, it came to a screeching halt in front of the bank. Two paramedics jumped out with a gurney in tow and rushed by her into the bank. Mason? She rushed in behind them. Standing scared inside the doorway she saw Mason holding a woman's hand and comforting her. She was relieved that it wasn't Mason; her mind played tricks on her. Death became very real and personal for her now.

As the paramedics arrived, Mason bent over and whispered something into the woman's ear. The elderly woman smiled and looked back at Mason and thanked him. He then stepped aside and let the paramedics work on her. After seeing Claire by the door and the look of terror on her face, he could tell she was scared and walked over to her.

"What happened?" she asked Mason as he arrived to her.

"I think she had a heart attack or stroke. They're going to take her to the hospital, but she'll be fine."

"What did you say to her?"

"I just told her she was going to be all right and not to worry, but she has to go to the hospital. She said okay."

"That was nice of you," Claire said, trying to gather her wits.

"It's nice when they have time left; sometimes they don't." As they wheeled the elderly woman out of the bank, she reached out to Mason, grabbed his hand, and thanked him. "DECEMBER 11, 2019" flashed into Mason's mind.

"You're welcome. I'll see you at the hospital before we leave," he told her. She just smiled back.

Before walking out of the bank, Mason grabbed a free sucker from a basket and handed it to Claire. "Here, these are awesome; it'll make you feel better."

Claire stuffed it in her purse and paused. "A sucker's not going to cut it; I need a coffee." They walked out of the bank. Claire looked in both directions and said, "This way." She took off down the sidewalk on a mission. Her mind raced. Can this get any weirder? she wondered.

Chapter 53

Eddie
Idledale, Oklahoma
June 9, 2017

Mason and Claire sat on the outdoor patio of Jolynn's Coffee Emporium. Claire's nerves were doing the rumba; coffee was probably the last thing she needed. She couldn't control her breathing or her impending fate. She wasn't used to *not* being in control. A feeling of helplessness shot through her like an arrow. It was a new feeling, one that left her vulnerable.

Mason tried to understand the stress Claire was under. After all, it's not every day you learn you're going to die in a few days, he thought to himself.

"Mason, the reason I was scared at the bank was because I thought you had something to do with it. I couldn't live with myself if someone got hurt because of you and I didn't do anything about it."

"What do you mean, 'because of me'?"

Grasping for straws, Claire made a last-ditch effort to prove him wrong.

"I don't know. Is there any way you cause the deaths?"

"God no; I hope not. It's exactly what I told you." Seeing the internal dissonance in Claire, he had to prove it to her somehow. A lightbulb went on in his head.

He sat up in his chair and said, "Wait, I have an idea. Let's go see the lady at the hospital."

"Now Mason, we have bigger things going on," she pleaded.

"I know. Trust me and let's go see her, then I promise we can go."

Claire saw how excited Mason got and was willing to try anything at that point. She finished her coffee, placed her cup on the table, and stood up. Exhaustedly, she agreed.

"All right, let's go do this," Claire said sadly.

After walking into the Idledale Memorial Hospital, Mason and Claire went to the emergency room front desk. "Hi, an elderly woman came in a little while ago from the bank. Is she okay?" Mason asked.

"Yes, she's fine, but she can't see visitors for a little while."

"All right, thank you. Oh, one more thing; do you have a cancer ward or a terminal ward?"

"Yes, up on the fourth floor we have a children's cancer ward."

"Thank you. Come on, Claire," Mason said, grabbing her hand. "JUNE 16, 2017."

"Ouch! You said we'd go right from the hospital."

"I know, we're still here. Come on." Reluctantly, Claire followed Mason to the fourth floor. As they got off the elevator, Mason started looking around. Walking down the hall, Mason started poking his head into rooms, but they were all empty.

A nurse walked by and asked, "Is there something I can help you with?"

"Where are all the kids?" Mason replied.

"They're in the play area; it's at the end of the hall to the right."

"Thank you; come on," Mason said.

"Mason, what are you doing? You can't mess with kids."

"I'm not."

As they turned the corner at the end of the hall, they came upon an area that looked like an indoor playground for children. Some were in wheelchairs, some were in their beds that were wheeled in, some were playing with their family members, and some were watching television, but all of them had one thing in common: they were all diagnosed with a terminal illness. As if Claire wasn't sad enough, now she felt sadder.

"Come on Mason, let's get out of here. This isn't right to be playing with kids like this."

"I'm not playing, Claire, but I am going to prove a point to you."

"You don't have to do this."

"Yes Claire, I do. Come on."

Walking by the children, Mason began patting them on the back, head, arm, or anywhere he could make contact. Turning to Claire, he whispered several of the dates to her as he got them. Until he came upon Eddie. He was lying in his mechanical bed in an inclined position so he could look out the windows. He didn't have the strength to walk, but he liked being around his friends. Every day his nurse would roll him into the play area to watch television and talk to the other children.

"Hi. What's your name?" Mason asked the bald-headed eight-year-old boy.

"I'm Eddie; what's your name?"

"I'm Mason and this is Claire."

"It's nice to meet you, Mason and Claire," Eddie said, stretching out his hand.

"It's nice to meet you too, Eddie," Claire and Mason said, shaking Eddie's hand.

"JUNE 9, 2017" flashed into Mason's mind, accompanied with the familiar shock.

"Ouch!" Eddie said with a laugh. "You shocked me."

"I think you shocked me," Mason said with a smile, playing with Eddie.

"Have you come to take me?" Eddie said.

"What do you mean?" Claire said, looking at Mason.

"No Eddie, not me," Mason said.

"Why do you ask, Eddie?" Claire asked.

"He was in my dream," he said, pointing to Mason.

"Eddie, it was probably someone who looked like him," Claire offered.

"No, it was Mason, and he had an owl with him."

"How do you know it was Mason?" Claire continued.

"Because he told me the next time I see him, he'll be with a pretty lady, and that's the day I would see my mommy again."

"Where is your mommy, Eddie?" Claire asked.

"She's in heaven with Jesus."

"Eddie, did Mason put you up to this to trick me?"

"He told me you'd say that."

"He did, did he?" she said, looking back at Mason as if he was busted.

"Yes, he said you'd have a red sucker in your purse for me."

Opening her purse, there was the red sucker that Mason grabbed from the bank. Slowly, she pulled it out. She stared at it in disbelief and handed it to Eddie with an uncertain smile.

"Thank you."

"You're welcome, Eddie," Claire said in utter disbelief.

Looking at Mason, she said, "How did you—"

"I didn't know," Mason said, cutting her off. "I figured I'd bring you here and if we saw a child, we could give it to them. It wasn't my dream, Claire."

As Eddie finished his sucker, Hannah, his nurse came by and asked, "Hi Eddie, are you ready to go back to you room?"

"Yes, can Mason and Claire come?"

"Sure, if they'd like to."

"Can you please? Please!" he said excitedly.

"I don't know, Eddie, we have to get going," Claire said.

"Mason, I don't want to go alone," he pleaded.

"Eddie, you're not going to be alone. I'm going to be here, like I am every day," Hannah said.

"I don't mean here, Hannah," he said as if she should know where he was going.

"We can come for a few minutes, okay Eddie?" Mason said.

"Awesome, you told me that too," Eddie said, reaching out and holding Mason's hand. "JUNE 9, 2017" flashed in Mason's mind.

"All right, let's get going," the nurse said, starting to roll Eddie's bed back to his room.

When they arrived back in his room, Mason and Claire walked to the opposite side of the bed that the nurse was on, so they wouldn't get in her way. Holding Mason's hand, Eddie looked at him in the eyes and smiled. Mason smiled back and said, "It's going to be all right, Eddie."

"I know, my mommy said to tell you thank you for staying with me."

"Tell your mommy she's welcome," Mason said with a smile. The nurse gave Mason a strange look, as if very confused.

Eddie looked at Claire and said, "Thanks for bringing Mason here, and he was right, you are pretty."

"Thank you, Eddie, that's very nice of you," Claire replied, stunned and confused, trying to smile. She didn't know what to believe. As the nurse plugged in the last of the machines, Eddie said, "It's time."

"Time for what?" Hannah asked.

"Time for me to go and see mommy. Besides, Mason has a lot of work to do."

Hannah, now getting visibly concerned, asked, "Eddie, what do you mean? Eddie?"

"Good-bye, Hannah, I love you," he whispered as his last breath expired. His eyes closed and he passed away.

"Eddie? Eddie!" the nurse called out, but he had gone. "Crash cart stat!" she yelled as Mason and Claire backed out of the way. Claire looked at Mason and back at Eddie and wiped a tear from her eye.

"Good-bye, Eddie," Mason said as he set Eddie's hand on his chest.

Emotionally beat, Mason and Claire walked out of Eddie's room and toward the elevators. They walked through a hallway called "the gallery." It had hand-painted pictures on the walls that the terminally ill children had painted. Saddened by the injustice of it, Claire walked slowly, looking at the paintings, and said, "It's not fair that children have to suffer like this."

"That's as hard as it gets," Mason said in a somber tone. Claire stopped at one picture and stared at it. When Mason realized that he was walking alone, he turned around to see Claire looking at a painting. He walked back and said, "What are you looking at?"

Not being able to say anything, Claire just looked at the picture and read the wall plate below it.

"Wow! That's just like the painting that Miram gave me," Mason said. The painting was a smaller version of an ancient city being ravished by owls and a blackened silhouette of a man walking away from it.

"That's not the odd part," Claire said. "The strange thing about this picture is that the date was two years ago and the little girl that painted it was blind. She died the day after she finished it."

"I'm telling you, Claire, I'm not making this stuff up."

"I— I guess not. I mean . . . how could you have known, two years ago?" Claire said with her voice trailing off in disbelief. Shaking her head slowly in amazement, she finally broke her gaze from the mesmerizing painting and conceded. "I swear, Mason, if you're lying to me one bit, I'll destroy you."

"Claire, I'm telling you the truth. Do you want me to find someone else who's going to die soon?"

"No, my brain can't handle any more. Let's go."

The drive back to Greenfield Ranch was a quiet one. The green rolling countryside that Claire had driven by a thousand times suddenly became alive and beautiful. Tree branches swaying in the wind looked as if they were breathing. Colors became vivid. Nature's secrets were now revealed. There's nothing like death to make people appreciate the little things in life. A deep breath of fresh air reminded her she was still alive—for now. Faced with her own mortality, her thoughts wandered.

We try to hang on for as long as we can in an attempt to keep our memories alive, she thought. What if, by some fluke, Mason is right? Then this is it? I hope he's wrong. As they turned off the main highway and onto the dirt road that led to Greenfield Ranch, Mason felt as if he had gone back in time again. While looking out his side window, something caught Mason's eye. "Stop the truck!"

"What, here?"

"Yes, stop the truck!"

Before the truck came to a complete stop, Mason jumped out and ran back twenty yards. Off to the right side of the road, Mason pushed branches away from an old sign that read, "Welcome to Greenfield Ranch." Underneath the greeting it read, "Population: 384." Mason's heart sank to the ground. As Mason stood looking at the sign, Claire walked up on him and asked, "What are you looking at?"

"Is this accurate? Are there 384 people here?" Mason asked.

"No, there's 385. Why?"

"385, not 384?"

"No, 385. What's up, Mason?"

"My dreams; they always have 384 dead something! Fish, sheep, buildings—384 dead something. I think it's telling me that that this town is in danger."

"What? That doesn't make any sense."

"It didn't until now. I have to figure out what's going to happen," he said.

"Come on, Mason, we need to get back," Claire said, not wanting to believe him, but after the day they just had, she would believe anything.

The last twenty minutes of their drive were completely silent. Mason couldn't stop thinking about the population of the town and his dreams. His dreams were trying to communicate to him. He was sure of it.

Exhausted from the long day, Claire pulled up to Marcie's and dropped off Mason.

"Mason, I am too beat to play games with you, so don't BS me; are you telling me the truth?"

Feeling pretty drained himself, he just replied, "Claire, I've never been more honest with anyone in my life than I have been with you." She finally believed him. She didn't understand, but she believed. That was the first step.

Chapter 54

Fortress
Greenfield Ranch, Oklahoma
June 10, 2017

"Wow Mason, you're up early!" Marcie said with a surprised look on her face, setting her coffee cup on the kitchen table. She watched as Mason came flying down the stairs. He looked like a man on a mission.

"Yes, I'm going for a run; I'll be back in a little while," he said, running out the front door, not wanting a response. Heading up the main dirt road he had every intention of checking out the old decrepit houses they passed driving out of the town yesterday. After three miles, he could see the old houses off in the distance and kept heading in their direction.

As he inched his way closer to the buildings, he waited until there were no cars in sight. Then he then darted off of the dirt road and sprinted through the tall grass another mile until he reached the woods. He was past the buildings, where he could hide and catch his breath.

Now walking toward the buildings through the woods, he could see them more clearly. Was it some kind of compound? There were seven two-story old buildings that formed the shape of an "H." They all looked like old barns. Did they make barns that large 150 years ago? he wondered. There were three buildings in a row almost touching each other, running parallel to another three buildings opposite of each other. There was one building in the middle of the two rows connecting the center buildings of each row with each other. Interesting design.

The wood looked old and was falling apart, windows were broken out, and the roofs had holes in them. They certainly looked like condemned buildings. As he was about to move in for a closer view, he heard the sound of an engine.

Turning around, he could see a vehicle approaching. Taking cover behind some brush, he watched as a pickup truck drove into the compound. Two men got out of the truck, looked around, then entered through the center building between the rows. "Now what would someone be doing in there?" he said under his breath. "I bet they're making meth," he concluded. "I bet that's what all the secrecy is about. They're making drugs."

Since it all made sense, it wasn't as interesting anymore. Slightly disappointed, Mason started to make his way back through the field, looking for an opportunity to get back to the main road, when he heard a truck approaching from behind him. He hid behind a bush again and watched as the truck approached. Another truck approached from the opposite direction. As they converged right next to where Mason was hiding, they stopped and began speaking through the rolled-down windows of the trucks.

"Hey, what's up guys?" the two men said from the truck that just left the compound.

"Just doing some routine checks; Mason is out running, so keep an eye out for him," the man in the approaching truck replied.

"We haven't seen anything; we'll let you know if we do."

"Sounds good. How's everything running?"

"Good; we had a motion sensor tripped, probably a deer."

"She's lucky she didn't get electrocuted," one of the men said with a laugh.

"Had she been any closer, she might have; those lasers don't miss very often," the man in the departing truck replied.

"All right guys, see you at Sid's later?"

"Yes, sounds good."

As the two trucks drove off in their opposite directions, Mason's thoughts became somewhat more serious. Electrocuted? Motion sensors? Lasers? What the hell are they making? As Mason pondered his next move, he looked closer at the woods. He could see trees camouflaging antennas, equipment mounted to branches, cameras, and motion sensors. This was no decrepit compound, this was a fortress.

I guess it's now or never, Mason said to himself. With the trucks out of view, he jumped up, sprinted back through the tall grass, and made it back to the main dirt road, just in time for one of the trucks that was out looking for him to drive up and pass him. As the truck passed Mason, he could see the driver put the phone to his ear and look in the side mirror, as if to call off the dogs.

"Hey, you made it!" Marcie called out as Mason walked through the door.

"What do you mean?" Mason said with a little paranoia.

"Your run? You made it back from your run."

"Yes, I guess so. I'm pretty beat. I'll see you later," Mason said, disappearing up to his room.

There's no way Claire is messed up with drugs, is she? he thought. That would explain why they pay for everything with cash. I think I just need to get out of here. The problem is that if something's going to happen on Friday I've got to try something, but what? he wondered.

Chapter 55

Just Say No
Greenfield Ranch, Oklahoma
June 10, 2017

Mason, now a regular face at the diner, watched Claire work. It took his mind off her death. The way she interacted with customers was uplifting. Everyone liked her. The world was a better place with her in it, he concluded.

"Thanks Natalie," Mason said as Natalie cleared his plate. He waited until Claire had a break before trying to get her alone.

"Claire, can we go somewhere and talk?"

"Sure, let's take a walk. Natalie, I'll be back in a while," Claire called out.

"What's on your mind?" Claire asked as they walked down Main Street.

"First of all, are you okay with yesterday? I mean, I dropped a bomb on you."

"You could say that. I guess part of me wants to believe you, but another part says it's insanity, literally." Claire's expressionless face told Mason all he needed to know. At least she was taking it seriously. He needed her to believe him if they were to try and stop whatever it was that was coming.

"Claire, I have to try and stop this thing, and I can't do it alone. If we're going to do this, you have to help. Are you okay with that?"

They stopped and faced each other. Mason figured he was on to something at the compound but needed information if he was to make decisions on what to do.

"I'm fine, or as fine as you can be, knowing you could die in six days."

"Good. Now there's something else, and I need you to level with me." He took a deep breath. Whenever he did that, Claire got nervous. Every time Mason didn't know how to ask something, he hesitated, and lately his hesitations were not good news for her.

"Sure, what is it?"

"I think I've figured out the town industry."

"You have?" Claire said curiously.

Mason hesitated again. He recognized how it sounded before he even said anything. "Don't freak out on me; I really don't care about that as much as I do about Friday."

"This sounds serious," she said, being coy.

"I'm serious. I know what you guys are up to."

"Oh, do tell."

"You guys are making meth or some kind of drugs, aren't you?"

That was exactly what Claire needed to lift her spirits. For a brief moment she was mildly entertained. It took her mind off of the impending doom, if even temporarily.

"Methamphetamine? Us? Here in this town?"

"Yes." Mason waited in anticipation to hear his assumption was correct.

"How did you figure that out?" Claire said, turning away from Mason momentarily to hide the smirk on her face. Mason took her turning away as a guilty plea.

"I knew I was right!" Mason said, clenching his fist, proud that he figured it out. He continued, "Maybe that's where the accident is going to happen. What are you guys making? Meth, ecstasy, maybe Georgia home boy?" Mason asked.

Not being able to control herself any longer, all she could get out was, "Did you say Georgia home boy?" with a loud laugh that she tried to cover with her hand. Recognizing that she was playing with him, he tried to convince her.

"Look, I get it. Maybe it's just marijuana—fine."

Claire let out another loud laugh that had passersby looking at her.

"What," Mason said, "is so funny?"

"Oh God, Mason, I have to sit down before I pee my pants."

"What?' Mason said as they sat on a bench.

"Mason, I can assure you that there are no drugs in this town. But that was rich." Not trying to make Mason feel any smaller, she asked, "Where did you come up with that crazy idea?"

"It's not important; I guess it is a little silly," Mason admitted, feeling a little embarrassed.

Claire's tone became more serious. Why would he possibly think that? she wondered. She hoped he was guessing but needed to know his basis for drawing that kind of conclusion.

"No, really, how did you come up with that?"

"Forget it, I'll figure something else out," Mason said, now visibly dejected.

"All right, enough. Mason, I'm sorry, but it was funny. I won't laugh anymore. Tell me, how did you arrive at that?"

"I went for a run this morning and I ran to those old buildings we passed yesterday off the main road and—"

"You ran where?" Claire said, cutting him off midsentence and becoming very serious.

"To the old rundown buildings that we passed yesterday."

Changing her tone, she advised Mason, "Whatever you do, do not tell anyone you've been out there; and for God's sake, don't go out there again."

"Why?"

"Are we clear, Mason? I'm not joking."

"Sure, but why?"

"Those buildings are booby-trapped and can kill you if you don't know what you're doing. You're lucky you didn't get killed."

"I know, by the lasers, right?"

"How do you know about those?"

"I heard some guys talking about how they don't miss."

"They're right, they don't," Claire said.

"What's going on out there?"

"That, I can't tell you."

"Why?"

"Because I don't know. It has to do with research. That's why it's highly protected."

"I get it. That would've been nice to know, don't you think?"

"We all know about it. You're not supposed to be looking out there. Whatever you do, don't tell anyone, because then you really could become an issue."

"An issue?"

"Just don't, all right?"

"Fine," Mason said. "Look, I don't care what you guys make here, I just don't want you to die."

"Neither do I, Mason. I need to get back to work. Will I see you later?"

"I have no plans right now, but my social calendar may be filling up, so I'd make plans if you want to book me," Mason said with a smile.

"Well, how about dinner at my house at 7 o'clock?"

"Hmm, I'll have to move some people, but I think I can fit you in. Am I walking?"

"No, I'll pick you up," Claire said as they both stood up off the bench.

"Great, I'll see you later." As Claire walked back to the café, Mason sat back down and soaked up the dry, warm Oklahoma sun and pondered their exchange. Georgia home boy? I'm an idiot, he thought.

Chapter 56

Honorable Intentions
Greenfield Ranch, Oklahoma
June 10, 2017

Mason climbed into Claire's truck and was hit with the sweet fresh scent of lavender fig. "Wow, you smell great, Claire, and look even better!" he said, noticing her makeup and dress.

"Thanks," she said. "Are those for me?" she continued, looking at the bouquet of flowers in Mason's hand.

"Oh yes, these are for you, and so is this," he replied, handing her a bottle of wine.

"The flowers are beautiful, thank you. We can pop this when we get to my place," she said with a smile, and then she leaned over and kissed Mason.

"Hope you like steak?" she said as they drove away from Marcie's on their way to Claire's house.

"If I was a vegetarian who worked for PETA, I think I'd like steak right now," Mason said, still a little frazzled from Claire's kiss.

Inside Claire's house, Mason watched Claire transform herself from a rough and tough tomboy to an elegant, beautiful woman.

"Claire, I have to say, you look utterly amazing," Mason said, setting the wine on the kitchen counter.

Walking over and putting her arms around him, she said with a kiss, "You're looking quite handsome yourself, Mr. Rhimes. Now, you crack the wine and I'll fire up the grill."

"Shouldn't it be the other way around? Shouldn't I be firing up the grill?" he replied.

Claire reserved her finest grill techniques for her house, not to be used at the café. A pinch of sugar caramelized the outside of the medium-cooked sirloin steaks. Then she smothered them in a creamy garlic pepper sauce; this was a steak Del Frisco's would be envious of. A twice baked potato, salad, and cherry pie completed the culinary ensemble. It was clear who the town chef was.

After dinner they sat outside on a loveseat on Claire's back patio and stared at the stars. The dim light from the chiminea and the smell of citronella drifted through the air. The harmonic sounds of crickets, the crackling of the burning wood, and an occasional howl of a coyote orchestrated the ambience.

It was almost too enchanting to talk. The night air was cool on their skin. Snuggled together under a throw blanket, they sipped their wine and soaked up the tranquil seclusion. They both knew the week ahead of them could get ugly, but for completely different reasons.

Claire broke the silence. "Mason?"

"Yes."

"Do you think we'll figure this thing out?"

"God, I hope so," Mason said, not taking his gaze off the stars.

"Me too," Claire said with her head resting on Mason's chest. "It would be sad to lose you."

"I hope that doesn't happen to either of us."

"Maybe we should go to Joe; I can get him to believe me," Claire said.

"Claire, I *showed* you and you were about to have me committed and put in an institution. What do you think Joe would do?"

"Mason, I'm so sorry for that, but I was a little freaked out."

"I know, I completely understand. Maybe if we both tell Joe he will listen," Mason said.

"Let's cross that bridge later," Claire said, cozying up to Mason.

"Yes, okay. Right now, I think it's best if maybe we just took our nightcap inside," Mason said with a smile.

"Inside? Why Mason, are your intentions honorable?" Claire said, teasing Mason.

"I can assure you that they are 100 percent honorable, ma'am."

"If I didn't know better, I'd say you're trying to seduce me," Claire said with a devilish smile and a romantic kiss.

"Yes ma'am, I can honestly say it has crossed my mind," Mason said between kisses.

"Well in that case, I'd have to agree; we should go inside." As they closed the door to Claire's bedroom, the large white owl that had been watching them while perched on top of a pinyon pine flew away.

Chapter 57

Critical National Asset
Missouri River
June 11, 2017

A week on the river tested the wills of Malik and Arsal. Between pulling over and waiting for the river to be clear and running mostly at night, the two were fatigued. The humming of the outboard motor in the middle of the night was slowly nursing Malik to sleep.

"Malik, wake up. I think there is a factory over there."

"Where?"

"See the lights?" Arsal said, pointing to a large factory on the bank of the river off in the distance.

"Yes, I see them. What is it?"

Opening the map, Malik pointed to a factory. "See, I think we're right here."

"That's not a factory, Malik, that's a power plant. And they'll have security around it."

"What do we do?"

"We'll need to stay as close to the opposite shore as possible. We only have a few hours of night remaining. We need to get past that plant while it's still dark. Steer to the west bank and go full throttle."

With the advent of dawn, the sun was rising quickly. Arsal and Malik were losing the cover of night. While their attention was on the massive power plant across the river, they didn't notice a plant security patrol boat come up behind them. The voice over the loudspeaker broke their gaze.

"You in the raft, slow down and turn off your engine."

Turning around, Malik and Arsal saw the patrol boat. Their hearts felt as if they were going to explode. They each had a bad feeling in the pit of their stomachs; an overt warning of their imminent situation. They looked at each with concern in their faces and knew they could not outrun the patrol vessel. Malik turned off the motor. Their small raft began to slow immediately. The patrol boat pulled alongside the raft.

"Good morning, gentlemen," a man in a law enforcement uniform said, looking down on the two men in the raft.

"Hello sir. Yes, it is a fine morning for fishing," Malik said.

"Where are you boys heading?" the man asked, surveying the packages on the raft.

"Just looking for a good fishing spot."

"It's all pretty good around here. You have a lot of packages for fishing. How long are you going for?"

"Just a couple of days. We probably just overpacked."

"Where are you guys from?" the officer asked, recognizing Malik's thick accent.

"We're visiting from Baghdad."

"You have your passports?"

"Sure, let me get them for you."

Malik looked at Arsal with the all too familiar glance where they knew where the security guard's line of questioning would end up.

"Here you go, sir," Malik said, handing the passports to the officer. "Is there a problem with fishing out here?" Malik asked. While Malik was talking to the security guard, Arsal nonchalantly picked up a handgun and placed it inside the pocket of his jacket.

"No, there's no problem with fishing. But do you know where you're at?"

"The Missouri River."

"See that structure over there?" the man said, pointing to the power plant.

"Yes, what is it?" Malik answered, knowing exactly what is was.

"That's an 800 megawatt power plant."

"Wow, it looks big."

"Yeah, it's big. It's a critical national asset." Seeing that the two in the raft weren't following the guard, he added, "In other words, it's pretty important, so we have security around it. I'm a guard that secures the river around the plant. So it's my job to know who's fishing around it. Let me call in and I'll have you on your way." The guard turned toward the radio, but before he could get to it, Malik tried to stall him.

"Sir, we're just out here fishing. Can we just be on our way?"

The guard turned back around to address Malik and stopped as if he had just looked into Medusa's eyes. Arsal was pointing his pistol directly at the guard's head.

Malik's tone changed from clumsy tourist to that of a killer. "Actually, sir, we'll be needing those back," Malik said, climbing onto the guard's boat. He pulled out his handgun and took their passports out of the guard's hand.

"Look boys, we don't need to get crazy. Take your passports and be on your way; neither of us need any trouble."

"Malik, what should we do?" he said, shaking his handgun.

"The problem is, he's seen us, and as soon as we leave, he'll call the police," Malik replied.

"No I won't," the guard pleaded. "I don't care what you're up to. I'm about to get off my shift; I won't say anything."

Arsal looked at Malik as if to ask, "What now?" With Malik turned slightly around to Arsal still on the raft, the guard lunged at Malik and tackled him onto the deck of the boat. Malik and the guard struggled to get the gun that Malik dropped. Arsal couldn't get a clean shot at the guard. Malik grabbed a wrench and struck the guard in the side of the head, knocking him back into the side of the boat. He then bent over to pick up his gun, but caught the guard's right knee square in the face instead.

While Malik was knocked back, the guard made a move for the microphone to the radio on the control panel. Before he could grab it, a gunshot penetrated his back and exited through his chest. The sharp pain stopped him immediately. He stumbled away from the radio toward Malik, who was lying on the deck bleeding from his nose and mouth. He knew he had been shot. He fell to his knees, holding his chest. In what would be his last act of defiance, he grabbed a knife off of a chair and plunged it into Malik's chest on his way to the deck. Malik felt the cold steel blade tear through his flesh. The blade tore right through his heart. Unable to focus, Malik's eyelids fluttered. Arsal pulled the guard's lifeless body off of Malik and saw the hilt of the knife protruding from Malik's chest.

"Malik!" Arsal cried out. Malik's breathing was too strained to be able to talk. Malik's eyes grew wide open and his short breaths stopped. His body became limp. Arsal knew Malik had died.

Sitting on the deck, Arsal's mind raced with questions. What do I do now? I can't do this alone. If they find me they'll kill me too. Maybe I should kill myself before they do. Wait, what would Malik do? He would remain calm; he always said to remain calm. He looked around to see if anyone had seen what happened. In the calm of the dawn hours, the river was otherwise quiet.

I need to dispose of the bodies, Arsal thought. He removed the knife from Malik's chest, remembering what he was told about making sure the bodies would not float. He stabbed the guard's body, tossed it overboard, and watched as it slowly disappeared into the water; however, he could not desecrate Malik by adding more holes in his body. Instead, he took the cell phone from Malik's pocket, took a pickax, and cut away at the floorboard of the boat until it began taking on water. He climbed back into the raft, started the small outboard motor, and said good-bye to his friend as the boat began to sink. He then made a call from Malik's phone.

"Hallid, this is Arsal. We've had a problem."

Chapter 58

Good for the Soul
Greenfield Ranch, Oklahoma
June 11, 2017

As Claire pulled into the café parking lot she could see Murph leaning against his car waiting for her. "Oh, I'm so busted," Claire said under her breath.

"Sorry I'm late, Murph; late night."

"This is the first time you've been late since I've known you. Must've been some night!"

"You could say that, Murph," Claire said as she smiled and unlocked the doors.

"By the size of that grin, I'd say it involved a certain someone," he said with a smirk.

"Don't be ridiculous, we just had dinner," she said, trying to deflect the obvious.

"I'm being ridiculous?" Murph uttered under his breath. "I think someone's in love, that's what I think," he continued while starting up the griddle. Claire, with her back to Murph, smiled and acted as if she didn't hear him.

Natalie came into the café an hour later and wanted details of Claire's night.

"Well, how was your date with Mason?" she asked eagerly.

"Awesome; we had dinner and wine."

"Oh, you naughty girl!" Natalie razzed.

"It's not like that!" Claire tried to explain.

"Yes it is. Then explain why you can't get that smitten grin off of your face."

"What are you talking about?" Claire said, completely dismissing Natalie's comment.

"I knew it! You two make a cute couple," Natalie continued.

"It's about time you get a boyfriend, Claire. Mason's an all right guy in my book," Murph chimed in from the kitchen. "Anyone who would ride with you is all right."

"He's not my boyfriend!" she cried out, completely blushing.

"Tell me about it! Come on!"

"No! We have to work."

"Later, you have to tell me about it, okay?"

"All right, later," Claire said, trying to hide her excitement. She hadn't felt like that in years. Her life was complicated, and Mason was a nice distraction from it all. Except the dying in a week thing. A somber chill went up her spine when she thought of it.

As the morning crowd began to thin, Claire decided it was time to wake up Mason and went next door to Marcie's.

"Good morning, Marcie," Claire announced as she walked through the front door.

"Hi, Claire!"

"What's sleepyhead up to?" Claire asked, pointing up to Mason's room.

"He left a little while ago. I think he got home pretty late, or pretty early, depending on how you look at it," she said with her all-too-familiar crooked smile.

"Did he say where he was going?"

"No, I assumed he was going to see you."

"Huh," Claire said curiously. "Was he acting all right?"

"Yes, he seemed normal, but last night was a different story."

"What do you mean?"

"He must've been having some dream. I woke to him yelling, and when I went to check on him he grabbed my hand and shocked the hell out of me."

"Did he say anything?"

"No, he just mumbled, 'Oh shit, no way.' It kind of freaked me out, so I went back to my room."

"Well I left my cell phone with him yesterday; I'm going to see if he left it in his room."

"Sure, go ahead. I've got muffins in the oven; I'll talk to you later," Marcie said, walking back into the kitchen, not really wanting to know why Claire wanted to get inside his room.

All right Mason, what are you up to? she thought as she began to ransack his room, starting with his luggage. Finding nothing pertinent, she noticed a small notebook with her name written on it along with *Joe, Frank, Natalie, Miram*, and *Marcie* added on the bottom of the list. The date June 16, 2017 was written above all of the names. What? Now it's up to six people? Looking under the bed, she saw Mason's black attaché case. "What have we here?" she said, pulling it out and opening it up. Seeing Mason's personal doctor files and newspaper clippings, she knew she hit the mother lode. She sat on the floor with her back against the wall and began reading.

Mason walked to Frank's to check on his car. "Hi, Mason," Frank said, walking out to greet Mason.

"Hi Frank. How's the transmission going?"

"It's coming along just fine; might have it done today or tomorrow."

"Awesome. I went to Idledale and got the money for it."

"Great, we'll settle up tomorrow."

"Hey, what's going on down there?" Mason asked, pointing down the street where people were gathering.

"That's our church service. It's about to start. Are you a religious person, Mason?"

"I think I am today, Frank," Mason said with a smile as he started walking down the street.

When the service was over, Mason walked out of the Greenfield Ranch Community Church and mingled with the crowd like he had been living there his entire life. If there was ever a stage to meet people, it was through church. Meeting people that he hadn't met, he shook their hands and greeted them—and obtained their death day. The common denominator was June 16, 2017. It flashed every time he met someone and came in contact with them. After encountering at least fifty different people who all had the same day, he had gathered all the data he needed and hurried back to his room.

He walked in through the front door and was immediately greeted in a loud voice by Marcie.

"Hi Mason!" she called out from the kitchen, no doubt alerting her friend to Mason's arrival.

"Oh crap!" Claire said, taking the hint. She scrambled to get the paperwork back together and threw it all back into the attaché case.

"Hi Marcie," he said, acknowledging her strange, loud behavior.

"Can you come here please, Mason?"

"Marcie, I really don't have the time for this, sorry," he said, starting up the stairs.

"Mason, wait! After all I've done for you, you can't give me two minutes?" she said, laying on the guilt.

"Oh man, she pulled out the trump card," Mason said to himself, stopping halfway up the stairwell.

"Fine, two minutes," he agreed and walked back down and into the kitchen.

Claire jumped at the opportunity and slipped out of Mason's room. She tiptoed down the hall past Marcie's room to a back stairwell that led to a back exit by the kitchen and waited.

"Here, try one of these muffins."

"Okay," he said, taking a bite of a tart blueberry muffin. "This is really good; you should sell these at Claire's," he continued as he finished it.

"It's my own special recipe."

"Well they're really good."

"Thanks, Mason," Marcie said with her sultry grin.

"Okay, gotta get going, but thanks," Mason said, rushing out of the kitchen, back to the front of the house, and up the stairs to his room. As Mason left the kitchen, Claire stepped out of the back stairwell, slipped past Marcie, mouthed "Thanks," and left through the kitchen door into the backyard. Circling around to the front door, Claire emerged and called out, "Hi Marcie, anyone home?"

Marcie, playing along with her, came out of the kitchen and gave her a hug and a sideways glare, as if to say, "What are you up to?"

"Hi Claire, nice to see you," Marcie announced.

Mason, playing right into their trap, heard Claire downstairs. Right on cue, he opened his door and said, "Claire! Come here, I've got to talk to you."

"Okay. Marcie, I'm being summoned. I'll talk to you later."

"Where's the fire, Mason?" Claire asked as she walked into Mason's room.

"Here, close the door and sit down. You're going to want to be seated."

"What's up? Where have you been?"

"I went to church."

"Our church?"

"Yes, nice people. However, they all have the same death day."

"I met fifty-some odd people and their days are all the same as yours." Looking around for his notepad, Mason couldn't find it. "Oh, where is it?"

"Where's what?" Claire said.

"Nothing. I bet Marcie's been snooping around. Anyway, I was talking to Frank this morning and saw that people were going to church, so I thought I'd go and try and get other people's days. Afterwards, I guess it's like a big social. Actually, it's pretty cool, by the way, you really should go to church more often. I started meeting people and all of their death days are the same."

"Which means that we're all in this together?" Claire said.

"It confirms that something is going to happen to all of you."

"Mason, didn't you say that you've never been wrong?"

Knowing where Claire was going with her line of questioning, Mason hesitantly gave the painful truth. "Yes, I did. But I can't help but want to try and be wrong this time."

"Then there really is nothing that we can do, right?"

Knowing Claire may be right, Mason knew he had to be optimistic. "I'm not sure, Claire, but I know we can't sit back and do nothing. If there was nothing we could do, then why would I be getting warning signs?"

Looking at the picture Miram gave Mason leaned against the wall, Claire probed further. "Mason, what's up with the picture?"

"I had a dream where I'm in an ancient city that gets ravished by a parliament of killer owls."

"A parliament?"

"Yes, that's a flock of owls. But the city looks just like the picture."

"Do you know what it means?"

"The woman, Amona, said I was the man in the panting and that I would know what it means. But I don't know. But I think it might be starting to make sense."

Testing Mason, Claire asked Mason questions she already knew the answers to after reading the papers in his attaché case. "Why you, Mason?"

"It's a long story, but in a nutshell, I had an accident when I was a kid, and when I came out of it I was able to see the date that people die. I didn't ask for it, and I'm not sure why he gave it to me, but he did."

"Who's he?"

"Ah Puch."

"Ah Puch who?"

"I know this is going to sound crazy, but I'm not sure you can think I'm any more nuts than you already do. He's the Mayan god of death. The doctor, Dr. Hogan, that I saw at the University of Oklahoma specializes in 'supernatural phenomenon.' It was he who helped me figure this thing out. We determined that the day I had my accident, I crossed over to another realm and made contact with Ah Puch. That day, June 1, was the feast day of Ah Puch. Somehow I came in contact with him and he bestowed this gift, or curse, or whatever it is onto me."

"That sounds pretty ostentatious, Mason."

"Here, I'll prove it," he said, reaching under his bed and retrieving his attaché case. Opening it up, he saw his missing notepad inside. "There it is. Funny, I'm not sure how that got in there considering I haven't opened this bag since I got here." Looking at Claire suspiciously, he asked, "Any ideas?"

"No, no, I have no idea how your notepad got in there."

"I never said I was looking for a notepad."

"I just assumed . . . Oh forget it! I'm sorry, Mason. I looked through it earlier when I came here looking for you," Claire said, coming clean.

"You looked through my stuff? After last night you still don't trust me?"

"No, I do! I mean yes, I'm sorry. I really am trying to believe you, Mason. It's just so hard to believe." Part of Mason felt violated, betrayed yet again by someone he was trying to help.

"Claire, that's a bunch of crap. You know what? I'm done with this shit. If you don't want to believe, then so be it. I'll be gone tomorrow when my car is done. So next Friday when you and your friends die, I won't be anywhere close to this town."

"Mason, I'm sorry. I am trying. You know, you've had twenty years to get used to it. It happens to you and you still struggle with it. You just can't expect me to understand it and accept it in three days."

Thinking about the true statement Claire made, Mason calmed down. "You're right. I guess it would just be nice for someone to not fight me on it every time."

"Okay, what do we do now?" Claire asked.

"I need to go to the library and check the weather. Maybe a tornado whips through here, I don't know. Let me go do some research and I'll meet up with you later."

With a newfound sense of partnership, Claire wanted to help. "All right, what do you want me to do?"

"Nothing right now; let me think about it. But keep in mind how difficult it was for you to accept it. I'm not sure I'd be telling people about it just yet."

"Believe me; you don't have to worry about me telling anyone."

Chapter 59

Lay of the Land
Greenfield Ranch, Oklahoma
June 11, 2017

Mason sat at a table in the town library tapping away on his laptop computer. He had been there all day, it seemed, when Claire came in to check on him. "Hi Mason. What's it looking like?" Claire said, walking up to Mason.

"Hi Claire. I'm not finding much. Here, check this out," he said, turning his monitor so she could see the map pulled up on his screen.

"These are the fault lines that run throughout the Unites States, none of which fall in this area. So it's unlikely there's going to be an earthquake. There's no volcanic activity around here either, so I'm guessing no kind of eruption. You are, however, located in Tornado Alley. So if the weather gets extreme, maybe a tornado rips through here."

"Yes, but the weather stations aren't forecasting anything significant anytime soon," Claire interjected.

"Exactly, so I'm leaning towards it not being a natural disaster. I mean, you're very dry and very hot out here, but I find it hard to believe that a fire would consume the town and nobody gets out. So although we don't know what it is, we have a pretty good idea of what it's not."

"So where does that put us?" Claire asked.

"I'm still not sure. What kind of gas lines, electricity, or power do you guys have here?"

"Believe it or not, we have state-of-the-art gas and electric here. We had it completely renovated and brought up to date a couple of years ago. I can't imagine it would be a problem with that."

"And you don't really have any industry here, right?" Mason asked.

"No, it's exactly what you see."

"So it's unlikely to be an industrial accident? Well then, I don't know. It's pretty difficult pulling up maps of this area. You guys are so small, there's no public topographical maps out there that I could find. Hell, I can't find anything on this town. So I guess we just keep looking."

"What do you need the topographical maps for?"

"Just to get a lay of the land. To try and figure if there's something else that we're missing."

"Wait here, I think I might know where one is."

A few minutes later, Claire placed an old rolled up map of the town on the table.

"Awesome. I'm not even going to ask where it was," Mason said.

"Good, because I'm not supposed to have it out."

"All right, let's check it out. God, this has to be over a hundred years old," Mason said, unrolling it.

"Yes, I think it's the original survey and the only one out there."

"Is that why you don't let anyone look at it?"

"I guess so. I've really never thought about it."

"Look for anything that has the potential to be or could cause destruction," he instructed.

As they examined the old map of the area before the land was developed, neither one of them could find anything significant. Growing weary and with hope diminishing rapidly, Mason, thinking out loud, asked, "What exactly does this green shaded area mean?"

"It looks like it shows where the town was slotted to be built."

"Yes, but we're over here, right?" he said, pointing to an area next to the lightly shaded area.

"Yes, there is nothing in that area now. We went through it on our way to the lake. What is that symbol?" Claire asked, pointing to a small triangle with a plus symbol inside it.

"I don't know, but there's got to be a legend," Mason said, flipping the large open map over. "Here, here's the legend." Moving his finger down the legend, he located the symbol and said, "It's where the church was to be built. It's actually a cross."

"Of course, that makes sense."

"I don't know, Claire. We'll have to just keep working on it," Mason said, sitting back and taking an exhaustive breath.

"All right, I have to put this map back," Claire said, rolling it up.

"Wait; let me check something for a second." Flipping the map around, Mason examined the legend again. "Interesting."

"What's that?"

"The thing about maps is that if it's on the map, it has to be in the legend. Like your church symbol or these proposed building sites," Mason explained, pointing to different symbols on the map. "But I don't see the green area on the legend."

"Yes, strange. I don't know what it means. But I better get this back before someone sees us," Claire said, rolling up the large map.

They walked to the front door of the library. With Claire still holding the map, she instructed Mason, "You go ahead, I'll put this back. I'll see you later."

Mason walked through the door and stopped by the window. Through the glass, he watched Claire walk to the back of the library. She looked around to make sure no one was watching and carefully slid behind a rack of books and disappeared. He stretched to try and get a better view, but couldn't see her.

"Can I help you with something, Mason?" a woman said as she was walking by the library and noticed Mason looking through the glass.

"No, I was just looking at the library."

"Well, it's easier if you just walk inside. The books aren't going to bite you, you know."

"Thank you, maybe later," Mason said, walking away very quickly. The lady gave him a weird glance.

Chapter 60

Greater Than the Sum of Its Parts
Greenfield Ranch, Oklahoma
June 11, 2017

As Claire was in her bedroom getting ready, there was a knock at her front door. She looked out the living room window and saw Joe, Frank, Jake, and Rod waiting at her door. She called out to them, "Come on in," while she finished putting in her earrings. The four of them walked inside Claire's living room. Joe took off his hat.

"Hi Claire," Joe said. "We wanted to talk to you about Mason."

"I figured that. What do you want to know?" She didn't mince words with them and she wasn't the least bit intimidated by them. There was always an edge to her conversations when Jake and Rod were present. She didn't particularly like them and she felt the feeling was probably mutual. She couldn't call Joe "Gramps" when they were around. There seemed to be constant tension with them, in this tension-less town.

"We understand that you went through his things?" Joe asked.

Knowing that Joe didn't ask questions he didn't know the answers to, Claire decided it would be better to be honest. "Yes, I did. I was trying to get information on him."

"What kind of information?"

"Nothing in particular, just general stuff." Which wasn't far from the truth.

"People are noticing that you're acting strange, Claire. Are you all right?" Jake said.

"I'm fine, Jake. God, small towns are way too involved in personal matters."

"So it's a personal matter now?" Jake asked.

"No, I mean yes. Look, I'm keeping an eye on him. I'm making sure he's not wandering around." Her disconcerting answer showed her frustration. The four men in her living room noticed it as well. They needed her to be a rock, but she showed them she may have vulnerability. That made them nervous. That was not good for the town.

"Are you sure it's not more than that?" Jake asked further.

"What do you mean more?"

"You know what we mean, Claire," Joe reiterated.

"He's a nice guy, there's nothing wrong with that," Claire said, trying to defend her actions—and hide her feelings. She had to stay strong. It was still a man's town and men were running it. If she didn't stay tough, she'd get eaten up.

"Don't get attached, Claire," Rod piped up. "He's leaving tomorrow."

"Tomorrow?" Her heart dropped to the floor in an instant. Her feelings were now completely evident to her. She tried hard to hide her deflated spirit, but they could tell. There's no hiding from that kind of feeling. Rod continued to pour on the salt.

"His car is ready; he needs to leave tomorrow."

"All right, then there's really nothing else to worry about, right?" Claire said, trying to be strong. Her darting eyes gave a different story. Her heart was pounding fiercely.

"What exactly was he doing in the library all day?" Rod asked.

"I don't know, checking emails."

"On Google Earth?"

"Maybe he's planning his trip back to Chicago; I don't know." She may have struggled with hiding her emotions, but in a battle of wits she could go the distance.

Recognizing that Claire was not cooperating, Rod said, "Whatever it is you're protecting for him, you had better be careful. This isn't a game, and you had better not lose sight of that."

She walked to the door and opened it; she was done with her interrogation. "I'm fine, Rod. Now if you'll excuse me, I have to go babysit one more time."

Joe put his hat back on and said, "Have a good night, Claire." She watched the convoy pull out of her driveway from the front door, thoroughly annoyed. Now the drink she was going for was a need, not a want.

Mason sat at the bar waiting for Claire. She wasn't usually this late. Sid diverted his thought temporarily.

"Hi Mason," Sid said, walking up from behind the bar.

"Evening, Sid."

"Jameson and Coke, right?"

"You got a great memory Sid, thanks."

"Ah, it's easy when it's a small town," Sid said, dismissing the compliment.

"Hey Sid, let me ask you a question."

"Sure."

Mason looked around to see if anyone was within earshot of him talking. He lowered his voice just in case.

"Being in a small town like this, do you ever wish you got out more and experienced the world? I mean, you guys really keep yourselves pretty isolated, which I guess has its pros and cons."

"Mason, most of us have traveled the world. We've done things, seen things, held other jobs, and at some point, just decided it was time to get back to our fundamental values. You know, the simple life. Most of us got sick of the crime, the hustle and bustle, the keeping up with the Joneses. You tend to lose yourself in the big cities. This town brings you back to what life is all about."

"I can see that, but unfortunately you still need money to survive. Kind of like a necessary evil. I just don't see how you guys do it," Mason said, shaking his head.

"I think we'd all be surprised what we could do if we had to."

"Hell Sid, it surprises me what people do when they don't have to."

"Here, here. You like living in the big city, Mason?"

Sid placed Mason's Jameson and Coke on a coaster in front of him. Mason took a sip and thought briefly about Sid's question, a more valid question than Mason had initially thought. Claire wasn't in the big city. Without her, maybe it's not worth it? he wondered.

"You know, you get bombarded on a daily basis with the thoughtlessness of human nature. Why we as humans do the things we do to each other blows my mind sometimes."

"That's why we're here instead of in the big towns."

"But don't we need the big town to a degree?" Mason asked.

"Ah, now that's a much deeper question, my friend. Do you understand what holism is?"

"Yes, it's like looking at the whole picture, I think?"

"It's the concept of the whole being greater than the sum of its parts. Take a car, for example. It is made of thousands of parts, but put them together and you get a car. Well, society is the whole and it's made up of hundreds of smaller groups: religious, racial, cultural, secular, sexual, generational, and it goes on and on. Now to complicate things, each group may have a different set of attitudes, values, beliefs, and educational levels. Now throw in money and economics and you have a very complex system or 'whole.' The problem is, the smaller groups think they're more important than the society as a whole. And because of that, they feel compelled to impart their worldview on the whole. In the old days, the system fought back. You know, shut them down. Now the system tries to accommodate everyone, and in doing so, the system is losing its identity along with its values. So do we need the big towns? Sure, but we need them to lead the masses, not corrupt them."

"Damn Sid, that's some serious stuff. Something tells me you weren't always a bartender?"

"Ah, I read a lot," Sid said, dismissing the open door Mason invited him to walk through about his past. Looking for an out, Sid was saved by the arrival of Claire.

"Hey Claire, good to see you. What'll you have?"

"Hi Sid, I'll have what he's having," she said, walking up to the bar and pointing to Mason.

"Hi Claire. Sid was just explaining holism to me."

"Oh yes, the idea that the whole is greater than the sum of its parts," she rattled off.

"What, is this entire town full of academics? Am I the only person that doesn't know what that is?" Mason replied.

"It's a psychology term. The body is a whole made up of parts, and if one part is affected, it affects the whole being. The same can be said about a person's persona."

"I bet you two are a blast at parties," Mason said sarcastically.

"Don't listen to him, Sid. We are the life of the party, right?"

"You know it, Claire; here's your Jameson and Coke."

"Thanks Sid." Turning her attention to Mason, she asked, "So did you get some rest?"

"Yes, I can get used to taking power naps off and on all day long. It'll be hard getting back to work."

"Well, speaking of work, it appears you'll be getting back after all; Frank said you car is ready."

"Really!" Mason said as his excitement trailed off, realizing what it meant. "I don't have to leave; I can hang out for a few more days."

"No, Mason. They're pretty much expecting you to leave tomorrow."

"Do you want me to leave tomorrow?"

"Don't ask me that, Mason." They both knew the answer to that question.

"Well do you?"

"No. But it's not up to me, and in the end aren't we just postponing the inevitable?"

"Maybe. Maybe not."

"What does that mean?"

"Part of me wants to stay and figure out the dilemma that you face, and another part wants to stay and hang out with you."

"That's sweet, Mason, thanks. I want to you to stay, believe me, but it's not that simple. People just don't stay here."

"Yes, but they do leave here, right?"

"Actually, no; it's complicated."

"What, are you telling me you can't leave your town? Now that might be a good story to write."

Joe interrupted before Claire could say anything. "There's no story, Mason; of course Claire can leave anytime she wants to," he said, walking up and putting his hand on Claire's shoulder. "But she's family and doesn't want to leave; right, Claire?"

"Yes, Joe," she said reluctantly.

"So Mason, your car is fixed."

"That's what Claire was just telling me."

"So you'll be leaving us tomorrow?"

"I was thinking I might stay a couple more days, Joe; that's not a problem, is it?" Mason asked in a very brash tone, thinking he'd put Joe on the spot.

Looking at Mason as if he wanted to beat him to a pulp, Joe leaned in and, in a threatening tone, whispered in Mason's ear, "Look, your car is fixed and this isn't a tourist trap. People don't feel comfortable with you here, and it's my job to make sure they're happy and safe. You are contrary to that feeling, therefore you need to leave. Are we clear?"

Not being intimidated, Mason politely informed him, "I think we're pretty clear. I'll be staying, and if you don't like it, perhaps you wouldn't mind reading about it in a national headline. See what that does to your tourism trade."

"Mason—" Claire started but was cut off by Joe. She knew Mason just started a firestorm. Joe's nostrils flared and his thick, burly eyebrows scowled. His glare at Mason showed he was no stranger to conflict. He leaned into Mason's face this time.

"Mason, I know we're just this little backcountry hick town, but you'd be surprised what I can do. You're going to want to reconsider your vacation plans. I'll talk to you later, Claire," Joe said as his evil glare sent a chill up Claire's spine.

"Mason, you have no idea what you've done."

"What, call out someone who isn't used to being confronted?"

"No, you just don't want to piss him off."

"I'm not worried about him; he doesn't scare me."

"He can be very difficult."

"What's the whole 'I'll talk to you later' thing he did to you? He's going to try and intimidate you."

"Calm down. No, he isn't. I know how to handle him. He's old school and isn't used to people questioning him. I'll deal with him, don't worry. Anyway, it's a great night; you want to take a walk?"

"Yes, I'm getting some pretty weird looks now."

Chapter 61

The Gathering
Greenfield Ranch, Oklahoma
June 11, 2017

Claire and Mason walked on a dirt trail taking in the warm summer evening air. Dusk rapidly approached. Mason finally calmed down from his confrontation with Joe in the bar. He noticed something odd.

"Check out that owl, Claire," he said, pointing to the top of an Austrian pine.

"Cool, he's just sitting there checking out the town."

"I guess they come out at nightfall, huh?" Mason asked.

"Yes, I guess so. I think it's amazing how they can perch on a flimsy branch and not bend it over."

"They're pretty cool birds. Oh look, another one on that tree," Claire said, pointing to another tree.

"Hey, there's another one, over there," Mason said, pointing to still another one.

"Wow, they're out in full force tonight I guess," Claire said.

"Wait," Mason said, stopping. "They're all over the place, check it out." He pointed into a thicket of trees.

"I don't think I've ever seen more than one at a time. In fact, I didn't know they even travel in flocks, do they?" Claire asked.

"I don't know; I didn't think so. At least I've never seen it. At least not when I'm awake. Oh shit!"

"What's the matter, Mason?"

"No, no, no," Mason said, looking down at the ground as if he thought of something potentially bad. "My dreams. That's when the owls descend on people and . . ."

"And what, Mason?"

"And, it's not pretty," Mason said. "We need to get back." His eyes shifted from tree to tree matching his rapid breaths. Owls were showing up all around them. What were they doing? This can't be like my dreams, can it? he wondered. His optimism overcame his fear. I've got to stop this, he thought. As they hurried back to Sid's, Claire watched one owl launch from its perch and go from treetop to treetop.

"Mason, that owl seems to be following us."

Mason looked up at the owl. The owl gazed back. What are you doing? he thought.

"Yes, that's odd. He's probably not following us," Mason said, trying to reassure Claire. She wasn't buying it.

"He's not hunting us, is he?" Claire asked, somewhat concerned.

"No, I don't think so." At least I hope not, he finished saying in his mind. They stopped outside Sid's at Claire's truck and Mason said, "I'm going to Frank's to pick up my car; I'll call you later if I come up with anything."

Claire watched the owl follow Mason down the street.

Mason cut right to the chase when he arrived at Frank's. "Hi Frank, I understand from the grapevine that my car is ready."

"Got her all fixed up and running like a top. Let me get your ticket and we'll get you all squared away."

"Great, thanks." Frank disappeared into a back room. Mason looked at the cluttered garage. A faded antique Pennzoil oil sign hung on the wall. It made him remember helping his dad change the oil in the Mustang when he was a child. Black blotches of oil stained the gray concrete floor. And what garage would be complete without the token Snap-On tool calendar? Mason wasn't sure Frank ever discarded anything. Frank emerged from the back room peering at the bill through the bottom half of his glasses.

"Here you go," he said, handing Mason the bill. "So you'll be leaving us tomorrow, I suppose?" Frank continued.

"I'm not sure. I might hang out a couple of days, I don't know."

Frank knew better. Word travels fast in small towns. He already heard of the confrontation Mason and Joe had at Sid's.

"It's an appealing little town, isn't it?"

"Yes. How would someone move here if they wanted to?"

"I suppose you'd have to find some property for sale and buy it."

"And I'm guessing you guys don't have much for sale right now?"

"I don't think we've had anything for sale for years. There's not a lot of flipping that goes on here."

"I guess not."

"Well, here are the keys; she sure is a beauty of a car."

"Yes, it was my dad's baby; he just gave it to me a couple of weeks ago."

"You take care of her and she'll take care of you."

"Thanks Frank, I really appreciate you fixing her up."

Mason handed Frank a wad of cash and fired up the car. The rumble of a car engine never sounded so good. His handcuffs were finally taken off. His tether was cut loose and he could finally breathe again. Now staying was his choice.

"You're welcome; have a safe trip back."

It felt good to get his car back. Mason noticed the owl perched across the street. It was meant for him. All he could think about were the owls attacking the town, like in his dreams. Driving down the vacant street, a thought crossed his mind. What if the people weren't here? Would the owls track them down wherever they were, or would they not be killed?

Pulling up to Marcie's, he went up to his room to think. While pacing back and forth in his room, he noticed a faint light outside through his window. Walking over and looking out, he noticed a person close the curtains in the small office building across the street. As he started to turn back around, he noticed the edge of the curtain being pulled back a little as if someone was watching him. Then it occurred to him that they'd probably been watching him since he arrived.

"Son of a bitch," he said under his breath. Closing his blinds, he laid down and began pondering his options. Do I leave, and they all die? Do I stay and try to get them to leave? If I tell them, they'll never believe me; hell, Claire barely does. The owls are coming and there is no way to fight them. Wait. Why are they watching me? What do they think I'll find? There's one way to find out.

Going down to the kitchen, Mason tried making noise to get the attention of Marcie, who was sitting in the family room.

Right on cue, she said, "Hi Mason. Do you need something?"

"No, just getting a glass of water," he said, walking into the family room. "What are you watching?"

"Nothing, I'm mostly reading. In fact, it's getting late. I'm probably going to go to bed. Are you heading out tomorrow?"

"Is it all right if I stay a couple more days?"

"I— I guess so."

Recognizing the hesitation in her voice, Mason clarified, "I've already talked to Joe about it, if that's what you're concerned about."

"No, it's fine. We're just not used to people wanting to stay in our town. But then again, not everyone has met Claire, right?" she said with her uniquely crooked grin. Getting a little embarrassed, he knew he had to take one for the team. "She is kind of special, isn't she?"

"Oh you have no idea, sweetie. Anyway, you stay here as long as you want."

"Thanks Marcie, you've been really great."

"It's nothing. I'm going to sleep. I'll see you tomorrow, unless one of your dreams keeps me up again."

"Sorry, I'll try not to dream."

"I'm kidding. Good night, Mason," she said, turning off the television and walking upstairs. Mason walked back to his room and closed the door. Peeking out his window, he could still the see the person watching him from the building across the street.

Chapter 62

Heart-to-Heart
Greenfield Ranch, Oklahoma
June 11, 2017

Joe sat on his back porch with a newspaper sipping his hot blackberry tea, a guilty pleasure only he knew about. It helped him relax before bed. The knock at his door was a big inconvenience, but he knew it could only be Claire at this time of the night. No one else would invade his personal time. He even expected it after the blowup with Mason earlier.

"Hi Claire, come on in. It's late. Are you all right?"

"Yes, I'm fine. I just need to talk to you." Joe could see the sadness in his granddaughter's eyes.

"Have a seat; can I get you some tea?"

"Thanks; that'd be great."

"This is about tonight, right?" her grandfather anticipated.

"Gramps, I have to talk to you."

"You haven't called me that for a long time; here you go," Joe said while handing Claire a cup of tea. He sat on the adjacent sofa.

Claire replied, "I know, and I hate it. Sometimes I feel like an employee rather than a granddaughter."

"It's the nature of our town and our responsibilities." He listened to his own words, defending the cold nature of his position. It bothered him.

"I know, but a small town is supposed to be more friendly, not less," Claire reminded him.

"We just have to be patient; things will get back to normal soon. This *is* about Mason, isn't it?" Joe's guilt of what his relationship with Claire had turned into snuck out like a Freudian slip. He quickly realized his slip. He shifted and fidgeted on the sofa. It made him uncomfortable.

Claire was too perceptive to not recognize her grandfather's unconscious concern about their relationship. She was pleasantly surprised that he was thinking about it. Secretly, what their relationship had degraded into bothered her as much if not more. But first things first.

"Yes, mostly," she replied. "He's not a threat to anyone. He's a nice person, not like some of the idiots I've dated."

Joe stood up and walked to the fireplace. "I know, Claire, but the timing is just not right. You have a little baggage too, you know. I'm sure Mason doesn't know about it, at least he had better not."

"No, of course not. But it's kind of nice to have a friend who doesn't know about all the crap I've been through. He actually likes me for me."

"Claire, he doesn't even know you." Joe said.

"He knows a different part of me. But it's still me," she pleaded.

"Well, either way, it's a good sign that you're able to build healthy relationships again. It shows that you're recovering appropriately from that last fiasco."

"I'll admit, it's a little therapeutic." It was also more than that, she thought.

"You know Claire, you may not believe this, but I miss talking to you. It's been a long time since we've sat down and talked about anything real."

"I know, I miss it too. You may not like Mason, but it's because of him that we're having this talk."

"I should thank him then, because we needed this; I needed this," Joe said.

"Yes, me too. But that is why I'm here. Joe, I can't just make him leave. He has to want to leave on his own."

"You're encouraging him to stay and you know he can't."

"I'm not asking him to move here, can we just give him a couple of days? That's all. Then I promise you, he'll leave." Joe stopped and thought for a minute. He looked at a picture of him and Claire from years earlier on the mantel above the fireplace. It occurred to him he was hurting the one person in the world he cared about more than anything. Seeing Claire practically beg for something she shouldn't have to made him feel like a bully. Humility overcame him. He didn't want Claire to remember him this way. Not as someone with no heart. It was time to turn their sinking ship of a relationship around. He turned back to her and smiled at the prospect of hope.

"Does it mean that much to you?" he asked.

"Yes it does; please?"

"All right, Claire," Joe said with a smile. He walked over to her and grabbed her hands. "I'll apologize to him tomorrow and we'll show him some small town hospitality. But by the end of the week, he has to go." Claire's eyes lit up with surprise. She jumped up and hugged him, squeezing the air out of his lungs. Her happiness broke the hardness around his now warm beating heart.

"Thanks, Gramps!"

As Claire pulled out of his driveway, Joe stood on the front porch and watched her drive away. The obvious soft spot in his heart for Claire emerged with a tear.

Chapter 63

The Gift of Wisdom
Greenfield Ranch, Oklahoma
June 12, 2017

With Marcie in her room and all of the lights in the house off, Mason quietly walked down the main stairwell and walked into the kitchen. Opening drawers until he found a flashlight, he slipped out the back door. Knowing that he was being watched, he had to be extra careful not to make a sound. Reminiscent of his surveillance work he did for his story, he slid along the back of the buildings, going from one to another until he was across from the library.

Making sure the coast was clear, he hurried into the library in one swift move, closing the door behind him. Looking out from the main window, he made sure no one was following him. "Now where did she go?" he said to himself, trying to find where Claire put the map.

Walking to the back of the library using his flashlight, he went to where Claire disappeared. "It's got to be here somewhere. Must be a hidden door."

He began moving books and racks but couldn't find anything. As he was walking, he heard the floor make a different sound. Looking down, he felt around until he found a small lip in the carpeting. Pulling it back, he saw a door in the floor under the carpeting. He opened the door and saw a stairwell leading into a basement.

Climbing down the stairwell, he wiped sweat from his forehead. His heartbeat pounded. At the bottom of the stairs, he shined his light around to see a large room with books, maps, filing cabinets, military clothes, and a large wide filing cabinet for large flat maps.

Pulling the light cord, he turned on the light and illuminated the old storage area. It's got to be in here, he thought, pulling open the wide drawers. Searching through the maps, he found the one Claire had brought down.

"What are all these other ones, though?" he thought aloud. "It's no use; there's so much crap in here, it's like looking for a needle in a haystack." He looked at one wall and noticed a steel door. Walking over to it, he saw it had an electronic keypad and was locked.

I wonder what's behind door number one? he thought. Knowing he wasn't getting in there, he continued to look around. He saw a map enclosed in glass hanging on the wall.

That's the same map that Claire brought up, he thought. Why is this one in glass? Looking at it closer, it was indeed the same map that Claire had shown him earlier—an old map of the undeveloped land that the town sat on.

There's the shaded area. No way! he thought. On top of the light green shaded area were the words "No Build – Indian Burial Site" that weren't on the version of the map that Claire had. You gotta be kidding me, they built on an Indian burial site, he told himself. How freaking stupid are these people?

Mason was now starting to get the picture. He put the maps away, turned off the light, and climbed out of the basement. As he closed the door and was putting the carpeting back, he heard someone walking into the library, talking.

"I don't care what kind of pressure you're under, you'll get it when I get mine; that's how it works," the man, talking on a cell phone, said. Recognizing the voice as Jake's, Mason moved and hid behind a book rack. Jake walked over to where Mason was hiding but didn't see him. A bead of sweat ran down Mason's cheek.

Jake reached down and pulled back the carpet that Mason had just replaced. He opened the door and went down into the basement. Mason's heart felt as if it was going to explode. With Jake down in the basement, he could now slip out. As Mason was about to start walking out of his hiding place, he heard a loud burst of air come from the basement.

An airlock? he thought to himself. He's in that room. Never being one to take the safe course of action, Mason slowly stepped down the stairs until he could see across the storage room and into the locked room, whose door was now open. A room twice as large as the storage area, it was filled with monitors, computers, phones, control panels, and a sea of blinking lights.

What the . . . Mason thought to himself. He watched as Jake jumped on a computer and started typing. He clicked something on and could hear all kinds of transmissions; they were too faint to make out, though. Seeing enough, Mason slowly made his way back up to the main library. As he made his way out of the library, he pondered going back on the street. If they saw him, they'd know he got out; then they would put someone on the back door. Therefore, he made his way back the same way he came. He made it back to his room at Marcie's. He needed help and decided to call Al.

"Hi, Al?"

"Hi Mason! How the heck are you?"

"I'm good. I have a huge favor to ask of you."

"You know it's pretty late, right?"

"Yes, sorry about that, but are you working tomorrow or actually today?"

"Oh, that kind of favor," Al said, changing his tone. "The one that gets me in trouble?"

"No, it's just a little information. Can you do it?"

"Sure, name it."

"I'm in a strange little town called Greenfield Ranch, Oklahoma."

"What do you mean by strange?"

"It's a long story, I'll explain later. Anyway, can you pull some records on it? I tried earlier today and I couldn't find anything."

"What do you mean records?"

"Just anything you can come up with. I tried the public databases and couldn't find anything. It's about sixty miles northeast of Idledale if you find that."

"Nothing? How does a town not have any public records?" Al asked.

"I don't know. That's why I want you to see what you get from the law enforcement side."

"All right, no problem. What about Claire—what's her last name?"

"Burnhardt, Claire Burnhardt."

"Okay, got it. Did they fix your car yet?"

"Yes, it's done."

"Great, then you'll be heading back?"

"Eventually, but I might stay a couple more days."

"All right. I'll call you tomorrow and let you know what I find out."

"Thanks a ton, Al. I owe you a Gino's for this."

"You know I take you up on those things, right?"

"I'm planning on it. I'll talk to you tomorrow."

"All right, good-bye."

As Mason hung up the phone, he lay down and relaxed. He thought about the secret room until he drifted into a deep sleep.

He was standing alone in the center of an ancient Indian city that appeared deserted. The pyramid structures climbed high into the sky and the stone huts looked decrepit. A warm breeze blew continuously. He heard the all-too-familiar screech echo through the city followed by the white owl circling above him. A week ago, he would have been terrified. Not this time—he just stared at the owl's magnificence. Then a deep voice called his name, "Mason!" Turning around, he saw a large Indian standing behind him. The large white owl flew down and perched on his staff. Startled, he asked the Indian, "Are you Ah Puch?"

"Yes Mason, it is I."

"Have you come to take me?"

"No Mason, I come to give you your final gift in your preparation."

"Preparation for what?"

"For the path you must walk."

"What path? Can't you just spare this town? They are good people."

"It's not up to me, Mason, it is up to you."

"What? I don't understand," Mason said. "What gift?"

"Mason my son, there is great wisdom in death." Reaching down with his right hand, he placed it on Mason's head. Immediately, as if downloading a file directly into his head, vivid imagery of war, pain, bloodshed, and death flashed at warp speed into Mason's brain.

"Receive the gift of wisdom, Mason!" Ah Puch cried out.

Mason's body arched and convulsed as if he was possessed. Every muscle in his body tensed up. He experienced vicious beatings. He could feel bullets penetrate his body. Knives stabbed him over and over. Fire engulfed him. He felt firsthand the pain and suffering of excruciating deaths. He had become witness to the atrocities of mankind throughout history. His heart pounded against his chest as if about to tear through. His short breaths were just enough to keep him alive. The last pain was that of suffocation. His throat was completely closed off. He struggled to breathe but couldn't get any air to his lungs. As his body was about to shut down, he screamed in agony and the bed bounced on the floor.

Marcie and Claire, who were downstairs talking, heard Mason's screams and ran into his room in time to see him tossing back and forth and then fly off the bed, screaming. Claire started to run to his side but stopped immediately, not sure if she should approach him or not.

"Mason! Mason, wake up!" she cried out as Marcie just backed away with her hand over her mouth in disbelief.

"Mason!" Claire yelled again. "Wake up!" With that, Mason turned his head sharply toward Claire and opened his eyes, revealing blood-red pupils that glowed with fury. Blood ran from the corners of his eyes and mouth. His arms and chest were black and blue and covered in bloody slashes. The surreptitious assault he had just undergone left him bloodied and beaten on the floor, gasping for air. Not yet awake, but not asleep either, he writhed on the floor in pain.

Startled, Claire let out a shriek and backed away. Mason's eyes closed and his body twisted two more times before it went completely limp. In shock, Marcie and Claire stood by the door, speechless.

Mason abruptly woke up, sweating and shaking. "Holy shit!" he said aloud, extremely disoriented. His eyes were wide open. Like a paranoid schizophrenic, he rapidly looked side to side and gasped for air. His heartbeat still pounded as he tried to regain his composure.

Claire tried to help again and asked, "Mason, are you all right? You're awake now."

Mason looked around and recognized his breathing starting to slow down along with his heartbeat. He started to get his bearings back. The injuries began to fade until they were gone. Mason felt different.

Claire asked again, "Mason, are you okay?"

Mason sat up against the bed from the floor and looked at Claire and Marcie. He couldn't talk yet. There was no hiding this one. They were privy to the most agonizing thing Mason had ever been through. As he processed what had just happened to him, he realized more than ever he must help the people of the town. He was indeed different.

Marcie looked at Claire and said, "He's all yours, honey," and walked out of the room.

Claire could tell he was back from wherever he had been. She walked over and sat next to him on the floor.

"Are you okay?" she asked, softly taking his hand.

"Yes. That was the most intense dream I've ever had."

"That was a dream?" Claire asked in disbelief.

"I think so. It was pretty intense, huh?" Mason said, rubbing his head.

"I'm not sure what that was," Claire said rhetorically.

"It was just an intense dream," Mason said, although he wasn't completely sure he believed it.

"I don't think so, Mason," Claire said hesitantly.

"Why do you say that?" Mason asked.

"Because when I called your name, you looked at me and opened your eyes."

"Yes, but I wasn't coherent."

"But your eyes, they—your pupils—were dark red, like the owl we saw. I've been around people with sleep disorders and I've counseled people on dreams, and that was no dream, Mason."

"Whatever it was, I'm all right now. But Ah Puch was right, death changes your perspective. We have to do whatever it takes, Claire. We only have four days." They got up off the floor and sat on the bed.

"But what are we supposed to do?" she asked

Mason stood up and looked at the floor while he paced. The gears in his head started to spin again. "We need to go to Miram's house," he concluded.

"What? Why?"

"I need to ask him a question before I give you my theory."

"You have a theory?"

"Yes."

"Does it involve me not dying on Friday?"

"Well, not exactly. But it may bring us closer to understanding why."

With a sigh, she replied, "Great, I can hardly wait."

Chapter 64

Indian Burial Ground
Greenfield Ranch, Oklahoma
June 12, 2017

After breakfast, Claire and Mason drove to Miram's house. Mason's demeanor had changed. Experiencing death humbled him. At least the physical pain people go through before they die ends in their own death and it's over. Mason's physical pain ended and the physical wounds healed, but how do you deal with the emotional aspect? he wondered. It was something he would have to figure out before it drove him to his grave. They pulled into Miram's driveway and walked to his front door. After ringing the doorbell, they waited. Mason remembered Miram's dead wife. He more than likely experienced the pain she felt before she died.

Miram opened the front door and greeted them.

"Hi Miram, do you have a minute?" Claire said timidly.

"Sure Claire, come in. Good morning, Mason."

They walked into Miram's living room. It was covered in Indian art and paintings by Amona.

"Hi Miram. Can I ask you a quick question?" Mason asked.

"Sure."

"Can you tell me about Indian burial grounds?"

"What do you want to know?"

"Just anything you can tell me about them."

"All right. They are sacred, not to be tampered with."

"Why not?"

"Because they are the resting place of the dead. It is believed that their spirits still visit the sites and it causes them great anger if it is disturbed."

"And the owl is the bird of the dead, right?" Mason asked.

"The owl is not to be taken lightly. In the Mayan culture, the owls symbolize death. In fact, every twenty-six years they gather at the sacred sites to honor their dead. Why do you ask this, Mason?"

"I'm hoping this is a twenty-sixth year. If it's not, we're in trouble."

"What kind of trouble?" Miram asked.

"Mason, you don't think—" Claire started.

"Yes, I do, Claire. I think this town is the city in the picture," Mason said, cutting her off.

"Thank you, Miram. Oh, one more thing. If a sacred site has been desecrated, what happens?" Mason asked.

"Usually, you have a choice to vacate the grounds or be cursed."

"Be cursed?" Claire asked.

"Have something bad happen or be killed."

"But you have a choice, right?" Mason asked.

"Usually; it depends how bad it was desecrated. If it's bad enough, the spirits might just kill them."

Mason's serious look spoke volumes to Claire. "All right, thanks Miram. Come on, Claire."

"Bye Miram," Claire said, being dragged out of his house.

Both of their minds raced on the drive back to Claire's house, but for very different reasons. Claire finally interrupted the mental tango going on in Mason's head. "Mason, will you slow down? What exactly is your theory?"

"All right, last night I snuck into the library and found your hidden basement."

"You did what?"

"I know, I'm not supposed to know about it. Don't worry, I don't care what's down there."

"You can't let anyone know that you know about that room, Mason; I'm serious." Claire shook her head and continued. "You can't sneak around out here, it isn't safe for you."

"Claire, I don't care what you guys make, I just don't want you to die."

"If they find you snooping, they'll kill you."

"They won't, don't worry. Anyway, the map you showed me had the green shaded area, right?"

"Yes."

"Well, there's an identical map in a glass case on the wall in there that I think is the original map. The one you showed me was a copy."

"How do you know?"

"Because the shaded area is labeled on the one enclosed in the glass and not labeled on the one you showed me."

"What did it say?"

"It said the shaded area is an Indian burial site."

"I think I would've known that," Claire said.

"Go check it yourself. You also saw the owls gathering in that area."

"Okay, so they want to pay their respects to the dead; then they leave, right?"

"I don't think so. In my dreams, there is always 384 dead something. Lately, my dreams have been like the painting; people getting slaughtered by ravenous owls."

"So you're telling me that we're going to die by being attacked by killer owls?"

"I know it sounds as crazy as everything else, but yes, I think we have to get you guys out of here."

"That's not going to go over so well."

"Neither is being torn apart by owls."

"Look Mason, I've got to get to the café. Let me think about this."

"All right, I'll drop you off."

"Is your life always this dramatic?" Claire asked.

"Surprisingly, it has its moments," Mason said as they drove down the main street.

Mason's cell phone rang. Reaching over, he saw on the caller ID that it was Al. "Hello."

"Hey Mase, I checked on that town you asked about."

"Great. What did you find?" he said, looking over at a concerned Claire.

"I couldn't find anything on a Greenfield Ranch. I found an Idledale, but it was pretty straightforward, regular town. Are you sure about the name?"

"Yes, I'm sure. Hang on, Al." They pulled into the café parking area. Turning to Claire, Mason said, "You go ahead, I'll be in in a minute." Claire nodded and went in.

"Okay, Al. Sorry, Claire was in the car."

"Oh yes, Claire. Now that's a different story. I ran an NCIC and a LEXIS/NEXIS on her and she's clean. So I had a friend at the bureau run her through the Sentinel database. That's when it got interesting."

"What do you mean?"

"She's clean on there as well. In fact, too clean. She has no known addresses, no credit cards, no bank accounts; nothing."

"Why is that interesting?"

"Because nobody is that clean. Think of it this way: you've been alive for thirty years. There are records from schools, jobs, addresses, mail that you receive, all sorts of things that say you've been alive. She doesn't have any of that. Either she's not alive, her name is different, or her records have been completely removed."

"Well I guarantee she's alive. Maybe she has a different name. I'll work on that and get back to you. And nothing on the town?"

"Sorry man, I couldn't find anything. Michele's dad is a pilot and she asked for one of his old aviation charts so we looked in that area. The only thing we saw in that area was an area tagged as an NFTA."

"What's that mean?" Mason asked.

"We didn't know either. So we checked the legend and all it said was that it was a 'permanently restricted no-fly' zone."

"NFTA, hmm? All right Al, thanks a lot."

"If you need anything else let me know."

"I will. Thanks a ton; I'll see you in a few days."

Mason entered the café and saw Claire talking to Natalie so he sat down in a booth. For the first time in his life, he felt as if he could use his gift. Now he needed to figure out how it could be changed. One step at a time, he thought to himself.

"Hey, so who was that?" Claire said, climbing into the booth.

"It was my friend Al."

"What did he want?"

"I had him check some stuff for me and he wanted to know when I'd be back."

"Yeah? What did you tell him?'

"I said I wasn't sure."

"What does Al do?"

"He's a cop in Chicago."

"Oh really? What did you have him check for you? If you have any unpaid parking tickets?" Claire asked. She laughed, appreciating her own humor, until she noticed Mason was not amused.

"Sorry, I'm just kidding," she apologized.

"I know, its fine."

The front doors to the café were busy with regulars coming and going. Joe walked in and headed for Mason's booth. "Good morning, guys."

"Hi Joe," Claire said, happily for a change.

"Morning, Joe," Mason said with a look downwards, avoiding eye contact.

"Mason, here's the deal," Joe said, cutting right to the chase. "I was an ass yesterday, and I'm sorry. You can stay here as long as you'd like."

"What? My guess is that Claire talked you into it?"

"Claire and I had a nice talk yesterday, and I figured some things out," he said, smiling at Claire.

"Thanks; I'm going to try and hit it before Friday if that's all right."

"That's fine. You two have fun," Joe said, walking away toward the door. He then stopped, turned around, and asked, "By the way, Mason, how's the car running?"

"Never better. Frank is pretty amazing."

"Frank's the best there is; see you later," Joe said.

"What the hell did you do to him, Claire?"

"You know, normally I'd feed you a line on how I beat him up. However, the fact is, I just missed talking to my grandfather and we had a really good heart-to-heart. He offered to let you stay, not me," she said with a smile.

"Well, since I'm not on lockdown, let's take Blue Lightning out for a run after breakfast?"

"Sure, I don't see why not; although, there's not a lot to see. We need to figure this out, and soon."

Chapter 65

No Deals, Just Complications
Greenfield Ranch, Oklahoma
June 12, 2017

The drive through the country on the dirt roads of Greenfield Ranch was a peaceful one. No matter how much at ease they felt, neither one could shake the thought of what was coming. Pulling over, Mason and Claire went for a walk in an open prairie.

"This is really nice out here, but do you ever get bored?" Mason asked Claire as they walked.

"Sure. It's kind of funny, though; we seem to want the opposite of what we are surrounded by. People from big cities want small towns and people from small towns want the big city."

"Maybe that's how we maintain balance," Mason offered.

"There's a lot of truth in that, I think," Claire said, stopping and leaning against a large rock outcropping. "You never told me about what Al was looking up for you."

"Oh yes, that's when Joe came in. It's nothing, really; I just had him run the town on the computer."

"This town?" Claire asked. The tone in her voice increased slightly.

"Yes this one, but he said he couldn't find anything."

"Mason, you're going to be the death of me, no pun intended."

"What do you mean?"

Claire got more serious. "What else did you tell him?"

"Nothing, why?"

"I told you before, Joe is very protective of us; he doesn't want any attention."

"Al's not a problem. He's the only person I trust 1,000 percent—I mean, except for you," he said.

"It's okay. What exactly did he do?"

"Why is it such a big deal? He ran your town name in the police computer and nothing came up."

"And that's it? He's not doing anything else?"

There was something Claire was concerned about. Maybe it was something about her. Taking the opportunity to waltz through the open door, he turned the questions around.

"Come on Claire, if you were driving down the highway and got pulled over, they would run your license, verify who you are, and let you go, right?"

"Sort of," she replied.

"What do you mean 'sort of'? That's exactly what they would do."

Claire took the bait. "Trust me, it's a bigger deal than that; and did you say 'me'?"

"What?" Mason asked, trying to buy time. He got the feeling that he may have overstepped some boundaries. It was too late to backtrack.

She didn't let him answer. "You said if they ran 'me'? God, tell me, you didn't have Al run me?"

"Well, kind of," Mason said cautiously.

"You have to call and tell him to stop looking!"

"Sure, but he said you're clean. There isn't a problem, right?"

"Wrong! Just tell him to stop, please!" she pleaded.

"Fine, I'll call him right now, but you know you're going to have to ante up eventually."

She conceded, "Let's hope not. Please, for me, just tell him to stop running us; I don't want to get into it with Joe and the others."

That was the answer he needed. She indirectly admitted there was more to her story. For whatever reason, though, she wanted to keep her private life private. A sentiment Mason could relate to. Mason called Al from his cell phone. As he waited for Al to answer, he could see Claire nervously play with her fingernails. She was concerned about something, but he didn't want to push it. He'd learned pulling personal private information from someone prematurely could have a very negative consequence. She'll tell me when she's ready, he thought.

"Hi Al," Mason said into his cell phone while Claire watched closely.

"Hi Mase, how's it going in Crazyland?"

"Good actually," he said and winked at Claire to reassure her. Whatever she was hiding, she was terribly troubled by it.

"Still no info for you on that town."

"Oh, it's not a big deal. Actually, I was corrected by Claire; it is in Idledale, I'm just staying on the Greenfield's ranch property."

"Oh, okay, so do you need me to check that out?" Al asked.

"No, it's good, Al. I appreciate your help, but you can stop checking; it all makes sense now."

"All right; are you sure? You sound kind of weird."

"No, it's cool, thanks. If I need anything else, I'll call you." After Mason ended his call with Al, he walked over to Claire and reassured her.

"Okay, he's backing off."

"Thanks." Claire let out a sigh of relief.

They walked further and sat under a large cottonwood tree, taking cover from the hot Oklahoma sun. An occasional breeze accented with Russian sage gave them temporary relief from the dryness. The calm trickling sound of a nearby stream gave them a reprieve from the pressure of their imminent truth. That is, until the haunting cry of a black crow calling out as it flew by caused a nervous chill to run up Claire's spine. Their reprieve would be temporary. Turning to Claire, Mason focused on their current dilemma.

"Claire, we need to figure out how we're going to get everyone out of here."

"That's going to be a tall order, Mason. Do we have any other choice?"

"I don't know," Mason said. "What I do know is that you have to get out of here. If everyone else wants to die that's their choice, but you have to leave with me."

"I can't just leave, Mason; these people are my family, my friends. I can't do that."

"Yes, of course, you're right. We need to get everyone out. But how do you get everyone out of a town?" he asked. "That's it!" Mason said, jumping up. "How do you evacuate a town?" he continued. "There has to be a threat of some kind."

"What are you talking about, Mason?"

"If we can convince the town that a tornado or fire or something is coming towards the town, they'll be forced to evacuate."

"I'm not sure it'll work on this town."

"Look, it's only for a day. After Friday they can come back, I think."

"What do you mean, 'you think'?"

"I've never tried this, so I'm not sure what to expect. I'll call Al and ask him how they get people to evacuate," Mason said, pulling out his cell phone. "No coverage? Let me borrow yours."

Pulling out her cell phone, she looked at it and noticed the same thing. "No coverage. That's odd," she said under her breath. Looking up as if a lightbulb went on, she said, "I think we need to get back to town."

They hurried back to the car, not saying a word. They jumped in and Mason broke the silence. "Now do you want to tell me what the deal is?" Mason asked.

"There are no deals, just complications."

Chapter 66

Blood Is Thicker Than Water
Greenfield Ranch, Oklahoma
June 12, 2017

Joe sat at his desk trying to figure out Excel. The IT guys made it look so simple. A knock at his office door was a welcome relief.

"Hey Joe," Jake said, walking into Joe's office.

Joe took his reading glasses off and leaned back in his desk chair, "How you doing, Jake? Come on in."

"Good, thanks. Hey, any reason why a Chicago police officer would be running Claire?"

Joe put his glasses down on the desk and brought his chair forward again. "What do you mean 'running Claire'?"

"They ran a check on her in NCIC and Lexus/Nexus, then shortly after that, she was flagged by the FBI."

"No, but I can make a good guess. What did they get?"

"I don't think anything yet."

"Get on the horn and find out what they're doing. We need to know what they're looking for ASAP."

"You got it," Jake said, slamming the door behind him as he rushed out of Joe's office.

Joe walked down to the first floor of the building and down the hall to Rod Thompson's office. He gave the token knock and barged in.

"Hey Joe, what's up?" Rod said with a vein protruding from his forehead. He hated being disturbed. Joe sat in the chair in front of Rod's desk.

"We're getting flagged in Chicago by the PD and a 'trip-wire' survey by their local bureau."

"What, are you shitting me?" Rod's disgust was evident.

"I wish I was; it's got to be Mason."

"That boy's becoming a pain in my ass," Rod said, taking a drink of bourbon. It was the only way he could calm the hornets crawling under his skin.

"To add to it, Miram said Mason and Claire were questioning him about Indian burial grounds."

"What? Why would they give a shit about that? Does he think he's on some kind of freakin' adventure? Get his ass out of this town!" Rod scolded.

"Look Rod, he's only got a few days and he's gone. He's all smitten with Claire. Let them have their fun. If he's with her, then he's not snooping around. Claire will break his heart and he'll leave on his own."

"Can we count on her?" Rod asked.

"I don't think that'll be a problem; he's not her type." Joe didn't lead on that Claire was far more into Mason than people thought. He wasn't about to ruin the happiness he saw in her. Blood is truly thicker than water.

"Make sure it's not. In the meantime, keep watching him and kill the cell tower. I don't want any more communication from Mason to the outside world."

"Good call. I'll keep you informed."

"You do that," Rod said, staring out his window. He watched as a crow picked at a rabbit carcass and flew away.

Chapter 67

Conversation with Allah
Rabwah, Pakistan
June 12, 2017

Aleem was ushered into Ahmed's palace by Ahmed's servant and found Ahmed sitting in his oversized sofa watching the television. As Aleem walked in, Ahmed sat up and placed his drink on the coffee table.

"Ahmed, great news!" Aleem said with a large grin on his face.

"For your family, I hope."

"Indeed, king. I have secured a—" stopping midsentence, he looked around at the servants standing by.

"Ah yes, leave us," Ahmed ordered of the servants in the room. "Now, you were saying?"

"I have secured a martyr who is excited to die for Allah."

"Good work, Aleem. Can he be trusted?"

"Yes, he is one of al-Qaida's men who is in a sleeper cell in Saint Louis. He has an uncle in Rabwah and is anxious to make him proud."

"Perfect. In my speech tomorrow night, when I address the people I will show what a hero he is. And I will bless his uncle. That will give hope to the people. They will see how change will soon be ours." Ahmed took a sip of his tea.

"What orders would you have me give him, Ahmed?"

"Have him contact Hallid. He will give him his orders."

Aleem left as excited as he was when he arrived. He may have saved his family. With Aleem gone, Ahmed stood up and stopped. He thought about his next move. Nervous and excited at the same time, Ahmed walked into his office and sat behind his large oak desk. He looked at the secure phone on the desk in front of him. His plan was materializing. He paused and thought about how the next call would forever change the world. Once this mission begins, there is no turning back, he thought. Ahmed's demeanor changed instantly. No pandering to his brother. No fake messiah claims to his people. No reckless disrespect. Behind the façade, Ahmed was quite serious, and quite calculating. With a very solemn disposition, Ahmed picked up his phone and called "Allah."

"Allah, this is Ahmed. How are you this fine day?" Ahmed said into the phone.

"I'm good, my friend. I presume you have good news for me?" the deep, calm voice on the other end replied. Allah knew the real Ahmed. The man behind the image. After all, he helped make Ahmed.

"Yes, we ran into a few problems, but nothing we couldn't handle," Ahmed replied.

"Good, so we're on schedule?" Allah asked.

"Yes, we had to pick up our supplies earlier than expected."

"What happened?" the man posing as Allah on the other end of the phone asked.

"Our men ran out of night and were spotted. They did what they had to, but we lost one."

"Sorry to hear that. There's always that risk; that's why we do it at night."

"It's all right. Normally they are good; this time they ran into drug runners that delayed them. Not to worry, though, we picked up the one transporter and the supplies. They are on their way to the site now."

"Is he going to be able to carry out the mission?" the man asked Ahmed.

"As luck would have it, the survivor is the one who knows how to set it up, and Hallid has secured another martyr to assist. It appears Allah is looking out for us after all," Ahmed said with a nonchalant laugh.

"How about the martyr; is he in position?" the man asked.

"He's waiting our instructions."

"Very good, Ahmed. How about the other matter?"

"The money will be in the account tomorrow," Ahmed affirmed.

"Good. As soon as I confirm it, I'll get you the exact coordinates."

"Very well, my friend. By the way, what are you going to do when this is all over?" Ahmed asked.

"I'm going to disappear and not worry about anything. What about you, Ahmed?"

"I will be the most powerful man in the world. Anything I want."

"That will come with a lot of responsibility. I hope you're ready for it."

"I am. I've never been more ready." Ahmed understood both parties were getting exactly what they wanted. Power and money: a narcissist's dream. It's a dark union of evil and extreme overindulgence.

"All right, I'll send you the coordinates tomorrow. After that you and I will never speak again. Peace be with you, Ahmed."

"I will be waiting. Peace be with you too." Ahmed hung up the phone and looked at a map of the world hanging on his wall. "Soon," he whispered.

Chapter 68

Almazorian Brief
The Pentagon, Washington, DC
June 12, 2017

Colonel Austin sat in his office working at his oversize cherry wood desk when he was interrupted by a knock on his door. A look through the side window showed Brian Dougherty waiting. He waved him in.

"Hi Brian. Come in, have a seat," Colonel Austin said to a straight-faced Brian Dougherty walking into his office. "What can I do for you?"

"I have some information for you on the Almazorians." Dougherty handed the colonel an informational brief.

"Great, let's hear it," Austin said while perusing the brief.

"The leader, Ahmed Mirza Almazor, is a descendant of Ahmed Ja'fari Almazor who started the Almazorians in India in the late 1800s. Ahmed Ja'fari Almazor claimed that he was the promised messiah that the Koran foretells."

Austin stopped reading and looked at Dougherty. "I thought Muhammad was supposed to be the last prophet?"

"Mainstream Muslims believe Muhammad was the last prophet and anyone else must be an imposter. Because of that, in the mid 1900s the Almazorians were driven out of India and were given safe haven in Israel, where they were sympathetic to their plight."

"Israel. I'm sure that went well for them," the colonel said rhetorically.

"Actually, for forty years they had good relations with the Israeli government. But as the senior officials of the Almazorians began to die off, the new, younger leaders decided they needed more from the Israelis. After a series of bombings in Israel in the late 1980s, they were run out of Israel and took up residence in Rabwah, Pakistan, where they still bitterly reside today."

Austin listened and processed the information. He tended to not underestimate anyone or any organization. In his mind, this was as viable a threat as any extremist.

Dougherty explained that the villagers didn't believe that Muhammad was the last prophet of Islam. The current leader, Ahmed Mirza Almazor, riding on the coattails of his great grandfather, had claimed that he was now the latest prophet sent by Allah. The problem was, he wasn't as smart as his father, grandfather, or great-grandfather.

The colonel cut right to the chase and asked, "So are they still considered Muslim?"

"They claim they are Islamic, but their doctrines are vastly opposed to mainstream Islam. Islam doesn't even acknowledge them," Brian replied.

The colonel rapidly analyzed the brief and concluded, "Are they a legitimate threat?"

"We don't believe they have the weaponry, technology, or the ability to accomplish anything near what Osama bin Laden did. That said, we believe that's what makes them dangerous. They are unpredictable."

"If that's the case, we must eliminate them and do it before a larger organization validates them by merging with them," the colonel suggested.

"That's exactly what we must do. They're like a small group of thugs that want to be a part of the bigger picture and will do anything to prove themselves, even coming after the US."

"Brian, we need to start formulating a plan on how to do this."

"I'll get on it." Dougherty said and left the colonel's office.

Chapter 69

Buying Time
Greenfield Ranch, Oklahoma
June 12, 2017

As Joe drove to Claire's house, he thought about how he would broach his conversation with her. After their recent heart-to-heart, he didn't want to revert back to their previous cold, impersonal relationship. With his responsibilities to the town, he had lost sight of what was important. The crunching of the gravel under his tires as he pulled into Claire's driveway let him know he was there. He dodged long overgrown oak branches, walked up the creaking steps to the front patio, and knocked on the door.

"Hi Joe," Claire said, hugging him as he came into her house. Something was up, and she knew it had to do with the cell towers being turned off.

"Hi sweetie," he said, kissing her of top of her head. "Let's talk, Claire."

"Why did you kill the cell phones?" she asked.

"It appears Mason has someone in Chicago snooping around for information on you and this town."

"On me?" Claire acted surprised.

"Yes, on you," Joe said calmly, having an idea she had already known that. He continued, "The bottom line is the higher-ups want him out, now. I bought you another day, but honey, he's got to go. I can only control so much, you know that. This is one of those things that has the potential to get blown way out of proportion, and we can't have that."

Claire admitted, "I know. He told me that he called his friend in Chicago and had him check out the town, but he said they didn't find anything."

"And they won't. The issue is that we don't want the attention. Remember, it's bigger than your heart."

"I know, but there's other stuff," Claire said.

"Like what? The Indian burial ground thing? We took care of that years ago, Claire. It's not an issue. Claire, we've already violated many town policies for you. Here's where we're at: either he leaves on his own or they'll make him leave."

"No! That's not an option. Leave him alone; he hasn't hurt anyone."

"But he knows more that he should."

"He doesn't know anything! He knows we're a weird little town, that's it." Joe recognized Claire getting excited about it and remained calm. Matters of the heart can skew a person's perception. But he couldn't roll over on this one.

"He also knows where we're located, and unfortunately, that could be a deal breaker."

"What if I leave with him, to get him to leave? It'll be like a vacation for me. Then I'll come back without him." Joe thought about it for a minute and found himself contemplating the idea.

"That could be an idea. I'll run it by Washington. In the meantime, be careful. This is garnering a lot more attention than it should be."

"Thanks, Gramps. I'd better get going; I'm heading over to Sid's."

"All right Claire, maybe I'll see you over there later."

Claire gave Joe a hug and walked him out to his car. Looking up, they noticed a large white owl fly up and take perch on her rooftop. They stood in amazement and gazed at the massive intimidating white owl staring back at them with dark red eyes. It obviously feared nothing. The bird stared at them with intent. By not breaking its imposing glare at them, it made clear it was not there by chance. Joe stared back, sizing him up. He slid his right hand to his hip where his untucked shirt concealed a Colt 45 handgun in its holster. Although he didn't believe in coincidence, how could an owl possibly be a threat?

"Interesting pet you have there, Claire," Joe said, breaking the silence.

"Kind of pretty, isn't he?"

"Don't think I've ever seen an owl quite like that in these parts," Joe observed, climbing into his car. Breaking her stare at the bird, Claire waved to Joe pulling out of her driveway.

Chapter 70

Bottoms Up
Greenfield Ranch, Oklahoma
June 12, 2017

Sid's was busier than usual. There was something in the air. Maybe a final gathering? Maybe they knew the fate that was rapidly approaching them. Maybe Mason's nerves were getting the best of him. An older woman looked at him from a table and her face turned into a skeleton. Mason looked away and focused on a man sitting in a booth by the window. When the man looked back at Mason, his eyes turned red and dripped blood. Still another man oozed blood from a slashed throat. The lines between reality and perception were promptly becoming blurred. Why is everyone looking at me? Mason wondered. His instinctual concern for the town was kicking into overdrive. His eyes shifted from one patron to the next. All looking at Mason. Reaching for him. Mocking him. Perhaps Claire is the only one I can save, he slowly deduced. As Mason's sensory overload was climaxing, Sid brought a short-lived reprieve.

"Mason, you okay?" Sid asked while placing his hand on Mason's shoulder.

"JUNE 16, 2017" registered in Mason's mind.

With a sharp glare to Sid, Mason replied, "What?"

"Are you okay? You look like you've seen a ghost."

Gathering his senses, Mason started to get color in his face again. Looking around now, nobody had any interest in him.

"No, I'm fine. Just thinking," was all he could muster.

Sid knew better, but whatever it was, it wasn't his problem. Sid placed a Jameson and Coke in front of him and said, "You look like you could use this."

"Yes, thank you. Hey Sid, if you wanted to leave this town, you could, couldn't you?"

"Of course Mason, this isn't a prison camp. Why do you ask?" Sid flipped a hand towel over his right shoulder.

"Do you guys take vacations?"

"Sure we do. What's on your mind?"

"I was thinking of asking Claire to come to Chicago for a visit, that's all."

"I'm sure she'd be delighted to visit Chicago," Claire said, standing behind Mason, smiling. "I'm just not sure she's been formally invited," she continued as she sat down at the bar next to Mason with a grin.

Sid smiled and poured Claire her drink. "You heard it from the source, Mason," Sid said with a wink and walked away.

"Hi Claire. I was going to talk to you about it."

"I know, I think it would be fun to check out Chicago. We have to make it past Friday first, right?"

"Yes, I've been thinking. Are you being completely truthful about the 'research facility'?"

"Mason, don't ask me about that stuff," she pleaded. "I can't answer questions about that stuff and I don't want to have to lie."

"So there's probably more to it than you're letting on?"

"There might be, but I really don't know what it is that they do. I just know that it's stuff I don't need to know about, so I don't know."

"The problem, Claire, is if it has something to do with you dying, then we have to know what's going on."

Claire started to clarify but was cut off by Mason. "I know, but—"

"Claire, you see Sid laughing with that couple?" Mason said, drawing Claire's attention to the end of the bar.

"Yes."

"His day is Friday just like yours. The couple he's talking to I met yesterday at church; their day is Friday also. Just like everyone in here, Claire. I don't care what secrets you guys have, I only care about you and your town disappearing."

Claire knew he was right. "I have to go to Joe; there is no other alternative. In fact, if you are right we'll need his help. We can't do it without him."

"Let's go talk to him now."

"No, let me talk to him first. He'll talk with me on a personal level that he wouldn't do with anyone else present." Just then, Joe, Rod, and Jake walked in and sat at a table with some other men. Seeing Claire and Mason, Joe made his way to them and said, "Evening Claire, Mason."

"Hi Joe."

"Hey Gramps."

"What, did I miss the funeral? What's with the sad vibes?" Joe asked.

"Oh, we've been talking and we kind of need to run some things by you," Claire said.

"Well, can it wait until tomorrow?"

"Yes, maybe first thing in the morning?" Mason asked.

"That'd be fine." Turning to Sid, Joe belted out, "Sid, whatever these guys are drinking, make it a double. They need it!"

"Thanks Joe," Mason said with a half smile.

"Yeah, ditto," Claire mimicked.

"Now if you'll excuse me, I'll talk to you two tomorrow."

As Joe walked away, Mason and Claire looked at each other and smiled. They both acknowledged he was right.

"You'll have to get to him early, and then I'll meet you both after you've had a chance with him."

"Mason, you have no idea what you're getting yourself into," Claire warned.

"I've been in some pretty heavy situations in Chicago; I think I can handle this," Mason said, fairly confident that a small town mayor couldn't get to him.

"I wouldn't underestimate him, Mason. He may be small town now, but he hasn't always been."

Sid placed two shots in front of them. "Bottoms up," Claire said, following Mason's lead.

Chapter 71

The Nest
Greenfield Ranch, Oklahoma
June 13, 2017

As Mason slept onboard his flight, the turbulence abruptly woke him up. Concern overcame the passengers. The "fasten seatbelt" sign came on and the pilot announced that there was a storm ahead that they could not circumnavigate.

People started to tighten down their seatbelts as fear moved through the cabin. The buffeting got worse and the passengers knew they were entering the storm. Mason looked out his window and saw the dark storm engulf the aircraft. On the wing, he could see the white owl's piecing red eyes staring at him through the window. Slamming the window shade down, Mason began to panic.

With a loud explosion, the airplane doors were ripped off and anything that wasn't anchored down began to be sucked out. The loud, wicked roar of the air rushing out of the cabin drowned out the cries of the passengers. The storm got louder and more violent, forcing the fuselage to bend back and forth. Mason looked over at the emergency exit opening and could see a crack shoot over the top of the cabin. The airplane's structure became overstressed. With the airplane in a full nosedive accelerating faster and faster, the fuselage began to break apart. The screams of the passengers were ear piercing.

With one final twist, the airplane broke in half, scattering people still secured to their seats flying to their deaths. The section Mason was in came crashing into the water below. As his section continued to sink, Mason held his breath and tried to get his seatbelt off. It was no use; it was stuck, he thought. He looked around under the dark dense water, but could not see anything.

Suddenly his seatbelt popped clear. As he turned around, he saw his mother under the water helping him. He reached for her, but she faded away. Starting to take in water, he quickly swam to the surface, gasping for air. A Coast Guard raft spotted him and pulled him inside the boat. "What's your name, sir?" one of the rescuers asked.

"Mason, Mason Rhimes," he replied, gasping for air.

"Well Mr. Rhimes, you're lucky to be alive; the other 384 passengers didn't make it."

"What? How many?"

"384."

Just then he looked next to him on his other side and was startled by Kelly sitting in the boat next to him. She placed her cold blue hand on his arm and told him, "Wake up, Mason!"

With that, Mason jumped up out of bed breathing deeply and rubbing his arm from the cold, burning sensation. Looking at the clock on the nightstand, it read 1:23 a.m. Sitting on the edge of the bed, Mason collected his thoughts.

"Why did she wake me up? What does she want me to do?" Mason decided to get another look around town. He got dressed and peeked out the bedroom window. He saw the person watching the house from across the street. He slowly snuck out the back door of Marcie's house again. Trying to decide which way to go, he looked up and saw his white owl friend.

"Okay 'whitey,' which way?" he asked, at which point the owl hissed and flew off toward the old buildings.

"Research, huh? Let's go take a look at the kind of research they're doing. I'll just stay out of the woods," he said to himself. Walking along the back of the buildings until he was out of sight, he grabbed a bicycle leaned up against a house and started riding up the dirt road toward the old buildings.

He blindly followed the owl until he turned due west off of the main road. Mason knew that was where he had to dump the bike and go in on foot. The tall prairie grass was familiar to him. As the scattered clouds moved in and out of the way of the partial moon, there was just enough light for him to see the outlines of the buildings. He made his way to a dirt road and followed it until he got close to the buildings.

He followed it right up to the buildings and hid behind an old pickup truck. He could hear a humming sound emanating from the complex. He snuck up to one of the broken windows on the corner building and peeked in.

What the hell? he thought. Inside the old barn-looking buildings were walls that climbed to the top. The old exteriors of the buildings were nothing more than shells. All they did was hide the steel buildings inside. He tapped the old wood only to realize it wasn't really wood. It was a fake building made to look old and to cover the interior buildings. "Like Disney World, huh? Interesting," Mason said to himself.

He heard the sound of the humming get louder, coupled with people's voices. Ducking down under the fake windowsill, he realized someone had opened a door. Slowly rising up and looking through the fake broken window, he noticed two men walk by and the door slowly shutting. Without thinking, he swiftly tiptoed around the corner of the building and entered the main door before it shut.

Standing in front of an unmanned guard desk, he heard someone coming. Not sure where to go, he had only a right or left option. Hearing the voices coming from the left and getting closer, he hurried to the right, to the end of the corridor, and took cover in a cubicle.

Hiding in the cubicle, he could see a guard walk up and sit behind the desk with something he heated up in the microwave. Mason crept through the darkened maze of office cubicles to a railing that surrounded the sunken center section of the building. He looked out and down through the massive building. The core section of the building was sunk at least three stories below the ground level.

He realized he was toward the top of the structure. Looking up two more stories revealed a fogged glass ceiling. He looked over the railing. The bottom level of the building was covered in a vast field of gigantic satellite dishes, hundreds of them all turning and rotating differently and independent of each other. The entire field was encased in glass from the bottom level to the ceiling.

Good God! he thought to himself. All right, I guess it's not marijuana, but what hell is it? On the levels above and surrounding the dishes were people working. The clear glass enclosure separated their work areas and the field of satellite dishes. Probably a safety thing, Mason thought. Maybe it's some deep space thing? Hearing a voice approaching, Mason jumped across the aisle and back into the cubicles. He could see a tall man wearing a white lab coat walking down the corridor talking on a cell phone. The man's right arm was flailing and trying to keep up with his mouth.

Mason could hear the man in the white coat say into the cell phone, "Look general, you get me more people and I can do it; until then, I've got as many resources as I can spare on Iran right now."

The man in the lab coat stopped a few feet from where Mason was hunched down, hiding. Mason could faintly hear mumbling from the man on the other end of the cell phone. The man in the lab coat continued his conversation speaking to a general on the other end of the cell phone.

"I understand, general, but I've already got sections of the world not being covered.

Look, I'll get Europe on it as soon as I can; it'll take me an hour. Yes sir, I know it's the middle of the day over there. I'm on it; good-bye." The man in the lab coat ended his call and continued walking down the hall until he came upon the security guard station.

"Hi Johnny, I'll see you later," the man in the lab coat said as he walked past the guard. "See you later, Randy," the guard replied as he continued eating his microwaved burrito.

Looking up at the cubicle he was hiding in, Mason saw a white lab coat draped over a chair. Taking it and putting it on, he grabbed some papers off of the desk and, as officially as he could, acted like he was reading them and walked up to the guard station.

"See you later, Johnny," Mason said, trying not to look at the guard as he walked past.

"Good night? Del is that you?"

"Yes, I'm in a hurry, got to get Europe up. I'll talk to you later," Mason said, rushing out the door that the guard opened for him.

"See you later; you still owe me fifty bucks from poker!" the guard yelled to him.

Mason just waved as the door slammed behind him. With no one looking, Mason darted out into the tall grass, losing the lab coat along the way. Getting back to the bicycle, he pedaled like he was possessed to get back to town.

Dumping the bike once again, he was about to sneak back into Marcie's house when he thought about the store. He stopped. I may not get another chance, he thought. He changed his plan and stealthily worked his way along the backside of the buildings along the tree line to the grocery store.

"I gotta see what's in that warehouse," he said to himself. He walked up and checked the back and side doors; they were locked. Contemplating breaking a window, he felt compelled to at least try the front door.

"No way!" he said to himself. Why lock any if you're going to leave the front door open? he thought as he entered the store. Walking to the back of the store, he went into the storage area. As he was about to try the steel door that led to the warehouse, it slammed open. Mason plastered himself against the wall behind it as Rod came barreling through it.

Missing Mason by no more than an inch, Rod went right into the main store and into his office. Mason quickly opened the door that almost flattened him and observed row after row of what appeared to be servers.

What the hell; there must be thousands of these things, he thought. The room was lit up like a Christmas tree with all of the blinking lights. As

Mason was looking in the room, he heard a cell phone ring. Slamming the door and slipping into the bathroom, he hid behind the open bathroom door. He prayed that Rod was not going to use the bathroom. As Rod pushed the swinging doors open, Mason heard him answer his phone.

"Yes?"

"Who, Mason? Tell them to go to the previous spot and start looking from there. No, he's got to be around there. When they find him, tell them not to do anything until they hear from me. Make sure they wait for my call. I just want to make goddamn sure I'm not anywhere near!" Rod said as he hung up his phone, turned, and started walking toward the bathroom.

The warehouse door flung open. "Rod, you need to take this," a man said excitedly.

"Can it wait until I take a leak?"

"No, you need to come now."

"Oh for crying out loud, what is it?" Rod said as he turned and entered the server warehouse. Mason took the opportunity to make a break for the front door. He hurried toward the front of the store and slipped out the same way he came in. He looked in all directions to make sure no one was following him. As he was about to make a move for the tree line to start heading back to Marcie's, he noticed a light on in the library.

Now what are they up to in there? he wondered. This place apparently never sleeps, he thought.

Torn between heading back and poking his nose around some more, the curiosity got the better of him. He made his way to the library. He entered and made his way to the back, where the hidden room was. Sure enough, it was open. Glancing down the stairwell, he could see the air-locked door open. He could hear someone talking, but couldn't make out what they were saying.

I have to get closer, Mason thought. Climbing down into the storage room, he knew there would be nowhere to hide if he got caught. Standing next to the open door, he peeked in. The room was much larger than he had thought. It's like the size of a basketball court, he thought. Like the warehouse behind the grocery, it was filled with high-tech equipment.

He could now hear multiple transmissions taking place. It sounded like an air traffic control tower. He picked out two men working and heard one man at the console speak.

"Captain Sandberg, standby. I'm connecting you now. Go ahead, the line is secure. You're welcome; have a good night." Then, turning to the other man, he said, "Hey Rich, where is Tom? Maybe he fell asleep on the can." They both laughed and Mason realized there might be another man in the bathroom.

Shit! I gotta get out of here, Mason thought. Slowly making his way up the stairs, he was almost out when the third man showed up. "Hey! What are you doing?" he questioned Mason.

"Nothing, just looking for a book," was all he could come up with.

"Hey Jake, we have a visitor!" Tom yelled.

"What the hell are you doing here, Mason?" Jake asked, walking out of the hidden room.

"Just getting a book," Mason said while walking up the last step, knowing Jake wasn't buying it.

Rich then chimed in, "Well well, what have we here?"

"He says he's out getting a book," Jake said, puffing up his chest.

"Oh, I think he's getting a little more than that," Tom said while the other two laughed.

"You weren't out by the old buildings tonight, were you Mason?" Jake asked.

"No, I just came here to get some books."

"At three in the morning? I'm sure you were. Claire's not here to help you this time?" Jake said, moving right into Mason's face. "I'm going to give you one chance to help yourself. You either go get your stuff and leave right now or you'll get a little more than you bargained for. And then you're going to get in your piece of shit car and get out of this town. It's up to you."

"And suppose I write a story about this town and expose your little secret?"

"And what little secret is that, Mason? That we scan space and look for signals? That we do communication and space research? You don't have a damn clue what we do, Mason! Good God, you can't even prove we exist! However, the town charter does allow us to eliminate any and all possible threats by any means necessary. And you, my amigo, just turned into a threat," Jake said, punching Mason in the stomach.

Mason keeled over and tried to catch his breath. Jake then grabbed Mason by the throat and, throwing him down, said, "Nobody is indispensible, Mason, not even you. This town is more important than the measly pittance your family will get when you end up having a bad accident out on highway 94."

"I've already called the police in Chicago; they know where I am."

"Oh Al? If he digs too deep, he'll have an accident as well. When are you going to figure this out, Mason? This isn't public corruption and you don't have any rights to protect yourself here."

"We'll see about that," Mason said back.

"People die all the time for reasons that would shock your puny little brain," Jake said, tapping Mason on the head. "If we need someone to be at a church on a certain day, a church member dies so everyone is there for the funeral; if we need to stop traffic we blow a water main; if we need cooperation from someone, little Susie comes down with a 'freak virus.' It's all around us, Mason; open your eyes."

"You'll never get away with this," was all Mason could muster.

"Now Mason, this is the point when you get more than you bargained for," Jake informed him. "Let's take him outside and use him as training, boys."

With that, they dragged Mason out the front door, kicking, and threw him down. Mason quickly jumped up and took a chance at running away. Tom tackled him in the street and began punching him in the face. Jake ran up and kicked Mason in the ribs. Rich punched him in the back, a direct kidney shot.

They all took turns beating Mason until he could no longer breathe or open his eyes. Jake walked up to Mason holding a pipe. He raised it over his head and said, "Lights out on the playground, Mason."

Just as he was about to swing, the white owl that had been watching over Mason screeched and swooped down at Jake. Jake looked up and, with laser guided precision, the owl's razor-sharp talons lacerated Jake's throat, dropping him to his knees. The other two watched in disbelief as the owl circled around and headed back. They ran for the door but tripped over Jake's lifeless body.

With the same precision, the owl screeched and slashed Rich's throat in the same manner as Jake's. Tom picked up the pipe that Jake dropped and swung the pipe recklessly in the air.

"Come on, you piece of shit bird, let's see how you like lead!" Next, he too heard the screech followed by the owl's talon slash through the back of his neck, severing his head almost completely off. The owl, shrouded in blood, flew away.

"What the hell is all the racket out here?" Rod said, barging through the front door of the grocery across the street. Stopping dead in his tracks, he saw Mason lying on the ground and three other men lying in the street, not moving. He ran over to them and saw Mason beaten to a pulp, Jake lying on the ground with his throat slashed, and two of his other employees lying next to the door with their necks slashed as well.

He heard Mason sigh and went over to him. Kneeling down beside Mason, he tried to talk to him. "Mason, can you hear me? Mason? Can you hear me?" Mason tried to speak, but was too battered. In and out of consciousness, he looked up and passed out.

"Oh shit, stay with me, Mason!" Running into the library, he called the ambulance. Then he called Joe.

"Hello?" a groggy Joe said, answering the phone.

"Joe, get down to the library now!" Rod said and hung up the phone.

Chapter 72

Complications
Greenfield Ranch, Oklahoma
June 13, 2017

Claire was awakened by a tapping at her window. She turned on the light to see what the noise was. She let out a short scream and jumped back into her pillow. The owl's red eyes stared at her through the window and tapped again. Staring back and scared, she asked, "What do you want?"

The owl tapped again. Looking closer, she saw the red blood on the owl's wings and chest.

"Oh my God! Is Mason all right?" The owl tapped on the window again. Then it flew away. Rushing to the window, she could see it circling.

"I get it; you want me to follow you. All right."

Getting clothes on and hurrying out to her truck, she followed the owl into town.

As she approached the library, she could see cars parked in the street, an ambulance, and people walking around.

What's all the commotion? she wondered, seeing people in the street at three in the morning. As she pulled up to the scene, she got nervous about

Mason. Jumping out of the truck, she ran over to where paramedics were working on Mason.

"Mason! Are you all right?" Joe grabbed her before she got to him.

"Claire, he'll be all right. Let them help him."

"What the hell happened?" Claire said, getting more hysterical.

"We don't know yet, but we'll find out, Claire, I promise. They're going to take him to the hospital and check him out. Why don't you—"

"No, I'm going with them!" she informed him. Not going with Mason was not an option.

"All right Claire, let us know when you get an update. We'll figure out what happened and call you later," Joe said.

"Thanks Gramps."

The paramedics lifted Mason onto the gurney and loaded him into the ambulance. Claire jumped back in her truck and followed after him.

As the ambulance drove away, Rod approached Joe. "Joe, we need to talk again. Let's take a walk."

"What happened back there, Rod? How did we end up with three dead bodies and one almost dead?" Joe continued.

"I have a feeling Mason got caught snooping around, and those boys roughed him up. The thing I can't figure out is how they managed to get their throats cut," Rod said, somewhat puzzled.

"Any idea what Mason saw?" Joe asked.

"Well, that's another issue. Turns out we think Mason made it inside the nest."

"Inside the nest or to the nest?"Joe asked.

"We think inside," Rod replied.

"What? How?"

"We don't know; security must've been relaxed. We just don't know."

"Damn it, Rod, if he made it to the nest that could be a problem. Do we know what he saw at the library, if anything?"

"Don't know that either. I was at the store when I heard a ruckus. When I came out there were four bodies lying in the street, three of them with their throats cut."

"Have we pulled the surveillance tapes yet?" Joe asked.

"Yes, I have guys going over them as we speak."

"Good job. Well, let's hope Mason is good enough to drive out of here," Joe said.

Rod clarified, "Let's hope he's good enough to drive out of here and has no information that would preclude him from being authorized to drive out of here."

"Yes, I guess there's always that," Joe said, pondering that scenario.

Chapter 73

Full Disclosure
Greenfield Ranch, Oklahoma
June 13, 2017

Claire paced the hallway outside of Mason's room while the medical staff worked on him inside. Her mind was in overdrive. She knew what the town was capable of and didn't want Mason to be chalked up as collateral damage. People "disappeared" all the time in the name of national security. She couldn't live with herself if Mason was one of them. Her mind was stopped by the creaking of Mason's room door as it opened. The doctor emerged from it somewhat disheveled. She could tell he was exhausted.

"Hi Doc. How's he doing?" Claire asked as Dr. Gedeon pulled of his face mask.

"Although he took quite a beating, I think he's going to be fine. There was quite a bit of internal bleeding we were able to stop. He has a couple of fractured ribs, some lacerations we were able to suture, and a lot of bruising. Right now he needs a lot of rest."

"When can I see him?"

"He's on some painkillers right now; I'd give him a few hours to sleep it off."

Claire left the hospital and drove to Joe's house. The drive was surreal for Claire. She was in too deep with Mason. She had no choice but to involve Joe. She pulled out her cell phone and called Joe.

"Hi Gramps, can we talk?" Claire said into her cell phone.

"Sure Claire, where are you?"

"Sitting in your driveway."

"Well, come in for crying out loud. I just put a pot of coffee on."

"Okay, thanks." She wiped away the last few tears and blew her nose. This was too close. Her heart couldn't take losing Mason. It was the first healthy relationship she had in years. It was nice to have someone care about her the way Mason did. She was all too soon reminded of her previous life. Why is it the people I care about end up getting hurt? she wondered. She reminded herself that was exactly what Mason thought about people he cared about. She walked up onto the front porch when the door opened up. Joe could tell by Claire's puffy red eyes that she had been crying.

"Come in, sit down. Well, how is he?" Joe asked, handing Claire a hot cup of coffee.

She sat on the sofa and stared intently into the coffee. She finally answered.

"Doc says he'll be fine. He has a couple of fractured ribs, some internal bleeding, but overall is okay."

"That's good to hear, Claire. He looked worse."

"That's for sure."

"Claire, we need to figure out what to do with Mason. We believe he made it into the nest last night."

"The nest? I told him to stay away from that place."

"What do you mean?" Joe's ears perked up.

"When we drove out of town on Friday, the buildings caught his eye as we drove past them and he started asking questions. I gave him the standard line and I thought it was over. Then Saturday he jogged out to them, but got scared away by someone. I think that just intrigued him more. He must have snuck out there again."

"Is that all he told you, Claire?"

Claire's exhaustion and hurt wouldn't allow her to think about her answers. She simply answered Joe's questions. "No, he also found the library room looking for a map of this area."

"Did he say why he wanted a map?" Joe was surprised Claire had kept that information to herself. That was a sure indicator of where her heart was. Joe was concerned how much she had disclosed. The conversation was going where he hoped it would not.

"This next part, Gramps, I really need you to trust me and not freak out on me."

"All right, Claire, it's okay. I'm on your side." He could tell she was broken. Whatever she said was going to be her truth. Right or wrong, it was what she believed.

Not having the energy to sugarcoat anything, she didn't beat around the bush. "The reason he's so curious about this town is that he believes we're all going to die on Friday."

"What Friday?" Joe's disposition flipped like a switch. Knowing the importance of the town and hearing that kind of prediction was cause for serious concern.

"This Friday, June 16!"

"And he thinks this because why?" Joe asked.

She took a sip of coffee and completely understood how it was sounding. A few days earlier, she had reacted like Joe was now.

"He has a gift or an ability to see things."

"And he sees that we're all going to die on Friday?"

"Yes, I mean no. I mean he sees the date that people die when he meets them. When he noticed that all of our dates were the same, he thought there was a natural disaster coming our way." Looking at Joe's reaction, Claire knew he wasn't buying it. "Look, I know how it sounds. I was about to turn him over to the police and have him committed in Idledale when he told me. Then I saw some pretty weird stuff and now I just believe him. I know he wouldn't hurt anyone."

"How did you know he was hurt this morning, Claire? Were you up at 3 a.m. with him?"

"Of course not. Why? What's going on?"

"We have a problem with the events that transpired at the library. We know someone else was there with Mason, but we don't know who."

"Gramps, do you really think I could've killed them?"

"I know you could have. What I need to know is did you?"

"No, I didn't."

"Then how did you know he was there?"

"This is really going to sound good," Claire said, looking at the floor.

"Claire, I've got three dead bodies. I have to know what happened."

"I don't know what happened at the library, all I know is that his owl friend or guide tapped on my window, and I followed him into town."

Staring at Claire, expressionless, as if she was completely crazy, Joe said, "Let's strike that last question."

"No Joe, did you hear me? That's what happened."

"Oh, I heard you. Mason knows when people are going to die, and his owl friend notified you that he was hurt. Did I get that about right?"

"Yes!"

"Claire, you're here recuperating. If the shrinks hear any of that, you're done. If you can't pass a psych eval, you're done. Does any of that matter to you?"

"Of course it does. But I'm not making this up! You have to believe me," Claire said as her voice trailed off. Looking out the window, tears began to stream down her cheeks.

"Claire, I'm sorry, but come on," Joe said as he tried to console her.

"I'm not sad that you don't believe me, Gramps, I'm sad that I know what he's gone through his whole life. I'm sad that I said all of the same things to him that you're saying now. I can only imagine the hurt that he's experienced from people like us. If we do all die on Friday, it won't be on my shoulders." As Claire gathered her emotions, Joe's cell phone rang.

"Hello?"

"Oh hi, great. Claire's right here. We'll be right down. Thanks, Bryn."

"Bryn from the hospital?" Claire asked.

"Yes, he's up and asking for both of us. Can we finish this later?"

"Yes, let's go."

They drove to the hospital and hurried into Mason's room. Claire ran up to the bed and hugged Mason.

"Ouch" he said, trying to smile. "Sore ribs."

"Oh, sorry; how are you?"

"I'm fine. Hello Joe."

"Hello Mason. Glad to see you're feeling better."

"Yes, much better."

"Do you feel good enough to answer some questions?" Joe asked.

"Gramps!" Claire started, but was cut off by Mason.

"No, it's all right, Claire. Yes, I'm fine."

"What the hell happened back there?"

"I was in the library. I know, I shouldn't have been there, but I was. Jake and two other guys pulled me out into the street and here I am."

"That's it?"

"Yes, but before that, Jake told me that they'd make it look like I had an accident out on the highway and that they do this kind of stuff all of the time. Those guys need to be stopped."

Looking at Claire, Joe paused before he spoke. "Mason, what's the last thing you remember?"

"Getting kicked in the head. Then I woke up to the paramedics talking to me."

"Mason, Jake and the other two guys were killed," Claire added.

"What? How?"

"That's what we were hoping you'd be able to help us with. Turns out their throats were slit. But we're not sure by who," Joe added.

"Sorry, can't help you on that one." Talking more softly, Mason asked Claire, "Did you talk to Joe about, you know?"

"Yes Mason, she did," Joe said, stepping forward. "Maybe now's not a good time to talk about it."

"Friday's not going to be a good day either. Joe, the owls are coming, and you don't want to be here when they do."

"Claire, I'll leave you two alone; I've got some work to do," Joe said, turning to Claire and completely dismissing Mason's warning. "Get some rest, Mason; we'll talk later," Joe said as he walked out of the room, obviously biting his tongue.

"Well, that went really well," Mason said sarcastically.

"Give him time to think about it; he'll come around."

"Claire, I have no idea what happened to those guys."

"I know; your friend tapped on my window soaked in blood? The very owl that I followed right to you laying in the street?"

"What?"

"The owl; the owl killed those guys to protect you. Then he came and got me. Rod said he heard a loud scream, like a cat being slaughtered, and when he went to check on it, you all were lying in the street and there wasn't a sound. Nobody running, no cars driving off, nothing. He said two guys had their throats cut and one had the back of his neck cut. And yours wasn't. It all makes sense; it had to be the owls."

"I can't believe you're actually trying to convince me, instead of the other way around," Mason said.

"I know; it's crazy!" Claire said, shaking her head. "I think I'm losing it."

"The first thing we have to do is get me out of here," Mason said, sitting up. "Ow, my head."

"No, you stay here," she said, pushing him back down. "The doc told me about your injuries."

"No, I'm fine; I just sat up too quickly. Hand me my pants, please," he said, sitting up again. Claire knew they were being watched. She grabbed a white lab coat and a surgical head cover and disguised Mason. They snuck out of the hospital, dodging people running in, more than likely searching for him. Making it to Claire's truck, Mason threw down the disguise on the ground and jumped in. They drove to Claire's house to figure out the next move.

"Come on, sit down and I'll make us some lunch," Claire said, helping Mason to a sofa in her living room. She then disappeared into the kitchen.

"Thanks, I guess I am a little sore," he said, sitting down. "However, I am starving."

"The doc said that you've recovered faster than anyone he's ever seen; he said you should've been in the hospital for a week. What do you make of that?"

"Good genes, I guess."

"I think there's more to it. He also said it would be a good sign when your appetite came back."

"Well, it's back all right."

"Good, because . . ." she started to say, stopping midsentence. As she walked back into the living room with a sandwich, she saw Mason fast asleep on her sofa. Setting it down, she pulled a throw blanket over him and let him rest.

Chapter 74

Assets
The Pentagon, Washington, DC
June 13, 2017

Late Tuesday afternoon in DC meant gridlock on the interstate. Only the rookies would even attempt leaving work at 5 p.m. The veterans knew you either left early or late. Colonel Austin knew he missed his opportunity and was in for another late day at the office. A hurried knock at his office door broke his thoughts. "Yes, come in."

"Good afternoon, sir," a serious and disheveled Brian Dougherty said, rushing into the office.

"Hi Brian, what have you got?"

"We've picked up a lot of intel that there is going to be a hit inside the US."

"Is it credible?"

"We believe it is, sir. We've secured an asset in the Almazorian command in Pakistan who has given us very good intel."

"What kind of access does he have?"

"Sir, he's the general of Ahmed's forces."

Austin took off his reading glasses and set them on the desk. He knew the potential of this asset. "Really. How did we get him?"

"One of our sergeants saved his daughter from getting hit by an army vehicle rolling through their town searching for the Taliban. He was so grateful for his daughter's life he invited the sergeant into his house for lunch. Once they got to talking, the guy changed his mind about Americans and said he might have information. The sergeant put him in contact with the embassy and we took it from there."

"If this pans out, I want that sergeant honored."

"Yes sir."

"What does this general want from us?"

"Amnesty and his family safe haven here with new identities. Turns out his eleven-year-old daughter is only one year away from 'indoctrination training.'"

"I see; when it was everyone else's children, not that big of a problem, but when it's his, now he's concerned. When the hell are those people simply going to start doing what's right?"

"Well sir, we'll need to exploit him, and soon."

"All right; did he indicate anything about the target?"

"No, all he said was they are smuggling some kind of short-range missile into the country through the northern border, and that the hit will cripple the country."

"What does he mean by that?"

"Remember a few years back in Russia, they hit an elementary school. Some analysts believe it might be something like that."

"Bullshit; he knows. What kind of general doesn't know what his army is doing?"

"He said he had no control over this attack. Ahmed has a source giving him intel, and he's keeping it close to his heart. He essentially is telling his followers that it is Allah."

"A source? What kind of source?"

"We're not sure yet; it sounds like it may quite possibly be one of our own."

"Have we checked with the NSA?"

"Yes sir, Islamic chatter has been picked up in the north US sector early this morning. By the time we triangulated the fix, they were long gone."

The gears in the colonel's head were grinding full speed. Thirty-five years of military service gave Austin a tactical advantage over most military personnel when it came to national security issues. He put his finger on it almost immediately.

"North sector, that's North Dakota. Did we decode the message yet?"

"No, we have people working on it now; all we do know right now is that they were Islamic."

"Have we dialed the ranch yet?"

"Yes sir, we advised them, but apparently there was a problem at the ranch last night."

"What kind of problem?"

"We're not sure yet; we're waiting on a report."

"I want to know as soon as you get it. In the meantime, maybe I'll give Joe a call. Excellent work, Brian. Let's stay on top of this."

"Sir, knowing that something was smuggled into the country through the north border, should we start moving people?"

"Not yet. We need to see where they're going first. Get everyone activated and keep them on standby. When and if it goes down, we'll have to move quickly."

"Sounds good. Oh, and one more thing, as if we don't have enough on our plate. The general in Pakistan has also indicated that he's been working with a spy in one of our army platoons. Apparently, Captain Martin has been telling them our moves for cash. Should we take him out?"

"Shit," the colonel said in disgust. "No, send in a plant and have him obtain some evidence. If this captain's lucky he'll get killed before his court-martial."

"All right colonel, I'll keep you updated."

"Thanks Brian."

Picking up the phone, the colonel pulled out a sheet of paper with phone numbers on it. Looking down the list until he found what he was looking for, he began to dial.

"Joe; hi, it's Mike, Mike Austin."

Chapter 75

Lifting the Kilt
Greenfield Ranch, Oklahoma
June 13, 2017

Curled up in a ball on the sofa, Mason slept for over two hours. The growing kink in his neck finally woke him up. The sharp pain in his chest as he sat up reminded him of his bruised ribs and of the importance of time. They both knew it was time to talk.

"Claire, about last night. I know you're not supposed to talk about it, but do you think we have a choice?"

"I've been thinking also, and I think you're right. I mean, at some point they trusted all of us with their secret, so what's one more person?" Claire confided.

"Who's 'they'?"

"First of all, Mason, I'll deny ever telling you this. And second of all, what I'm about to tell you is the absolute truth, no more lies. 'They' would be your government."

"I figured they were somehow tied into it. So what's the deal?"

"The deal is we're essentially an undercover town. We don't exist; that's why it was imperative that your friend Al stop searching for us. Every person in this town is an agent from some government agency—the CIA, FBI, NSA, DIA, CTU, or the military intelligence units. There are sixteen different intelligence-gathering organizations in the US."

"Okay, why? What's the point?" Mason replied, listening intently.

"This town, Mason, is the communication hub for all sixteen of those government agencies as well as all communication that takes place in our country. All government communications are routed though this town. We are 100 percent secure and we record 100 percent of all communications that take place in the country at any given time. Those satellite dishes are exactly that, dishes that monitor communications. The servers and mainframes are stored in the back of Rod's grocery. They're supercomputers with amazing capabilities."

"That's not a problem, Claire. Why so secret about it?"

"When this town was set up seventeen years ago, the plan was to just be a backup system in case of an emergency. But after upgrading the systems over the years—and believe me, every time a system is improved, we are the first to get it—they realized the potential was far greater than anything they could have imagined."

"What do you mean?"

"We realized that our satellites were so precise that we could actually monitor all communications throughout the world, not just in our country."

"So you're able to listen in on any communication, anywhere in the world, at any given time?"

"Yes. In fact, if you had an argument over the phone, and you knew the date and some of the verbiage used, we could retrieve it. Think of fingerprint databases. You put in eight points from a fingerprint and it'll search millions and millions of prints at an unbelievable rate. Communications are analyzed in a similar way."

"So when I overheard people saying they need to 'get people on Iran' or 'Europe is up' they were talking about listening in on people's communications?"

"Yes, we have stopped literally hundreds of terrorist plots, assassination plots, murders, and all kinds of other things. We have the ability to know what people are thinking as long as they verbalize it or put it in some kind of electronic media."

"But how do you sort through the average mope calling to tell their wife they're on their way home?"

"Think broader, Mason. We're not concerned with the average mope unless they do something to draw attention. Imagine what kind of knowledge we would gather if we could listen to world leaders? Well, we can and we do. We know who's bluffing and who's not."

"But what about privacy?"

"Ah, now you're getting the big picture. Can you imagine if this got out? 'Your government is spying on you!' would be the headlines. Do you realize, Mason, your president doesn't even know about this town. Some of his advisers know, but he can't. We don't entirely trust him."

"And you found my story hard to believe?" Mason said sarcastically.

"That's why it cannot get out and will not get out, Mason. They will protect it at all costs."

"So what agency are you with?" Mason asked serenely.

"The CIA."

"And let me guess, Claire is not your real name?"

"No, Claire is, but Burnhardt is not. Everyone here has an alternate identity."

"How much of what you told me before was true?"

"Surprisingly, a lot. I used a lot of half-truths. For example, my education is all true, my job working for the State of Maryland was true, it was true about Rulon Woodley, and all the BS about the job I had was all true. I just left out that in fact I killed Rulon, and that's when I was recruited by the CIA."

"So what's with the town then?"

"Well, another advantage, or byproduct, that was observed when they set up this town was that we could hide people here. So when agents got burned in the field and they had to hide their families, they brought them here. If we needed to hide an asset or get them acclimated to our culture, we'd bring them here and train them to be 'American.' That worked out so well that the CIA started using it as a training ground. After their recruits would get out of the 'farm,' they'd do a stint here on the 'ranch' and hone their undercover skills. They get to actually live and practice their undercover craft."

"How did you end up here?"

"I was on an assignment in Prague as a professor trying to recruit an asset who was a visiting Russian professor working in the biochemical industry. There's a whole cycle on how to recruit people, and when it came time for me to reveal the 'real' me, he freaked out and blew my cover and it got ugly. He ended up getting killed, undercover organizations that we had established were burned, and I had to flee. When I left, they ran me into Canada, and the US denied any part of it.

"The Russians still have an outstanding contract on me. Fortunately for me, they still think I'm Canadian. So when I got back to the US they sent me here to hide out for a while."

"Wow, you're like a hot James Bond!" Mason said, lightening up the tone. "And everyone knows about this place?"

"No. That's another interesting thing. Everyone knows it's an undercover town, but they don't know exactly what the objective is. They know who they report to, but they don't know who everyone else does. For example, Natalie and Murph report to me, but they don't know who I report to, and I have no idea if anyone reports to them. It's a big system of checks and balances; and there's a system of protocols if anyone violates them, like I'm doing now. A lot of people here have no idea what we really do. You've heard of a safe house, right?"

"Sure, that's a house where people are protected, right?"

"Yes. Most of the people think this is a 'safe town.' In the intelligence gathering circles, Mason, everyone understands and accepts that there are levels of clearances. And you don't ask questions about things that you either don't need to know or don't have the clearance to know. In other words, there is no 'I was just curious' in this field. If you don't have the need or the right to know something, you don't even ask. You also know that if you do ask, you're not going to get the truth, so what's the point."

"That would explain why you don't need uniformed police," Mason said.

"Yeah, this wouldn't be the best town to try robbing. It's a lot of info, but do you kind of follow what we're about, Mason?"

"Yes, I do. Could you imagine if the ACLU got wind of this?"

"We'd be shut down, and our country would spiral down to oblivion. We have a hard enough time maintaining the security of our nation with this system in place; could you imagine if it were removed?"

"It's hard to believe that 384 people can run all this," Mason posed.

"That's just here on site. We've had as many as nine hundred and as few as one hundred. Overall, the system probably employs several thousand."

"So I'm guessing you report to Joe; is he really your grandfather?"

"Yes and yes. Most people probably think it's our cover, but then they probably don't care."

"So now the million-dollar question; now that you've told me, what happens?"

"Good question. I'm not sure; we'll have to check with Joe on that one. You know more than most of the people in here. Most people don't even know what the nest is, let alone having actually seen it."

"Well, we'll have to talk to Joe then."

"Just like in asset recruitment, you have to be prepared for any situation. The minute Joe knows that you know, Mason, I really don't know how he's going to respond. I do know there are several black ops guys here for security. Remember, the secret is everything and the black ops guys don't play twenty questions, they just do their job."

"I wonder if it was Jake and his guys?" Mason asked.

"More than likely they were, because they were willing to kill you. Another option might be for you to join us." Surprised at the option, Mason thought about it for a minute. Then it occurred to him, there may not be much of anything to join in a few days.

"So I guess you're right about not getting people to evacuate," Mason said, focusing on the issue at hand. "The problem is, I've heard people commenting on the number of owls they've seen."

"Everyone's talking about them, Mason. Now what do you think?" Claire asked.

"You're right; we need to go to Joe. He might know how to get people out of here."

Mason stared at his drink with the gears going a mile a minute in his head. The ante had just gone up. Nothing was as it appeared. Was the couple sitting in the booth really a couple? What did the older man sitting by himself do to be here? Everyone here had a secret, and now so do I, he realized.

Chapter 76

The Gauntlet
Greenfield Ranch, Oklahoma
June 14, 2017

Joe sat on the front porch of his house reading a newspaper and sipping a cup of coffee. He liked mornings. The chirping birds were peaceful; it reminded him that there was still good in the world. Neither Claire, nor Rod, nor even Washington could spoil his happy place. Unfortunately, it would be short lived. One way or another, someone would attempt to ruin it; it was the nature of his world. He tried to soak in the scenery nonetheless. His peace ended with the ringing of his phone. There was no avoiding it, but he was in no hurry to answer it, either.

"Hi Joe, Rod here."

"Any word on the surveillance tapes from earlier?" Joe asked.

"You're not going to believe this, but a goddamned bird landed on the camera and we didn't get it."

"What do you mean?"

"We see Jake and the other two beating the snot out of Mason, then a bird lands on the camera blocking the view, and when it flies away all four of them are lying in the street."

"Unbelievable; kind of figures with the week I'm having," Joe said exhaustedly.

"Don't worry Joe, we'll figure it out. Is Mason all right?"

"Yes, they released him earlier; he's over at Claire's now."

"I guess it's too late for her to not get personally involved, isn't it?" Rod asked, almost rhetorically.

"I'm afraid that ship sailed a while ago," Joe replied.

"Any idea what we're going to do about that?" Rod asked.

"No, I'm still working on it. I am, however, open for suggestions," Joe replied.

"As soon as I have a practical one, I'll let you know, my friend."

Joe watched two brown owls fly by. What are they doing? he thought while their perfect flight path took them to a high branch. They always seemed to take high positions to get better views. His attention was quickly drawn to Claire's truck pulling into his driveway. "Let's see what this is all about," he mumbled under his breath. He sipped his coffee and stood up.

"Hi Gramps," Claire said with a hug.

"Good morning, Joe," Mason said in succession.

"Morning guys; come on inside. I'll put on some coffee. Have a seat. I figured we weren't done discussing this thing," Joe said before retreating into the kitchen.

Mason and Claire sat quietly waiting in the living room. A framed picture of a much younger Claire with what appeared to be her mother rested on the mantel above the fireplace. The house was meticulously clean. Everything was in its right place, almost too perfect. The large front picture window gave an expansive view of mature trees and rolling hills. When Mason's eyes made it back around to Claire, they both realized their minds were racing in preparation for a battle. A smile from Claire was reassuring. As Joe walked in with two cups of coffee, Claire threw out the first disclaimer.

"Gramps, before you start, there is something you have to know; it may help in your decision." Five days ago Joe would've taken that as an insult. Not now. He sat down, took a deep breath, and prepared himself for whatever bomb she was going to drop on him.

"All right, what is it?"

Hesitantly, Claire gathered her words and carefully told Joe, "I told Mason a lot."

Joe set his cup on the coffee table and bit his tongue. This had potential to be bad. Those were probably the most deafening words she could've said, but not completely unexpected.

"Define a lot," Joe calmly replied. His overt attempt to use restraint was a good sign, Claire thought.

"He knows pretty much what I know."

"That is a lot," Joe said, not completely surprised, but troubled nonetheless. He scratched his head and contemplated this game changer. Grasping at straws, he sent up a Hail Mary. "You mean a lot about you or a lot about us?"

"He knows about us and what we do."

Joe's fear from when he first met Mason had come to fruition. Matters of the heart are a tough proposition. His mind raced. In this line of work, we don't get the luxury of even having matters of the heart, he thought. This one issue he didn't have a contingency plan for.

"You know that violates some pretty serious protocols?"

"I know, but—" Claire started and was cut off by Joe.

"There is no 'but,' sweetie. The protocols are in place for this very reason. Obviously, Mason knows too much. Now we have to figure out what to do."

Mason spoke up. "Look Joe, I don't care about any of the work you guys do here, I just care about you guys not dying in two days."

"That's well and good, Mason, but we keep detailed records of who exactly knows about this place."

"Fine, I'll fill out your background forms or whatever it is that you do," Mason offered.

"Look guys, don't get defensive, I'm on your side. For the first time in a long while, I've seen my Claire happy. I don't want to ruin that; there are just so many checks and balances, it's practically impossible to cover it up. In fact, I'm running late. I have a phone conference and we have a rush order from Washington I have to get busy on."

"What's going on?" Claire asked.

Looking at Mason and hesitating about whether or not to say, he finally gave in. "We got a pretty good threat last night that we need to find and, if possible, track."

"Do you need me?"

"No, you stay with Mason."

"Gramps, what about what I just told you?"

"Look Claire, we'll figure this out. But don't tell anyone else; the minute everyone knows that Mason knows, his life will be in danger. We'll discuss it later, all right?"

"All right. Thanks, Gramps."

"I'll meet you guys later," Joe said as they all left his house. Claire and Mason went back to Claire's house to think.

"Well, he took it better than I thought he would. Of course, he also probably knew I'd tell you," Claire said.

"Yes, at least he didn't recommend killing me. You know, Claire, I've been hesitant to bring this up, but what if I'm wrong?"

"What do you mean?"

"What if it's not everyone? I mean I've met a lot of people, and they're all the same, but I haven't met everyone."

"Okay, what does that mean?"

"I guess it really doesn't change anything. Whether it's 60 or 384, it doesn't matter. We need to know why."

"How are we going to do that?" Claire asked.

"There's one way to find out. Come on!" Mason said, fervently walking toward the door. Jumping into Claire's truck, Mason directed Claire to drive back into town.

"Are you going to tell me where we're going?" she questioned.

He told her to pull over by the edge of the street by Sid's Bar. A little confused, but getting more used to it the more she knew about Mason, she pulled over.

"Kind of early for drinks, don't you think?" she asked, knowing they weren't going to drink.

"No, we're going to take a nature walk."

"A what?"

"I want to go to where the owls are gathering and see if we can get some answers."

"You want to talk to the owls? Like Dr. Doolittle?"

"Yes," he said out of desperation.

"This should be interesting," Claire said, getting out of the truck.

They walked behind some buildings and made their way to the heavily wooded area, where the old Indian burial ground was located. The morning rays of sun punched through the trees like a Pink Floyd laser show. The early morning fog dulled the hue of the foliage, but it didn't hide the hundreds of owls in the trees keeping close watch over their sacred grounds. Like walking a gauntlet, they made their way into the woods.

"I'm not sure this was a good idea, Mason," Claire said, grabbing Mason's hand and getting more concerned the further they walked in. Two brown and black owls dove down and flew in between Mason and Claire, forcing them to separate and dive to the ground.

As they laid on the ground looking up, the two owls landed and stood between Claire and Mason, staring at Claire as if they were holding her at bay.

"I'm guessing they want you to stay here," Mason offered.

"No way! I'm coming with you." As she made clear her bold intention, the two owls tilted their heads down and hissed at her.

"Oh shit, or I'll just stay here," she countered.

"Claire, you'll be fine; if they wanted to hurt us they would have by now." Then the familiar white owl flew up and took perch on a branch near Mason.

"I'm thinking he wants me to follow him, alone."

"It would appear that way. You go ahead. I'll just be here talking to my friends," Claire said, trying to hide her fear.

"All right, just don't make any sudden movements."

"Okay, does a sudden bowel movement count?" she said sarcastically.

"Funny. Hopefully those aren't your last words." As Mason slowly stood up off the ground, the white owl leapt from its perch and flew further into the woods with Mason following. After fifteen minutes of following the white owl, Mason finally said, "All right buddy, where are we going?"

With that, the owl soared off into the woods, losing Mason.

"Hey! Wait up," Mason sighed and stopped. Realizing the owl was gone, Mason looked around and thought, Great, now what? Just then, he heard the crackling of branches and leaves.

Out from behind a cluster of bushes emerged a daunting Indian warrior covered in tribal warrior face paint. His black, flowing hair poured out from under his feathered headband. His broad shoulders and bustling muscles would instill fear in any generation. Startled, Mason took a step backwards and asked, "Who are you?"

"I am Ma'xu. I am your friend, Mason; your protector; your guide."

"My spirit guide?"

"Yes Mason."

"Am I asleep?"

"No, you are very awake, my friend," the guide said with a laugh. "However, you should not be here; these are sacred grounds."

"I guess I knew that. I just needed to look somewhere for answers."

"Answers to what?"

"Answers to what's going on. Are you going to slaughter these people?"

"Mason, I don't make that decision. I am Ah Puch's messenger; I only carry out his will."

"His will is to kill innocent people?"

"No, he will not destroy innocent life; he will let nature take her course on them. He will only destroy people when they have become so corrupt that their death is the only way to save them."

"Then what about these people? What are they guilty of, lying in order to protect millions of lives from the real bad people?"

"Mason, all I can tell you is to broaden your perspective. Think of the larger good and trust Ah Puch."

"With what? He gives me this 'gift,' and then doesn't let me do anything with it? So that people will be more at ease when they die? I mean, what's the point to this ability if I can't help anyone?"

"Ah Puch would not have given you the gift if you couldn't use it to help people."

"Wait, so you're telling me, I can change someone's death day?"

"What I'm telling you is that Ah Puch has not limited your ability; you have."

"You can't throw me into a game and not tell me the rules."

"There are no rules, Mason."

"Well then, how about an instruction manual or some guidelines?"

"You need more wisdom, that's all."

Getting frustrated, Mason tried to simplify things. "Look, let's make it easy; how do I change someone's death day?"

"Every event leads to another, that leads to yet another, and so on. Every event has a consequence, some large and some small. You need to figure out whether you are engaged in the event or the consequence. When you can discern between the two, Mason, that is when you are being ruled by wisdom."

"In other words, I need to know what else comes with this situation; I need to . . . broaden my perspective," he said as if a lightbulb went on in his head.

"Yes Mason, you're getting it. It's good that you struggle to understand; the humility will serve you well later on."

"Wait, what's later on?"

"That's for another time, my friend. I can see that you're ready for more wisdom." With a deep intense look, Ma'xu walked toward Mason.

"More wisdom? You're not going to do the Vulcan mind probe thing, are you?" Mason said, although he knew from his dreams what was going to happen. Ma'xu raised his hand to Mason's head. Mason braced himself.

"Oh crap, you are . . ." Immediately, an intense shock flashed through Mason's entire body. Every muscle in his body went immediately tense. Centuries of war images, pain, suffering, and death were being burned permanently into his memory. He felt the pain of being shot. Of being stabbed. Of being killed. Knowledge of human behavior and historical events filled with death and suffering was burned into his mind until he couldn't take it anymore. He collapsed from the pain. When it was through, Mason, on his knees with his head hanging down and gasping for air, looked up at the Indian and asked, "What did you do to me?"

"Only a small part of wisdom, knowledge, and compassion can be imparted onto you. The rest you need to learn; that is why I cannot give you the answers. I opened the pathway that connects us. You and I are one, Mason." With that, the Indian morphed into the white owl, let out an extraordinary cry, and flew off.

"Wait! What about the town?" Mason yelled from his knees, not yet having the energy to stand.

"It's not about the town, Mason; look for the signs," the Indian's voice said inside Mason's head.

"What? Where are you?" Mason said, looking in all directions for the Indian. "Did you say that?" Mason thought out loud.

"Yes, Mason, you will see what I see and hear what I hear. Go brother, be well."

Stumbling to his feet, Mason shook his head and squinted. Looking through the trees, he could see buildings off in the distance. Are those the buildings in the town? he thought to himself. How can I possibly see that?

Suddenly, his energy came back to him and he felt completely rejuvenated. His senses were acutely refined. He followed a fly flying in slow motion. He could see the fly's blackened eyes looking back at him. Following each movement of the fly, he felt the fear of the fly before reaching out and snatching it out of midair. He opened his clenched fist and allowed the fly to fly away. Whatever the Indian did to him, he liked it.

Walking back to Claire, he noticed she was still sitting in the exact location she was when he left. "Okay, let's go," he said, walking up to her, giving her his hand, and pulling her up.

"It's about time—" Claire started to say, and then stopped. She looked into Mason's eyes and saw his pupils fade from red back to black. It stopped her in her tracks. Mason was different.

"What?" Mason said to her.

"Nothing," she said, looking concerned at the white stripe that had appeared in Mason's hair on the right side of Mason's head. "Are you all right, Mason?" she hesitantly asked.

"Yes, I'm fine. We had a nice chat. And you, did you have a nice time?" Mason asked confidently, looking at the owls staring at them. Mason felt a kindred spirit with the owls.

"What? Are you kidding?" she replied.

"No, they like you," Mason reassured Claire as they walked back to the car.

That's comforting, she thought. Wait, they like me; like I like Thanksgiving turkey?

"No Claire, like you're a good soul."

"What? How did you hear that?" Claire asked.

"You said it pretty loud."

"No I didn't. I didn't say anything out loud," her voice trailed off.

"Obviously you did. Let's eat; I'm starving," Mason said, discounting Claire's curiosity.

"Okay, are you going to tell me what you talked about with the owl?" Claire asked, knowing exactly how it sounded.

Chapter 77

Austin's Warning
Greenfield Ranch, Oklahoma
June 14, 2017

A coded message from Colonel Mike Austin popped up on Joe's computer screen as he was sitting at his computer in his office. "Requested surveillance video" was the subject header. Clicking on the video icon and watching the video, Joe couldn't believe his eyes.

"What the hell?" Playing it again, he watched in amazement. Just then, the phone rang and he answered, "Hello?"

"Hi Joe, it's Mike Austin."

"Hi Mike, I just got the email you sent me."

"Good; hopefully that's what you need."

"I'm not sure it helps or not," Joe said, bewildered as he watched the clip again.

"Is that the Mason character we talked about yesterday getting his ass beat in the video?"

"Yes, our surveillance was blocked by a bird; that's why I wanted the NSA's Globalhawk surveillance."

"Looks like Mason has a friend; any idea what that's about?"

"That, Mike, would take a while to explain, and even then, I'm not sure you'd believe me."

"After being in this job for thirty years, Joe, you'd be surprised at what I'd believe. I'd keep an eye on him; it's awfully coincidental that your town is now on the radar right after this guy shows up. In fact, didn't your mechanic say that the vehicle looked sabotaged?"

"Yes, he did; and did you say we're on the radar map?" Joe asked.

"Yes. In fact, I've got another matter that I need to discuss with you."

"Sure, what is it?"

"Any reason your location would get a hit by our NSA friends?"

"Our location sends out intel all over the world. I'm sure we get flagged a lot."

"That's not what I mean," Mike said. "Your actual coordinates were decoded coming out of the Midwest region yesterday."

"Out of the Midwest US?"

"Yes, and we have obtained intel that a terrorist group smuggled some kind of explosive into the country from the northern region heading south."

"What kind of explosive?"

"We're not sure what exactly; we're working on it. But what we do know is that there has been a threat made to our country."

Joe's mind was running a mile a minute. "Certainly we did a trace, right?" he finally asked.

"Yes, but that's part of the problem we're running into," Austin replied. "We traced it to the Kansas City area, but that's as close as we could get. The rest of the coding information was deleted before we could get it."

"Kansas City? That's us. And you say the authentication data was deleted?"

"Yes."

"But that's impossible to eliminate," Joe said.

Austin continued, "Unless you have *physical* access to the servers; and we both know where all of the servers are housed, don't we, Joe?"

Joe knew where the colonel was going. Austin laid his assessment out as if playing a game of chess. He continued to walk Joe down his methodical passive indictment.

"It's impossible for most people, but your outfit is not most people. Here's what I see: The call came out of your region, with your coordinates, to an area where we had a terrorist breech, and the only people who know how to hide critical ID information work for you in your town. I wish I was missing something, and if I am let me know. Otherwise, you and I both know the answer to this situation," Mike said regretfully.

"Yes, I know, there's only a handful of people that know how to do that, including me?"

"Yes, and unfortunately including Claire."

"Mike, we've known each other a long time—" Joe started and was cut off by Mike.

"Don't even start, Joe; you know the deal."

"I know, Mike; just give me forty-eight hours to figure this out before you initiate the secondary protocol. I'm not trying to buy time to cover for anyone; I just want to know who sold us out before we all get eliminated. You would want to know the same thing if it were you. Just give me forty-eight hours to get to the bottom of this."

"Joe, we have to find out what the hell is going on out there."

"I agree. In the meantime, hold off on the Twin Rivers Initiative plan."

"Don't screw me on this, Joe. You got forty-eight hours to report something back. If I don't hear anything, consider it a go," Joe ordered.

"Thanks Mike, and one more thing; keep this surveillance tape between us. The fewer people that know about it, the better."

As Joe hung up the phone, he leaned back in his chair and watched the video clip again. The troubling part of the video clip wasn't that a single owl attacked and killed three men. It was that when the killing was done, the owl stopped midflight, turned and looked up at the satellite, and screeched. Its talons dripped blood as it was suspended in flight. Then it flew off.

Chapter 78

The Greater Good
Greenfield Ranch, Oklahoma
June 14, 2017

Mason sat in a booth in the café with Claire. After finishing dinner, they discussed the importance of their situation. The death day was in two days. There was no time for guessing; he needed direction. It occurred to him that after talking to Ma'xu, maybe Dr. Hogan would be able to help. Dr. Hogan was probably the only other person who would believe him.

"Hi Mason!" Dr. Hogan said, answering his phone. "Almeda says to tell you hello also."

"Tell her hi for me," Mason replied.

"I was hoping you'd call. Did you make it back to Chicago?"

"No, I had car problems," he said. Then, looking at Claire, he continued, "I'm visiting a friend up state."

"Nothing serious with the car, I hope."

"No, it's just an older car so it took longer to get parts, but no worries. I wanted to talk to you about my deal."

"Your gift?"

"Yes, I had an interesting talk today; do you have a minute to discuss it?"

"Oh yes, by all means, tell me about it."

"Well, first off, it was with an owl that transformed into an Indian who said he was my spirit guide."

"Oh, hang on Mason, let me put you on speaker so Almeda can hear this. Okay, go ahead; so an owl revealed to you that he is your spirit guide?"

"Yes, and he told me that only I limit my ability, Ah Puch doesn't. He also said that Ah Puch wouldn't give me a gift that I couldn't use to help people. I guess I'm curious what your take with this whole 'I'll give you this ability to know when people are going to die thing, but I'm not going to let you know how to change the outcome.' Any advice?"

"Mason, it sounds like your gift is somewhat of a paradox, is it not? You feel as if the very things you know are things that cannot be changed; therefore, what's the point of knowing them in the first place?"

"Yes, exactly."

"Good, Mason. The real question then becomes, how do you overcome a paradox?"

"I have no idea."

"The first thing you must do is define the contradiction that makes it a paradox. Then examine the facts. In your case, you know the date on which people will die. That is a fact, therefore it becomes a truth. The second part is that you cannot change the date of their death. However, how do you know this? Because you've tried with someone? Because the outcome was not agreeable to you? According to your spirit guide, this is not a fact; therefore, it becomes the nontruth contradiction of your paradoxical dilemma."

"English, Doc! What exactly does it mean?"

"Yes, yes; sorry, I get carried away sometimes. I think what it means is in your case, you have to know the greater purpose. For example, in Christianity, Jesus had to die so that people may live; you know, for the greater good. Dying and living thus become a paradoxical relationship. Jesus knew his greater purpose. Had he stopped his crucifixion, who knows where or even if Christianity would exist today?"

"But if I am able to change someone's day, then didn't the initial truth just change?"

"Yes, exactly, this leads us to dual nontruths."

"Doc, you're killing me. Please?"

"Sorry, here's the bottom line. The ultimate goal isn't just to stop people from dying, it's the understanding why they may need to die," Max said. "Furthermore, if you can accomplish the same purpose without the dying part, perhaps it's possible to stop or change a person's death date."

Mason nodded his head in agreement. It was starting to make sense.

"The guide kind of said the same thing. He said to understand and make the distinction between events and consequences to those events. Okay Doc, let me see if I understand this. If I can figure out what event is going to be caused later on because of someone's death today, it's possible that if I can cause that event without their death, they may not have to die, thus changing their death day?"

"Precisely. An event today may serve a greater purpose six months from now. You have to put something in motion that will render the same event that would've been caused, had the person actually died." Max continued, "For example, say the forces that be need an individual to attend college for some purpose. But the individual doesn't want to go. Now say that the mother of the individual always wanted her son to go to college. Fate may cause his mother to die knowing that that son, in his guilt, will go to college in her memory. Now if you knew that was the goal and could find another way to get him in college, she may not have to die."

"I see, but you have to know what the ultimate goal is."

"I think you've got it, Mason!"

"I think it's easier said than done. I guess I need to start broadening my perspective."

Almeda then added, "Mason, did he talk anymore about Ah Puch?"

"He said that Ah Puch doesn't kill innocent people. He only does the people who are so morally iniquitous that killing them is the only way to save them. Kind of like putting them out of their misery, that they don't know they're in. If someone said today that we need to kill someone to put them out of their misery, we'd call them sociopaths."

"Probably true, Mason," Max said.

Almeda continued, "Mason, I did some research on Ah Puch, and although he is blamed for a lot of death and destruction, most of the incidents he's blamed for the Mayans claim he had nothing to do with. As for the owls, those are his past messengers. There is only one messenger alive at any given time. Once his 'messenger' dies, he becomes a spirit who takes the form of an owl. Ah Puch then passes on his 'gift' to someone else that he selects in order to help him. I think you were the one selected to take over when the last one died."

"Wow, all those owls were past messengers?"

"It is a great honor to be selected, Mason," Almeda added.

"That must be why they keep calling me brother. Thank you guys, you've been a tremendous help."

"You're welcome; call us anytime," Max said.

"I'm sure I will again. Thanks. Good-bye."

"Well what did they say?" Claire asked anxiously, sipping her coffee.

"Kind of the same thing that the Indian said: know the greater purpose. My problem is, how are you supposed to know the greater purpose if you're not part of it?"

"Obviously, you are a part of it, you just don't know how. I say we just trust him; if he wants you to do something he'll let you know."

"You're probably right, but we don't have a lot of time to wait for the signs," Mason conceded.

Chapter 79

A Bee's Sting
Rabwah, Pakistan
June 15, 2017

Ahmed and Macmul sat by the pool eating breakfast. Their usual banter was almost nonexistent. This day was different than most. The attack they were planning on the United States was drawing near. The ante was as high as it had ever been. The realization of what they were about to embark on was front and center. More importantly, they could not back down. They had talked themselves into a corner and committed themselves. This would change the world political stage forever. The United States would forever be knocked off of their throne. They would not go down without a fight, though. A servant interrupted their breakfast.

"King, General Aleem is here to see you."

"Oh, he worries too much; bring him to me."

Aleem walked up with an awkward smile and disingenuous excitement and said, "Hello Ahmed, I apologize for the intrusion, but we are drawing near to our triumphant day!"

"Ah, there's the Aleem we know; not so worried anymore, no?" Ahmed asked, making a mental note of his false excitement. Aleem almost immediately noticed the serious nature of Ahmed. He changed his demeanor to match Ahmed.

"Still concerned, but still excited. Can we talk in private?"

"Yes, of course. Leave us, all of you!" Ahmed ordered of the servants. "Macmul, you stay, for you will share our glory. Now what is on your mind, my friend?"

"We know the missile made it into the Unites States, but has it reached its launch site?"

"It should make it today, Aleem. Then they will set up the link so that we will see the launch live."

"How will we know it was effective, Ahmed?"

"We will watch CNN, like everybody else!" he said to Macmul with a gregarious laugh. "You saw how well they covered Osama's attack; ours will be no different."

"Shall we put a martyr in the location to report back just in case?"

"Yes Aleem, perhaps you are right," Ahmed replied. "Macmul, get a camera on the target so that we can see Allah's glory firsthand. In the meantime, Aleem, prepare more martyrs; we will need them in the coming months. This will be a mere bee sting compared to the swarm that will follow."

"Yes sir," Aleem said with a bow. He began to walk away when Ahmed called out to him once more.

"Aleem, one more thing."

Turning around, he answered, "Yes, Ahmed?"

"You will find out from our American spy that you have been working with how much damage we did."

"Yes sir, of course," Aleem said nervously. He couldn't help but think, as long as the Americans haven't arrested him yet.

After Aleem left, Macmul spoke to Ahmed.

"Aleem asks a lot of questions, Ahmed; are you sure you can trust him?" he asked.

"Aleem? His loyalty has never been in question. I have killed with him on the battlefield, shared drink and women, and have planned attacks. I wouldn't worry about him; he's just concerned because I didn't consult him."

"Perhaps he needs more drink and women. I know it helps me relax!" Macmul said, raising his glass to Ahmed.

"Ah yes, Glory to Allah," Ahmed agreed.

Chapter 80

The Video
Greenfield Ranch, Oklahoma
June 15, 2017

Joe paced in his office trying to figure out his next move. He knew there was a mole, and he knew he had less than two days to find them. He stopped and looked out his office window; everyone that walked by became a suspect. Who could he trust? Who would do such a thing? Why was Mason there? So many unanswered questions, and very little time to investigate. A knock at his door followed by the entrance of Claire and Mason disrupted his thoughts.

"Hi Gramps," Claire said, walking into his office.

"Hi guys; come on in and close the door, please," he said in a solemn tone. "Thanks for coming over so quickly."

"What's going on, Joe?" Mason asked, picking up on Joe's acute sense of urgency.

"Here, sit down," he said, pointing to the chairs in his office. "There are some problems we're experiencing, and I'm hoping you could shed some light on them, Mason."

"Sure, what's going on?"

Turning on his computer, Joe turned the monitor around so Claire and Mason could view it.

"I want you to watch this video surveillance clip and tell me what you think." Joe clicked "play" with the computer mouse. They watched how the events outside the library unfolded. Mason was severely beaten and saved by the owl. It was hard for Claire to watch.

"My God, Mason, why didn't you tell me what happened?"

"I did up until right there," he said, pointing to the screen when he was knocked unconscious. "Then I didn't remember anything."

"Keep watching, it's coming up," Joe said. "Right there! What the hell is that?"

Leaning in with mild disbelief, Claire, glued to the monitor, said, "It looks like an owl attacked Jake."

"It's not just attacking, Claire, it went right for his throat and slashed it, as if he knew exactly what it was doing. Then he comes around and does it again on the next guy. Then on the third guy, he damn near cuts his head off from the back. What kind of owl does that?"

"One that is protecting me, I guess," Mason said.

"Owls don't protect people, Mason," Joe rebutted.

Hesitantly, Mason clarified, "They do if they're your spirit guide and in their human life they were a warrior."

"Claire, is he fucking with me? We have a serious terrorist threat against this town and he wants me to believe 'his spirit guide' and not his trained owl are killing people!"

"Gramps, he's telling you the truth," she pleaded.

"Wait, Joe, what did you say?" Mason asked.

"That you've got a trained owl that killed three of my men."

"No, about a terrorist threat?"

"Um yes," Joe said, calming down and deciding whether he should say anything about the threat.

"Gramps, what do you mean?"

"We believe that we may have been compromised and that we may be the target of an attack."

"What? When did this happen?" Claire said, standing up.

"Right about the time Mason arrived in this town."

"Joe, I'm just trying to help. I—"

Cutting Mason off, Claire pressed Joe. "How do we know it's credible?"

"I got a call from Washington yesterday. The NSA picked up chatter containing our coordinates and the call's authentication data was removed."

"That's impossible," Claire said.

"That's what I said, but if someone had gained access to the server and had the right know-how, it could be done quite easily. Mason, what exactly were you doing at the library on Monday night?"

"Gramps, you don't think that Mason had anything to do with this, do you?"

"I don't know what to believe. But remember your training, Claire; there is no such thing as coincidence. In fact, we make coincidence happen; we are the irony incarnate to the rest of the world. All of this started when Mason arrived in this town. Now I'm going to ask you again Mason, what the hell are you doing here?" Joe said, leaning over Mason's chair.

"Joe, I know how this looks—"

"Then don't bullshit me!" Joe yelled, cutting Mason off. "What the fuck are you doing here? I need answers!" The vein in Joe's forehead told Mason that Joe was not kidding around.

Starting to get concerned, Claire jumped in between Mason and Joe. "Joe, you killed the cell tower, so he couldn't have made the call; even if he got to the server, he wouldn't have a clue what to do when he got there. My God, Joe, you saw his grades from high school through college. He's not a computer whiz, he's a reporter."

"You saw my high school grades? You know, I didn't apply myself like I could have. I had a rough time after—"

"Shut up, Mason!" Joe barked out. "Then what was he doing?"

"Joe, I was snooping to see what the mystery was. I wasn't even sure what I was looking at; all I knew is that you guys had a lot of high-tech equipment," Mason offered. As Joe listened, he sat down in his chair behind his desk, regrouping from his offensive attack. His efforts to break Mason were thwarted.

"I need answers, guys, or Washington will destroy us," Joe said, as if he was at his wits' end.

"You don't mean the secondary protocol?" Claire asked.

"Possibly, Claire. I bought us forty-eight hours, from last night. They'll be expecting a report from me soon." Claire sat back down. She turned pale, as if she'd seen a ghost. With her head in her hands, she just whispered "no" over and over.

"What exactly is the secondary protocol?" Mason asked.

"It's a self-destruct sequence that once initiated, there is no stopping it," Joe answered.

"So everybody has to leave the town, right?" Mason asked again, as if he found a way to get people out of the town.

"Not necessarily, Mason. There is no countdown like in the movies. The order is given, it's done, and the collateral damage is assessed afterwards," Claire told him.

"Collateral damage? Like people?"

"Yes Mason, like unintended consequences," she continued with a sigh.

"They can't do that, can they?"

"They can, they have, and they will again if they deem it necessary," Joe said. "It's another way of making sure the level of compromise is contained; if nobody survives, nobody can further compromise anything."

"Claire, I'm thinking that our problem isn't the owls ravaging the town people. I think Joe was right; the Indian burial ground wasn't disturbed when they built the town."

"What about all the owls showing up, then?" Joe asked.

"Miram said every twenty-six years, the owls go to the burial grounds to show their respect for the dead. They must be doing that," Claire said. "This means we're not going to get eaten!" Claire continued, sarcastically.

"Yes Claire, but it doesn't change your day. Which means one of two things: either a terrorist plot kills you or your employer, Uncle Sam, does."

"Great," a dejected Claire said.

"We need to hit them one at time," Mason said. "What do we know about the terrorist plot?"

"We're pretty sure we're the target. And if we are, then someone from this town is in on it," Joe summarized.

"All right, if we can find the person responsible and stop it, we solve that problem. If we solve that problem, perhaps Uncle Sam won't need to light us up, right?"

"It's a stretch, Mason, especially if we only have one day to do it," Joe said. "Even if we do stop it, the problem is once we're compromised, we don't know how far it goes."

"Well we can't do nothing; we need to find the mole," Claire said.

"But remember, unless it's one of us three, and God help us if it is, everyone is suspect," Joe reiterated.

"We can start by getting the daily access reports. We need to see who has access to the servers," Claire said.

"That information is so classified, Claire, if it got out that I released it, I'd spend the rest of my life in jail," Joe said with reservation.

"Gramps, we don't have a choice. Besides, you're not releasing it, we're just going to look at it. It'll never leave this office."

"All right, I'll let you use my computer. In the meantime, Rod has something to see me about."

"Gramps, since it's all out in the open now, can you tell me something? Do you report to Rod or does Rod report to you?"

"We are both part of a system of checks and balances. What he thinks and what I think, and what's actually real, may be very different things."

"You're not going to tell me, are you?" Claire asked, already knowing the answer.

"Let's just say, I'm not 100 percent sure what he has access to, but I know he's never seen what you're looking at. I'll see you later."

As Joe left his office, Claire and Mason started going through the classified details of the people in the town.

Chapter 81

The List
Greenfield Ranch, Oklahoma
June 15, 2017

Joe pulled into Rod's driveway. This was as much stress as the ranch had ever experienced. There was no way Mason wasn't connected somehow, Joe was convinced.

"Hi Joe, come on in," Rod said as Joe was about to knock on the front door.

"Hey Rod, just wanted to fill you in. Washington's sending us some replacements for Jake and the other two," Joe said as he sat in a chair in Rod's living room.

"Good, we need them. Washington's going to have to get us some help if they want us to produce miracles," Rod said. "Anyway, I talked to Austin in DC; he's concerned about Jake's incident."

"We're trying to figure out what Mason knows and what he saw," Joe said.

"We do pretty important work here, Joe, you know we can't compromise that because of Claire's feelings."

"I know, Rod, but we can't cut him loose until we know what he knows."

"Cutting him loose may not be an option, Joe. I need to know I can count on you when the time is right. We may need to move Mason along, if you know what I mean."

"I understand that. I think Claire does too."

"Maybe we should take him out now before it gets any worse?" Rod suggested.

"We can't take him out until we know he hasn't had any more contact with anyone else. In fact, Claire's the only one he'll confide in. I'm thinking of letting Claire take a vacation and leave with Mason to get him out of here. Then, when all of this blows over, we'll tie up that loose end."

"You know what I think about loose ends, Joe—cut them off." Before Joe could plead his case further, Rod beat him to the punch. "But I know, we need to be diplomatic about it."

"That's right, Rod; let's be smart about it."

"Mason seems like a decent enough guy, although I don't think he's right for Claire. She's an ass kicker with a serious side for action. I think if Mason had a clue what she was really like, he'd wet his pants and run," Rod said.

"You don't think he could get used to our world?" Joe asked.

"No way! That guy wouldn't have a clue what's what in our world," Rod said pretentiously. "Hell, he's the reason we have to keep this information top secret. Most of the world doesn't want to know what we do; they want the hamburger, they don't want to know where the hamburger comes from."

"I guess that's where we come in, huh?" Joe asked.

"You bet. We're the good guys, Joe."

"All right, Rod. Well, we both know how trying to force Mason to leave went. It would be better if he'd leave on his own. Once he gets back to his life, I'm sure he'll forget all about us," Joe said, telling Rod what he wanted to hear.

"If it'd get him out of here, let's do it. Besides, Claire could use the break."

"I'll let her know," Joe said, getting out of his chair. "I'm going to get back to work now; gotta see who's saying what to who."

"Okay, any word on the threat?" Rod asked.

"Not yet. We know it came out of the North Dakota region, but we're still working on it. It seems like Washington relies more and more on us instead of just good ole fashioned field work."

"We've stopped hundreds of terrorist attacks, and now they've come to expect it," Rod said.

"We'll do what we can; hopefully it's enough. I'll talk to you later, Rod," Joe said, walking out of Rod's house and heading back to his office.

It didn't take long for Joe's office to look like an explosive went off inside it. Piles of paper littered the floor and the top surface of Joe's desk. Joe's office had never looked that unorganized. Mason was in his element looking through records and making a complete mess in the process. As noon approached, there was no sign of slowing down. After they completed the list, they determined sixteen active people had access to that server room. However, only seven were actually at the ranch presently; the other nine were on assignment somewhere else.

"Okay, so we have to track down seven people, right?" Mason finally concluded.

"Really only five, because Joe and I are on that list also."

"Great, let's go talk to them."

"It's not that simple. I can't let on that I'm looking for info. I especially can't let on that you know anything," Claire cautioned.

Joe returned and walked into his office. "What the hell happened to my office?" he asked. Claire ignored his question and redirected him to their findings before he could process any more of the mess. She rose out of Joe's chair and handed him the list of names.

"We've narrowed it down to five people; now we're trying to figure out how to interview them without them knowing it."

"Good work," Joe said, studying the list and sitting in his chair.

"Wait a minute," Mason said. "Do we need to interview them? I mean, really all I have to do is come in contact with them. Whoever it is should have a different day. We just need to get to them."

"Will that work?" Claire asked. "Gramps, you could call them in and Mason could come in contact with them here."

"I could do that, but Mason, this sounds ridiculous."

"It'll work Joe, I know it. What have we got to lose?" Mason pleaded.

"This is nuts, but all right. I'll call them in and have Mason see if he can 'identify' them from the beating. Who's first?"

Chapter 82

Off the River
Bank of the Missouri River, Atchison, Kansas
June 15, 2017

Arsal called Hallib while Saied unloaded the packages from the raft that were smuggled into the country. "Hallib, I have just met Saied."

"Good, no more problems?" Hallib replied into the phone.

"No, you were right. They don't look in the rivers too much."

"Saied will drive you to the final launch site; call me when the feed is hooked up."

"I will; hail Allah!" Arsal closed the cell phone and climbed inside the minivan. "Saied, you have the live feed equipment?" he asked.

"Yes brother, we will bring the downfall of the Americans to our brethren in the homeland. Then we will return heroes. First, change into these clothes and shave off your beard; we must fit in. Here is your new name," Saied said, tossing him a bag of clothes and a new passport.

Rabwah, Pakistan

Amidst the large banner-size self-portraits on each side of the podium on the elevated stage in the village square, the people waited with anticipation for their leader. Ahmed Almazor called the emergency village meeting, but wouldn't tell anyone what it was about. Although the villagers became accustomed to Ahmed's speeches, people were starting to question his true abilities. They also knew that to question him directly would most certainly end in death. Instead, they listened and then participated in the party that ensued after every speech. Under another calm, cloudless night, the villagers waved their pictures of Ahmed and waited for their cult of personality to arrive.

One by one, ceremoniously, Ahmed's advisors walked out onto the elevated stage above the people in the village square and stood behind the pulpit. Ahmed emerged to a riotous cheer and made his way to the microphone.

"Peace be with you, my fellow Almazorians. I have great news to share with you on this glorious night. I tell you, by tomorrow night, the Americans will bow to us! Allah has revealed to me their deepest secret, one that I will destroy tomorrow. We are in miraculous times, my friends. We will be witness to Allah's greatness as he delivers the great Satan to us on their knees. But I tell you, the time has passed for Satan to convert and join us; the time has passed for forgiveness; the time has come to conquer him for good! Tomorrow, we will gather again in this square. We will eat, drink, and watch our conquest as it takes place. Then we will celebrate and take our rightful place in the world!"

At that, the crowd started to cheer, "All hail Allah, all hail Allah!" Ahmed walked away from his pulpit pumping his fist in the air. The somewhat contained crowd began to riot. People began burning American flags, drinking, and firing their guns in the air.

"Nice job, Ahmed," Macmul said, climbing into Ahmed's private limousine.

"Oh Macmul, tomorrow will indeed be great. Now call ahead, make sure the candidates for indoctrination training are ready. I'm feeling extra good tonight!"

"Yes, Ahmed, but I don't think there are any more candidates available."

"Do I have to do everything? Then make them younger! Tell them that Allah has found favor with them."

"Of course Ahmed, sorry," Macmul said, dialing his cell phone.

"There's nothing like celebratory indoctrination," Ahmed said, resting his back and closing his eyes for the ride back to his palace.

Chapter 83

Dead Ends
Greenfield Ranch, Oklahoma
June 15, 2017

After the people on the list were checked, Mason, Claire, and Joe sat in Joe's office, deflated. Night was approaching and their ideas went cold.

"I just don't get it, guys; none of them had a different day. They are all on Friday," Mason said, from his chair in Joe's office.

"Maybe someone else got in there and messed with the servers," Claire said.

"Either way, we're running out of time," Mason said.

"Speaking of time, Mason, do we know a time?" Joe asked.

"No, just the date—tomorrow."

"Claire, I'm sorry, but we just don't have the time to run a formal investigation. I think you and Mason need to leave."

"There's no way I'm leaving here without you or all the other innocent people."

"We can't just caravan out of here, Claire; the mole's going to know, and God knows what kind of damage they can do if they get out of here. Right now we know that the mole is contained."

"Are you willing to sacrifice a lot of innocent people to keep them contained?" Claire asked.

"Here's another thought," Mason interjected. "Whoever the mole is will have an exit plan, which means the innocent people die, but the mole still gets away, with the information of this town."

"Good point, Mason," Joe said.

"Wait, Gramps, what about a lockdown? We basically turn this entire town into a jail until it can be investigated."

"That'd be a great idea if there was a way to round everyone up without drawing attention, because the minute we do that, they're gone."

"Yes, but at least we will know who it is," Mason said.

"Yes, but once they're out and they know that we know, they'll go into hiding. The bottom line is we need this to stop here, one way or another."

"What about Washington?" Claire asked, already knowing the answer. "Can't they do something?"

"I've already talked to them; they know the situation and are going to follow protocol. They don't care about us. But I'm not going to sit here and watch my granddaughter die for no reason."

"Gramps, there's got to be another way," she pleaded while Mason closed his eyes and replayed the events of the last few days.

"We'll keep trying, but tomorrow morning I want you two out of here," Joe said.

"Wait!" Mason said, jumping out of his chair as if a lightbulb just turned on. "When I was in the ambulance, one of the paramedics had a different day."

"Are you sure?" Claire asked.

"One of the paramedics that worked on me in the ambulance had a different death day, I'm sure of it."

"Who's that, Ryan and Trey?" Joe asked.

"Yes," Claire said. "We have to go to them; we don't have time to call them in."

"All right Claire, you guys go check them out. I'm going home to try to figure something out if that doesn't work."

As Claire and Mason waited at Trey Clements' front door, Mason was nervous about what to do.

"Claire, should I just grab him or what?"

"No, just reach out and shake his hand and thank him for helping you."

Just then the door flung open. "Hi Claire, hi Mason. What brings you out so late?" Trey said.

"Oh, nothing," Claire said. "Mason just wanted to personally thank you for helping him, so I drove him over."

"Yes, thanks for fixing me up," Mason said, extending his hand.

When Trey grabbed Mason's hand, the familiar shock accompanied by "JUNE 16, 2017" appeared in his head.

"You're welcome, Mason. I'm glad you're feeling better," he said, shaking off the shock that he felt also. "Quite the handshake you have there, Mason."

"I get that sometimes. I think it's the dry air."

"Trey, we have to go; thanks again," Claire said, dragging Mason off the front porch.

They climbed back into Claire's truck. Her nervous anticipation was eating her up. She wasn't sure she wanted to know. She was used to being in tough situations, but she thought that life was far behind her. Intel was what always got her through, and that's what she needed now.

"Well?" was all she could muster.

"No dice, he dies tomorrow," a dismal Mason said.

By deductive reasoning, it had to be Ryan. Claire was not happy about it, but she wouldn't have been happy about anyone from her small town being a traitor. Her mind began to play out potential outcomes, all ending badly. Her thoughts shifted to her own self-doubt. Have I been out of the game that long? she asked herself. Why didn't we see this coming? What does this mean to our national security? Her brief moment of guilt morphed into anger. Someone betrayed their country. Someone betrayed their town. Someone betrayed her trust. It was personal now.

"Let's go confirm it's Ryan. On the one hand, I hope it's him so we can finish this thing, but for Teagan and their baby, I hope not." They pulled out of the driveway and drove down the road to Ryan's house. Claire didn't want to believe it, but she was going to attack it head on. They walked to the front door. Giving a sobering look at Mason, she knocked on the front door.

"Hi Teagan, is Ryan around?" Claire asked at their front door.

"Hi Claire, it's almost eleven. Do you want me to wake him up?"

"Yes please. I'm sorry, it's pretty important."

"Hey Claire," Ryan said, walking up behind Teagan. "What's going on?"

Feeling awkward with Teagan standing there, Mason butted in, "Hey Ryan, I had a question about when I was in the ambulance with you."

"Sure; what's up?"

"Did I say anything to you when I was in there?"

"Like what?"

"I don't know, anything?"

"No, you were pretty much out of it."

Teagan was irritated by the intrusion and Mason noticed it. He had to do it now. Mason moved in next to Ryan and placed his hand on Ryan's shoulder. Thinking it was something important, Ryan just stood there and listened. "JUNE 16, 2017" flashed.

"Did I say anything about Claire?" was whispered into Ryan's ear. Pulling away from Mason and looking at him puzzled, Ryan just said, "No, I told you, you were out cold."

"All right," Claire said, cutting out any additional banter. "Sorry for the intrusion. Let's go, Mason." Claire pulled Mason by the arm off the front porch and dragged him to the truck. She looked at him and waited for the verdict.

"No, his is tomorrow also. I just don't get it, something's going on. I know one of them was different."

"Maybe they changed," Claire said.

"I don't know," a confused Mason said. "Maybe it was the doctor instead, or a nurse."

"Think, Mason, we don't have a lot of time! Let's get back to Joe's office; the answer has to be there," Claire said, getting more disheartened.

Chapter 84

Final Preparation
Launch Site, Southeastern Kansas
June 15, 2017

After killing a farmer and his wife who owned the farm where the launch site was located, Arsal finished stacking tree branches up against the missile. The site setup was complete. A large rectangular platform housed a six-foot-long missile now standing up ready to be launched. A camera and video link was established. The missile was perfectly camouflaged. He called Hallib.

"Hallib, the missile is on the pad, the coordinates have been entered, and the link is up."

"Good, Arsal, stand by. The next time we speak, glory will be ours. You need to begin your mental preparation, so to be ready when the call comes. The next time we talk, it will be for real. There will be no room for error. Prepare yourself."

"Okay, but after I launch the missile, what do I do?"

"Just wait. I'll have one of my men pick you up and get you to the transport immediately. They will get you back to the homeland." Arsal closed his cell phone, kneeled down, and began to meditate.

Pakistan

June 16, 2017, 9 a.m.

A knock at Ahmed's bedroom door startled the partially nude girls passed out throughout the large room. "Pardon the intrusion, my lord," Ahmed's servant said as he entered the room.

"What is it?" Ahmed yelled, turning over on his bed and rubbing his eyes.

"General Aleem is here to see you."

"Yes, yes, of course, send him in; the rest of you leave, get out of here," he ordered the young girls.

"Good morning, Ahmed," Aleem said, walking into the bedroom.

"Hello Aleem, what is it?"

"I'm sorry, Ahmed, but is not today the day we attack the Americans?"

Changing his demeanor, Ahmed smiled. "Yes Aleem, today we take our rightful place in the world. After today, I promise you, everyone will know who we are; every nation will know where Rabwah is."

"I must admit, Ahmed, I was a little skeptical; but you have shown the entire village how great you are."

"Allah has blessed us, my friend; make sure the preparations are in place for the celebration. I want the entire town to witness our glory."

"The monitors are in place and we've already tested the link; the missile is ready for your command."

"Good, Aleem," Ahmed said, climbing out of his bed naked. "Let's get something to eat and get prepared for tonight."

Chapter 85

Death Day
The Pentagon, Washington, DC
June 16, 2017, 11:20 a.m.

Mike Austin walked into his office first thing Friday morning to his phone ringing off the hook. He sat down in his chair, looked at the caller ID, and contemplated whether or not to answer it. He wasn't one to shirk duty.

"Austin here."

"Mike, this is Joe; we have to talk."

"Good morning, Joe. You have some answers for me?"

Joe hesitated and Mike was well aware what that meant.

"Joe, you more than anyone know my hands are tied here."

"Look Mike, they don't all have to die. Let me evacuate the people that know nothing about it," Joe pleaded.

The colonel listened to Joe plead his case. Although he was sympathetic to Joe, national security trumped any loyalty.

"Joe, you don't know who knows what, and we can't risk it. I need you, Rod, and Claire out of there, but that's it. I'd prefer that Mason doesn't make it, but something tells me Claire's not going to let that happen, is she?"

"I don't think so; we'll have to deal with him later."

"Just keep them together. I activated the contingency plan two days ago, Joe. It'll be online by noon and we'll be ready for the switch. Make sure you're out by then."

"I understand," Joe said sadly as he hung up the phone. He knew he had to get Rod the information and begin planning for the self-destruct sequence.

The drive through the small downtown was chilling. Was this it? Memories flooded his mind. The town may have been a front. Their purpose may have been hidden. But the people and their deaths were very real. The few people he passed in his car waved hello to him. He waved good-bye to them. This was the last he would see many of his friends. The decision he hoped he'd never have to make was front and center. He pulled into Rod's driveway and walked up to see his friend. He knocked on the door.

"Hi Rod," Joe said in a somber tone as he entered Rod's house.

"Hi. What's up?"

Joe noticed some boxes and a suitcase in Rod's living room. "Boy, you don't waste any time, do you?" he continued.

"What do you mean, Joe?"

"You're already packed and ready to roll."

"Yeah, I talked to Austin last night and he wants me in DC today for a briefing."

"A briefing? You're packed for a trip to DC?"

"Yes, and I'd love to chat, but I'm in kind of a hurry."

The red flags flying up in Joe's head didn't make sense, until it did make sense. Rod also picked up that something wasn't right. Both men became somewhat defensive.

Joe's tone shifted to that of a more serious nature as he said, "Mike didn't tell me about that."

Getting irritated by the exchange, Rod became short with Joe. "What, all of a sudden you and Mike are tight? You guys exchange information during pillow talk?"

"No, but we've been friends for twenty years, and he would've told me if a senior guy was leaving."

"Well obviously he doesn't tell you everything," Rod said, getting annoyed with the questions.

"What the hell's the matter with you, Rod? I don't like it any more than you do, but headquarters made the call."

Rod stopped his packing and asked, "Made the call?"

"I'm sorry that you were left out of the loop, Rod. This is a funny business we're in; we're not always sure who knows what."

"Made what call?" Rod asked.

Those three words echoed in Joe's mind. Joe recognized from Rod's behavior that Rod didn't know what was going on. Rod walked closer to Joe and asked, "What the fuck are you doing here, Joe?"

As his gut tightened up, an eerie feeling came over Joe. "Where are you going, Rod?"

Chapter 86

Closer Look
Greenfield Ranch, Oklahoma
June 16, 2017, 9:55 a.m.

With the morning sun pouring through Joe's office windows hitting Mason right in the face, it abruptly broke him of his slumber. Lifting his head from Joe's desk and wiping the drool from the corner of his mouth, he looked over at Claire still sleeping in a chair with a three-ring binder lying open on her chest. As he unfolded his arms off the desk, he bumped the mouse to Joe's computer, waking up the monitor.

On the monitor was the video from Colonel Austin that Joe showed them earlier. Examining the still image of him lying in the street bloodied, he curiously hit "play" to watch it again. Wincing with every blow, he painfully watched the video surveillance of him getting beaten. After the owl killed the three men and flew away, Mason sat back in his chair and pondered why that happened and why he wasn't dead. As Mason sat there staring at Claire peacefully sleeping, something caught his eye on the computer monitor.

"What the hell," he said under his breath. "No, no, no; you gotta be kidding," Mason said, now intently staring at the screen. The video had kept playing. "Claire!" Mason yelled. "Get up! We have to check one more person."

"What?" Claire said, coming out of peaceful sleep. "What's going on?" she continued as her senses returned. Her reality returned. "Oh shit, what time is it?"

"Come here, you gotta see this," Mason said, replaying the video for her.

"I know, Mason, we've already seen this."

"No, just keep watching. I thought it was over after the owl flew away. But keep watching."

They both intently watched the screen while Mason narrated, "Keep watching; there the owl flies away."

"And you're lying there almost dead," Claire observed.

"No, keep watching," Mason instructed.

"What am I looking for, Mason? It's over."

"That's what I thought, but here it comes, see?" Mason said, pointing to the left side of the screen.

"See what? Rod comes out and checks you, and then goes to call the paramedics. We already know that."

"No." Backing up the video, Mason pointed out one more thing. "Right there, I reached up and touched his arm. It wasn't the paramedics whose day was different, it was Rod's."

"Oh my God! No way!"

"Yes way. I remember now, his day is different."

"And he would have access to the servers," Claire added. "In fact, if he could remove the authentification data, he could certainly remove his name from the access list. Shit! How could I have missed that? We got to call Joe." Claire pulled out her cell phone and dialed him twice.

"There's no answer; let's just head over to his house," Claire said.

Chapter 87

The Mole
Greenfield Ranch, Oklahoma
June 16, 2017, 10:15 a.m.

Rod was becoming more irritated by Joe's semi-interrogation.

"I told you where I'm going. Why don't you tell me what you're doing?" Rod said, getting in Joe's face. It was a mixed-motive negotiation. They both were not sure what the other was doing. Neither were people who minced words. Joe struck the first verbal blow.

"You're the mole, aren't you Rod?" Joe asked, moving away from Rod.

Looking down and contemplating his next words carefully, Rod gave Joe an admission. "I wouldn't say mole; maybe turncoat, traitor, deserter, spy. All of those, but mole sounds so negative."

"It is what it is, Rod; you betrayed your country."

"Not before they betrayed me!" Rod yelled.

"Your country's never betrayed you."

"Bullshit! When we were in Israel in '82, you let Carol die, and you know it."

"No Rod, when I reported that we were on our way to get her out of that market, it was the truth. While we were on our way over, we were told the market had been attacked and everyone was dead, so we turned around. There was nothing we could've done."

"There's always something that could've been done. You saved your own ass, and now it's time for you to lose someone close to you."

"Rod, what the hell have you done? We can still stop this thing!"

Rod's admission pushed himself to the edge of lunacy. With Rod walking closer to Joe, Joe grabbed a fireplace poker from next to the fireplace and swung at Rod, hitting him in the arm as he blocked his head.

Pulling out a handgun from his waistband, Rod taunted Joe by pointing it in his face, causing Joe to drop the poker.

"You know what they say, Joe; never bring a fireplace poker to a gunfight."

Joe grabbed Rod's arm and, pushing it upwards, a shot rang out. With his right arm, Joe delivered a crushing elbow to Rod's face, breaking his nose and causing Rod to drop the gun. With blood freely flowing out of his nose, Rod rushed Joe and took him to the floor. Rod began punching Joe endlessly until his face, too, was bloodied. Joe kneed Rod in the groin and pushed him off to the side.

Seizing the opportunity while Rod was trying to catch his breath, Joe reached for the gun on the floor, but was stopped short by Rod pouncing on him. Joe rolled over on top of Rod and, as he delivered blow after blow to Rod's ribs and face, he could hear the crackling of bones breaking.

Rod rolled over and was within reach of the gun now. Between the swelling, the blood, and the repeated blows to his face, however, it was impossible to focus. Instead, with his hand flailing for anything, he felt a steel pan on the coffee table. Grabbing it, Rod swung up at Joe and struck him in the side of the head; he knocked him unconscious. Joe's limp, bloodied body fell off Rod and onto the floor. Rod grabbed the gun and pointed it at Joe, waiting for him to move. Wiping the blood from his face, exhausted, Rod stood up and grabbed his suitcases.

When Joe didn't answer at his house, Mason and Claire drove frantically to Rod's house. They pulled into the driveway and saw Rod loading his bags in his truck. They saw Joe's car in the driveway, but didn't see Joe.

"There's Rod. What's he doing?" Claire asked.

"Looks like he's loading suitcases in his truck," Mason said.

As they got closer, they could now see the disheveled appearance of Rod covered in blood.

"This isn't good, Claire," Mason said.

When Rod noticed Claire's truck pulling up, he jumped in and tried to drive off.

"Hold on, Mason, that son of a bitch isn't going anywhere," Claire said as she started driving straight for Rod's truck. "Get down!" Mason yelled as Rod's left arm came out of the driver's window, pointing a gun at them. Flashes of light came out of the barrel and multiple gunshots riddled Claire's windshield and truck. Ducking down, Claire peeked back up and put her truck on a collision course with Rod trying to escape. "Hold on!" she yelled as they crashed into the side of Rod's truck.

"You go find Joe, I'll get Rod," Mason ordered while he wiped blood away from his forehead.

"Be careful," Claire said. "Here, use these," she continued, throwing Mason a pair of handcuffs.

Mason looked inside the cab of Rod's truck and could see Rod lying on his side, not moving, "I'll be all right; he's not going anywhere. You go get Joe."

Claire ran into Rod's house. "Gramps?" she called out. The front room was a mess. Broken pictures and turned over tables littered the room. She could see blood spattered on the wall. A momentary feeling of horror befell her. She saw Joe lying on the floor face down with blood coming out of the corner of his mouth.

"Gramps!" she cried out, running to him. "Gramps, wake up! Can you hear me?" She shook his lifeless body.

Mason ran in and asked, "Is he all right?"

"I don't know; he's not moving."

Mason kneeled down next to him and checked for a pulse. "He's got a pulse; we need to get him to the hospital." He pulled the keys to Joe's car out of Joe's pocket and said, "Come on, help me get him into the car."

The jostling of Joe's body was apparently all Joe needed. "Hey, what are you doing? Put me down," Joe said, wiggling out of the clutches of Mason and Claire.

"Gramps! You're alive!"

"Of course I am. What are you guys doing here?"

"It's Rod, but I guess you know that too," Claire said.

"Yes honey, I didn't know until I got here. Where is he?"

"He's outside handcuffed to the steering wheel," Mason said.

"Gramps, we have to get out of here."

"I know, Claire, you two need to get out of this town; they're going to destroy it."

"I'm not leaving without you," Claire said.

The three of them walked out and looked at the front end of Claire's truck smashed into the side of Rod's. "Come on, I'll drive you two to Mason's car, then you leave."

"Joe, what about—"

"No, Mason!" Joe said, cutting him off. "You two get out of here, go to Idledale. I'm going to the office."

"But Gramps, what are you going to do?"

"I'm going to give the evacuation order. Then I need to call Washington and see if I can stop them from pulling the plug."

Chapter 88

Glorious Day to Change the World
Rabwah, Pakistan
June 16, 2017, 2:15 p.m.

Ahmed sat by the pool of his palace sipping his tea. As he waited for his brother and his general, he considered today to be a defining point of his life. Today I attack the Americans, he thought. I will be the most powerful man in the world. I will be a hero to the Islamic world. His ego was blinding. His self-indulgent, narcissistic episode was briefly interrupted by the arrival of his brother.

"Macmul, come in, sit down. Today is a glorious day to change the world, is it not?"

"Indeed, Ahmed, you have orchestrated a grand plan."

Aleem arrived within minutes of Macmul.

"Pardon my tardiness," he said as he approached Ahmed and Macmul sitting by the pool.

"Aleem, come sit," Ahmed replied. "Not to worry, today we make our mark on the world stage."

"Yes, it is exciting. The plans are set. They just wait your word," Aleem said before accepting a drink from a servant girl.

"Good, my friend, then we shall prepare for the attack. Is the square ready for the villagers?"

"Yes, the screens are up and the word has been given to be in the square for an important message tonight."

"Forgive me Ahmed, but looking at the feed, it appears we are going to attack a small town?" Aleem asked.

"Ah, Aleem," Ahmed said, putting his arm around him. "This is no ordinary town. This town has very important equipment in it. When we destroy it, the American government will no longer be able to communicate among themselves. We will open the door. There will be mass chaos; then our Muslim brothers will be able to attack at will. The Americans won't have any idea where it's coming from."

"Are you sure it will work? I mean, won't they just be able to use cell phones?" Aleem asked.

"Yes, they will try, and we will be able to listen to them. You see, Aleem, the American government uses a different system than everyone else. All of their communications go through this network, and by taking it out, it shows them that we know how they work and that they are not invincible, or impenetrable."

"But how do you know this?"

"Allah has revealed it to me," Ahmed said with a laugh. Aleem looked at Macmul and wiped a drop of sweat from his brow. Macmul smiled and winked at Aleem, as if acknowledging that they knew it was something else, but they knew not to question him in front of his servants. They also knew that regardless of how Ahmed got the information, it had to be reliable for him to do what he was doing. Looking at the servant girls devilishly, Ahmed announced, "Now that that's all worked out, let's have an early afternoon indoctrination session, shall we?"

"Yes Ahmed, a little pre-celebration celebration," Macmul said.

"Ahmed, I cannot, I have to finish with the warriors," Aleem said.

Ahmed and Macmul stopped in their tracks with their servant girls in tow and looked at Aleem straight-faced. Their silence spoke volumes. "I thought the plans were ready, Aleem," Macmul said.

"They are, mostly; I just want to double check to make sure there are no problems tonight."

"Aleem, your duty is admirable," Ahmed said. "These women are a gift from Allah; to not partake may anger him. The preparations are fine."

"Yes Ahmed, very well then, I can check on them later," Aleem said, taking a servant girl in each arm and disappearing into the palace.

Chapter 89

Evacuation
Greenfield Ranch, Oklahoma
June 16, 2017, 10:55 a.m.

Joe dropped Claire and Mason off at Marcie's and drove down to his office.

"I'm going to run in to the café and get something; you go get your stuff quickly, and give Marcie the heads-up," Claire ordered as she ran to the café. "Natalie, Murph!"

"Hi Claire. What's going on, are you all right?"

"No, Joe is about to hit the evacuation order; go get your stuff. I'll meet you at the evacuation point."

"Is this a drill?" Murph asked.

"No, I'm serious, now go!" Claire ran back out to meet Mason standing by his car, staring up at the sky. "Oh my God, Mason, are those—"

"The owls? Yes," Mason said, finishing Claire's sentence. "They're leaving," Mason continued as they watched the wave of thousands of owls flying away.

"Maybe they know something we don't," Claire said.

"No Claire, they know the same thing we do. We gotta get out of here now."

Joe burst into his office and grabbed the ringing phone. "This is Joe."

"Joe, it's Mike. Are you about to be out of there?"

"Mike, I was just about to call you. I found out what happened. Can you stop the secondary protocol?"

"Sorry, old friend, it's already in the works; you have to get out of there."

"Mike, they don't all have to die. Rod's the mole."

"Can you guarantee containment? Do you know how much he leaked?" Austin asked.

"Well, no, but the people here aren't the problem."

"Where's Rod?"

"He's handcuffed in my car; we can debrief him later," Joe pleaded.

"There's another problem. Our source out of Pakistan said a small government communications town is going to be the next target; that, Joe, is you, and they're hitting today."

"Mike, do not let these people die. I need fifteen minutes."

"Joe, I'm not pulling the strings here; the bureaucracy is larger than you and I. I can tell you that the ranch has been offline since 0300 this morning. And you know what that means. I'm calling to give you a heads-up; get the hell out of there."

"Can you stall them?"

"The sequence has already begun; you have ten minutes. Get whoever you can to the evacuation point, and Godspeed, Joe." Joe went directly to a picture on the wall. He pulled it open, revealing a large red button sunken in the wall. After pulling the button, ear-piercing sirens resonated throughout the town. The townspeople knew what it meant. They dropped what they were doing and the mad scramble for the evacuation was under way. The townspeople rushed to their houses and grabbed what they could. The evacuation order was meant to be immediate. There was no need to pack. The people took only what they could carry. They knew they only had minutes.

Chapter 90

No More Bluffing
Rabwah, Pakistan
June 16, 2017, 8:56 p.m.

The crowd gathered in the square and waited with anticipation for their leader to speak. They didn't know what the purpose of the meeting was. But then, they rarely did. In the back of the stage, Ahmed met with his brother.

"Ahmed, are you ready?"

"Yes Macmul, it is a beautiful night for killing Satan," a preoccupied Ahmed said, almost discounting his brother. He looked to the heavens, closed his eyes, and prayed. His brother and others quietly watched Ahmed in his preparation. Ahmed concluded his prayer. His mental preparation was complete. With his eyes glossed over, he looked through people as if they were not there. He walked out onto the stage to a cheering crowd. He let them feed his conceit for several minutes. When he raised his arms, the crowd went quiet.

"With the light of a full moon and stars as our guide, tonight we make history. Tonight, my fellow Almazorians, Allah will show great favor on us. No longer are we a small, insignificant village. We will all witness the fall of the great Satan." Just then, the sheets covering two large screens were removed. A hush fell over the crowd. On one screen was a missile standing on its launch pad; the other had a satellite view of a distant small town in the middle of the day.

"Allah has given the order. Aleem, launch the missile!" With his order, Aleem made a call, and all watched the two men on the screen prepare the missile for its launch. With a final push of a button, the two men ran out of the view of the screen. Smoke started pouring out of the underside of the rocket, and then with a loud explosion, bright yellow and white fire scorched the earth and the missile took off. The crowd let out an enormous applause while watching the missile disappear off the screen.

Greenfield Ranch

Mason waited in Claire's driveway while she grabbed her things. She emerged from her house with a large duffle bag and threw it into the backseat of Mason's car.

"Is that all your stuff?" Mason asked.

"Yep, everything else is the government's, and they can have it. Come on, I'm thinking the owls have the right idea," Claire said, jumping into the passenger seat.

"What about Joe and Miram?" Mason asked.

"Once the order is given everyone knows what they need to do. They're on their own, and so are we," Claire replied.

Mason drove out onto the main road where a convoy of cars and trucks was trying to make its way out of the town. Looking into the rearview mirror, Mason's heart started to pound. A few loud explosions signaled the commencement of the destruction. Within seconds, the explosions amplified and began at a rapid ear-piercing pace. The deafening explosions began to rock the town behind them. The ground shook and trembled. One after another, the explosions were tearing apart the town.

Those son of a bitches really did it," Claire said in disbelief, turning around in her seat. "Mason, how are the tires on this thing?"

"Fine, why?"

"You'll want to take the next right; I think we're going to do some off-roading."

"What? Why?" Mason started to say until he could see the road behind him exploding faster than he was driving.

"Oh shit! Come on, Blue Lightning, show me what you got," Mason said under his breath, pushing the accelerator to the floorboard.

"Who the hell blows up the road?" Mason said.

"It's like blowing up the runways; nobody comes in and nobody goes out," Claire said. Mason could see cars being blown off the road in his mirror. The explosions were quickly approaching Mason's car.

"You'd better hurry, Mason," Claire said.

"I'm trying."

"Try harder!" she yelled. Mason jerked the car to the right, fishtailing off the main road as the explosions raced by; the shockwave lifted the back end of the car three feet off the ground and spun it 360 degrees to a screeching halt. Sitting in the car, not saying a word, they let the dust settle. The distant sounds of explosions still decimated the town and roads.

"That was close," Claire said, calmly staring out the front of the car.

"Yes, that was," Mason said, looking out at the crater-filled road, stunned at what just happened. "Any ideas on how to get out of here?' he continued.

"Yes, this dirt road will wind itself out to the main highway. Only a few of us know about it; just follow it."

"Fasten your seatbelt. Here we go," Mason said, still not sure where he was going.

Chapter 91

The Owl Sings
Rabwah, Pakistan
June 16, 2017, 9 p.m.

Ahmed and the crowd watched intently as the missile was launched as planned. When the missile could no longer be seen on the one screen, all eyes moved to the other one. Without warning, deafening explosions began tearing up the small town. The crowd cheered as the damage was being inflicted onto the town.

"Yes, thank Allah!" Macmul said, patting Ahmed on the shoulder. The cheering crowd turned into a frenzied crowd.

"Yes, my brothers and sisters, be witness to Allah's wrath!" Ahmed shouted. The crowd began firing their guns into the air and drinking. Ahmed fed off their passion like a shark at a feeding frenzy.

"Eat, drink, live, my brethren! Tonight you are witness to the hand of Allah!"

While watching the buildings explode, Aleem became concerned; walking up to Ahmed, he whispered in his ear, "Ahmed, what kind of missile did we use?"

"Who cares, Aleem? It worked; look at the destruction!" he said excitedly. As they watched the screen, the explosions finally ceased. All that remained was rubble and smoke. Then, like an encore, a lone missile with a tail of white fire could be seen flying into the town and exploding as it hit the ground. After the display of explosive pageantry that was just unveiled, the missile explosion was like a firecracker after a Fourth of July fireworks show.

Aleem looked at Ahmed and Macmul, puzzled. "What was that?" he asked to anyone who would answer as they all stared at the screen.

"Was that our missile?" he continued. The crowd was too caught up in their celebration to notice; they continued with their orgy of defilement.

Like the crazed dictator that he was, Ahmed took credit for the destruction. Stepping up to the microphone again, he yelled, "All hail Allah! All hail Allah!" As he yelled, the light from the full moon became dim.

The cloudless night became overcast with what appeared to be a fast-moving fog. The crowd began to stop the celebration and everyone looked up. When the clouds moved closer, they realized it wasn't clouds at all. Thousands of owls made their way over the village. Not a sound came from any of them. The silent stirring of air was all that could be heard. With military precision, the owls flew over the village following one much larger white owl. With the crowd now silent, they watched in awe as the massive birds encircled the village from the air. Ahmed, in his arrogance, taunted the usually feared birds.

"Look, the birds of the dead have come to pay homage to me!" With that, the crowd started to cheer, until they heard the ear-piercing screech of the lead owl. They became quiet again. The lead owl let out another mighty screech, at which all the owls let out deafening cries and descended on the villagers. The owls' razor-sharp talons tore at the villagers' flesh like scalpels. Their powerful beaks wrenched the flesh of the people until it tore away from their bodies. Blood poured out of their bodies and covered the square. The screams of the people echoed off of the mountainside. Like a precise squad of assassins, the owls massacred everyone in sight.

Ahmed pushed people out of his way and ran for the limousine. He climbed in and told the driver, "Go! Go!" The lead owl smashed in from the side window and perched on the seat across from Ahmed. His brilliant white feathers were covered in the blood of Ahmed's countrymen; the blood matched the bird's eyes.

They stared at each other. Ahmed cautiously reached behind his back for his handgun. Before he could pull it out of his waistband, however, the owl screeched, dipped his beak, and leapt across the seat. Its talons sliced Ahmed's arms and face. Ahmed tried to defend himself by punching the owl. However, he was no match for the massive owl. It stabbed and tore his skin at will. The owl's beak stabbed Ahmed in his face several times before hitting Ahmed's eye socket and ripping out his left eyeball. Ahmed screamed in pain as the owl mauled him. Ahmed's white garment was soaked in his own blood. The owl finally concluded its barrage of torture by slashing Ahmed's throat from ear to ear with its talon. It then turned its attention to the driver sitting in the front seat with his back pressed against the driver's door. The horror he just witnessed paralyzed him. His eyes were as wide open as they could get, locked on the owl in fear. There was no escaping. If he tried, it would surely lead to his death. He watched in terror as the massive bird looked back at him. In a final effort, he tried to reason with the owl.

"Please, I'm not anything like them. I drove because he'd kill me and my family if I didn't. I have a wife and kids who are at home and have nothing to do with this. Please, don't kill me," he pleaded with the owl.

He slowly opened his door and got out of the vehicle. He opened the back door for the owl. He then dropped to his knees and bowed in respect for the owl. The owl looked at him and hissed. It opened its beak as if it was getting ready to screech. Then it stopped, closed its beak, and flew off, sparing the driver's life. It joined the massive swarm of owls as they flew off together as quietly as they had arrived, leaving the streets cloaked in blood.

Chapter 92

The Morning After
Idledale, Oklahoma
June 17, 2017

The morning light shining through the motel window hit Claire in the face and woke her up. She sat up and looked around. Mason was still fast asleep. She felt her arm to see if she was still alive. She was indeed. A sigh of relief ran through her body. Still unsure, she couldn't wait to see what would happen next. She had to wake Mason.

"Mason, are you awake?" She gently tapped his shoulder.

"Huh, yes, what is it?" he said, rolling over.

"Good morning," Claire said with a nervous smile.

"Good morning; what? Good morning! Is it morning? You're . . ." He sat up.

"Alive? Yes, I'm sorry to disappoint you."

"No, that's great, but I don't understand," he said, rubbing the sleep from his eyes.

"Well here, check my day now," she said, leaning over and kissing him.

"Hmm, I may need to get another look," he said, kissing her again.

"I don't get it; you have a different day now."

"That's good to know, but I don't want to know, so keep it to yourself."

Confused but pleased, Mason climbed out of bed and walked to the motel window. He pulled the curtains back and looked out. Cars were driving by, people were walking, and it looked like any other day: full of life. He closed his eyes and took a deep breath. He opened them again to make sure it wasn't a dream. It was real. Claire walked up behind him and put her arms around him. She whispered in his ear, "Are we all right now?"

"I think so. I mean, I've never had this happen before."

"I need to try and get a hold of Joe. I afraid he didn't make it," Claire said.

"I hope he's okay. Let's go get some coffee and try and see if we find him," Mason replied. As they walked down the street, Claire feverishly looked for anyone from the town. She didn't recognize anyone. When they came across a small café, Mason stopped Claire and tried to get her to focus.

"Claire," he said, turning her stretching neck to face him, "we need to relax, get some coffee, and start making some calls. The answers will come. We need to stop and think about this."

"You're right," Claire conceded. With one last-ditch effort, they looked in vain in all directions but saw no one from Greenfield Ranch. They walked into the café and sat down in a booth by the window. The coffee was the perfect anti-anxiety medication.

Mason reassured her, "We'll find them, don't worry." Lightening the air, Mason proposed a toast: "Here's, as they say, to the first day of the rest of your life, literally."

"That's one cheesy toast that I'll gladly accept," she said, touching her coffee cup to Mason's.

Their toast was briefly interrupted by a loud customer sitting at the counter talking to the owner of the café. The customer was excited about what he had experienced the day before.

"No, we drove in on 94 yesterday and I'm telling you, shit was blowing up!"

The owner replied to the customer, "We got a call yesterday telling us that they were doing military training exercises up there; they do that stuff all the time around here."

"Well, someone should go check it out and make sure everyone's all right," the customer said.

"With the military dropping bombs up there, I'm not going anywhere near that area."

"Yeah, good point," the customer said. He finished his coffee and continued, "Have a nice day," as he left the coffee shop.

Bringing their attention back into their booth, Mason casually asked Claire, "A military training exercise, huh?"

"That's how we explain everything."

"Well, where's the evacuation point?" Mason asked.

"It's an abandoned Air Force base about fifty miles west of here. They'll be able to airlift everyone out and get them debriefed."

"Is that where we're going?" Mason asked.

"No way; most of those people know that after you showed up, we had to evacuate. I don't think you'd be received very well."

"I guess not, and I suppose we can't just walk away, either?"

"No, they will find us," Claire replied.

"It's really not that hard to find people," a deep voice sitting at a corner table said, lowering his newspaper and looking over at Mason and Claire.

"Gramps!" Claire said, jumping out of the booth and rushing to hug him. "I'm so glad to see you!"

"Me too, honey," Joe said, standing to greet her.

"Hi, Mason," Joe said, extending his hand to Mason.

"Hi Joe. Thank God you got out before it blew." January 16, 2037 resonated in Mason's mind.

"It was tight, but I managed," Joe replied.

"Did we lose anyone?" Claire asked.

"No, everyone made it to the evac point."

"So what happens to the technology that you guys had?" Mason asked.

"There's a contingency plan in place; it was activated early yesterday, so at no time was coverage ever compromised."

Mason caught an image of an owl on the television behind the counter.

"Excuse me, could you turn that up?" Mason said to the waitress standing by a television.

All three of them looked up at the television screen mounted on the wall behind the counter. Shepard Smith from the Fox News channel began to report the story.

"And in a freak story out of Rabwah, Pakistan, a small village was attacked by a group of killer owls. Yes, you heard that right. The small village is located in the Suleiman Mountains of Pakistan. The lone surviving witness reported that during a village celebration, a group of angry owls descended and mauled the villagers. In the end, 384 Almazorians were killed. No one seems to know what triggered the attack, but killer bees, look out, you may have some competition. In other news . . ."

"Did they say 384 died?" Claire asked.

"Strange, isn't it," Mason said.

"If I wasn't watching it right here with you, I wouldn't have believed you," Joe said with a puzzled look on his face. "Are you guys going back to Chicago?"

Looking at Claire and smiling, Mason said, "We were thinking of taking a vacation?"

"Oh we were, were we?" Claire said, surprised.

"Oh Claire, one more thing, I almost forgot," Joe said, reaching into his briefcase and pulling out a stack of papers.

"What is that?" Mason asked while Joe thumbed through them.

"This, Mason, is Claire's new identity. Here's Claire Burnhardt's death certificate and here's Claire Barnett's birth certificate, passports, and bank documents."

Looking at Claire's death certificate, Mason said, "Looks like Claire did die yesterday. Does everyone in the town have a new identity?"

"Yes Mason, that's how it works. In fact, because of your help, I'll give you a one-time offer. If you want to disappear and start over, I'll get you a new life with new documents; or if you'd like, you can join us in our new town."

"But you can't tell me where it's at, can you?" Mason asked.

"I can tell you it's warm, but that's it. Claire doesn't even know the location yet."

"Does she have to go?"

"That depends on her," Joe said, smiling at Claire.

"Can we get back to you on that?" Claire said.

"No problem, Claire. You still know how to get a hold of me?"

"You bet I do."

"All right, you two have fun, and whatever you do, don't piss off the owls," Joe said as he hugged Claire good-bye.

"So a vacation, huh?" Claire asked.

"What do you think about the Caribbean?" Mason said mischievously.

"I have a feeling I'm going to find out," Claire said with a smile.

Chapter 93

A New Messenger
Tikal
899 AD

Tikal did not turn out like Ma'xu had expected. So many dead. So much pain. So much wisdom for the teenage warrior. Ma'xu sat on the ground sobbing when a strange sound befell him. Looking up, he saw a great Indian tribal leader standing above him with a large owl perched on his staff. Startled, he fell back onto the ground.

"Be not afraid, Ma'xu," the large Indian said. "I am Ah Puch. You are troubled about the grave misfortune done to your Mayan brethren, no?" he asked.

"Yes king," Ma'xu answered while never lifting his head.

"Your brothers became corrupt, Ma'xu. They dishonor and disrespect the great one. They disgraced and shamed themselves. They have forgotten from whence they came. Ma'xu, go to your village and tell the people what you have seen; that they will believe."

"Yes king," Ma'xu said. As he rose and turned he remembered his gift. "Wait! Ah Puch," he said, turning around and seeing the large Indian god still standing there. "I mean king," Ma'xu said, bowing his head.

"Yes, come forward Ma'xu. What is it?"

Kneeling down on one knee before Ah Puch, Ma'xu bowed his head and lifted his hands upward to Ah Puch holding the leather pouch with the onyx owl inside. "My village has made you a gift."

Ah Puch reached down and took the leather pouch from Ma'xu and opened it up. Removing the onyx owl Ah Puch examined it carefully. Smooth, black, and beautiful. Looking back at a humble Ma'xu still kneeling and with head bowed, he ordered, "Rise, Ma'xu, and come forward."

Ma'xu knew the legend of what happened to those who offended the gods. Nervously, he rose. Standing brave and small before the god of death, Ma'xu was willing to accept his fate. He said, "Yes, king."

"Your courage and your humility will serve you well when it is your time to replace your father. Your village will have one hundred years of prosperity and protection from your enemies, and your descendants shall be many. You will be revered as a great leader."

"Thank you, king, I am but a . . . Why me?"

"Because your heart is pure, Ma'xu. Be sure to keep it that way. Don't let power corrupt you. Use your wisdom, Ma'xu. With great power comes great responsibility."

"But, I have no wisdom. I am not my father. How will it be so?"

"Your village has pleased the gods. Go and sacrifice the fattest calf in my name. And Ma'xu, one more thing," he said, looking intently into Ma'xu's eyes.

"Anything, king."

"I have a gift for you, my young leader. Death is rich in wisdom; become wise, Ma'xu." Reaching down to Ma'xu, Ah Puch placed his right hand on Ma'xu's head. An electrical jolt shot through Ma'xu's body, paralyzing him with pain. As Ma'xu convulsed from the shock, images of slaughtered Indians were rapidly being burned into his mind. One after another, images of war, Indians dying, the physical pain they felt, and the emotions they experienced were cascading into Ma'xu as if he were experiencing each one firsthand. After what seemed like an eternity, Ma'xu collapsed and passed out.

When he awoke, it was dusk. Shaking off the sleep, he looked around. He took a deep breath. He attempted to stand up, only to stumble back to the ground. Rubbing his head, he looked around again, taking in the still of impending night. As his senses began to come back, he clenched his left hand into a fist and realized he felt strong.

Rejuvenated, he stood up again. This time his senses were acutely refined. He squinted and realized he was looking past the city and across the valley. How could this be? he thought. He heard a rhythmic beating. What is that? he wondered. Looking off into the woods, it was getting louder and stronger. A wild black stallion emerged out of the woods and stopped as it made eye contact with Ma'xu.

They stared at each other as if they knew each other. Ma'xu could not only hear the stallion's beating heart, he could now feel it. Walking to the horse, Ma'xu looked over the beauty of the horse. He looked it in the eyes as if talking to it and ran his hand over its mane. A strange sensation, he thought, seeing great distances, hearing a horse's heartbeat. What has happened to me?

He picked up a rock and threw it. Ma'xu watched in amazement as the rock sailed out of sight. The words of Ah Puch echoed in Ma'xu's mind: "Don't let power corrupt you." He then realized that Ah Puch had changed him. He had given Ma'xu a gift. "One that I will not abuse," he said to aloud to himself.

Stroking the long muscular neck of his newly found mustang, he whispered in its ear confidently, "You are now called Death, named after the great Ah Puch. We are one and the same, my friend. You for me and me for you."

Ma'xu was different. He felt no fear. He started his journey a timid boy on foot and would emerge a wise leader on a black stallion called Death. As Ma'xu looked up at the darkening sky, he noticed a large white owl circling overhead. The massive bird locked its blood-red eyes with Ma'xu and began to descend. Twelve hours earlier, Ma'xu would have taken cover. Not now. Ma'xu stepped back away from the stallion and watched as the bird came straight toward him, almost beckoning it.

As the owl approached, it slowed down and hovered above him. Staring intently at the owl, Ma'xu mounted Death and yelled up to the owl, "Take us home!" With that, the owl swiftly changed direction and began flying toward the forest. Death took off following the owl in a heated sprint while Ma'xu screamed out an Indian warrior cry, "QueYaaaa!"

The End

Since 1997, David Maloney has been actively working in the field of Forensic Science as a Forensic Chemist, Senior Criminalist, and, most recently, a Crime Scene Unit Supervisor. He has testified in court as an expert witness over eighty times and has active formal certifications as a Medical Death Investigator, a Senior Crime Scene Analyst, and a Bloodstain Pattern Examiner. Demonstrating his commitment to lifelong learning, he has amassed three bachelor's degrees and two master's degrees from three different universities. He has been an adjunct professor at four different colleges and universities in Colorado since 2001 and has a commercial pilot license.

When he's not studying, writing, or being an advocate for the field of Forensic Science, Maloney enjoys mountain biking and hiking in the Rockies. He currently resides in Colorado with his family and can be reached by email at dcm@davidcmaloney.com or via his website, www.davidcmaloney.com.